Blending Chords

Blind Rebels book 2

amy kaybach

Content and trigger warnings:

Reviving the Rhythm - Blind Rebels book 2

Edited by: Editing Fox

Edited by: Nice Girl Naughty Edits

Cover: Emily Wittig Designs

Copyright © 2022 by Amy Kaybach

R

For my parents for their support.
For my fellow rockers who live through the music whether playing or listening.
But especially for those who doubted I could do it- including myself.

Contents

Note to readers

Thank you for coming back and reading book 2! It means a whole lot that you're willing to give these characters of mine a chance! I hope my book provides you with an escape because that is what I want when I read. But most importantly I hope you love these Blind Rebel boys like I do.

I had the most fun writing this book. Gibson is a little older and a lot of fun to write. He stole my heart; I'm hoping he steals yours as well.

I mentioned it in my note to the readers in "Bridging the Silence," but these books are meant to be read in order. That order is: Bridging the Silence, Blending Chords, Reviving the Rhythm , and lastly, Finding Harmony. Don't forget to read the epilogue.

I love to connect with readers. Check out the "About amy kaybach" in the back of the book for ways to reach out to me.

- Amy

Chapter 1

Arista

Standing sideways in front of the full-length mirror in my sister's bedroom, I examine the outfit she helped me pick out for my interview. It's sensible; a light gray layered ruffle skirt, paired with a white, long-sleeved button-up blouse and a matching gray sweater. The neutral heather gray color plays well with my shoulder-length, natural blonde hair and emphasizes the gray flecks in my hazel eyes. You'd never catch me wearing this while being a nanny. Running after a toddler in a skirt can't be comfortable, and white while watching a child this young, I might as well buy a lifetime supply of bleach. But according to Evelyn at the agency, this is no ordinary client, so the interview outfit needs to be classy.

The requirements of this job fit me well. I have the requested early childhood development degree. I'm fine with signing a non-disclosure agreement, and I am more than willing to travel for extended periods of time. I'm happy to be a live-in, as it helps me save money that I can use to rent a place when this nanny assignment ends.

They all end eventually. My last family dismissed me because the wife thought I was after her husband, which I

1

absolutely was not. I was sad to go because the little girl was precious. She was six when I was dismissed. I wasn't a live-in there.

All Evelyn will tell me is that the placement is for a single-parent musician. Since this is Los Angeles, it could be anyone. It doesn't matter who it is, I need this job.

"Very professional, Ris. It's a good look on you." My sister Viola stands in the door, watching me as I examine myself in her clothes. Right now, I'm not making enough as a substitute teacher to afford rent and food, so I had to move back in with her and her husband Todd.

Hopefully, this job will be the key to getting out of her house. I love my sister dearly, but I can't live with her much longer because of him.

"I don't know. This feels too formal. I'm interviewing to be a nanny, not an executive secretary." Wearing a skirt was Evelyn's idea. Normally, I wear slacks for the first interview. Of course, normal first interviews aren't at a house in the Hollywood Hills. Not for me, anyway. "I don't want them to think that I'm this impractical, wearing a skirt. I'd never watch a child dressed like this."

"I think it's exciting that they picked you as one of the candidates to interview." My sister is ever the optimist. "But if it doesn't work out, Ris, it's okay to stay here. We're happy to have you."

I shake my head. "No. I need to get out of your hair. I don't want to be in your way. I should be on my own at this age." I don't look her in the eye. I've never been good at lying to my sister, but there are things she doesn't and can't ever know or she'd hate me. I couldn't deal with that because she's the only family I have left.

I hug my sister. I love her to death. She looks and acts older than she should, and part of that is my fault. Having to raise a young, rebellious, grieving teenager when you're twenty-eight and a newlywed wasn't easy on her. She should have been raising her own kids. Not me.

I can't believe I ended up back here when I promised myself I was gone for good after I left for college. But my return is temporary, just until I get myself together and get a full-time nanny position.

"I have to nail this interview in the hills." I pull away from my sister and smooth my hands down the skirt again.

"I better go, you know, with traffic and all. Thanks for letting me borrow your car, Vi. I'm not sure mine would've made it, and even if it did with no air, I'd be sweaty and gross before I got there." Poor Penny may be on her last legs, but she's all mine, even if I don't have the money to sink into the repairs that she needs. Hopefully, this job will help with getting her into the classic Volkswagen shop and getting her fixed-up into the diamond I know she can be.

Vi hugs me and presses a twenty-dollar bill into my hand as she pulls away. "Some just-in-case money." I nod, even though I hate the thought of taking her money. "Good luck, kiddo. Not that you'll need it. You're fantastic."

She hugs me tight again and I close my eyes and soak it in. Vi's more like a mom to me than a sister. She stepped up and took care of me when our parents died and I don't want to disappoint her any more than I already have.

"Thanks, Vi. I'll be back soon."

The traffic heading into the Hollywood Hills area is slow, and the weather is hot. I'm so glad for her car's air conditioning and automatic transmission. This would be a killer in my Bug. I wind my way through some of the side streets until I find Hills Overlook. The houses up here aren't just bigger, they are palatial, so much so that you can't even see most of them from the road because they are hidden behind fancy fences with security gates and cameras.

Who is this person?

I finally find 1420 Hills Overlook and pull up to the gate. I press the pad and a friendly voice comes over the intercom, asking for my name.

"Arista Addington. I'm interviewing for the nanny position. I'm from the NAC agency. Evelyn sent me."

"Of course. Follow the driveway to the left and park out front."

The grand black metal gate rolls open, and I follow the extended driveway that forks off in two directions. One fork appears to go to a standalone building, which I assume is a garage but looks bigger than my old apartment building. The other fork heads toward an amazing two-story house. It's got a Spanish Adobe feel to it and judging by its location, I'm guessing it has amazing views of the whole valley below.

Who the hell am I interviewing with? Madonna? She doesn't have any children that are two that I know of. Gulping a long drink from the cool water I picked up at the convenience store thanks to Vi's cash, I take a second to collect myself. I grab my purse, a copy of my resume, slip my confidence into my back pocket, and get out to face this interview.

I got this.

I hope.

The door opens before I reach it. They were probably watching me gather myself in the car. A woman answers the door. She's my age, maybe slightly older, and has violet-colored hair cut in an A-line bob.

"Hi, I'm Kady. Come on in." When she turns sideways, I can see a slight baby bump on her petite frame. The home is beautiful, decorated in a rich dark gray with white and burgundy accents. It's got a very put together yet masculine feel. I follow her to a small sitting room area directly off the main entrance.

"Before we start the interview, the agency should have told you to expect a non-disclosure agreement. We'd like you to sign it now before we go any further into this process. It's a standard agreement, basically stating whether or not we hire you, you won't disclose any specifics of your work with anyone, including anything in this interview. Doing so could be cause for immediate dismissal and possible litigation." She slides a document across the coffee table between us, along with a very expensive pen that has a pleasing weight to it.

She tilts her head at me. "Do you have any questions?"

I scan over the document. I've read a few of these before and this one is no different from others I've signed. "This seems fairly similar to what I'm used to seeing." I take the weighty pen and sign and date the paper, the flowing ink thick and dark.

She returns the agreement to her folder that she sets on the table. "Great. It'll be a few minutes before the interview starts. Cal is upstairs with Gibson, and they'll be down soon. That's a fantastic skirt."

"Oh, thanks, I don't remember where I got it, but it's a favorite of mine." I know exactly where I got it, but like hell am I admitting I'm wearing my sister's clothes.

"Skirts like that never go out of style." She smiles warmly at me. "So, Gibson just turned two. He's waking up from his nap, so this is the perfect time for him to meet you because he's usually happy when he wakes up."

"I can't wait to meet him."

She smiles at me. "The position is for a live-in nanny. Evelyn told you that, right? One that is willing to travel when the band is on tour." She tilts her head as she watches me for my answer.

I nod. "It's the perfect arrangement for me. I'm very willing to travel, assuming that rooms and meals are covered."

She smiles widely at me. "Oh, definitely. Cost of travel is covered by the band's label, as are your rooms and meals. You'll also get a per diem stipend for anything you might need during the tour, all on top of your usual wage. You can also expect that Cal will cover all of Gibson's needs on the tour. You'll have

5

access to a credit card specifically for anything that he might need."

"Perfect." I reach into my bag and pull out a copy of my resume with references. "I wasn't sure if Evelyn provided you with a copy of my resume, so I thought I'd give it to you so you can go over the information about my experience or in case you want to contact any of my references." She takes the paper, her cheeks turning pink.

"I think you misunderstood. I'm not Gibson's mom. I'm his aunt. Well, not even really an aunt, just a good family friend. He calls me Kaykay. I'm just here for, uh, moral support. Cal makes the ultimate decision, of course." I can feel myself pale. I've already made a mistake. Great, there's one strike against me right there.

"I'm sorry, I didn't mean to assume—"

Kady chuckles softly. "Don't be. I can totally see how you got there." Her smile is genuine, and I relax a little. "I just wanted to be sure that you realized." She looks at me. "Want some water?"

I nod and shift on the couch. It's suddenly hotter in here and my gulp of water prior to coming in is long gone.

She leaves the room, returning a few minutes later with a glass of water. As she hands it to me, the heavy footfalls of boots coming down the staircase across from the sitting room sound. I look up and there is Callum Donogue standing at the bottom of the stairs. As in *the* Callum freaking Donogue from the Blind Rebels. His long, dark brown hair is pulled into a low ponytail at the base of his head, and a couple of days of dark scruff graces his jaw. He wears tight black jeans, a faded rock t-shirt and black boots. In his arm is the most adorable blonde-haired boy, his fingers curled into his dad's hair.

Chapter 2

Callum

Gibson woke up from his nap in a good mood. Yesterday, that wasn't the case. I change him, put a clean shirt on him, and pull on some pants.

"Nooo!" He pulls at the pants I tug up. He wants to go in the pool. This kid is half fish, I swear. But we have these damn nanny interviews. "Noo! Pease! Okay!?"

"Sorry, Gibs, no pool right now. Maybe tonight." He throws his head back with a pained expression. "I know. I don't want to do these interviews either. But we need help, buddy. And so far, the other three people were all hard noes."

I think back to when Sammy caught me sleeping on the couch while Gibs crawled around on the floor. He called in the troops, and Mav and Kady somehow convinced me that a nanny would solve all my troubles. I'm still not sure that's the case. I should be looking after him; he's *my* son.

He whimpers and I pick him up. "Maybe Kaykay will get you some frozen fruit." Frozen fruit slushies and popsicles have been my saving grace lately. They started out as a way to numb his gums as he was getting those molars, but now, I think he just likes them because they are sweet.

He nods his head. "Foot. Pease! Okay?"

"Sure, buddy. Let's go find Kaykay and see about that fruit."
I kiss his head and we head downstairs.

"Kaykay?" he whispers.

"I bet she's downstairs. You think so?" He loves Mav's wife,
Kady, and she loves him. She'll make a great mom when she
has her baby. Gibson's lucky to have someone as caring as Kady
in his life, since his own mom abandoned him.

"Kaykay! Kaykay? Foot pease!" he sings.

We hit the first floor. When I look up, I'm taken aback. I see
Kady, but only in the periphery. I'm focused on my next interview. She's going to be another hard no because there is no
freaking way on God's green earth that I can live with someone
as beautiful as the woman sitting on my sofa. Nope. I'd never
keep Sammy or Kill away from her. Not that she'd stay long
enough for any of us to get attached to her, anyway. I know her
type, love them and leave them.

Her long blonde hair sports a glittery clip or some shit. Her
full lips are the perfect shade of light pink with just enough
gloss. She's like a roadside sign. Caution: Supple Curves Ahead.
Her eyes are a warm hazel, mostly green with bits of brown and
gray in them. I'm so thoroughly fucked, probably because I
haven't fucked in a long time, after becoming a father to a cock-
block personified.

I'm sure I'll find something amiss with her so we can move
on to the next interview.

Gibson tucks his head into the crook of my neck because of
the stranger. Who would have thought any son of mine would
be shy? I'm hoping the books are right and this is some sort of
stage. He's completely at home with the rest of the band, with
Kady and her friend Hayleigh.

"Kaykay? Foot? Pease!" he whispers. My son is food driven.

The nanny candidate steps up to me and shoots out her
hand.

"Hi, Mr. Donogue. I'm Arista, but I prefer to be called Ari." Her smile is like sunshine, all shiny and warm. If I look too hard at her, she'll burn completely through me. But fuck, she even smells good, like some sort of exotic spicy vanilla.

It takes me a second, probably two, to respond. "Uh, hi. Call me Cal or Callum. I've never gotten used to being called Mr. Donogue."

Her hand is still extended towards me. I take Ari's hand and shake it and I swear there is a zing that goes right through me, straight to my crotch. Maybe it's just one of those static discharges, but I can't help feeling it deep down.

"Nice to meet you. Let's move to the kitchen so we can be with Gibson, my son." I motion for Ari to follow us.

In the kitchen, Kady sets Gibs up in his highchair with a homemade frozen fruit pop and we all sit around the table.

"So, uh, Ari, you seem kind of young to be an experienced nanny," I note.

Ari's eyes widen slightly, and Kady says shrilly, "Cal! You can't say things like that in an interview!" Kady kicks me hard in the shin under the table. That'll probably bruise. She turns to Ari. "I'm sorry. He's not good at this," she says with an apologetic look on her face.

"Don't apologize. I'm not as young as I look. I'm twenty-five. You can call any one of my references and find I'm good at what I do."

I glance through her resume. She may be twenty-five, but she seems like she's still too young to have the education and experience she already has.

"I got my GED when I was sixteen and went to community college and got an associate degree in early childhood education. So, when my previous classmates were graduating with their high school degrees, I already had an associates degree and was working for the agency as a fill-in nanny while working on a Bachelors in education. I hold a passing CBEST

9

test score which allows me to substitute teach between nanny jobs. I've worked a couple of long-term sub positions. The substitute teacher field here in LA is cutthroat and can be unsteady work. Not to mention with classroom sizes the way they are, I rarely feel I'm making a difference."

She's saying all the right things, and judging by Kady's lit-up face, this nanny-for-hire is making a good impression. I can't, however, seem to look away from her supple lips.

"Is there a reason you don't teach full-time, if that is what your degree is geared towards?" Kady kicks me again, in the same damn spot on my shin.

"I prefer not to be confined by state requirements on how and what to teach. Plus, as I mentioned, I prefer more face-to-face time with kids in an individual setting" A well-practiced answer if I've ever heard one, but I nod. This will all have to be vetted.

"What was your longest gig? Just curious." I lean forward, elbows on the table.

Her licking her lips grabs my attention. I'm making her nervous, good. "I worked for almost a year and a half with the family at the top of the list of references. They were my first long-term placement, but it wasn't a live-in situation since the children were older."

Wait, no live-in experience? I scan over her list of references and realize she has absolutely no live-in experience at all. She's not as experienced as most of the other candidates so far.

"Have you ever worked in a live-in situation before?"

She shakes her head. "No, this'll be my first as a live-in. I can handle any rules, routines, and tasks you'll have me for. My purpose is to provide stability and complement the environment you're creating. You control everything." Ha. I'm not in control of anything anymore. I gave that up when I became a father.

"And you're sure you're willing to travel? We'll be leaving for a mini tour in a just over a month. It's only a three-week stint, but any tour is grueling. A lot of time in confined spaces like hotel rooms, planes, and tour busses. You'd be responsible for Gibson for large parts of the day and night. Off-days would be few and far between when we're traveling, but you'd be compensated for not having them, of course."

She nods and swallows, but still manages to maintain her cool exterior. I have to give it to her, I'm trying to scare her, but it doesn't seem to be working.

"You'll be on your own to provide appropriate activities and meals. Not to mention, having to deal with the media and overzealous fans."

Her eyes grow larger. I'm finally getting to her. Good.

"The label provides security, but you'll need to keep a cool head and make appropriate snap decisions to keep Gibson's safety and security at the forefront at all times. It's a shit-ton of responsibility to take on for a toddler that's not your own." I cross my arms over my chest as I lean the chair back on two legs.

"I'd never jeopardize your son." Her words are firm, and she doesn't break my eye contact, but I see hurt flicker through those hazel eyes. Is she hurt because I insinuated that she couldn't keep the best fucking part of my life alive? Too damn bad.

"I assume you don't have a boyfriend, a family, or much of a social life to be able to take on this kind of responsibility to the degree required?" I tilt my head and scrutinize her face. She gives nothing away. Another kick to the same spot on my shin from Kady has me shifting in my seat.

"I can do this." I can't tell if she's trying to convince herself or me, and it's not lost on me that she didn't answer my question. Maybe it was a bit off the mark.

Kady's eyes tell me she is astounded at my ruthless rudeness. After all the interviews before Ali, or whatever her name is, got here, Kady chastised me for being unengaged. This is me being engaged. I might be a bit hard on her, but Ali needs to know what she's in for if this job is to be hers.

I can't possibly be considering her for this job. She'd be living with me! Fuck.

I glance over her resume, making sure she has first aid and CPR requirements that are up to date. Looks like she just renewed them.

"Have you ever performed CPR or first aid on a child in your care?"

She shakes her head, indicating no, but doesn't answer me verbally. When her eyes meet mine, they are damp with new, unshed tears.

Something in my gut doesn't sit right with her reaction to this question. Father's intuition maybe. I need more information.

"Have you ever been in a situation where you should have rendered first aid or CPR on a child in your care and didn't?"

She shakes her head again, with more fervor. "No," she gasps out, her voice thick.

She's oddly emotional for someone who was so cool and collected before.

"Have you ever had to render first aid or CPR?" I keep pressing on. I'm going to crack her.

She nods and a few of the tears that had been threatening escape down her face come to fruition. "Yes."

That's all she'll give me? Oh, hell no. "Was it successful?"

She shakes her head and I'm about to ask for more details again when Kady kicks me yet again, drawing my attention away from the possible nanny and to her. "Stop," she mouths at me when I look at her. If her eyes had lasers in them, I would already be a lump of ash.

"I was thirteen. It was on my dad after a car accident." Her eyes don't lift from the table. "Nothing about that situation is relevant to this interview." She quickly swipes a hand across her cheeks. She takes a deep, shaky breath and then looks back up at me. Her face is almost hard now as she regards me stoically. I'll give it to her. I may have rattled her cage, but she didn't wallow or try to use some sad story to her advantage.

"Well..." I look over at Kady as I slap my hands on the table and rise. "That's all I have." I glance across the table at Kady, who glares at me. "Am I forgetting anything?"

Kady shakes her head slowly. "Not that I can think of." Her voice is cautious.

"Do you have anything for me?" I ask Ali.

She shakes her head as she rises. I escort her to the door. "I'll be in touch with the agency when I've made a decision."

She turns to me when we arrive at the door, raising her head high and sticks her hand out. "It was nice to meet you, Callum."

She's the picture of bravado, but her eyes are full of doubt and something that looks a lot like disappointment. I'm not clear if that's in me or herself.

Her lips part like she wants to say something, but then her face takes on a stoic look again and she turns and walks to her car.

Kady yanks the door from my hand and shuts it gently. "What the hell was that, Cal?" She spins and looks at me. "You barely said or asked anything for three interviews and then this one you tear into the poor girl's personal life? She's probably going to cry all the way home. Her dad, Callum, as a thirteen-year-old. What were you thinking?"

"Quit being melodramatic, Kady." There's a bite in my tone that's not usually there, and to make it even worse, I get defensive. "You're the one who said I needed to be more active in the process. I'm not going to let just anyone live in my house and care for my son. There's nothing wrong with asking about a possible caretaker's CPR and first aid experience."

Kady blinks at my outburst. Dammit. She's trying to help; I shouldn't have been so snappy with her. She's more than just Mav's wife. She's a godsend to me and Gibson, and I'm treating her like crap.

"I didn't mean that the way it sounded, Kady." I reach out and touch her arm. "I appreciate everything you do for me. Shit." I'm exacerbated. I don't want a nanny, but I do need some help, especially with the tour coming up.

Gibson looks up from his highchair, melted red fruit pop all over his face, and grins a huge grin. "Shit!" He holds up his hands, looking at the mess he's made.

Wouldn't you know it, his usage and pronunciation are fucking spot on. I've given the guys absolute hell about cursing around him, and in the course of three seconds, my son learns his first curse word from me.

Kady leans in. "Just ignore it. The more reaction he gets, the more he'll say it."

I nod and look her in the eye so she can see I'm serious. "I mean it. I'm sorry. I shouldn't have snapped. It's just—"

"I know this hasn't been easy for you." One thing I've learned about Kady since she's come into our lives as Mav's woman, and now our bandmate, is that she's quick to forgive. She wraps her arms around me in a hug. "But you were super hard on that poor girl."

"I know." It wasn't my finest moment. I drop my head.

"I thought she was the best suited so far," Kady says, going over the resumes in her folder. "Both for you and for Gibson."

"She's never done live-in before, never toured before. She seems super young. I don't know how this'll work." I shake my head.

"Cal," Kady starts slowly, grabbing my arm. "She's twenty-five. The same age as Sammy. You realize lots of people Sammy's age have children Gibs's age, right?" She chuckles and pulls me into a hug.

"Think on it and we'll talk about your options tomorrow when you have a cooler head. I've got to get home to Mav."

I nod, but don't meet her eyes. "I didn't mean to snap."

"I know. We'll talk tomorrow." She kisses Gibson and then heads out.

Gibs looks up and grins his biggest grin for me. "Shit!" I try not to laugh because he's proud as fuck of his new word.

Chapter 3

Arista

I take the coffee from the barista leaning out of the small hut, glad for the liquid sustenance. I'll need it today. Middle-schoolers are the root of all evil. When subbing, I prefer the lower grades, but I'm desperate to get out of Vi's house as soon as I can, so I'll take any job I can get right now. This position isn't ideal. Taking into account morning traffic, it'll take me nearly an hour to get there and get home, but it's a week-long assignment so I'll earn some money to put into my apartment deposit fund.

I need out. If it was just Vi, it wouldn't be a big deal. The longer I'm there, the more hinky Todd makes me. He hasn't tried anything with me this time, which is good, but I know it's just a matter of time.

At lunch, I scroll through all my social media while eating my peanut butter and jelly at the park across from the middle school. My cell phone vibrates in my hand, surprising me. Evelyn, from the agency, is calling.

Hopefully she's found more interviews for me. I need something steadier than these subbing gigs if I'm going to be paying rent. It's been over a week since my last interview.

"Good afternoon, Evelyn. How are you?" I use my professional nanny voice, soft but firm.

"Ari, I'm not interrupting, am I?" She's aware I sub between placements and knows I wouldn't have answered if I were in the classroom.

"No, of course not. I'm enjoying my lunch before heading back into a classroom of rambunctious middle-schoolers." We both laugh.

"I won't hold you up. I'm calling because you've been offered a trial position as a nanny starting on Monday." Her usually cool voice hints at a level of excitement I'm not used to from the ever-professional Evelyn Masters.

"A trial position?" I've only interviewed for the Donogue position, but he clearly regarded me as too immature to care for his son. Plus, he was kind of asshole-ish toward me.

"Mr. Donogue called first thing this morning asking if you'd accept a trial period as his live-in nanny. The trial will be for a month. If all goes well, you'll be the permanent nanny. But at any point during the trial period, Mr. Donogue has the right to terminate you immediately. If that happens, you will be paid for the entire month, regardless."

I'm speechless. With the way he acted during the interview, I was sure that I wasn't even on the short list.

"Ari? Did I lose you?"

"No, I'm here, Evelyn. Surprised, but here. I didn't think Mr. Donogue would be offering me a position at all. He didn't seem convinced I had enough experience."

You could push me over with a feather right now. When Evelyn offered me a chance to interview for this position, I was all over it, sight unseen. A live-in situation would get me out of Vi's house without me having to make up even more lies about why I wanted out. Now that I've interviewed for the position, though, I question how compatible I will be with Mr.

Donogue's needs. But it gets me out of the house for at least a month. He can't be that bad, right?

"I'm committed to subbing through Friday, will that be an issue?"

"No, you'll start on Monday. If you accept, of course."

"Sure. I mean, yes, Monday works for me." I still can't imagine Callum asking for me, but I'll take it. A placement is a placement, and this one pays more than a semi-permanent teaching gig, without the politics involved in teaching. Even if I only make it the month, I'll have enough to get a place with roommates, probably.

"Great. Mr. Donogue will be in touch sometime toward the end of this week. You can ask him any questions at that time." She pauses. "Don't forget, you represent this agency while working for Mr. Donogue. Don't disappoint me, Ari."

"I won't, Evelyn." This job will get me out of Vi's house and since room and board are included, the money I'll be making, I can bank away. It's perfect.

What's not perfect is dealing with these middle schoolers for another four days.

R

THE FRIDAY AFTERNOON bumper-to-bumper traffic on the 405 is making me crazy. I've already been on the road for an hour and I'm not even halfway home.

Stuck in traffic leaves me time to overthink everything about next week. I still haven't heard from Mr. Donogue. Maybe Callum's changed his mind. Evelyn said he'd call this week to iron out details about starting, yet I've heard nothing.

I probably cursed it because I started packing up my stuff from Vi's and now I've jinxed the dream nanny job.

Vi's given me a corner in the garage to leave my boxed up

stuff I can't take with me for now. I figure I won't need much more than clothes, laptop, my makeup and toiletries. Oh, and I can't forget my Kindle. Assuming I'll get at least one day off a week, I can come back and get anything I might need but forgot.

But what if I don't hear from Callum? Do I just show up at his house at 8:00 am on Monday morning? I pulled myself out of the active substitute list with the local school districts. Now I'm beginning to regret that decision.

My phone rings as I'm walking into Vi's condo. Usually, I send blocked numbers to voicemail, but this could be Callum.

"Hello, this is Ari," I answer, praying it's Callum and I still have a job on Monday.

"Hi, Ari! Is this an okay time to talk?" Not Callum. I recognize the voice, but not who it belongs to.

"Um, sure." Who *is* this? I hate not knowing who I'm talking to.

"Sorry it took us so long to get back in touch with you." Oh right, it's Kady.

"That's alright." I flop onto the couch, wondering if this is my kiss off, and he's sent her to soften the blow.

"I know Cal was supposed to call you, but the band actually ended up flying out to New York for a few days unexpectedly. They'll be back Sunday." Aha. Mystery solved.

"Oh, that makes sense. I was wondering why I hadn't heard anything."

"I'm still in Los Angeles, staying with Gibson, actually. Cal would still like you to start Monday, but we thought you could move some of your stuff in on Sunday, so when you arrive on Monday, Cal can get right to immersing you in Gibson's schedule."

"That's a great idea. I can do that. The room I'll be staying in is furnished?" Please be furnished, I don't want to have to buy furniture.

19

"Of course. It's basically a miniature master suite. You have a queen-sized bed and a little sitting area. There's also a TV that's already set up, so you don't have to worry about bringing one of your own. You'll have your own bathroom. The closet space is generous." This is going to spoil me. I don't have my own bathroom at Vi's place. I've learned while living with her again to take up as little space as possible, so I don't have much to bring and now I don't even have to worry about buying a bed.

"Sounds perfect. Can I ask you a question? It's about an expectation so you might not know the answer and that's okay." I bite my lip. I feel silly asking, but I don't want to start off on the wrong foot on Monday. Somehow, I doubt that Callum would be very forgiving.

"Of course."

"Am I expected to wear any sort of uniform? Some clients prefer their nannies to dress a specific way. I probably should have asked Evelyn." The contract sent over mentions nothing about a dress code. I double-checked this morning.

"I can't imagine Cal expecting any sort of uniform. Wear whatever you feel comfortable in, as long as it's not revealing."

"Oh no, I wouldn't do that." I'm not a revealing clothing type of girl, but she has no idea. "I just wanted to make sure if I needed something specific, I'd have it before Monday."

"I'll double-check with Cal and let you know on Sunday, but I'm sure you can wear whatever's comfortable. I'm looking forward to seeing you again and getting to know you. I know the interview was kind of awkward." She could say that again. "Can we start at about 10:00?"

"I'll be there."

℞

I PULL my Volkswagen Beetle to the gate at Callum's house and Kady's voice comes over the speaker, greeting me.

"Hi. It's me, Ari, with my stuff."

"Oh, hey, Ari, you're in a different car. I didn't recognize it. Come on up. I'll meet you in front to help you." And with that, the large metal gate begins to roll open.

By the time I'm parked in front, Kady's standing on the stoop. She's obviously pregnant, so there is no way I'm letting her carry anything of substance.

"It's great to see you!" She greets me enthusiastically with a hug. I'm not much of a hugger, but when in Rome you hug the pseudo-aunt to your little charge.

"Thanks. I don't have much. Just a few bags of clothes and some personal belongings. My sister is letting me stow what I don't need in her garage." I yank out my large duffle bag that contains most of my clothes and set them next to the car before grabbing my laptop case. I hand it over to Kady. "If you can get this for me, I have the rest."

I follow her into the house with my bag and a box, but this time we go straight upstairs and turn to the right at the top. She opens the second door on the left into a very large bedroom.

"This is the second master. It's slightly smaller than Cal's. I hope it's big enough for you." The room is huge, immaculate, and decorated with the same gray walls that run throughout the rest of the house. It's all very neutral, so I can totally work with that.

"Kady, I'm pretty sure it's bigger than the living room and kitchen of my sister's condo. This is amazing." She laughs and sets my laptop down in the chair. Everything I could possibly need is in this room.

"Your closet is through here." She leads me into the en suite bathroom that has a huge walk-in closet on the left. I set my duffle bag and box down on the floor of a closet that would make Vi cry because it alone is more closet space than her

21

entire condo. The room and bathroom are bigger than the first apartment we lived in after my parents died.

"While Gibson naps, let me give you a quick tour of the house and grounds. After he wakes up, the three of us are going to lunch and then shopping to pick you up some things to make the room more you. All on Cal. I can help you unpack and set up when we get back."

"Across from you is a guest bedroom." We move farther down the other end of the hall, passing the stairs.

"This," her voice drops to a whisper when she motions to the room across from a bathroom down the hall from my room, "is Gibson's room." She opens the door, careful not to make a noise, and I can make out his little sleeping form, butt up like a stink bug, in his crib. The room is darkened, but I can tell it's decorated in monochromatic gray and white.

"Across from Gibson, we have another bathroom, and this room here is another guest room. Sammy stays in it when he's here." She points to the door at the end of the hall. "That is Callum's room."

She stops in her tracks and turns to look at me. "I have to ask. You know who Callum is, right? And the band?" Her stare is intense and protective.

"I know their music and admit I could probably pick the members out of a line-up, but I'm not a groupie or anything. When I got the interview, all the agency told me was that it was for a single-parent musician. I didn't know who I was interviewing for until Callum came downstairs." I don't want her to think I am here because of who Callum is. She nods and continues our tour.

We head downstairs, where she shows me a large, open concept kitchen overlooking a large family room with probably the biggest TV I've ever seen. I don't know how I missed it when I was here for the interview. There's a large table with a highchair pulled up near the head of it. In the corner is a box with a few toddler toys in it. We see an office off the kitchen, and in there are the first glimpses of Callum, the musician. There are some Grammys on the shelf with a couple of other awards. There's also a guitar that hangs on the wall. I'm not sure if it's some sort of prized guitar or just a decoration. There's a closed laptop on the wooden desk and some built-in shelves behind it.

She then takes me down a different hall that has a home gym that rivals the one Vi pays to belong to. There's a treadmill and an elliptical that are both top of the line, a weight bench, and towards the rear of the room is an exercise ball, a small trampoline, and a good-sized mat. Across from the gym, Kady points to a closed door. "This is Cal's music room. It's sound-proof, which is a good thing, considering your room is right above it."

We head back through the kitchen and out the back door. "This door has an alarm on it because of the pool. There's also a special cover on the pool that protects kids from drowning. It's easy to operate. That reminds me, I hope you brought a suit because Gibson loves to swim."

The backyard is huge, and as I assumed, it all overlooks the valley. With the outdoor kitchen on the patio, this yard is made for entertaining. There is a small area off to the side with a covered sandbox surrounded by a dump truck, sand molds, and shovels. This house is huge, I knew that driving up, but it's not as pretentious as I had assumed it would be. I mean, sure, it has an impressive gym and a music room. But the living areas feel comfortable. I can see myself fitting in here.

After my tour of the house, Gibson wakes up. He eyeballs me wearily as I change him. I rub his leg as I smile at him, trying to ease his wariness with soft words. Then Kady loads him into her SUV, and we head out together. Gibson happily babbles in his car seat in the back. "He loves being in the car. We need to get you your own bedding. That guest bedding is functional, but you're not a guest. You need something *you* love. You'll be more comfortable if you make the space your own. You'll also need some towels. Do you have a swimsuit? If you don't, we'll pick up a few of those for you too."

"I have a few, actually. I'm okay there." I don't relish the thought of being in the pool with Callum there, but if the little guy likes water, I won't deny him.

Kady shakes her head. "Cal was going to put you in the bedroom nearest Gibson's, the one Sammy stays in, but I told him you'd need your own bathroom." She shakes her head.

"This nanny thing is new to Cal, so you might find you'll need patience with him, but he's a great guy, very loyal to his band and family."

We hit an upper end department store with Gibson in a stroller and head right for the bedding section.

"Do you have any favorite colors?" We peruse the different bedding options.

"I like lavender, lilac, those in the light purple family. I also like turquoise. But not together."

"That makes sense." Kady giggles. "Ooh, check out this one." She pulls out a beautiful comforter covered in a pattern of lilacs. I reach out and touch it. It's the perfect weight, not too heavy to be stifling, but not too light either. And it is beautiful. I follow the edge to the tag and just about choke. At nearly three hundred dollars, I can feel my eyes bug out of my head.

"Do you like it?" Her head tilts as she looks at me.

"Like it? I love it. But not at that price."

Kady takes it from me and folds it neatly and sets it back on the counter, then takes a new one that hasn't been fondled and sets it in the cart.

"What? You're not paying for it. Cal is." She smiles at me when I make a face at her. "It's beautiful, and if you love it, you should have it. You need to treat yourself to something pretty."

I shift between my feet. It feels wrong to spend that much

on the spread, even though it is beautiful. I can't imagine a world where I'd be okay spending that kind of money on a bedspread.

"He can afford it, trust me." She carries on to sheets, picking out a few different sets in various shades of purple or pink, not even looking at the price tags.

She does the same with towels, but I draw the line at the $75 fuzzy throw pillow.

"For the chair in the sitting area. Wouldn't it look cute with that purple chenille throw tossed over the back. You could snuggle into it for reading or watching TV. And they'll look cute in the chair when you're not using them." She holds up the fuzzy pillow that matches the comforter perfectly.

Is it cute? Absolutely. But who the hell needs a fuzzy pillow that costs $75? For a fuzzy throw pillow? No way.

I shake my head and take the pillow from her, placing it back next to the other fuzzy pillows. At the checkout, I bend down to pick up the small stuffed shark that Gibson had been playing with to put it on the stand. And somehow both the fuzzy pillow and chenille throw ended up in the cart and are currently being scanned by the sales associate.

When I look at her, she just shrugs. "The chair needs them to live its best life." She winks and pulls out a black card and hands it over to the salesgirl.

After we shop, we head to a pizza place for lunch. Gibson sits in a highchair playing with the crayons the pizza place gave him. I grab one and color on the paper tablecloth in front of him. I draw a person. He thinks that is great fun and starts emulating me.

"He likes you already. Gibson isn't usually so friendly with people he doesn't know." I look at him and he grins and tries to hand me a different color, so we swap, and I doodle more in front of him.

"Gibson, can you say Ari?" He looks at Kady and tilts his

head. Kady puts her hand on me. "This is Ari. Can you say Ari?" Gibson looks over at me, shakes his head and gets back to coloring.

"It's great that you are so close with him. That Callum feels comfortable leaving him with you for a few days."

She nods and looks at me torn, like she wants to tell me something but doesn't feel comfortable sharing. "The members of this band are super close. We're more like a family, really. They're very bonded with each other. So, Gibson is close to all of them. Sammy and Mav are just as much uncles to him as Killian is. Gib's probably won't ever understand that they aren't all blood. It's just how the band is." She watches him color. "Once everyone is comfortable with you, you'll be part of that family too."

Her hand moves to her rounded stomach, and she smiles softly. Her smile then turns serious as she looks back up to me. "Promise me something."

When I don't say anything, she continues. "Promise your sole intention is to look after Gibson. That you don't have any ulterior motives for taking this position. That you aren't coming into Cal and Gibson's lives to make a quick buck by selling some fabricated half-truths or for status or—"

I stop her train of thought. "I have no delusions of grandeur here. I'm here for Gibson. That I guarantee." It's also about proving to Callum that I can be trusted with his son. I don't like being easily dismissed by judgements.

She tilts her head as she listens to me. "My references speak highly of me. Some of that experience comes from high-profile clients. I'm not stupid. I know going against the NDA not only means I'll be fired, but it also means dismissal from my agency. I take every placement very seriously."

Her lips curl up slightly and she nods, seemingly convinced. "It's nothing against you. I already like you. But Callum doesn't trust easily. It's why hiring a nanny has been so hard for him. I'm afraid if someone else in his life breaks his trust." She shakes her head, and her lips pull down into a frown. "He'll never trust again."

Gibson smacks his hand down on the table. "More. Peas. Okay?" He looks at Kady and then at me, his eyes squinting slightly as he takes me in. I give him another piece of breadstick.

When we get back to Callum's place, it takes a little under two hours for Kady and I to unpack my clothes, wash all my new sheets and towels and get it all put away. Gibson plays on the floor most of the time, but towards the end gets a little restless.

"Sim, Kaykay! Sim! Pease? Okay!"

She smiles. "Told you he loves the pool. Come with me while I change him into his swim diaper." I follow her into his room. It has a hand-painted mural of different musical instruments on the crib wall, all in white and red on the gray walls. There's an area with toys and a dresser/changing table, and a nice rocking glider between the crib and the dressing table.

"Cal would like you here at 8:00 am on Monday. Here is a gate code for you." She hands me a slip of paper with a six-digit number on it. On the back is a phone number. I look back up at her. "That's my cell. Call or text me, whether it's Gibson-related or not."

Chapter 4

Callum

It's not often I'm awake earlier than Gibson. I slept like shit last night. I tossed and turned, worrying about the nanny. Our flight back to LAX was late, and that didn't help. Deciding to give up on trying to sleep, I pull my ass out of bed and successfully shower without waking my son.

I'm surprised and slightly terrified she agreed to this trial position. I'm just not ready to commit to a nanny. I thought Arista would be offended by the interview and not take the position. Obviously, I was wrong.

Last night Gibs wrapped his arms around my neck, hugging me as tight as his little arms could when I finally got home. I don't often leave him overnight with someone, let alone three nights, so I missed him just as much as he missed me.

Kady prattled on about purchasing bedding for the new nanny, something about helping her make the space her own, all on my credit card. I didn't listen too closely because I was busy soaking up all I could of Gibson before his bedtime, because I missed my little man.

After he went to sleep, Kady lectured me on making the nanny feel at home, in my freaking house. I thought the nanny

28

was supposed to fit into our family, not the other way around. Still, Kady went on and on about what a good fit Ari will be and how much Gibson already likes her. Part of me hopes she's right because I don't have it in me to go through interviewing nannies again. The other part of me worries she'll be a distraction because I'm not going to lie, she's beautiful in a natural way and it's hot. It doesn't help that I haven't been with a woman for, well, I can't even remember how long.

Is that why I'm so freaking nervous? This is my house, my kid, and my rules. If anyone should be nervous, it's her. The agency talked me into a clause that says if I fire her before the trial is up, Ari gets paid for the full month, but I have a feeling that's more of a protection for the agency than the nanny.

I'm not even sure how this nanny thing works. Do I have to explain stuff to her? Hopefully, she comes in like Mary Poppins and just does the job. When I suggested that to Kady, she slapped my arm and went on about how I needed to quit joking. Thing is, I wasn't really joking. I want her to fit with minimum effort on my part.

"Daddy, sim! Pease? Okay!" Gibs runs up to me with his hands in the air.

"Sorry, no swimming. It's too early. Ari should be here soon." He cocks his little blonde head to the side and looks up at me in recognition. He knows her name. Of course he does. Kady and Ari spent time with him on Sunday. I can't believe he already remembers her.

I pick him up out of his highchair as soon as my phone registers someone coming through the gate. He's been done eating for a while but has been happily playing with the last strawberry on his tray. I quickly wipe the yogurt remnants from his face before heading to the door.

She drives up in the ugliest Volkswagen Beetle I've ever seen. It looks like a 1973 maybe 74? The patchy maroon paint looks as if it's been through a war, patched up and then

29

involved in another war. It sounds rough too. She won't take my son anywhere in that contraption. Ugh, I don't even want to look at it. I make a mental note to make room for it in the outbuilding.

As she comes up the walkway, she slows to a near stop when she notices us waiting and looks at her watch. She thinks she is late. Hardly, she's a good ten minutes early, and it's irritating me.

She sticks her hand out. "Thank you for choosing me, Mr. Do—Ugh, Callum." I shake her hand firmly with my free hand.

"Here." I pass Gibson into her arms without warning. She takes him without question, her eyes big. But Gibson doesn't fuss or complain, which surprises me with the stranger danger stage he's going through. "Follow me."

She does as told, following me to the kitchen.

"Gibson has been waking up at about 7:00 this week. The week you interviewed, it was 5:30. You can never tell with him lately."

I reach across her to pull open the cereal cabinet, and my hand brushes her shoulder. A charge zaps between our bodies. What the hell was that?

"He usually has fruit and cereal for breakfast. Sometimes I give him a little yogurt." I show her where all his stuff is in the kitchen. I lecture her on what I want him to eat and what I don't. I show her where all his snacks are. I stop and show her his stroller in the entryway closet.

After that, we launch right into where and how he plays, his nap times and anything else I can think of. I go quickly and she follows me around but isn't afraid to pipe up with questions when she doesn't understand.

I try not to concentrate on how her jeans hug her in all the right places, only accentuated by the way she carries my son on her hip as he plays with her long blonde hair that has a natural wave to it. He does the same thing with my hair.

"He loves to swim, but I prefer to be the one who takes him in the pool for now." She nods and looks like she wants to say something but doesn't.

"What do you prefer to be called again? Arista? Ms. Addington?" I think she mentioned it in the interview, but I didn't retain it.

"Ari is fine, for everyone, even Gibson." She smiles at him, and the little traitor puts his head on her shoulder. She smiles down on him, her eyes softening at his loving gesture. I can't believe he's already this comfortable with her. This isn't good. I don't want him too attached to her, because when she leaves, he'll be devastated.

"The door to the patio is alarmed even though he can't reach the knob yet." I show her how to disarm it as we move through it. "When he's outside, he gets 100 percent of your attention."

"Of course." She adjusts Gibson on her hip, and surprisingly, he still seems comfortable there.

"He loves the pool and will wander towards it if you aren't paying attention. I have a pool net installed to protect him should he fall in. I'll show you how to work that later. I think that's everything. Am I missing something?" I look at her.

She shakes her head. "You were very thorough and you're here if I have questions. Right, Gibson?" She looks at him and he nods his head but gives her a weary look that he usually reserves for encounters with overly friendly strangers. I struggle not to roll my eyes at her comment.

"Wow, we've been at this longer than I thought." I can't believe Gibson hasn't fussed about being carted around on the tour of the house. How can he be that comfortable with her already?

"He's ready for his morning nap. Put him down and come find me in the kitchen and we'll go over a few more things." She nods and heads upstairs with him. He grips her neck tightly, looking over her shoulder at me as they walk away with a 'What the hell, dad?' look.

It's killing me not to follow her up there. I'm drawn to her, but also have a deep need to critique her, fault her for every difference in her technique.

I turn up the volume of the video monitor in his nursery. I probably should have mentioned that I have the nursery recorded. Leaving the light off in his room, she changes his diaper, then sits in the chair with him.

"Do you want me to read you a story?" He shakes his head and crumples his face like he's about to cry. She gently rocks him in the glider, looking quite maternal in his space. I don't like it.

"I know I'm new to you, but we'll become fast friends once we figure each other out," she says quietly, and he shakes his head. I didn't tell her he has a stuffed dog that he sleeps with. I contemplate going up there and showing her. But I don't. Instead, I watch Mary Poppins to see if she figures it out.

"UffUff." He says it quietly with a slight whine. It's his name for the stuffed dog Sammy gave him about a year ago. He loves that damn dog and insists on sleeping with it. I try to keep it in the bedroom because otherwise he'll carry it all over the house and leave it somewhere.

"UffUff?" she asks him and he scrunches his nose up at her. He nods his head. "UffUff!"

She looks around the room. "What's UffUff, buddy? Is that UffUff?" She points to his toy box.

He shakes his head and wiggles, trying to get away, and lets out a cry when he's unsuccessful, but Ari doesn't panic. She just continues to rock him slightly.

"UffUfffff." He strings out the last uff, letting her know he really needs his dog. She walks him around the room asking if various things are 'UffUff,' all while Gibs gets increasingly agitated.

Gibson finally catches sight of his stuffed dog on the shelf by the changing table. I probably tucked it there this morning. He reaches for it. "UFFUFF!"

Ari gives him a huge smile and hands him the dog. "Is this UffUff?" He nods and clutches it to his chest. They return to the chair and rock. As much as I want to fault her, she kept him calm during the search. The last time that damn stuffed dog went missing, he screamed at the top of his lungs for thirty minutes while the whole band looked for it.

She kisses his head and puts him in the crib. "Sweet dreams, Gibson."

He rolls onto his stomach and sticks his butt in the air, his preferred sleeping position since he was tiny. She closes the door, but not completely. I flip the video monitor off and move quickly to the table as she comes down the stairs.

"It went well," she reports. "We had a missing UffUff, but we found him." She smiles at me brightly as she comes back into the room.

"Good." I motion for her to sit across from me at the table. "You're fully responsible for his breakfasts and lunches. Sometimes his dinners, depending on what's going on with the band. I've already made them aware I'm not leaving until I'm comfortable with you, so the band will be meeting here for a while." I throw that in, hoping to see her get giddy with the idea of seeing the band. To my surprise, she doesn't.

I stop and look at her. "You'll need to keep him out of our hair when we're working. If we are working at bedtime, you'll be responsible for that too. If I'm not busy, I'll do bedtime."

"Understandable." She nods.

"You probably have foods you like. I have a housekeeper who comes in twice a week, and she does our shopping on Sundays. I leave her a list in this drawer." I reach over and open the drawer and pull out the list. "Add anything you like to the list. If you notice any of Gibson's foods or things like diapers are running low, please add them to the list." I can't help firing this stuff off at her. I don't want to get to know her. I just want her to do her damn job. By being brusque, I can eliminate the need for pointless chatter.

"Okay," she says quietly. "I have some questions, if you have a few minutes." She seems nervous to ask, and that just pisses me off. I nod, letting her know to ask her questions.

"Does Gibson have any allergies or health issues I should be aware of? Oh, also, I assume I get at least a day or so a week off, while we are at home anyway. Is there a particular day? And am I allowed to use the pool myself without Gibson, like on my day off or after he's in bed? What about your home gym? Am I allowed to put Gibson in a stroller and walk the neighborhood with him? Is there a nearby park he likes?" She fires off the questions so rapidly I barely catch the last few.

"Wow, that's a lot of questions." I run my hand through my hair. "No, Gibson doesn't have any allergies or health issues. Yes, you get a day and a half off. I'm not an 8-5 kind of guy, as you can imagine. Just tell me what day you'd like off and what half day you want off. It doesn't matter to me if it's morning or evening. Think about it and let me know." She nods, but stays quiet. Probably hoping I'll answer the other questions.

"There is a park up the hill on Meadow Court. You're more than welcome to walk there with Gibson, although he has his own play area in the backyard too. If I'm home, I'd appreciate you letting me know when you take him somewhere."

"I'm sorry, I don't remember the rest of the questions." I offer her a lame half-smile, even though I don't mean it. I can't believe I let Kady talk me into hiring her.

"Am I allowed to use the pool and the home gym when I'm not watching Gibson? Oh, and I didn't ask this, but I just thought of it... are there any rooms you consider off limits to me? I know you said Gibson can't go into the music room, but am I allowed to say, sit in the sitting room and read or come into the living room and watch TV?"

These questions are ridiculous and this time I can't control the roll of my eyes.

"The only places that are off limits for you are my bedroom and the music room. You can use the gym and the pool and the other rooms of the house."

"Thanks." She shifts in her chair.

I give her a set of house keys, and we exchange numbers.

"It goes without saying, my number is not something you should give out or sell." I glare at her hard. This will be the first true test of her trustworthiness.

"I'd never do that." She looks down at her phone for a minute.

"I don't know that, do I?" Her head snaps up at the bitterness in my tone. She has that look again, like she wants to say something but then thinks better of it. Good.

She finally breaks the awkward silence since my snippy remark. "Sunday and Wednesday mornings work okay for you?"

It takes me a minute to figure out she's asking about her off time. "That works for me." It's not lost on me that it's the same time that the housekeeper works. Does she not trust me with my own son? I've done just fine on my own for two years. I grit my teeth. Who is she to judge me? I run my hand through my hair. I should be the one with issues since I'm the one trying to trust someone with my son's well-being and heart. She better not fucking hurt him.

Chapter 5

Arista

Today has been very transactional so far. I get the distinct impression Callum wants me to fail or wants me to give him a reason to fire me. Well, I won't give him one. I don't need his friendship to be a kickass nanny to his son. Gibson is all that matters here.

Callum startles me as he stomps in the front door, when I hadn't even realized he'd left and tosses my car keys to me. "Your car is parked in my garage, which is the large building to the right of the driveway. If you need to take Gibson anywhere, use the Tahoe. Keys are in the same drawer as the shopping list. His booster seat is already installed. That car of yours is a deathtrap." His somewhat disgusted look tells me he thinks I'm crazy for driving it. How dare he insult *my* baby.

"Penny is not a deathtrap. She's a classic car! And moreover, she's *my* classic car. Hide her in your garage if you must, but I'll be using her on my Wednesdays and Sundays." I probably shouldn't be talking back to him since he is my boss. How pretentious of him to call my car a death trap just because she's an older lady.

"It's a classic deathtrap." He says it under his breath, but I certainly hear it.

Oh, fuck no! No one puts down my Penny. I will defend her to the death; she is all mine. Someone like Callum Donogue wouldn't understand that. I haven't seen the inside of his garage, but I'm sure it's full of fancy performance cars that he doesn't even know how to drive. He seems like the rock star who has so much money he'd pour it into cars he doesn't have time to drive. What a waste of both cars and money.

"Penny runs fine." Mostly, but I don't give him the satisfaction of knowing that. "And for your information, classic VWs are known to be fairly safe, even today. We can't all afford this year's huge ass SUV or luxury sedan." I slap my hand over my open mouth when it flies out before I can stop it. I immediately regret it. I'm giving him a reason to fire me. He slightly curls his lips upward. Shit. I've played right into his hand.

"Regardless of the safety rating or capabilities of your piece of shit car, under no circumstances are you to drive *my* son around in it. If you need to take him somewhere, you will use the freaking Tahoe." His tone is as icy as the glare from his dark blue eyes. Part of me feels like a scolded child, decidedly put in my place.

"Understood." I refuse to meet his stare because I don't want him to know that his words hit their mark. I knew he was going to be an arrogant asshole, I just knew it.

My cell phone vibrates with an incoming text in my back pocket. As much as I want to grab it and use it as a shield, I don't. It vibrates again with another one. Even though it's on vibrate, he must hear it because his eyes narrow.

"I'd also appreciate it if you'd keep your attention on my son and not on your phone." That's unfair. I haven't made one move to take the phone from my pocket.

"You didn't give me a chance to put it or my bag upstairs

when I got here this morning. I'll do that now." I turn on my heel, pick up my bag, and head upstairs to my room.

Kady: How's it going so far?

I throw my purse on the bed and put my phone on charge, ignoring Kady's text. She is the wife of Callum's bandmate, so as much as I like her, I'm not naïve enough to spill my guts about anything. I'll answer her tonight after Gibson's gone to sleep for the night. I don't need Callum hearing about how I'm texting his singer's wife all day long.

I'm halfway down the stairs to see if Callum has any other instructions for me when Gibson gives a cry. Thank goodness. Kids I can deal with, their grumpy, asshole dads not so much.

"Hi, kiddo. Remember me?" I set him on the changing table. "I bet soon you'll be learning to use the potty like a big boy. I'll ask your dad about his plans for that." I dress him in the same outfit he had on, chatting to him about 'RuffRuff' and his toys, trying to get him comfortable with me.

His weary eyes tell me we're not there quite yet. He's not upset with me, which surprises me, but he's just not comfortable with me. I thought when I came to get him, he might cry. He didn't, but Gibs doesn't hold me as trustworthy enough to get his full attention yet.

"Sim? Please? Okay?!" he asks, looking up at me with these gorgeous long lashes around his dark blue eyes. He's going to be a looker, like his dad. He's already a ton more polite, and he's only two. He'll have the girls beating down his doors as a teen.

"Let's ask daddy if he has time to go swimming with you."

I find Callum downstairs, still lurking in the kitchen. I approach, holding Gibson to my hip. "Gibson asked to go swimming. I was wondering if you have time for that now? I wasn't sure what to tell him since you said you didn't want me to take him into the pool."

"Are you freaking kidding me?" I jump at the voice from

behind me in the living room. I hadn't realized there was company over, or I wouldn't have asked.

Callum shoots his curly-headed drummer a glare that would make the meanest of dogs tuck their tail between their legs and run.

Sammy just stares at me. "Can you swim?"

I nod.

"Do you know CPR and all that first aid shit?" he asks.

"I'm Red Cross certified. It's a requirement of the agency I work for and a good idea in general."

His hair bounces as he turns to Callum. "What the fuh, feck, man? You let me take him in the pool all the time and I'm not certified in shit. Why not her?"

"It's my first day. It's natural for either of them not to trust me yet." I look over at Callum. "I'm sorry, I didn't realize you had company. I'll take him out to play in the sandbox." I head back upstairs to get his hat and slather him in sunblock. I tuck the tube in my back pocket so I can reapply if I need to.

"No sim." He seems resigned to the fact that he won't be swimming.

"Maybe you and daddy can swim later." He nods as he waits for me to uncover his sandbox. We sit in the sand and Gibson is content to pour sand out of cups and I show him how to use the molds. I make a mold of a crab. "See Gibson, crab!"

"Cab," he imitates and then scoops his next cup of sand out of the middle of my crab. After playing in the sand, Gibson moves on to playing with his tractor that sits on the lawn nearby, only to cap our playtime off with some more sandbox fun.

"Okay, buddy, it's time to wipe off the sand and have lunch. Does that sound good?" He nods.

"Unch. Gooood." I can't help but smile at his eagerness to talk.

"Do you want to walk or be carried?" He looks up at me

when I ask him the question. Cal must not give him the option to choose.

"Walk!" He starts towards the door, and I grab his hand.

"When we walk outside, we hold hands." His little fingers grip my hand.

When I finally put Gibson down for his afternoon nap, Cal isn't around when I come back downstairs. I grab a bottle of water for myself and go up to my room. I pull my laptop out and set it up on the desk. It has a window view of the front yard and I notice that there are a few cars in the driveway. I assume they are all in the forbidden music room.

I text Kady back since Gibson's asleep.

It's fine. Gibson's taking his nap with RuffRuff.

And then I shoot one off to my sister.

Hi V. All is well. Baby is napping. I'll call tonight. Xoxo

I organize my bathroom area and rearrange my shoes. I try to settle into my chair with my Kindle, but I can't concentrate. I'm too restless. A mug of tea would help.

I do a brief search of the kitchen but don't find any, but then again, I don't dig too hard. I feel awkward and unwelcome here, so rooting through the cabinets is not something I'm comfortable doing. I'm unsure if Callum means for me to be this uncomfortable or if it's just because this is all new to him. Gibson, at two, seems more adaptable to change than his father at this point. I shouldn't judge. Maybe I'm projecting my first day jitters into the situation.

I add a couple of my favorite snacks to the shopping list, and include my favorite pretzels, fig bars, and cheese sticks. By Wednesday I should know how dinner will work for me and can pick up some easy freezer meals if I'm not included in dinner.

Moseying out onto the back patio, I move a chair from near the pool to the edge of the yard that overlooks the valley. I pull Gibson's monitor out of my pocket and set it on the lawn in front of me and just enjoy the view. At least it's peaceful out here. I'm just about to take my shoes off when I hear Gibson stirring from the monitor.

I grab some snacks, water, and the sunblock I left on the counter and pack the stroller. Callum is still missing in action, so I text him.

Walking Gibson to park. Should be back in an hour.

I strap Gibson and RuffRuff into the stroller and we all head uphill to the park Callum mentioned. Gibson loves being outside, but what little boy doesn't? We swing, which I find out quickly he doesn't like. So instead, we slide and play in the sand. A slightly bigger kid comes over to Gibson and tries to show him how to climb the rope ladder, but Gibson is uninterested, in both the rope ladder and the other child. He doesn't seem to have much experience interacting and socializing. I'll make some friends of the moms in the area and arrange play dates for him.

After our snack, we play a little longer and then I load a sandy Gibson back into the stroller with RuffRuff and we take the scenic route home. Gibson spends most of the time babbling or pointing and screaming, "CAW" at every vehicle we pass. I love it. He's ditched his shyness and is showing off his vocabulary to me. And as a bonus, I feel better having some fresh air in my lungs and away from under the stifling mood in the house. This will be something we do a lot.

As soon as I unload Gibson and hand him his dog, he runs around in the great room as I put his stroller back. When I turn to join him, the entirety of the Blind Rebels are lounging in the room. If that doesn't make me do a double take. Since when did this become my life? I want to tell Vi all about it when I call her tonight, but I know I can't because of the nondisclosure agreement.

Gibson hands RuffRuff to the drummer, who is deep in conversation with him and the stuffed dog.

I stand there for a few seconds. Callum looks up at me and over at Gibson, as if I'm neglecting my job.

"I'll get him out of your hair. Sorry." I head towards Gibson.

"He's fine," Cal says to me. "Everyone, this is the nanny. Ari, this is everyone." He waves his hand around the room, then turns back to his brother, continuing where they left off, effectively dismissing me.

"Hey, Ari, I'm Mav." The lanky singer comes to me, hand extended. He oozes arrogance and confidence, the combination coming off as charmingly cocky. He's as stunning as he is in the pictures, with eyes the color of a chocolate bar. He's not my type, but I can see why some are so attracted. "You already know my wife, Kady."

I shake his hand. "Nice to meet you."

He smiles. "Seems my buddy, Cal, here has completely lost his manners." He kicks Cal's boot as he passes him and leads me toward the drummer. "Sammy, this is Ari."

The drummer pushes some errant blonde curls from his face. "Hey, Ari. We kind of met earlier. I'm Sammy." He smiles up at me from his conversation with Gibson.

Gibson points to me. "Awee?" My heart swells and I can't hold in the smile that breaks across my face. It almost makes up for the uncomfortable awkwardness that's been gnawing on my insides most of the day.

Sammy grins at him and then at me. "That's right Gibs, that's Ari."

Gibson nods in that serious two-year-old manner of his. "Awee." Sammy ruffles his soft curls, and Gibson giggles as he pulls back. "Messy!"

Mav leads me over to the Donogue brothers as they sit near each other talking. "You already know this rude asshole." He waves a hand over Callum. "I apologize again for him. He's apparently so sleep-deprived he's forgotten how to properly introduce people." He shoots my boss a glare.

"I didn't forget, jerkwad. I didn't think person-to-person introductions were important for the nanny. You don't know my housekeeper's name, do you?" Callum glares at Mavrick and the singer glares right back, his face awash with an incredulous surprise.

Callum's comment cuts me deep, so deep I feel it viscerally. I'm not important enough to introduce by name. I work hard on remaining the stoic, unseen domestic he deems me to be.

"It's Greta. She has a 22-year-old daughter who goes to UCLA on a full ride scholarship studying film production. She used to come on Mondays and Thursdays, but now comes on Wednesdays and Sundays." The singer stares at Cal, effectively shutting him down.

"Anyway," Mavrick continues, refocusing his attention back to me after giving Cal another scathing look. "Ari, this is Killian, Cal's much nicer twin brother." Killian lifts his gaze to me. They both have the same dark blue eyes, but Killian's are stormy where Callum's are icy and hard. Killian's hair is dyed jet black and is much shorter than his brothers, and he seems softer somehow. He's not all hard edges and tension like Callum.

"Hey, Ari." Even his voice is softer than his brother's. Killian lifts his chin in greeting and then gives me a soft smile.

"Hi. Nice to meet you."

He nods and glances back and forth between his brother and me.

"Well, I know you all are busy. I'll take Gibson upstairs to play." I scoop up my little charge, situating him comfortably on my hip.

"Noooooo. Down." Gibson arches his back in protest. "Down. Down," he whines, reaching for Sammy, who tries to placate him by handing him RuffRuff. "Down. Pease."

"I know, kiddo. Let's go upstairs and you can show me your favorite toys." I start towards the entry hall and the staircase.

Callum follows me to the stairs and corners me near the

43

closet where he keeps the stroller. "Before you go up, I'd like a quick word." He hisses quietly at me, probably aware that his bandmates are watching us. By his tone, I doubt he's here to apologize.

"RuffRuff does *not* leave the house ever, not even to the backyard. If he gets lost, Gibson will never sleep again." His quiet words are as cold as his glaring eyes, which pin me into the corner.

My heart starts to pound in my ears. I can't help but close my eyes, which is a mistake because I can suddenly feel Todd towering over me in the garage.

"You know, I should charge you to store your crap here." I can smell the burning alcohol coming from his breath as he towers over me.

I open my eyes quickly and Todd vanishes and Callum's in my face instead, glaring at me with his hard, dark blue eyes.

"Sorry. The dog never left the stroller. It's my job to track things and keep them safe. But no problem. RuffRuff stays home from now on." My tone is calm, and my words are soft as I am holding a squirmy, grumpy two-year-old. The whole band watches silently while Callum reprimands me.

"Let me know if you want me to take care of Gibson's dinner." I turn quickly and continue upstairs with Gibson.

I end up preparing and feeding Gibson his dinner while the band eats tacos at the table. Gibson seems to like the chunks of grilled chicken and his veggies from his approved list of foods. While he eats with the band, I keep an eye on him and clean up the little mess I made from fixing his dinner. I'm starving and drained mentally and physically. And I really need to talk to my sister about tomorrow. I put away the pan and grab more of the chicken I prepared for Gibson and deposit it on his tray.

Not sure where to position myself since there is no room at the table, I sit at the breakfast bar where I can keep my eye on Gibson.

They eat and talk like family. Kady waves at me. I shoot her a brief smile but keep my focus on Gibson, not wanting to give Callum another reason to scold me in front of everyone. I purposely ignore everyone at the table because I know I'll turn as red as a beet, the sting of Callum's reprimand in front of everyone still fresh.

They all chat and eat and tease each other. Gibson starts playing with his food, which is my cue that he's done. I clean his tray, then Gibson, the best I can as he wiggles away from me.

I unbuckle him, but Callum swoops in and lifts him out of the highchair before I can.

"I got him. You're done for today."

I give a curt nod after his cold dismissal and head straight to my room. I don't even look towards the group at the table, despite feeling all their eyes on me as I make my way up the stairs. I know if I do, the tears I'm holding in will spill and I don't want to give Callum the satisfaction.

I flop face down on the beautiful lilac bedspread, letting it dry my quiet tears. I expected to be tired since my first-day jitters turned into a lack of sleep last night. I even expected to be somewhat off kilter as I learned my way around a new house and family.

What I did not expect was a blatantly hostile boss. One who not only dislikes me but seems hell bent on looking for any excuse to fire me or drive me to quit. He may fire me, but I won't quit.

I don't know how long I have my solo pity party, but when I sit back up, it's gotten darker. The sun is slung low on the horizon and out my window I notice the band members in the driveway getting ready to leave.

I change into my workout clothes, grab my phone, and make my way to Callum's gym. Tucking my earbuds in, I pray he's not in there.

Thankfully, he's not. His home gym is bigger, and the equipment is way cleaner than my sister's paid gym. I figure I might as well make use of it. I use the elliptical until I'm winded, then jump rope until I'm winded again. Sitting on the mat in the far corner, I do my yoga stretches. Then I lay there on the mat and contemplate my working arrangement.

I don't know what I did to make him angry or why he bothered to hire me if he didn't want me here. But if it continues like this, I might be forced to quit. Again. And that alone makes me want to cry. I need to talk to my sister, but it's not like I can tell her about Callum.

Chapter 6

Callum

Mav: *Quit playing asshole rock star for the nanny. That's not you.*

Sammy: *Why so harsh with Ari? Gibs loves her. He's a great judge of character.*

Kady: *I've never seen you treat anyone as badly as you treated Ari tonight. You know I love you, but I don't like you right now. She probably doesn't either.*

Good. I don't want her to like me. I want her to quit. I can't be around her, she's too perfect. She's smart and amazing with my son; he's already in it with her. She's fuckin' beautiful. That long blonde hair in a ponytail is just made for pulling, and those legs make me think things I shouldn't. It's just too much for me to handle, her living with me and Gibson. This is why I didn't want to hire her in the first place.

"Aww done!" Gibs holds his hands up, asking to be lifted out of the tub.

I chuckle. "Not yet buddy, we gotta rinse you off first." I tip him back and get the shampoo out of his hair. He hates this part, even though I use that tearless baby shampoo stuff and take special care not to get water in his eyes. "Now you're all done."

I softly sing as I towel dry his soft curls. He sings the lyrics back to me, his head on my shoulder as we finish drying. He seems more tired than usual. Hanging with Ari most of the day tired him out, and a worn-out Gibson is a Gibson that sleeps well. Despite my misgivings about Ari, things went better than expected.

Until the band showed up anyway, when I couldn't reel back from being the dick I'd been all day. The only person who didn't give me any shit about how I treated Ari was my brother. He didn't offer any opinion on Ari. Everyone else went on and on about how great she is with Gibson and how well Gibson gets along with her already.

Across the hall and back in his bedroom, we put his pajamas on and sing one more song. 'Twinkle, Twinkle' is our nighttime standard right now. His eyes are heavy when I tuck him into his crib and slide RuffRuff beside him. He slings his arm around his dog and smacks his lips. I need to convert his crib over to a toddler bed, but part of me will miss knowing he can't get up and wander around the house while I sleep. I'll probably have to start sleeping with my bedroom door open so he can find me. I should have put Ari in the room across from him.

Heading downstairs, I grab a beer and pull open the drawer with the shopping list to make sure Sammy didn't add a bunch of crap. A couple of months ago, I ended up with 15 pounds of Belgian dark chocolate and an unbutchered pig thanks to Sammy's shenanigans. There is unfamiliar writing on the list, a smooth but slightly bubbly script that has to be Ari. Her items are small, mostly snack type things.

She didn't eat dinner tonight. As a matter of fact, I don't recall seeing her eating at all today and she's been here since 8:00 am. I should have let her know to help herself when she first arrived. I thought that was how it worked. She eats my food. I also should have included her in the taco order. Sammy suggested it, and I immediately shot him down. The human vacuum that is Sammy even offered her half of his tacos, but she politely turned him down.

Well, she shook her head no and headed to the breakfast bar where she kept her eye on Gibson, but didn't engage with any of us. Of course, I didn't give her much reason to want to engage with us.

Movement in the living room catches me off-guard and startles me so much I almost shout and my heart pounds out of my chest. Ari has changed into workout clothes and has a light sheen on her face. She's been in the gym. She moves quietly through the room, her face creased with frustration, maybe? No, more like disappointment. Earbuds in, she didn't hear me moving around in the kitchen. She's so in her head, she doesn't notice me at all as she slips out the back door and onto the patio.

I take my beer and head upstairs. After a quick peek in at Gibson, I grab my acoustic from the stand in the corner and slip out onto my balcony. Music always helps me think, or distracts me from thinking, whatever I need most at the time.

Reaching into my back pocket to get a pick, I hear talking and then remember Ari's outside by the pool. Peeking over the ledge, her legs poke out from the covered portion of the patio under my balcony, her bottle of water next to her lean, tone legs. Her black spandex pants leave nothing to the imagination, and they make me want to slide them down those sexy legs of hers.

"I miss you too, sis, but I'm sure Todd is glad to have you to himself." She gives a humorless laugh. "If this doesn't work, I should have enough to get a cheap place with some roommates." She listens. "You've done enough. I'm an adult and shouldn't have to run to my sister for every little thing." She sighs and crosses her legs at the ankles. "Yeah, I know."

I shouldn't be listening, but I can't help myself. Maybe she'll say something that I can use against her non-disclosure agreement. That would be an easy way to get rid of her. I should be watching my son, not a stranger, even if she's a beautiful one that he is already comfortable with. Mav's right though, I'm not an asshole. And treating her as shitty as I did today has me feeling like crap.

"I'm not upset. I just used the home gym. I'm a sweaty mess." She lets out a little laugh. "It's free and nicer than the one you belong to. A good way to work out my frustrations." Her hand brushes across her knee while she listens.

"No. I mean, yeah. I didn't sleep well, so I'm sure it's that. You know how I am when I don't get enough sleep." She sniffles a few times. Fuck, she's crying. *Dammit.* I hang my head down into my hands. I was king of the assholes today. I didn't need Mavrick's text to point that out. My gut sours knowing that I'm the one responsible for those tears.

"Plus, you know with tomorrow being the..." She stifles a sob, then listens for a spell. "I was going to, but I don't feel right asking now. I have half of Wednesday off. I'm going to pick up some stuff. We can go then, 'kay?" She leans forward and grabs her bottle, and it disappears under the cover my balcony provides. "Yeah, I know. I'll be busy with the baby, so that'll help." She stands and I move back towards my door so she can't see me up here if she looks up.

I've been a dick, yes, but I'm not sure I like that she wanted to ask me something but didn't feel comfortable because of my attitude.

"Yeah. I'll see you then, sis."

"Love you too." A few minutes later, I hear her feet softly on the stairs and the door to her room shuts.

R

I WAKE WITH A START. I stopped setting an alarm when Gibson was born. I didn't need it anymore. But now it's 9:04 am. My first thought is Gibson must be sick. He never sleeps this late. Then I remember Ari. She has the monitor I usually keep in my room. No wonder I didn't hear him.

As I make my way to the kitchen, the smell of breakfast makes my stomach growl. I stop the minute I get into the kitchen. It's not just clean, but immaculate, and there is a plate at the breakfast bar I assume is for me. There are scrambled eggs, a piece of toast, some orange slices, and strawberries. I make myself a cup of coffee and sit to enjoy the breakfast laid out for me. This is something I do not deserve. Not after the way I made her first day hell.

The house is quiet, eerie considering Gibson doesn't have volume control yet. They aren't in the yard, and there isn't a text or note letting me know that they went to the park or for a walk.

As I take the last bite of my eggs, I hear the muffled laughter of my son and what I can only assume is Ari. It's so faint, I barely hear it. Christ, even her giggle is beautiful, and it pulls at my chest.

The sound is coming from the hall. They aren't in the music room, or I wouldn't be able to hear them at all with the sound-proofing. But the gym seems like a weird place for a two-year-old. Peeking through the window in the door, I see Ari cross-legged on one end of the exercise mat and Gibson standing at the other end. They're rolling a big exercise ball that hasn't been touched since Becka lived here, back and forth between them. Well, Ari does most of the rolling.

"Big Baw!" Gibson hugs the large ball and laughs. "Frow!" He hits it with all his might, and it rolls off the mat. "Uh-oh!"

He runs after it and Ari laughs. She's quick to her feet and helps him navigate the ball back to the mat. She's all smiles and so is Gibson. My chest warms that he's so happy with her and she seems just as taken with him. She's so natural with him. Her smile lights up her entire face, and oddly, I want to be the one to make her light up like that. I shove those feelings immediately back down. I can't think like that about her. She's here for Gibson only.

They move over to the small trampoline, which was also something Becka claimed she needed but never used. Not the first thing she thought she wanted, then ditched.

Ari holds Gibson's hands and helps him climb up on it. She helps him bounce on it, encouraging him to jump. I would have never thought to bring him into the gym, let alone help him use some of the equipment.

"Hump!" Gibson yells and then tries his best at a jump, but only one of his legs leaves the trampoline. Ari encourages him to jump again and jumps on the hard floor next to him to show him how. He watches her and tries to emulate her, but he loses his balance and starts to fall backwards off the trampoline. Quick as a flash, Ari has him before he even fully leaves the trampoline, saving him from the fall.

"Oopsie." She rights him and they laugh, like it was nothing. Like she didn't just save my toddler from what could have been an injury all on instinct, like a mother would do. Fuck, if that doesn't warm me to her and hurt my heart at the same time, because she's already more like his mother than his actual mother.

She helps him flop on his butt on the trampoline so he can feel the bounce, then back to his feet and encourages him to flop down again. He does and cackles a full belly laugh and I can't help but smile, and apparently neither can Ari. Her full, unfiltered smile robs the breath from my chest. It accentuates her natural beauty, making her hazel eyes sparkle.

She catches me watching them, and the smile immediately falls from her face. Expressionless, she watches me watch her. She actually stiffens, like she's steeling herself against me, even though I'm not in the room. It's as if she's expecting me to yell at her, like I did yesterday.

This room isn't exactly childproof, and I would have never brought him in here. She's not only watching him carefully but engaging him, and he's having a blast.

To cover my stalker-like peeping, I push the door open. "Hey."

Gibson looks up at me, his face lighting up. "Daddee!" He runs at me, opening his arms to clutch my legs in a tackle-hug. I love his tackle-hugs the most.

I swing him up into my arms. "Good morning, buddy." I nuzzle into his neck and breathe him in. He smells like oranges and vanilla and his lavender baby wash from last night.

"Moanin." He flails his arm towards the mat. "Big Baw!"

"You were playing with the big ball?" He nods.

"Humps!" He bounces in my arms to emulate his jumps.

"I saw you working on your jumps. That was awesome."

"Aweshome." He parrots me, Daddy's little sponge.

During our exchange, Ari stands nearby, quiet, with a slight frown on her face. I put that frown there yesterday, and it's still here this morning. I'm queasy thinking of how I've treated her. It's created a wall between her and I, an awkwardness that's making living together wholly uncomfortable and we're only on day two.

I give her a rundown of my plans for the day, which includes leaving the house for a few hours, and she nods along, responding to me only when necessary. "You should probably keep your phone on you so I can update you if our plans change. With Sammy, I never know."

Her forehead creases deeply. "Okay." She draws out the last syllable, accentuating her confusion. "Yesterday you told me I shouldn't have my phone on me, so I can concentrate fully on Gibson."

I grimace. I did say that, only not as kindly as she states. I shrug. "I changed my mind."

Her only reply is a curt half-nod and a quiet, "Understood." She's nothing but professional, but she's also so shut down and aloof that I can see her walls from here.

"You and Ari have a good day, okay? Daddy's got to work at the studio." I don't. I'm hitting the beach with Sammy to surf for a few hours. Let them bond without me here, hovering over them. I need to get out of here and get some perspective, as Sammy said. Perspective comes from the ocean for Sammy.

"Awee!" He holds his hands out to Ari and she takes him.

"Let's go get my phone from upstairs. Say bye to your daddy." She seats him on her hip.

"Buh-bye, dadda!" He does his version of a wave, holding his hand up and opening and closing his fist as she carries him out of the room.

I scrub my hand over my freshly shaven face. Fuck, things are worse than I thought. I really fucked up yesterday. I was short with her, but I didn't think she'd be giving me the silent treatment today. I need to fix this somehow.

R

I'M GONE LONGER than I expected. After surfing, Sammy talked me into lunch because he's always hungry. I'd almost forgotten what it was like to sit and just have lunch without Gibson with me. Sammy doesn't mention Ari the entire time we're together, but I have a feeling that he wanted to.

The rest of the day at home is awkward. Ari is great with Gibson. The two are never far from each other. During his nap, she stayed upstairs. Watching them play before dinner, I could tell Sammy's right, he loves her already. But she's increasingly distant towards me and my stomach churns, knowing that distance is my fault.

"Hey, Buddy," I pick him up out of his highchair after feeding him dinner and Ari watches us from her seat at the bar where she stayed while Gibs and I ate alone at the table. There's plenty of room at the table without the band here, but she still sat off to the side and she didn't eat dinner again.

Isn't that exactly where I put her yesterday with my words about her being the hired help? I didn't invite her over, nor did I offer her anything to eat two nights in a row. I feel like a total d-bag. *There is no feeling like one. You are one, stupid.* I have a strong suspicion that even if I did invite her to eat with us, she'd stay over at the breakfast bar, foodless.

"Maybe Ari will take you swimming while I clean up." It's a peace offering. I'm trying to show Ari I trust her. I need to talk to her tonight. Apologize. This is my way of breaking some of the icy wall between us.

"Sim! Awee! Sim! Pease, okay?" He wiggles until I put him down, and when I do, he rushes over to her.

"Are you sure?" She looks at me warily, her forehead wrinkling with suspicion as she picks him up and seats him on her hip like she's been doing it her whole life.

"He loves it. He has this floatie shaped like a boat. I'll get it out of the shed while you two get ready."

When they return, he's got a swim diaper and a hat on. Ari has a coverup tied tightly around her, leaving me to wonder what's underneath. She sets Gibson down and tells him to hold her leg while she pulls her coverup off.

Jesus. It may be a simple navy colored one piece, but she's... yeah, I need to stop thinking about my nanny like this. I can't be this attracted to her; I hardly know her. It's not stopping all the inventive ways of removing that bathing suit from her and envisioning what's underneath that runs through my head like previews to a movie.

I watch from the kitchen as she carefully situates him in the floatie I tossed in the pool and sets him adrift. She stays right by him, chatting him up. He splashes her. At least she's laughing again.

After I finish cleaning up, I join them in the backyard with a beer, while Gibson squeals with delight as he splashes Ari.

She goes underwater and pops up on the other side of him. "Agin! Agin!" She does it again, and he laughs some more. However, her laughter has stopped since I've joined them out here, which makes my heart sink even deeper into my stomach.

He's so damn happy with her. And I have so much time now that I'm not chasing him around 24/7. Almost too much time because it's hard not to sit here and think about Ari.

After about thirty more minutes of pool time, Ari wrestles him out of his floatie. She wraps his favorite pool towel around him and flips the froggie hood over his head as she rubs him dry.

"Ibbie. Ibbie. Foggy." Gibson tries to mimic a frog as she dries him off.

I can't help but laugh at him. He's always the best part of the day, even the ones where I feel like shit for treating Ari like crap. "Yep, you're daddy's little froggy." I stand and take him from her so she can dry herself off. She turns from me as she does and promptly pulls her coverup over herself and tightly secures it.

"I've got him for the night if you want to stay out here and enjoy the evening or swim or whatever." Ugh, could I be more awkward in my own home? But I do remember her asking if she could use the pool, so she must like to swim.

I tickle Gibson, and he squirms in my arms. I hope she's out here when I come back downstairs so we can talk.

"Actually..." She stands in front of me, fidgeting and biting her lip. She's so uncomfortable just trying to talk to me that my gut churns. Is she quitting? I mean, I wanted her to initially, but she's so good with Gibson and he loves her already that now I'm not sure I want her to quit.

"Since tomorrow's Wednesday, is it okay if I pull my car out front tonight? I'm leaving early, and I don't want to disturb anyone in the morning. I'll be back by one."

"Sure, go ahead." Fuck. I was such a dick about her car that she's nervous just to ask me if she can take it out of the garage. What have I done? I'm not this asshole guy that she sees in me.

She leaves and I don't see her for the rest of the evening. I thought she might come back out like she did last night and sit on the patio. I was going to join her and apologize for Monday. Maybe chat with her and try to get to know her, so this living together thing is less awkward.

R

ARI LEFT BEFORE either Gibson or I were up. Surprisingly, I didn't even hear her bucket of bolts car start up. Gibson's been looking for her all morning, and it hurts my heart just a little. He's already attached to her after only two days. If this nanny thing goes wrong, which I am sure it will, he'll be devastated.

At ten to 1:00 pm, a vehicle pulls up to the front gate, but it's not Ari's Beetle. It's an older blue sedan of some sort. The gate log on my phone shows it's Ari's gate code being used on the pedestrian gate at the end of the driveway. I flip to the security camera. Ari's standing outside the driver's door, chatting. The driver is female, but her sun visor is down, and I can't see her face from the camera view. After a few minutes, the two embrace and Ari pulls out some shopping bags, and with a slight wave to the driver, she heads through the gate and up the walkway.

She lets herself in and Gibson's head turns from where he

sits on the floor in the living room with his toys. When he sees her, he immediately drops his car and pushes up to a stand.

"Awee! Awee! Aweeeee!" He takes off running for her and she quickly sets her bags on the floor so she can pick him up as he attempts to tackle-hug her.

"How's my favorite munchkin?" She tickles him and he wraps his arms around her head and gives her a big slobbery open mouth kiss on the end of her nose. She smiles and kisses him on his forehead. "That good, huh? Want to help me put my stuff away in the kitchen?" He nods and dives into one of her bags when she sets him down. He pulls out a box of tea.

"I hope you don't mind, I brought a few of my favorite teas and my mug from home." She glances up at me as she takes the box from Gibson. I flinch internally. She's living here and feels like she needs permission to have her favorite beverage on hand.

"Thanks, kiddo. You're a great helper." Encouraged by her words, Gibs reaches in her bag and holds up another box of tea for her and she praises him again.

She's dressed nicer than she has been the last couple of days. Dark jeans and a purple silk top that brings out the green in her hazel eyes. I hope that doesn't mean she was at a job interview. Or wait, if she gets another job, she won't be working here. So maybe it's a good thing. Damn, I don't know. I'm confused as fuck. She looks even more beautiful, which I didn't think was possible.

"I can keep them in my room, so they aren't in your way." She reaches down for another box that Gibs has pulled out.

"You can put them here." I clear a small area in the cabinet over the coffeemaker and relocate the few things that were there. "There's plenty of room." She nods her thanks at me and begins putting away her things.

"Oooh, cold!" Gibs has moved on to the next bag and is holding up a cheap microwavable meal, not even the substantial ones that have a dessert in the corner, but the kind that are perpetually on sale.

Ari squats down to his level. "You're right, these are cold. Let's put them in the freezer so they stay that way." Gibs nods and hands them to her one at a time as she puts them in the freezer. She sat by us for two dinners and didn't partake in either. She kept an eye on Gibson and made sure he ate and tended to him as needed, but otherwise kept to herself. As a matter of fact, I didn't see her eat *anything* at all the past two days. I hope she at least made herself some breakfast yesterday when she made it for me. The only thing I've seen her do is refill her water bottle using the fridge's waterspout. I shake my head at myself. *Nice manners, Cal.*

I still need to have that talk with her, but she's gathering the rest of the bags. "The rest of this goes up in my room. You want to help me up there too, munchkin?"

He heads towards the stairs and reaches for her. "Hands!"

She takes his hand but pauses to address me. "Don't worry, there's nothing he can get into in my room." Her voice isn't cold, but the aloofness in it bothers me even more than it would have if she had been icy towards me. I deserve icy, but the not-giving-a-shit vibe rolling off her is what's alarming me because I don't want her to start feeling that way about Gibson.

Ari and Gibs climb the stairs together with the rest of her bags, and I can hear Gibson's occasional giggle from down here. The next time I see them, Ari is wrestling Gibson's stroller out of the closet while he is trying to climb in.

"Buh-bye, daddy." Gibson holds up his hand and opens and closes his fist.

"Where are you going without giving me a kiss?" He runs over to me and gives me a wet, open-mouthed kiss on the cheek.

"Ari. Pawk." He pats my shoulder.

"Ari's taking you to the park again, huh?" He nods and I

pick him up and walk over to the stroller that she dislodged from the closet and snap him in. "Bye, buddy, have fun. I love you."

"Wuvs daddy." He smacks his lips and then covers his mouth with his hand. His version of blowing a kiss. I blow him a kiss and Ari gives me a curt nod and leaves for the park.

When I leave for Mav's in Malibu, I detour around the park to see what they are doing. Ari's standing next to the smaller slide, trying to coax him down. I need to talk with her tonight. This awkwardness is doing us no favors, and I don't want it to start affecting Gibson.

Oh, who am I kidding? I'm going to have to eat crow and apologize for being a dick to her for the last two days. As it is, Kady will be all over my case for not already doing it, and there's no chance in hell she won't mention it when I arrive at their house.

Chapter 7

Arista

When Gibson and I get back from the park, Callum's already gone. I shouldn't be so relieved, but I am. I even let out a huge breath I didn't realize I was holding.

After going to the cemetery with Vi this morning, I'm not in the mood to deal with his cutting remarks. The only reason I came back at all was because of Gibson. Well, and because I need the money. But Gibson has a huge part of my heart and I already love the little guy. He's such a sweetheart, unlike his ass of a father.

I give Gibson his dinner and heat mine in the microwave. We play a little before I give him his bath. We sing, I read him a story and put him and RuffRuff in his crib. I'm exhausted from getting up so early and being on the go all day, but I force myself to use the evil stair climber downstairs, then take a shower and curl up with my Kindle in bed. I don't think I even made it a chapter before falling into a deep dreamless sleep. At least I didn't drop my kindle on my face.

Enjoying the solitude of being the only one up early the next morning, it's my favorite time in Callum's house so far. My tea warms me from the inside out as I enjoy some me time on the patio with the newest book on my e-reader. This is when I feel most like myself in this new environment.

Just as I bring my cup of Lady Gray tea up to my mouth for another sip, I hear a raspy, sleepy rumble. "Mornin', Ari."

Startled, I jump and shriek. It causes me to dump my steaming hot tea onto my shirt. "Ahh! Hot!" I stand quickly, trying to pull the hot shirt away from my skin, forgetting about the baby monitor on my lap, which goes skittering across the patio. "Oh no."

When scrambling to reach for the monitor before it ends up in the pool, I somehow knock my mug off the arm of the chair, and it shatters around me as it explodes against the textured concrete patio.

It's my favorite cup because it was my mom's favorite coffee mug. I can't help the tears that instantly bubble out as my head hangs down. I don't even attempt to hide them from Cal, although I don't want him to see my ultimate breakdown.

What else could go wrong? My boss hates me, yesterday was the anniversary of my parents' death, my Volkswagen threw her transmission, which I can't afford to fix right now, and not only did I destroy my mom's favorite mug, but I'm sure I've busted what is no doubt a very expensive baby monitor.

"No use crying over spilled tea, Ari." His voice is light and almost humorous. Ugh, now he's mocking me. He lays a hand on my hunched shoulder and a hot tingle travels down my spine. Squeezing my eyes shut, I refuse to let him see me break.

I suck up the tears the best I can, throw my shoulders back and whip around to face him. "Whoa." He grabs my shoulders, stopping my movement and holding me in place. "Don't move. Your feet are bare and there are shards of the mug everywhere. I'll be right back." He takes a few steps towards the house but turns back towards me and scolds me like a child. "Don't move."

He returns with a broom and a grimace. Instead of starting to sweep, he sets the broom on the chair and stands with his back to me. "Hop on."

"What?" I don't get what he means.

"Gibson's awake. Hop on and I'll piggyback you into the house so you can go upstairs and get him while I clean up."

"You can't be serious." Surely, he didn't just suggest he carry me on his back to the house.

"Quite. Come on, Ari, hop on up." He squats slightly to encourage me to wrap my legs around his waist. Sensing my hesitation, he continues. "If you stand there and wait for me to sweep up all the glass, he'll be in full meltdown mode by the time you get to him. Trust me on this."

"For the love of God," I mutter, as I awkwardly grab his shoulders and hoist myself up onto his back. I'm almost overwhelmed by the intensity of his spicy scent. It's something I've only smelled lightly on Gibson. I fight the instinct to nuzzle my head into his back because I'm oddly comforted by the scent. That would be crazy weird. He's my freaking boss, the one who hates me. He sets me down in the kitchen and then turns around and heads back out to the patio without a word.

"Awee! Beckfist time! Pease, okay?" He is standing at the corner of the crib with his arms up, waiting for me to swing him up out of his crib. I wonder if he was about to try climbing out. I dress him and head downstairs. Once he's buckled into his highchair, I give him his fruit plate and yogurt and watch him eat. I show him how he can dip is fruit in the yogurt if he wants. He likes that and continues dragging his apple slices through the yogurt.

Callum sits at the table across from Gibson and me. I should be apologizing for breaking the nursery monitor.

"Can you come find me after he goes down for his morning nap? I'll either be in the gym or the music room. I need to talk to you." Frick, here it comes; the talk about all the reasons I am not fit for this job.

"Of course, Mr. Donogue." He winces at the formality of my reply, but says nothing. He watches Gibson for a few minutes and then nods and leaves us to our day.

We start with playing in the sandbox.

"Wuvs, Awee!" He hugs me around the neck and I breathe in his lavender body wash and feel tears threatening to escape. In a little over three days, this kid has wormed his way into my heart. It's the best part of being a nanny, loving someone else's kids unconditionally and having them reciprocate that love. I give my all to melt into families and give their children stability and love, only to be dismissed because someone doesn't like me, or I'm too good at my job, or too pretty, or not willing to put out.

"Humps! Humps!" He jumps up and holds out his hand. He wants to go and jump on the trampoline.

We make our way down to the gym, and Callum is there working out. Great, just what I want to deal with right now, knowing that soon Gibson will be sleeping, and I'll be fired. I wonder if I'll get to work the rest of my contract out or if I'll be leaving immediately.

"Awee! Humps!" He leans forward and pounds on the glass in the door, which catches Callum's attention, so I open the door.

"Is it okay if Gibson jumps on the trampoline? We won't disrupt your workout." Callum's wearing a tight blue tank top and a pair of dark blue basketball shorts, his hair tied back low against the back of his head. It's the most un-put-together I've seen him since I've been working here, but it's kind of hot. His toned legs are shiny with sweat and the right one sports a tattoo along the side that runs from knee to ankle, but I can't see the details from this angle.

Callum nods. "Sure. I'm almost done." He nods and takes a drink from a green refillable bottle.

"Dink, daddee! Dink. Pease?" He holds out his hands until Callum puts the pour spout to his lips and squirts in a little. Gibson smacks his lips and sighs, then starts wiggling to get down. "Humps, Awee!" I put him down and let him lead me to the trampoline.

I help him climb up and he proceeds to flop onto his butt and giggle. I show him my jump, and he works on trying to jump. And then flops down on his rear again and giggles some more. His giggle always makes my heart smile, so pure and unadulterated.

We move on to the big exercise ball and we roll it between us. He seems to think rolling it off the mat is hilarious because I jump up and chase it, trying to capture it before it interrupts Callum, who seems to be watching us interact more than he's doing anything else.

"Uh-oh, baw gone!" He runs after it. Callum watches Gibson and I play for a few minutes and then finishes up with his weights and leaves the gym. I let Gibson tire himself out good before heading upstairs and putting him down for his nap. Spending a few extra minutes watching him sleep, I wonder if this will be the last time I watch my little froggy snooze.

When I rap on the door to the previously forbidden music room, I don't get an answer. I wait a few minutes and then knock again, a little louder. Still no response, so I quietly push the door in. Callum has showered, his damp hair hangs loose around his head. He sits with his guitar on his lap and large silver headphones over his ears. His black t-shirt is well worn, so much that the band logo on the front is hard to recognize. His legs are now clad in tight black jeans. Callum's tongue is between his teeth as he plays, but I can't hear the music, just his fingers squeaking against the strings. He obviously can't hear me either, so I stand there awkwardly for a minute until he notices me.

"Oh, hey, Ari. Come on in." He removes his headphones and sets the guitar in a stand and shuffles some papers off the couch along the wall, moving them to a table. I swallow hard, sitting on one end of the couch, and he joins me on the opposite end. He sits sideways, facing me, his legs crossed like a child.

"I've been trying to find time to have this conversation with you since yesterday." He sighs and scrubs his stubbly face with his hands. He picks at the tread of his sneaker.

I hold my breath. Here it comes. I'm getting canned after less than a week.

He lifts his head, and his dark blue eyes connect directly with mine. "I apologize for treating you so poorly these last several days." He grimaces and glances away from me, only to return his gaze. It takes my brain a hot minute to realize that I'm not being fired, that instead he's trying to be nice to me.

"There's no excuse for how I've acted with you." He shakes his head. "It was rude. I was rude." The lines on his forehead deepen into crevices.

I open my mouth to speak, but he holds up his hand. "Let me get this out, then you can tell me whatever you need to." He waits for my nod before he continues.

"Thing is, that's not me. You probably don't believe me, and I wouldn't blame you one bit with the way I've treated you. Ask anyone who knows me well, like the guys. They'd tell you I'm not the pretentious rock star asshole I've shown you. I can show you three different texts Monday night, making sure I realized what a jerk I was being to you." He sighs and his shoulders hunch.

"You probably guessed it, but I didn't want a nanny. Gibson is *my* son, and *I* should be the one taking care of him. I don't trust anyone else to do the job because they aren't his dad. That's nothing against you, it's just how I feel."

He pauses and motions around the room filled with musical instruments. "This lifestyle with the late hours, the traveling, the parties, it's hard with a kid. I've been handling it with help from my Aunt Sandy, but she's getting on in years and Gibson's an active toddler."

He looks up at a black-and-white picture of a younger Gibson resting back against Callum as his hand holds Gibson secure, across the stomach. The photo shows not just a content baby Gibson, but also illustrates Callum's protective, loving nature.

"Gibson, he's everything I didn't know I wanted." He looks back at me. "The other guys don't necessarily understand, I don't think, since they aren't fathers." He sighs.

"If this doesn't work?" He motions back and forth between us with his hand. "I leave the band. Music has always been my life, fuck, it probably saved my life a time or two. But it's not more important than my son."

Tears try to spring from my eyes at his confession and self-resolve. I can't speak, not just because it might cause them to fall, but also because I got more than I ever expected out of this conversation.

I came in here prepared to defend my job and my abilities. Now I'm playing catch-up and don't know quite how to handle all the information being given now that Callum's opened up to me. Yes, he's been an asshole towards me, but Callum Donogue is not just a man struggling, he's also struggling with asking for help.

Is any of this my fault? No. Nor is it an excuse to treat me like shit. But sitting this close to him, I'm hearing more words out of him than I have since I met him, all in his normal tone, not the clipped asshole one he's been using with me. He's not the cocky, asshole rock star, but a flawed, struggling father needing help but unable to ask for it.

It makes a little more sense to me now. I couldn't figure out what I had done to cause him to react to me like he had. But he's extending an olive branch out to me. No, not quite an olive branch, more like an outstretched hand asking for help. Both are hard for most men, but for some reason, especially for this man in front of me.

My silence must make Callum uncomfortable because he glances up at me through the dark brown hair that has fallen into his eyes as he continues to fuss with his shoe. When I still don't say anything, he clears his throat, straightens his shoulders and glances again at the picture of his son as if he takes strength from it.

He returns his eyes to mine, and they are softer and more emotion-filled than I've ever seen. "I'm truly sorry. Please don't quit."

Chapter 8

Callum

My stomach clenches so tight it hurts. I didn't mean to say all that. I sound so fucking desperate, so vulnerable when I've spent my life trying to be strong. Music has been my life almost as long as I've been alive. It's not as easy to leave it as I make it sound. But there's no question, Gibson is more important, *the* most important.

If I don't put him first, who will? His mom, who signed away her rights to him before he was two months old? Hardly. I've heard women say that they didn't know it was possible for their hearts to live on the outside of their body until they had a child. I understand that feeling, because all my heartbeats are for him. He's the most important thing in my life, even above the band, which fucking says a lot because they are my family.

Ari takes a breath and opens and closes her mouth a few times, like she's thought better than to say something. That's my fault. I've been a snarky asshole for the better part of three days now.

"Just say it. Don't censor yourself because I'm your employer. Say anything that's on your mind."

"I was going to say that you *are* an asshole, but I've decided that isn't necessarily true." She looks at me like she can see me on the inside, which disarms the hell out of me.

"For whatever reason, asking for help is hard for you. Somehow, my presence represents some sort of perceived failure on your part, but that's only how *you* see it, not anyone else." Another exacerbated sigh falls from her lips. "It's not a reason to treat me like crap, Callum." She sighs, but at least she's back to using my first name.

"If I'm being honest, if I didn't already love your son, I wouldn't have come back on Wednesday afternoon." Shit, that stings. A small part of me wondered if she'd bother to come back after she left so early and quietly on Wednesday. If she had left for good, it would have been my fault because I was a total asshole to her. That's not the kind of person I want to be, not the kind of model I want my son to grow up with.

"I love working with your son, and I'm not a quitter, but I came really close to not coming back." She stares at me until I return her gaze.

"As a stranger coming into your family dynamic, I can tell you that Gibson is a curious, talkative, and loving little boy. That's because you've done an awesome job already. I'm not here to replace you. You'll always be his father. You're a good one, and it's obvious you're his whole world." She pauses and looks up at the picture of Gibson that hangs on my wall. It's one of my favorites. He's on my lap, resting against me and smiling at something. All you can see of me is my tattooed hand across his midsection, holding him safely to me.

"My job is to give Gibson the care, stability, and love that you would when you're not able to be with him and to give you peace of mind that he's being cared for to your standards."

She looks back at me. "We should be working as a team for Gibson, but right now you're openly hostile towards me, oftentimes for what seems like no reason. It's hard for me to even want to be a team with you when I feel belittled and afraid that my slightest misstep will have you jumping down my throat. Or letting me go." Her eyes are suddenly glossy, like she's about to cry. But she doesn't let her tears fall. I'm not proud to be the one that put them there and I feel even worse that it's not the first time she's cried because of my fucking attitude.

"If I do something you don't agree with or something you don't like, just tell me. We can talk about it. I'm a reasonable, levelheaded person. I can take constructive criticism. What I can't take is the stress of walking on eggshells around you, Callum, afraid that you'll chastise me for breaking a rule I didn't know about in the first place."

I blow out a sigh but don't comment right away, because I don't know what to say. I'm not usually like this. Watching her integrate so seamlessly into Gibson's routine and work her way into his heart was a huge red flag to me, but it shouldn't have been. I didn't want her that close to him so quickly. It means that when she leaves, the more it'll hurt him. But she's also shown me that he needs her fun-loving touch.

She lets out an uncomfortable laugh at my silence. I think she's trying to ease the tension in the room.

"Try looking at this from my perspective for a second. It's not easy to come into this situation and not be intimidated. I mean"—she waves her arms around, indicating my house—"before moving in here, I lived with my sister and her husband in a condo in North Hollywood that'd probably fit entirely in your kitchen, living room, and half of your music room."

She drops her previously animated arms. "Maybe it's naiveté on my part, but just because this is your life"—she waves her arms around again—"doesn't make you any better than me."

I never said I was any better than her. Likely, the opposite is true. Killian and I didn't have the most upstanding upbringing. We didn't know our father. Our mother literally abandoned us before we were teenagers. We've both struggled to understand and feel love. My goal is to stop that cycle for my son.

She shifts on the couch, moving to the edge as if she's ready to get up. "I'm staying the duration of the month trial because I need the money. Unless you fire me before month's end, you're stuck with me for the month at the very least. I'm hoping for longer, for permanent. Regardless of how long I stay, let's at least try to figure out a way to work together and be a team for Gibson."

She stops and looks at me hard. "But if the asshole really is you? We won't become a team. I work well with children, but not unreasonable, asshole-y adults. Sadly, I fear Gibson will be the one to suffer the most."

"I don't know your background, but as you know, I have a degree in education. Your son may only be two, but he's in the middle of the largest developmental stage he'll go through in his life. There's a reason they call these the formative years, Callum. Gibson is actively learning from everything he sees and hears. He's a pint-sized living, breathing human sponge, soaking in everything about life and sorting through it to get a basic understanding of how the world works. Whether Gibson is playing alone or with others, or just observing how others interact with each other around him, he's always taking it in, always learning." What she's saying makes sense, but it's nothing I would have ever thought to consider.

"If you're constantly an asshole to someone, you may find yourself raising a mini-asshole alone in your fancy house while your bandmates tour and make albums or whatever." She lets out a humorless laugh.

I never even considered Gibson paying attention to conversations he wasn't a part of. I can't believe this fact about my son is just now clicking with me. Am I that stupid that I didn't realize this? I don't want my son to treat women like I've treated Ari. I'm not a very good role model for him.

She shrugs as she stands. "I'm sorry I ruined the nursery monitor this morning. Please replace it out of my pay. I should get back upstairs so I can hear him when he wakes up."

Ari heads across the music room. I don't want her to think I haven't been listening to her.

"I want to be a team, Ari." My words to her are a quiet resolution. I want this to work for my son. He needs someone with the kind of resolve Ari's shown me the last few minutes. It's clear she is here solely for the well-being of my son.

She stops at my words but doesn't turn around.

"I want this to work."

She nods back silently, then carries on upstairs.

R

FOR THE NEXT TWO DAYS, I stick around the house with Ari and Gibs, working on the teamwork Ari talked about. It's hard because the more I'm around her, the more incredibly attractive and fucking tempting I find her. I try to remember she's here for Gibson, not me. I need this to work so that I can make the music that I love. I need to just stay away from women in general; they fuck with my head.

I won't ruin what she is to Gibson by caving into temptation, because the more we are all together, the more it's crystal clear that Ari is the person I want watching my son. Watching her interact with Gibson makes me interact with him in a deeper, more meaningful way. She's always teaching him something, even when he doesn't know it and I'm always learning how I can be more purposeful in my interactions with him. If he asks for a ball, she repeats to him that the ball is green. Teaching him colors when he's two is not something I'd have ever thought to do. Isn't that why I decided on Ari in the first place? Because she had the background to know shit I wouldn't know how to do?

Gibson loves her with all that he is, and while I love seeing him connect on that level with Ari, it still scares the ever-loving crap out of me. He loves her almost as much as he loves Kady, which is a lot, and he's known her his entire life. He doesn't open himself up to a lot of people, something he probably gets from me. He keeps his circle of trust tight because I do.

He loves Sammy, Kady, and me. He kind of likes Mav. Even though Mav loves him, they still have a somewhat tenuous relationship. Mav teases him without realizing and I think it confuses Gibson. Gibs tolerates my Aunt Sandy and usually tolerates Killian, but Killian doesn't tolerate Gibs. Theirs is another relationship on a string and one I'd love to strengthen to a rope or a chain.

If you're not within his circle of people, then Gibson regards you with a shy curiosity but doesn't get too close. He hasn't even gotten close to Greta, my housekeeper, and she's always leaving him little surprises in his room. I don't know if he doesn't realize who Greta is or if he just doesn't feel a need to get that close to her. Something else he's probably gotten from me.

Everything Ari does is for his enrichment and growth. She's always giving him choices to make, something else I would have never thought to do. Does he want an apple or a banana today? Does he want cereal or yogurt? And she tells him she loves him, a lot. Both are things I need to do more of. Because I do love him. He's my damn world.

Ari returns from putting Gibson down for the night and sits on the end of the couch nearest my chair.

I hand her cell phone back to her. "It's all configured and working with the new nursery monitor system. And I added the gate remote to your phone so you can use it instead of punching in a code each time."

"Thanks." She opens the app to the nursery monitor and

watches Gibson for a few minutes. "I still feel bad about the baby monitor I broke."

"I was planning on upgrading it anyway. This just spurred me to do it sooner. And now, no bulky receiver." I reach out and touch her arm to reassure her and it zings all the way through me to my groin. Shit, that was a surprise. I can't remember a time when a single touch made me feel like that. "It's not a big deal, Ari, really. Any big plans for your day off tomorrow?"

She shakes her head. "My sister and I are going to lunch, but I'll be back by the early afternoon. Just reading, I guess. Maybe catch up on my laundry."

"Greta can do your laundry." She'll refuse the help, just like she refuses to eat with Gibson and me. It doesn't stop me from asking every night, but each time she insists on sitting at the island with her crappy little frozen dinner, despite me making plenty of food and setting a place for her. I thought I told her food was on me on her first day here, but she buys her own frozen meals and continues to eat them. "Greta has enough to do. I'm perfectly capable of doing my own laundry."

I nod, not doubting she can do her own laundry, but having Greta do it should be considered a perk for her, just like me buying her food. I don't say anything, though.

"I cut up some watermelon into Gibson-sized pieces and put it in a baggie in the fridge. He's really liking watermelon lately. I left his bowl next to the fridge, so you don't have to go into the cabinet for it. Oh, and I put diapers on the shopping list because he's running a little low. You should have plenty for tomorrow, though." She looks like she's trying to remember something. "I think that's it."

"Thanks, Ari, for everything you do." She nods, but I don't think she hears the sincerity in my thanks. I'm trying hard to make this work, become the team she mentioned. I want her to know I have already learned so much from her, but I feel weird telling her that, like she'll think I'm some sort of weird stalker.

"I hope you'll join us tomorrow afternoon. We're having a barbecue. We do it a few Sundays a month when we aren't touring. Sometimes it's here, sometimes it's at Mav's place in Malibu. It's just the band and whoever Killian is currently sucking face with. There's always good food and music. Gibson will be there, of course, but you won't be responsible for him. Come relax and hang out with us." I touch her arm to let her know I'm serious, and for some reason, my heart beats faster. I really want her to come to the barbecue.

She shrugs, not committing one way or the other. "Maybe." She unfolds her legs from under her and rises from the couch. "I'm heading upstairs. Goodnight, Callum."

R

THE NEXT MORNING, Ari is coming out from a workout as Gibson and I are entering the kitchen.

"Awee!" Gibson holds his hands up, wanting her to take him.

I expect her to ignore him since it's her off day, but she comes over and plants a kiss on his head. "Ari is stinky and needs a shower. Have a good breakfast, munchkin."

Gibson wrinkles his nose and repeats, "tinky," which makes Ari laugh. She only laughs when she's with Gibson. He watches her go up the stairs as I take him into the kitchen.

I repeat Ari's usual breakfast routine. "Do you want Cheerios or yogurt today?"

He regards me for a moment. "Chee-ohs."

"Cheerios it is." I put some in a bowl.

We don't see Ari again until 10:00, as she is preparing to leave. "See you later," she says, more to Gibson than to me.

She waves and Gibs waves in his signature style. "Buh-Bye, Awee! See waiter." When she closes the door behind her, he runs into the front sitting room and crawls up onto the couch by the window. He watches her walk down the driveway through the bay window. "Buh-Bye, Awee!"

Gibs looks up at me. "Awee buh-bye."

I pick him up and his arms go around my neck. "Yeah, Ari went bye-bye, but she'll be back later, buddy." He nods, but I wonder how much he really understands.

Ari arrives back at the house at almost 2:00 pm. She puts a to-go container in the fridge and heads right upstairs. I'm unsure what the protocol should be today. It's her off-day, and I don't want to pester her, but I don't want to be rude and not acknowledge her either.

"Awee!" Gibson looks upstairs.

"Yeah, she's home, buddy, but today's Ari's day. You're stuck with daddy today." He wraps his arms around my neck as I carry him upstairs and put him down for his afternoon nap.

I'm disappointed when she doesn't join us for the barbecue. I don't see her for the rest of the evening. Kady gives me a lecture about how I'm not doing enough to incorporate her into our life.

By the next week, Gibson seems to understand that Ari has times that she is off. He also thrives with the routines she's built for him. They are easy enough to stick to on her off days and they make it easier for him to transition from activities. His vocabulary is blossoming. He seems to use more and more words and says them clearly. Ari's constantly talking to him.

When she's on duty, we're a well-oiled machine. I've loosened up on being such a jerk. It's still hard to resist her, so I've locked down my attraction, but that's only made it stronger. I'm determined to keep this solidly in a friend-zone.

I've also learned little things about her while working together. She drinks tea the way Mav drinks coffee, first thing in the morning, as if it's her life's blood. She has one cup in the morning and sometimes a different one in the evening. She does yoga at least three times a week during Gibson's morning nap. I've changed my workout schedule to match hers. Sometimes we banter back and forth in the gym, but mostly when she's doing her yoga, I leave her alone. Don't think I haven't noticed how damn flexible she is.

In the evening, she sits on the patio or in the living room and scribbles into a notebook. I can't tell if she's drawing or writing because I mostly watch her face as it smooths into a dreamy look as she gazes off into the distance or at the television. Then a storm will pass over it and it's back to scribbling. The few times I've asked her what she's doing, she just shrugs it off, which I have learned is my cue to mind my own business.

Ari's cutting up carrots and radishes for Gibson's lunch, her hair in a loose bun while she chops. She's always doing something while he's sleeping. Thinking about her and those yoga positions yesterday is making me want to bend her over the counter and see just how flexible she really is. I shake those thoughts out of my head.

I grab a carrot from her pile and munch it. "So, what happened to your car? You never brought it back." She's probably keeping it at her sister's because I lambasted it, not one of my prouder moments.

She doesn't even look up at me as she continues to add to her pile of carrot pieces. "The transmission blew out. Unfortunately, getting it fixed isn't something I have time for right now, or even really need since I drive your Tahoe if I need to take Gibson somewhere." She sighs and continues to chop. "Penny's sitting in my sister's driveway for now." She shrugs. "I'll fix her up the way she deserves one of these days." Her voice is almost wistful as she thinks of her beloved bucket of bolts.

Her attachment to that ancient Volkswagen fascinates me. I don't get it, but I can tell her car means something to her. It's just another thing that makes Ari, Ari.

She has a huge heart, but she keeps it to herself. My favorite moments are the ones where she doesn't realize I'm watching her and Gibson interact. She's very maternal with him. I've seen her hug him and tell him she loves him more than once. And I love it when she tickles him. Between his shrieks of delight and her infectious giggles, I have no doubts about her. He's attached. Last night he told her he loves her and gave her a kiss before he went to bed.

With me, she's still on her guard. She doesn't often open up to me, not about anything personal anyway, and she almost never laughs. She reserves that for Gibson.

Chapter 9

Arista

When he's not preoccupied with being an asshole, Callum's a normal guy, if there is such a thing. Gibson is the center of his world. Even when I'm not directly interacting with Callum, I feel him observing my interactions with his son. In the evening, he'll often ask about things I do and the reasons behind them. Then he'll try to emulate me.

When Callum asks me about something I'm doing with Gibson, it's more out of curiosity than questioning my motives, abilities, or education. Not only am I helping Gibson transition from toddlerhood to childhood, but I'm also helping his father learn ways to assist him along the way. At least he's becoming friendlier.

He watches me transition from one pose to another while I'm doing my yoga. He's watched me the last few times I've been in his gym, and I'm not sure how I feel about that.

He finishes up on his weights and comes to the edge of the mat in the back of the gym and sits cross-legged at its edge.

"Teach me some of this yoga stuff you do. Why do you do it?" His head is cocked as he sits there.

"Yoga helps me stretch my back and keep my back pain at bay. But it's also wicked good for your balance, flexibility, and mind." I've never mentioned my back pain to Callum before. I hope I don't regret doing that.

"Wicked good?" His lips turn up as he questions my wording, to which I respond with a shrug. "What do I do first? I'm putty in your hands."

"You're hardly putty. Let's see how flexible you really are. Take off your shoes and socks. Yoga is meant to be done barefoot."

He quickly complies. "Okay, let's do this." He claps his hands together and rubs them.

"First, we sit and breathe." I sit on the mat and cross my legs underneath me.

"Breathe?" He sits cross-legged in front of me, his eyebrows raised. "That's, uh, weird." His lips turn down slightly and his eyes dart to his left towards the door.

"It's not as weird as it sounds. You've never really focused on it before because breathing is something we do automatically. We'll be focusing on the natural breath. There are four parts to each breath you take; the inhalation, the retention, the exhalation, and the suspension." I go through what each part of the breath is with him and then we practice holding each in our awareness.

We move into some beginner poses. Callum has some nice guns and is strong and fit, but he is not very flexible. A giggle bubbles out of me as he tries the extended triangle pose and ends up tipping forward and nearly landing on his head.

He grimaces at me. "I'm not good at this."

"Sorry, I shouldn't laugh. We all start somewhere." I move down to my back to show him the bridge position, which he easily aces.

"So back pain?" he asks with a slight grunt as he thrusts his hips off the ground, which is oddly erotic, so I look away.

"Yeah, yoga keeps me limber, which helps with my back pain."

"Tell me about this back pain. How did you injure your back?" He turns his head to look at me as I perform the perfect child pose next to him.

"I've had back problems since I was a teen." I'm not giving him anything to hold against me, so I won't give him and specifics. I don't think he'd fire me because of my back problems unless it got to the point that I couldn't properly care for Gibson, but I'm also not stupid enough to give him ammunition.

"It doesn't keep you from working." It's a statement and not a question, so I'm unsure if he expects a follow up to it.

"I guess I've learned to live with it to some degree. I focus on things I know help, like yoga." I stare at Callum as my head is positioned on the floor. "Jobs where I am required to stand on my feet, like retail, do not help." I can't believe I gave him that. I won't give him anymore. I sit up to indicate we'll be transitioning into our last pose.

I lay on the floor on my back. "This one is called corpse pose. A lot of yogis say it's the most important pose. While we lay, we concentrate on breathing like we did before we started."

I glance at him out of the corner of my eye, and he lies there, eyes half-closed as he breathes in, holds, breathes out, and waits before starting the whole cycle again. He looks peaceful. I focus on my breathing for a few more minutes, and by the time I sit up, Callum is snoring lightly, completely relaxed, head slightly lolled to the side.

I've been there, so mentally and physically tired that I've fallen asleep on the mat, especially when I was first learning. I consider leaving him here, but that seems cruel somehow.

I nudge him gently with my foot. "Callum?" Nothing. He's out. His face is soft in this relaxed state, and he looks younger when he's asleep. Do we all look younger when we sleep or does Callum wear all his stress so that it ages him? His long, dark locks fan out slightly on the mat, and I resist the urge to run my fingers through it to see if it's as silky as it looks.

I nudge him a little harder, this time in the ribs. "Callum?" I say it a little louder and he snorts and opens one eye. When he realizes where he's at, he sits up, probably a bit too fast.

"Sorry, I, woah—" He props himself on the mat against the swimming in his head. "Head rush."

"You sat up too quickly. And don't worry about it. I think everyone's fallen asleep at the end of yoga at some point." He looks at me with an eyebrow arched in question. "Even me."

He finally stands up. "Thank you. I might add some of that stuff to my workout."

I nod at him.

"I really like this." He motions back and forth between us.

"Yoga? I can recommend a studio if you want." He sure didn't seem to like it when he was grunting and moaning through some of the positions, and I sure as hell can't picture him in a class full of people. "I'm definitely not a professional when it comes to teaching it."

"No, us, being friendly. Being friends." He pops up from the mat with ease.

I nod again, not looking at him.

"We are friends now, right?" He steps closer to me so that his salty, spicy scent envelopes me. I shrug but add a little half-nod to it because it's hard for me to reconcile my asshole employer with this Callum, but I do like this new rapport with him.

He puts his hand on my shoulder, and its warmth radiates through my shirt. "Is that a yes?"

"Yeah," I whisper, then clear my throat. "Friends." I can almost envision more with this Callum, and I kind of like the idea. But I can't feel this way. He's my boss.

I concentrate on visions of him from the first couple of days and those biting comments and steely glares of his to remind myself there is nothing good there, so I'm not as tempted by him, but it doesn't really work.

My phone alerts with the telltale rustling of a waking Gibson. "Duty calls," I say as I take a step back, and Callum's hand falls back to his side.

Chapter 10

Callum

Does she feel the energy we just exchanged? I sure as fuck did, it tingled all the way to my balls. Can't say that's ever happened before. It makes me want to touch her again to see if it happens. But what if it does?

She scurried out of here like her ass was on fire when Gibson woke up. Maybe the connection I thought we shared is a one-way thing. Even if it wasn't, it's not like we can act on it. She's my nanny, and I won't take that away from Gibson. He trusts her implicitly. He loves her. I want him to have that kind of connection with the person caring for him. It's exactly what I'd want in a nanny, someone that my son loves and trusts. With the way her face lights up when she sees him, even on her days off, I'm pretty sure she loves him right back. That tells me all I need to know; the person to care for him is Ari.

After my shower, I end up on the patio. Gibson and Ari are playing in the sandbox. "Hey, Ar?" She looks up at me from being crouched in the sand as Gibson packs sand in an old set of measuring cups that Kady gave him. "I forgot to mention the guys are coming over. We're going to write this afternoon, but we'll eat first. We're getting tacos. What kind do you like? Assuming you like tacos."

"Who doesn't like tacos? I'll take shredded or ground beef, crispy if they have them. Two is plenty." I nod and text Sammy to pick up at least four more so that Ari and Gibson can join us. I'm surprised she agreed. Usually, when we ask her if she wants something when we get takeout, she shakes her head and politely declines the offer. Maybe she's warming up to us, to me, after all. Then again, it could just be that she really likes tacos.

I deposit Gibson in his playpen and start laying out napkins for lunch. Mav and Kady stroll in with Kady carrying a tray of cupcakes that I take from her immediately. "Why are you making Kady carry things in her condition?" I glare at Mav.

"She bought them. She wanted to carry them." He shrugs. "Where's Gibs?" Mav looks around.

I nod over to the playpen, and he's already lifting Gibson into his arms. "Where is Ari?"

"Upstairs showering. Gibson dumped a cup of sand on her head and then in the name of trying to help, he rubbed it into her scalp."

Mav looks at Gibson with big eyes. "Did you do that, Gibs?" Gibson shakes his head, adamantly denying it. "I didn't think so." He looks around.

"Ari's having lunch with us?" Kady rubs her stomach as she tucks into Mav's side. I like seeing Mav this way. He's fully invested in Kady and their baby.

I nod.

"Oh, good. We had so much fun together last Sunday, shopping for the baby and having lunch together."

"Yeah, she'll be down shortly. And the tacos should be here soon too."

"Did someone say tacos?" Sammy and Killian walk in carrying a huge amount of food as Ari comes downstairs, hair still damp. Sammy pulls out some tacos for Ari and hands them to her as he divvies up the Mexican food on the kitchen table.

"I only wanted two!" She looks at me.

"One is for Gibson to try, and the other's a spare in case he tosses it onto the ground or something. I thought it might be fun to see if he likes it, since he's never had a taco before. They aren't spicy unless you put the salsa on," I tell her. "I don't know how much of it he'll eat."

The guys and Kady stare at me like I've grown a second head.

"I thought you didn't want him eating fast food?" Kady ventures.

"It's a damn taco. It has cheese, lettuce, and meat in it. He might not even like it. We'll see." I shrug. "It's not like I'm suddenly feeding him a steady diet of Oreos and fries."

I snap Gibson into his highchair as Ari sets the taco on Gibson's tray and we all watch him try to figure out how to eat it. Gibs ends up splitting it open and fisting the shredded beef and lettuce into his mouth. He then picks up the taco shell and bites it.

"Do you like it?" I ask him. He nods but sets the taco shell down and pokes at it, like he's not sure what he's supposed to do with it. Ari piles some apple and banana on his tray, and he forgets the crispy taco shell and dives into his fruit.

Sammy hits the table a few times, getting our attention. We turn to him, expecting one of his usual gems. But he looks odd. His eyes are wide with panic and his parted lips are dry.

"Shit, he's choking." By the time I realize what's going on and stand up, Ari has Sammy out of his chair and grasped tightly around the middle as she thrusts up several times from behind him. She can't get the right angle, so she readjusts her grip on him and thrusts up two more times and he finally ejects a wad of taco to the ground. He goes slightly limp in her arms and gasps, pulling in large, ragged breaths. Mav shoves a chair under his ass, and he droops to the chair.

"Are you okay? Do you want us to call the paramedics?" Her words are quietly reassuring as she rubs her hand up and down his back gently.

He shakes his head a few times. "No." He clears his throat. Ari hands him his soda. He takes a few tentative sucks from his straw. "I'm good." He pauses between sips. "I'm okay." He nods again and Ari continues to lightly rub his back.

"Fuck! That was fucking scary." He looks up at us gathered around him, his eyes wet. "I had no air. None."

Sammy shifts in his chair and lurches forward, hugging Ari around the waist tightly, his head against her abdomen. Her eyes open wide as a surprised "oh!" escapes her lips.

"You saved me. Thank you." His voice is gruff, with his head still buried in her midsection.

She pats his back awkwardly from the adjusted angle. "Hey, no problem. If I didn't do it, Callum or Mav would have." She pats his back. "Are you sure you're okay?"

Would we have? I didn't know what to do. I should know shit like this. I'm responsible for someone else. What if it had been Gibson?

He nods into her and finally releases her and settles back in his chair. "Thank you."

Kady moves to clean up Sammy's mess, and Ari gravitates back to Gibson. I glance at her as Killian and Mav fuss over Sam. Ari's pale and takes a couple of deep breaths, with her eyes closed before reaching down and releasing the buckle keeping Gibson in his chair. She picks him up and mumbles something about getting him cleaned up as she makes her way towards the stairs, like she didn't just save Sammy's life. Just another thing to add to that file cabinet in my head. The one that I keep locked that has all the reasons Ari is amazing and attractive to me.

When she doesn't return, I check the nursery cam, and she is sitting cross-legged on the floor with Gibson, rolling vehicles together along the carpet that looks like a town with roads. They make quiet vroom noises.

"You watch Ari from your phone?" Killian announces to the table as he looks over my shoulder. "Isn't that against the law?"

"No, dickhead. I can look into the nursery from my phone. Ari and Gibson just happen to be in it. I was wondering what they were up to."

He looks at me with a cocked eyebrow, like he thinks I'm spying on her or some shit. "She has the same app and access. I was wondering why she didn't come back down. I guess he's still not down for his nap yet. Are we going to work on some music or what?"

R

I ASKED Ari to attend the label party three times. It's here at the house and I thought she might enjoy mingling and wine and food. The most I got from her was a non-committal "maybe" accompanied by her one-shoulder shrug. If I've learned anything these last several weeks, it's that "maybe" usually means no. I can't force her to come down if she doesn't want to. People started arriving an hour ago. Right after, she fed Gibson and took him upstairs.

Kady smiles at me, her rounded belly obvious in her tight purple dress. "Where's Ari?"

"Upstairs. Before you blame me, I invited her three separate times. I don't think she'll come downstairs." I shrug.

Sammy walks in the front door, shedding his jacket in the closet, then joins us.

"What's happening, fuckers? Where's Ari?" He peeks around us, scanning the room.

"She's not coming down," I say, and his face falls. Since she

89

performed the Heimlich on him, they're best buddies, even though she cracked two of his ribs in the process of saving him from death by taco.

"Says you." Kady starts up the stairs.

"Kady, leave her be. She worked all day. Maybe she's tired. Maybe she doesn't like parties. God knows I don't." My words don't stop her ascent up the stairs.

Mav leads me to the bartender that's set up in the corner of my living room. How I got talked into being the host of this party, I'll never know. I hate these things. The label uses them to ramp us up for the mini tour. And having a party at my home isn't something I love the idea of. This is my private space.

"Two shots of Cuervo for him. One whiskey neat for me." He shoves the shots at me after the bartender finishes pouring the second one. "Drink up, loosen up, and enjoy our party, man. This is to celebrate us."

I nod and throw one of the shots back, the liquor burning on its way down. I'm not a tequila guy. I'd much rather just have a few beers and get my mellow on, but Mav's right, I need to loosen up to get through tonight. We're all familiar with the kind of things that go on at these kinds of functions and there was a time I was more than happy to take part in the sex and drugs part of rock and roll. I'm over it now. I have a son to think about. I haven't touched anything more than Advil since I found out Becka was pregnant. Indulging these days is the occasional beer in the evening, maybe two if it's one of our weekend barbecues.

"We hit the road in two weeks. Ari's been here nearly a month, so please tell me she's the one. You're running out of time if she's not." His look is guarded but hopeful.

"Yeah. She's the one. She loves Gibson. I have no doubts she'll do great, and I think Gibson will too, if she's on tour with us." I pray the hoopla of the tour doesn't get in the way of that and doesn't jade her or affect Gibson.

Mav claps my shoulder. "That's fan-fucking-tastic man. I was sweating bullets that you were going to find a reason to dismiss her." His relief is evident in the way his whole body relaxes. "We were taking bets, man. Kady wins."

"Bets? Really?" He shrugs. If the roles were reversed, I'd have been the first one on the list with my bet. "You're such an asshole."

"Not as much as you are. Come on, let's get into some trouble." He starts to mingle through the crowd. The label said there'd be about fifty guests and judging by the turnout, that seems an accurate count. It's been a long time since I've had so many people here, definitely before Gibson.

At some point, Kady and Ari both join the party. I catch a glimpse of Ari, wearing a tight black skirt I've never seen before and that silky purple top she wore on her first Wednesday off with ballet flats. Her blonde hair is down and straight, swept over one of her shoulders, exposing that long, beautiful neck.

She spends most of the party by the pool, enjoying some wine and chatting with Kady. Sammy brings every person he meets to her so he can introduce them to the woman who saved his life. Her cheeks flame each time he introduces her. A couple of times he even makes her demonstrate how she did it on him, in a skirt. Her long, sleek legs keep drawing my eye and probably the eye of every guy here, causing an unfamiliar tightening each time I think about it.

The party goes into the night. We even perform a few songs by request of Darren. We set up on the small stage the label had assembled near the patio and play our newer songs, the stuff that we've been recording in the studio, and a few older fan favorites. Darren smiles and nods, liking that we're making him look good. But I only have eyes for Ari. She nods her head and sways to the songs, enjoying our impromptu concert.

After we're done playing, Kady makes her way to Ari, the two of them chatting and laughing. Knowing that they're friends only solidifies me in knowing that she is the one I want taking care of Gibson. I have to offer her the nanny position full-time and soon because her month-long trial is up in a few days.

Mav sticks different tequila-based drinks in my hand several times through the evening, while I schmooze with the label's guests. I'm not totally shitfaced, but I'm loose enough that the small talk isn't a chore. I'm actually damn happy. Which makes me want to look for Ari. Because she makes me fucking happy too.

Searching for her near the pool, Mav grabs my shoulder and stops me. "We've got a problem." I can't find Ari, that's the fucking problem.

"What?" I turn to Mav when I see Jax, our head of security, escorting someone I don't know from upstairs. "Who the hell is that? And what are they doing upstairs? Gibs!"

"You got more problems than that. Someone was coking up in the main bathroom." Mav grimaces. When the hell did this small label party get so fucking out of hand? Cocaine in my house? I'm no angel, but that shit should not be in my house.

"Who the fuck is doing that?" I head to the main bathroom. No one is around by the time I get there, but the powdery evidence is cut all over the counter. "Dammit. My son is in this house. What the hell?" I don't need strangers slinking around upstairs or doing coke in my bathroom. I shouldn't have allowed this party in my house.

Ari sets her wineglass on the kitchen counter and heads to the staircase. "Where are you going?"

She waves her phone at me. "Gibson woke up."

"Dammit. This is why we have the parties at Mav's fucking house." I look around for Jax, since he's head of damn security. He should be taking care of this. It shouldn't have even made it into my house. Where the fuck did he go?

I find him down the hall. "I have a fucking kid upstairs and people are wandering around up there, while others are coking up in my bathroom? How is this happening? Why aren't you doing your fucking job?" The warm fuzzies I was feeling from the alcohol have turned in to a dull awareness that what is going on in my house could get my son taken from me.

"She didn't make it past the top of the stairs, Cal. Aiden is posted outside Gibson's room, so she wouldn't have gotten anywhere near him. Only you and Ari are allowed in his room. I'm dealing with the bathroom incident. We've got it under control, Cal. Are you?" Jax stares me down in his cool, collected way while Mav adds another drink to my hand. I don't like the insinuation that I'm not under control. I'm a fucking adult.

"Jax knows his shit, Cal, calm down." Mav drags me outside to the patio where most of the guests are oblivious to the shit going on inside. "Just chill." I slam back the drink he gave me, probably a little faster than I should have.

"I don't know what I'm more pissed about, the drugs or the person upstairs. Probably the person." I seethe. "I gotta check on Gibs."

I head upstairs, meeting Ari on her way down. "He didn't even fully wake up. The alert probably sensed the activity in the hall or whatever. I'm not sure how it works." She puts her hand on my shoulder. "He's good. I promise. And Aiden's right outside his door. Go back to your party."

By the time the party starts to officially wind down, it's nearly two-thirty in the morning. I can't remember the last time I was up this late. Fatherhood has turned this night owl into an early fucking bird. There have been no other incidents and Gibson doesn't wake up again. The band, Ari, the security, and a few of the caterers are the only ones left.

I'm not sure who's drunker, Mav or myself. I haven't had more than a beer or two here and there since Gibson was born. I don't know why tonight was any different, but it felt good to let loose for a change and not be the responsible one. Thanks to Mav and his friend Jose Cuervo.

That Jose's a shady motherfucker; his hangovers are the worst, but I give absolutely no fucks tonight. I welcome the easy numbness for the night and will deal with the hangover tomorrow. The party's over, thank fuck. This'll be the last one I host.

Sammy follows Kady to the kitchen. I saddle right up where he was, next to my Ari.

"Hey, Ari, you enjoyin' your beautiful self?" I still sound pretty with it, at least I do in my head. I'm not as sloshed as I thought. Good. We need to talk about some stuff, Ari and me, I just can't remember what.

She nods and scoots away slightly. "Thank you for inviting me."

"You live here too. You should have fun. We should all have fun. Fun for everyone! The tours are fun. But not really. You'll find out soon enough about that."

I wave my arm around, and shit, if the world doesn't slide sideways for a minute. Fuck, how many drinks did I have tonight?

"Are you okay, Callum?" I've never noticed before that when she's concerned her nose wrinkles between her eyes. It's adorable and makes me want to kiss that wrinkly nose of hers.

"Okay? I'm fuckfantasticking. No! That's not right." I shake my head and that causes the world to slide again. No more of that. "Fan-fucking-tasticking? You get the idea. I'm damn great." I wave my arm again and she nods, her nose wrinkling up again. I lean in and lightly kiss her adorable wrinkly nose and fuck if it's not as good as I've been dreaming it'd be. If just giving her a peck is that good, how good would kissing her the way I've been wanting to be?

"Callum..." She pulls back again and looks at me. She's not horrified. At least it doesn't seem like she is.

Now, on to kissing that mouth of hers.

Two Kadys stand next to us at the table. "We're going to head home, Cal. Mav's blitzed." Kady sounds kind of miffed.

"Sure. I'd tell you to be careful and be safe, but too late. You're both already knocked up." I laugh and two Kadys turn back into one. "And I was the second person to know. Not even your husband knows that I knew before he did." I snort with laughter at my funny joke.

But instead of laughing with me, Kady looks pissed. *Uh-oh.* "What did I say?" I look over at both Aris and they stand and walk with Kady out to the foyer.

I finish the last of my drink and walk into the kitchen, looking for more.

"Woah, Cal. You're pretty fucked up, huh?" Sammy and his new twin watch me pour myself another.

"What do you mean? I'm just a little buzzed. I didn't know you're a twin too, Sammy." It's not like Sammy doesn't drink sometimes, so what the fuck gives? Everyone drinks but me. The one time I have a little too much, everyone wants to make a federal case out of it.

He points at my glass on the counter. "You missed the cup." He takes the bottle from me. "You've hit your limit." He grabs a kitchen towel and mops up my spill.

"Where's Ari?" I ask him. "She's beautiful, huh? Tell me she's as beautiful as I think she is. I want to kiss her again. On the mouth this time." Sammy's eyebrows pull together like he doesn't like something.

"Um, yeah, she's pretty. I think she's in the living room." He doesn't look at me. "Are you okay, man?" Sammy squints at me a little. "Maybe you should go to bed, Cal. It's late." He leads me to the stairs. "Just go on up to bed. I'll tell Ari goodnight from you and me both, okay?" I nod and head upstairs.

I get to my bedroom, and I realize I never got to talk to Ari, and more importantly, I didn't get to kiss her again. I need my lips against hers like yesterday. But really, I need to tell her that she's pretty and I like her. Like her, like her. Sammy's a fucking sneak. Tricking me into going to bed so he can have all the fun with Ar.

"Fuckin' Sammy! He doesn't get her to himself." I head back downstairs. Fuck if I don't almost fall halfway down the stairs. Something is wrong with the gravity in this house, I swear. Maybe I am a little bombed. I make it to the living room and flop down next to her and lay my head on her shoulder. "Hey, pretty girl."

"Sammy said you went to bed." She stiffens slightly. I must have startled her. But she still looks so beautiful with the way her cheeks each have a few freckles. I never noticed that before either.

"I needed to talk to you." My words slur together.

"I'm about to go to bed. What do you need?" She turns and looks at me so I can't rest my head on her shoulder anymore. What the fuck did I want to ask her?

Chapter 11

Arista

I 've never been much for parties. In college, I was focused on getting my degree, so I didn't party much. A friend hooked me up with the agency, and the rest is history. I wanted to stay in my room tonight. I don't know any of the people at this party except Cal and the other band members.

Kady came up and insisted I come down for a little while. She told me that I didn't have to stay if I didn't want to but, she wanted to chat with someone that she knew. She helped me pick out something to wear and styled my hair quickly.

I walked down the stairs behind her. I was so out of my league at this party. After all, I was just the hired help. Callum's words from the first week still sting, even nearly a month later. He had no way of knowing my previous assignment for a washed-up C-list actor and his pretentious wife, ended because the wife suspected that I was after her husband. First off, he was far too old for me, and secondly, I watched as he relentlessly pursued their maid as well as me. The wife was not only very hands off with her own children, but she was also hands off with her husband. Thankfully, I got released from that job before he did anything crazy with me, like he did with the maid. Officially, I was released because "the chemistry" wasn't there, but I got the feeling that the maid was jealous that he had turned his eyes toward me. Their house had a weird dynamic, and I was relieved to have been let go.

"Ari!" Sammy, his curly blonde hair bouncing as he approaches, hugs me like I was his long-lost friend. Now that I think of it, he treats me as if I'm a long-lost friend too. Sammy is the kind of guy who makes a friend out of everyone he meets. "I'm so glad you're here."

"I work here, Sammy," I deadpan. His smile falters for a second, until he realizes that I am just joking.

"Ha, good one. What's your poison, Ar? We have everything you could want to drink." He and Kady guide me over to a bartender set up in the corner of the living room, where I order a glass of Moscato, one of the few alcoholic beverages I'll drink.

I mingle by the pool. Mostly, I stand and sip my wine, while every ten minutes or so Sammy introduces me to people with, "This is Ari. She saved my life the other day. Seriously, I was choking on a taco." Then he goes on to tell the whole story.

"Ari, this is Darren, our Monumentus Records label rep."

Darren is a short man with dark hair that's parted on the side and slicked over the top with some sort of greasy tonic. His eyes are dark, almost beady, and he wears a blue suit with no tie and the shirt underneath has the first three buttons undone. If you had asked me to pick out the label representative, I would have picked him.

"Ari, it's a pleasure." He holds his hand out as if to shake, so I stick mine in his, only to have him turn it and kiss the top of my hand. I stiffen slightly, not wanting to encourage him.

"Ari saved my life the other day. She's amazing. I was choking on a taco. It was scary as shit. I had no air, Dar, none. And she performed this special hold thing, what was it called, Ari? The Hamlin maneuver?

"Heimlich, Sam, Heimlich." I correct him as Sammy and Darren both look at me.

"That's right, Heimlich. Anyway, it was close man. She's my hero." Sammy hugs me for the umpteenth time this evening. His hugs are just friendly, thankful ones, and not something I have to worry about.

"Well, thank you for saving Sammy, Ari. What is it you do when you aren't saving choking drummers?" Darren checks me out as he asks.

"She's Cal's nanny. Gibson loves her." Sammy wraps an arm around my shoulders and squeezes.

Darren says nothing but nods and disengages from our little trio. And just like that, I've been dismissed again like the domestic I am.

"You don't have to tell everyone at the party, Sammy." I can feel my cheeks heat up. It's nice to know he appreciates me saving him, but being introduced as his guardian angel every time is just a bit much.

"I gotta go get ready. We're playing a small set." He nods to the corner of the yard and there is a small stage set up over Gibson's turtle sandbox.

"Hey, I'm part of that too," Kady says in my ear. "Will you be okay?"

I nod.

"Great. When I'm done, I want to ask your opinion on a theme for the nursery. Enjoy the show."

Fifteen minutes later, some lights illuminating the little stage come on and the band takes the stage, Mav front and center. Callum and Killian sit on opposite sides of Mav, with acoustic guitars. Kady has a keyboard and sits between Cal and Mav. Sammy is behind them all.

I've never seen the Blind Rebels in concert, and while I doubt this is what a typical show is like, I'm transfixed. I'm not sure if it's the music or the wine, but I can't help swaying back and forth to the music, getting more and more into it.

Mavrick Slater's vocals are welcoming and sultry at first but then powerful as they play some of their harder stuff, which is different to hear played on acoustic instruments. Everyone in the audience is moving to the music, even Darren, who now has a leggy brunette saddled up to him.

My eyes drift over to Callum as he plays and sings harmony to Mav's vocals. His eyes scan the audience, then land on me. There's something in his stare as he plays and quietly sings that makes my body heat. I move back and forth harder, wanting him to know I'm enjoying the music and his playing. I've never really heard him play before. When he's in the music room, I can't hear what's going on in there. I have heard him sing softly to Gibson at night before, but this is different. The way he gazes at me as he plays feels like he's playing just for me.

"Thank you all for your support." Mav closes the session as we all clap. The band carries their instruments back to the music room, except for Kady, who leaves the stage and seeks me out.

"So, what did you think?" Kady smiles at me.

"That was amazing. I haven't seen you guys live before. I really enjoyed it."

"Well, that's nothing. Wait until you see us in our full arena show glory with lights and a sound technician. You should get to see it at least once on the tour," she shares with me. Callum hasn't told me if I'm hired for the position, since I still have a few days on my one-month temporary assignment with the band.

"I hope so. So, what did you want to ask my opinion of?" I admit, I am curious.

"I just wanted to show you some nursery themes for the baby before I show them to Mav. I wanted your thoughts."

She pulls out her phone and shows me a couple of ideas

she has for themes. One is for a gender-neutral music themed room done in black and white. There is also a nursery in soft blues and greens with trucks and planes and one done in bright pink and purple with little skulls.

"The pink one with the skulls is adorable. Could you adapt it for a boy if it turns out to be a boy?"

"Oh, it's definitely a boy. Didn't I tell you?" I shake my head and she grabs my shoulder in excitement. "Darn it. I thought I mentioned it. But I agree, that one is adorable. I thought Mav might like the skull theme too. They do have the same theme in black and grays, so let me see if I can find it." She scrolls through her phone. "Here it is."

I look at it over her shoulder and it's just as adorable as the pink and purple version of it.

"I think that's perfect. It's just as cute."

Her smile brightens as she sticks her phone into her back pocket. "We're so excited. He wasn't planned, but he's been the best surprise." She gives her stomach a gentle touch as her smile brightens.

Kady introduces me to a few people that Sammy managed to miss. I'm on my third glass, and because I'm a lightweight when it comes to alcohol, I know I will have to stop now, or I'll regret it in the morning. I can't remember the last time I was up this late. I should probably go to bed because Gibson will be up early. There is some sort of commotion in the house, but out on the patio it's hard to tell what's going on.

My phone vibrates in my back pocket. Shit. Whatever it was woke up Gibson. I head inside to check on him. A man introduced to me by Kady earlier as Aiden from the Blind Rebels' security team is stationed outside Gibson's door. He's a wall of a man, with close cropped dark hair and dark eyes. He stands when I approach.

"I got an alert that he woke up. I'm just checking on him." I wave my phone at him, another way I know I've got to cut myself off from the Moscato.

Aiden nods and steps to the side as I quietly enter Gibson's room. He's lying in his favorite stinkbug position, RuffRuff near his head. His eyes are closed, and his breaths are long and even. He's still asleep. Thank goodness. I stay for a few minutes and watch him sleep. There's always a peace I get when I'm around Gibson, especially when he's asleep.

Halfway down the stairs, I run into Callum, who's stomping up the stairs, and seems surprised when I'm coming down. He must have received the same alert about Gibson waking up.

"He didn't even fully wake up. The alert probably sensed activity in the hall or whatever. I'm not sure how it works."

He still seems upset and looks beyond me towards the top of the stairs. Resting my hand on his shoulder, I try to keep him from charging into his son's room, which will surely wake the toddler. "He's good. I promise. And Aiden's right outside his door. Go back to your party."

I didn't intend to stay to the end, just like I didn't intend to have two more glasses of wine, but both happened. I'm still not sure what happened right before Gibson woke up, but I am sure I'll feel the wine tomorrow.

Sitting on the couch, I watch as the caterers start quickly picking up all the food and dismantle the bar set up in the living room. Callum's drunk, like really drunk. As he flops on the couch near me, I can smell the alcohol coming out of his pores, both pungent and sweet. The scent nauseates me, and I close my eyes and for a second. I'm not sitting on Callum's couch, but I am back in Vi's first apartment as Todd whispers threats to be quiet while he's pressed against me with his hand over my mouth. I'm not that little girl anymore. He can't hurt me here. I take a deep breath and open my eyes.

"Hey, Ari, you enjoyin' your beautiful self?" Callum's words are slurring but still understandable, and a happy, loose grin graces his face. It's something I've never seen before. I can see Gibson in his father's easy smile. It's little boy adorable, but on a gruff exterior of a man.

"Thank you for inviting me." I nod, not wanting to upset or offend him.

"You live here too. You should have fun. We should all have fun. Fun for everyone! The tours are fun, but not really. You'll find out soon enough about that."

Callum flings his arms out and almost topples himself off the couch.

"Are you okay, Callum?"

"Okay?" He drags out the last syllable on his slur. "I'm fuck-fantasticking. No! That's not right." He pauses, his dark blue eyes momentarily losing focus, but he smiles instead of getting frustrated. "Fan-fucking-tasticking? You get the idea. I'm damn great."

I can tell he is. He's looser than I've ever seen him, thanks to the alcohol he's had tonight. I've been here a month and I've never seen Callum drink more than the occasional beer, always in the evening after Gibson's gone to bed. At least when he's drunk, he's a happy-go-lucky one, unlike Todd.

He smiles at me with the most adorable, goofy grin and leans in and kisses the tip of my nose. It's a friendly kiss, one that I'd love to think was for me, but Callum clearly has tequila-glasses on.

"Callum..." I back off from him. Sober Callum would probably be mortified that he kissed me, even something as innocent as one on the tip of my nose.

Thankfully, Kady interrupts us, and I don't have to worry about how to stop Callum from going too far in his state, because tomorrow would be awkward.

"We're going to head home, Cal. Mav's blitzed."

"Sure. I'd tell you to be careful and be safe, but too late. You're both already knocked up. And I was the second person to know. Not even your husband knows that I knew before he did."

Callum thinks what he's said is funny, but by Kady's face, it isn't funny to her.

"What did I say?" He looks between Kady and me. I'm not exactly sure of the context of this conversation, but Kady is obviously hurt by Callum's comment, so I stand and walk her out with Killian helping corral her intoxicated husband into the backseat of their car.

"Are you sure you'll be able to get him inside?" I watch as Killian pours Mav into the backseat and tries to buckle him in. My only worry is that getting Mav into the house might be hard on pregnant Kady.

"If I can't, he can sleep in the damn car." She rolls her eyes at her very drunk husband. "It'll be fine. Mav doesn't usually do this. I think he and Callum were having a 'who can get more drunk' contest."

"Okay, text me if you need help. I can come by and help you." I watch my friend fasten her seat belt and drive out through the gate.

When I return to the couch, I pull out my phone and check on Gibson, still sleeping in his crib.

Chapter 12

Callum

When I get back downstairs, Ari is sitting on the couch, staring at her phone, a small grin pulling her lips up. She's beautiful, but when she smiles, even just a small smile, it lights the night with sparkles. What's on her phone that's making her so happy?

I flop onto the couch. Okay, maybe more like fall onto the couch, not even hiding the fact that I'm trying to see what she's staring at on her phone. It's the nursery app, and she's watching Gibson sleep. *She's watching my son sleep. She loves him like I love him, not just because she's getting paid to watch him.*

"You love my kid. You take such good care of him, Ari." I look at her. The area between her eyes is wrinkly again and gives her an adorable look. She looks amazing in this purple top. Purple is her color. "I tried so hard not to like you, but you're so good with him." Her eyes soften just a little with my admission.

"You're a beautiful person, Ari. Inside and out. So beautiful that it's hard to be around you." I snort and giggle like a girl because I'm so sloshed... "Get it? It's hard? As in—" I lean in and consider taking her hand and pressing it against my groin, so she can see that it's hard for her and it's no joke. Even as inebriated as I am, I think twice about that and decide to just kiss her instead. So, I close my eyes and lean in to make the contact my lips desire, to finally taste Ari's lips and hopefully her mouth.

"Fuck on a stick! He's so obliterated, Ar. I'm sorry on his behalf." Killian grabs my arm and pulls me away from her before our lips touch. "Get off the couch, asshole. I thought Sammy put you to bed already."

He gets me to a stand, but I sway back and forth. Is the earth losing its gravity or is it just my house? Shit, I hope Gibson's not floating out of his crib.

"I don't need you to put me to bed, Kill. Ari's my nanny. Right, Ari? She can put me to bed." I turn to look at her on the couch, where she won't make eye contact with me.

"Is the gravity okay in here? Do we need to go make sure Gibson doesn't float away?" I ask Killian.

"We'll check on him and then get you to bed," Killian assures me while he tries to push me upstairs.

"Ari—"

"You're making her uncomfortable, you dick. Ari could sue your ass for harassment." He's still got a hold of my arm. "Fucking hell, Cal. We have a tour coming up. You can't go harassing your damn nanny this close to the tour."

Killian turns to Ari on the couch. "He hasn't gotten this drunk since the band broke up. I'm fucking sorry, Ari."

Why is he apologizing to her? I'm confused and my head feels like it's stuffed with cotton balls.

"What the hell is going on?" I turn to slug Killian but miss his face and hit his shoulder. He turns me and pushes me towards the stairs, but grabs me by the belt loops on my jeans when I start to fall forward.

"I'm gonna put his drunk ass to bed. He apparently can't handle his liquor anymore. I shouldn't be driving, so I'm crashing here tonight in the room across from Gibson's. Sorry for what Cal said. He'd be ashamed if he wasn't drunk off his ass." Killian pushes me towards the stairs.

"What did I say?" I ask Killian, but he shoves me up the stairs and pushes me down on my bed, hard. Or maybe I'm so messed up, I lose my balance and fall onto the bed. My room is spinning. What the fuck is wrong with earth today?

"You're such a dumbass." He grabs my foot and pulls my boot off with such force that I think he's going to sever my foot and then the asshole does the same thing to the other one. "Sleep it off and leave Ari alone."

R

MY HEAD POUNDS to the rhythm of Sammy's drums as I open my eyes just a little. I'm in my bedroom, so I'm damn sure Sammy and his drums aren't here. It's a headache from hell threating to explode my skull. Sitting up causes the world to spin and I hold on tight to the edge of the bed, waiting for it to stop spinning while I try to keep the acid churning in my stomach from rising.

Fucking Jose Cuervo. I knew better. This is exactly why I stopped drinking the hard stuff; the aftereffects suck. The last thing I remember clearly is playing the acoustic set at the party, then doing some mingling with a glass in my hand. The rest are just half memories. Fuck! Did I kiss Ari? Twice? I have a fuzzy memory of kissing her on the nose and wanting to kiss her more. Did I? Another vague memory of Kill pulling me away from her. Cussing. Fuck, what did I do?

Once the bed's stopped spinning, I head to my bathroom and take a shower. I feel a little better after I pull on some clothes. Shit, I acted like a drunken fool. I hope Ari's still speaking with me.

When I get downstairs, Gibs and Ari are outside playing in

the sandbox that just last night was covered over by a makeshift stage for us to play on. I have a clear memory of Ari swaying back and forth to the music. She was having fun enjoying the music, and it was a joy to watch.

Ari pulls Gibs in for a hug and he hugs her back and then places his hands on each side of her face and squishes them together until Ari puckers up into a fish face.

"Ishie!" Gibson's squeal is loud enough that it penetrates my brain from outside. My head gives a few hard thuds to go along with the headache as he runs around her and then sits back in the sandbox and digs his fingers into the sand.

I need coffee and something in my stomach to help combat this hangover. Sticking a coffee pod in the machine, I open the fridge and find some of the appetizers left over from the party. Perfect. As I'm popping them in the microwave, my email tone pings my phone.

Leaning against the counter, I sip my coffee with one hand and check my messages. It's probably the finalized schedule for the mini tour we leave on in a little over a week. That reminds me, I need to talk to Ari about what to expect and ask if she anticipates needing anything specific for Gibson while we tour.

To: cdonogue@blindrebels.com
From: AnonymousMail@anon.com
Subject: Your So-Called Nanny
Attachments: image1.jpg, image2.jpg, image3.jpg

Callum- You may want to reconsider your nanny. She was the one doing coke in your bathroom last night (see attached pictures). I've personally observed her doing this several times while alone with your child.

When she takes him to the park, she is on her phone with her dealer or meeting up with him. The last time (on Tuesday), Gibson *wandered after another child and nearly got to the sidewalk of the park before your nanny even noticed. And let's not even mention the times the dealer met her at the park so she could buy her drugs.*

If you love your son, I'm sure you'll get a new nanny.

WHAT THE ACTUAL FUCK? I remember yelling at Jax about the coke in the bathroom. That was Ari? Why didn't he tell me? Is that what she does while Gibson's napping?

I click on the first attachment and there it is. The bathroom just off the kitchen by the stairs. Ari bent over the counter with a straw to her nose. The next one is similar, she's just in a slightly different position, cutting the drugs on the counter with a razorblade.

My heart drops from my chest to my stomach. I would have never thought Ari could do this. I can't deny these photos, though. It's clearly her. It's clearly the bathroom near the stairs and that's the cocaine I saw. A glutton for punishment, I open the third email and it's Ari chasing after Gibson in the park, and he's dangerously close to the street.

I worried last night that having coke in my house could somehow get my son taken away from me. Little did I know how careless I had been trusting my son, my whole fucking world, to a coke user. I drop my coffee cup and it crashes to the ground and shatters.

"FUCK!" I scream. How could I be so stupid? I knew this nanny thing was a goddamn mistake. Fuck if I will let Gibson pay the price.

Chapter 13

Arista

I sip my Lady Gray from my usual seat at the island, phone opened to the app that monitors Gibson's nursery. He'll probably sleep for another thirty minutes or so. At least that's my hope. Any longer than that and I risk running into Callum and I'd rather avoid him for a while.

I don't know how much he'll remember of last night, but I can't help but feel awkward about what came out of his mouth. He kissed my nose. He muttered something about wrinkles and then sucked the tip of my nose into his mouth like it was a lollipop made just for him. I don't know what's worse, that he obviously enjoyed it or that I did too. He probably won't remember any of it. At least that's my hope.

My head throbs as Killian's words from last night come back to the surface.

"You can't harass your damn nanny this close to the tour."

I've made a critical error, again. When will I learn that these people are not my friends? To Callum and his friends, I'm just someone to keep the kid occupied while they live their rock star lives, someone to keep Gibson safe while they party. I let myself think that they were my friends.

Please sleep, I silently beg both father and son, hoping to give the aspirin time to ease the constant throbbing of my too-much-wine-and-emotion headache.

"Hey, Ari." Killian pads into the kitchen, dressed except for his bare feet. His slightly damp hair hangs just right. He heads straight for the coffee machine and makes himself a cup.

He doesn't look too bad, considering he thought he was too drunk to drive himself home last night. Or was it this morning?

While he waits for the machine to warm up, he lifts himself up to sit on the kitchen counter. He watches me watch him.

"You sleep okay?" he asks, his head cocked to the side as he studies my face, his legs swinging in small circles from the countertop he sits on.

"Yeah fine. Just waiting for Gibson to wake up." I wave my phone at him like a dork, as if that will explain what I'm doing, when it's obvious I'm nursing a headache from too much wine and not enough sleep.

"Yeah, me too. Slept fine. I'm not waiting for Gibson, though." He shrugs from his perch on the counter. There is something about the way he says his nephew's name that causes me to pause, but there's too much pounding in my head to question him about it.

I return my gaze to my phone and watch Gibson sleep, oblivious to the world around him.

"Don't hold it against him." Killian's voice is suddenly lower and raspier.

My head turns back towards Killian, but he won't meet my eyes. Instead, he swills the coffee he just made like it's water, not speaking again until he's drained half the cup.

"He was drunk off his ass last night, Ari. For the first time since the band broke up, I think. The things that he said, he didn't mean them. Or maybe he did, but he'd never act on them sober because he's Callum, but also because he's Gibson's dad and doesn't want to mess anything up for his son." *But what about you? Did you mean what you said about just being the damn nanny?*

"You've seen him the last month. Gibs is all that matters to Cal." He runs a hand through his damp hair. "Cal's been that way since he was born, and he should be."

"But yesterday, we all saw glimpses of old Cal. Pre-Gibson Cal. The carefree guitarist of a band at the top of its game, the larger-than-life rock star. And it was fucking good to see him. That Cal is someone you'd like. Well, you would if he wasn't shitfaced and being sexual with you."

Killian's gaze returns to mine. "I mean, I can't say that I blame him. You're hot. But for some reason, Cal thinks it's either one or the other ever since Gibson. Either he's a dad or he's a rock star. He's either an ass or he's nice." Killian shakes his head.

"He'd never admit it, but Becka abandoning them really fucked with Cal's head, but not because he loved her. We were, uh, well, let's just say Cal and I were raised mostly by our Aunt Sandy. We know what it's like to not be wanted by the people who are supposed to love you unconditionally." He shrugs as he sets down his empty coffee cup. I'm not sure if Killian expects me to respond or not or what I should say.

"Anyway, he'll be a grumpy asshole when he wakes up. More so than normal. He'll feel like shit from the massive hang-over he will no doubt have, but also, he won't know what to do with how he acted with you. If he's too unbearable, take Gibson to the park or something and text me. Mav and I will come straighten his ass out."

He shoots me a text from where he stands. "Cal gave us all your number when he hired you, in case of an emergency. Now you have mine. Use it. Whether he's a dick today, tomorrow or two Wednesdays from now." He stares at me. Killian's eyes are the same color as his brother's, but Kill's are guarded and almost a little sad.

"I will." I stand when Gibson starts to stir in his crib.

Killian stands up straight. "That's my cue to get outta here. See ya, Ari. Text me. Seriously." And with that, Killian slips on his shoes at the door and leaves.

Gibson is his cheery, talkative self this morning, and he makes my heart happy despite the dull pounding in my head. We play in the sand outside. I know I'm just prolonging what will inevitably be an argument, but if I can keep it from happening in front of Gibson, all the better.

"Cwab Awee!" Gibson shrieks as he presses his plastic mold into the sand, then pulls it off. "See Cwab!"

"That's an awesome crab buddy. How about a fish or a turtle?" I offer him up the other sand molds.

But he has other ideas and stands up and puts his chubby, gritty hands on my cheeks and presses them inward until I pucker my lips. He cackles when I cross my eyes and move my lips while puckered. "Ishie Awee. Awee ishie!"

I lean in to give him a fishie kiss with my puckered lips, and he screeches and runs around behind me. I've got to take this kid to an aquarium. He loves fish.

"Get me Awi!" He runs around wanting to be chased.

My head gives another dull throb, but I get up and chase him around the yard and once I catch him, we both collapse in a fit of giggles as I tickle him. We freeze when we hear breaking glass and curses coming from the kitchen.

"Uh-oh." Gibson utters quietly. "Cwash." His eyes are big and on me.

"Sounds like daddy dropped something and it broke, huh, kiddo?" I reassure him.

Gibson nods and seeks my arms, so I pull him to me and give him a hug. "Boken?"

"It's okay. Sometimes things break. It's an accident." I pat his back.

"Assident." He nods his understanding and pats my shoul-

113

der. His pronunciation makes me giggle. This kid is so quick to pick up words. I love him to pieces and squeeze his warm little body to me.

Part of me wants to go in and face Callum to just get the awkwardness from the party over with. He'll apologize and I'll pull back. They aren't my friends. Callum is my employer and I think I lost sight of that for a minute being romanced by the rock 'n' roll lifestyle. A big part of me wants to stay out here with Gibson, oblivious to the man throwing a rockstar-sized tantrum in his kitchen as the cursing continues and then more glass breaks.

Gibson pulls back from me. "Help daddy." He starts to wiggle out of my hold. I stand and pick him up and hope that Gibson's desire to help his dad won't end up causing more ire from Callum. I don't want him to direct his anger towards Gibs. I don't think he would, but from what I hear out here, he's really pissed off.

We slip into the kitchen to find Callum surrounded by broken coffee mugs and dishes, cursing under his breath. His fists are balled up at his sides as he turns to face Gibson and me, his eyes are steely as they lock onto mine.

"Daddy. Uh-oh, boken! Assident. I help!" Gibson starts to wiggle again, trying to escape my grip, but judging by the deathly stare I'm getting from Callum, setting Gibson down is not in either of our best interests right now.

"I got it, buddy." He seethes as he speaks, spit flying from the corners of his mouth. "Daddy wouldn't have had an accident if someone had cleaned up the breakfast dishes before playtime." His narrow eyes glance sideways at me as he pulls out the trash can and drags it over to the sink. I left a few things in the sink with the plan of washing them while Gibson napped, same as I do every day.

"I help!" Gibson reaches out for his dad, who ignores his request. "Help daddy!"

"I said no." He snaps at Gibson, his tone scathing and one I've never heard him use with his son before. Gibson buries his head in my neck at Callum's harsh words, his little fingers pulling my hair tight.

Those three little words have Gibson seeking comfort elsewhere, when usually the first person he seeks comfort from is his dad. I need to get him out of the line of fire before Callum destroys this little boy's trust in him. Killian wasn't wrong about Callum being embarrassed, but it's not an excuse to lash out at your child. I turn sideways so that Gibson is as far away from his dad as possible.

"I get you're not feeling well, and may be embarrassed by what happened last night, but don't take it out on Gibson." I keep my tone even since I'm holding Gibs but look at Callum harshly to get my point across.

"These are sharp." He softens his voice, noting his son's response to his words. "You could get cut."

He then steadies his gaze on me, his dark blue eyes icy cold. "Put my son in his playpen and go pack your shit. I want you out of my house. Today. Now." His tone is unforgiving, but the words he says tear a hole in my soul.

"What?" He might as well yank my heart from my chest and set it on fire. I worked hard to become part of this family, and now I'm dismissed because someone has a hangover, and his ego is bruised.

"Why? Because you broke some dishes? Because you're embarrassed or regretting things you did yesterday? Is that any reason to fire me on the spot? It seems a bit much, even for you." He is my employer and I'm holding his son, but no one else will stick up for me. It's ridiculous to send me packing for no reason, absurd even.

"No. Because you are not who I thought you were, Arista." He says my name like it's a bad taste in his mouth. He holds up his phone, showing a photo of me bent over the counter of the bathroom by the stairs. I squint at the small screen and step closer to get a better look, taking his phone in my free hand. It looks like I'm snorting something up a small straw.

My stomach drops as far into my gut as it can. "That, that's not me." The words that come are barely a whisper. It's not. But it sure looks like me.

"Bull. Shit. Pictures don't lie, Arista," he grits out, his jaw clenched tight. "Before lunch. Out. I won't have anyone using drugs caring for my son."

I gently set Gibson down in the cordoned off play area in the living room, leaning into him as I set him on his feet to breathe in his lavender scent just in case it's the last time.

"I've never used drugs in my life, Callum. I'll submit to a drug test right this second, lab of your choice." Panic bubbles up in my chest. He can't possibly believe that photo is real, that I would use illicit drugs, ever.

"Now, Arista." He repeats, his eyes still cold.

"I don't know where you got that, but it's not me. I didn't even go into that bathroom last night. I swear I didn't." Hot, fat tears break loose from my eyes and roll down my face.

"I won't say it again. Get your shit and get out of my house. Now!" He screams the last word, causing me to jump, and Gibson let out a cry from the corner of the room. Callum's jaw is tight, and his face is red. I don't know what hurts more, that he thinks I would do cocaine in his house, or that he doesn't believe me or trust me when I say it's not me.

Why would someone send him something like that? His face says it all, though. He *doesn't* believe me.

I turn on my heel and head upstairs, directly into the walk-in closet I once reveled in having. I pull all the clothes from their hangers in one violent swoop. Where did he get those pictures? Who would do that to me and why? Why can't he ask himself if he really believes I would do that to his son?

Hot tears burn my eyes. Now I'll have to go back to Vi's.

I stuff what I can in my suitcase, but most of this stuff was brought in duffle bags that I took back to my sister's house. I make my way downstairs and into the kitchen. Callum and Gibson are nowhere to be seen, all the better. I grab a few plastic garbage bags from the pantry off the kitchen and return upstairs.

I can't believe he's firing me because of some doctored photos. They have to be because there is no other explanation. My hands shake as I push my toiletries into one of the bags right on top of some clothes. He doesn't believe me. Him thinking that I'd do cocaine at all tells me that Callum didn't know me at all, professionally or personally.

I pause and look down at the two very full trash sacks containing everything I couldn't fit in my small suitcase. There is something about my life in trash bags being dragged out to the curb, but I'm too hurt to put it all together. Hurt that burns in my chest and turns into a hot bubbly anger just under the surface.

I drag my belongings out the door and down his long drive. I'm pulling the last one through the pedestrian gate when Sammy's huge Jeep pulls up to the keypad. For a moment, I wonder what he's doing here. But then I realize it's not my business anymore. I have more important things to worry about, like where I'm sleeping tonight.

I don't want to move back in with Vi and Todd. If I live with him any longer, I'll lose the rest of myself, but I don't know that I'll have much of a choice right now.

I close the metal gate. Pulling my suitcase behind me, I kick the lighter trash bag in front of me as I go all the way to where the driveway meets the road. I flop onto one of the bags under the tree to wait for my ride share, who, according to the app, is stuck in traffic.

I send off texts to a couple of friends, asking if I can crash on someone's couch until I can find something.

"Ari?" Sammy's blonde curls bounce as he jogs down the driveway toward me, his monster of a Jeep abandoned at the gate, driver's door still open. "Whatchya doing out here?" He tips his head, his eyes narrowing as he notices the trash bag I am sitting on.

"Taking out the trash." My sarcastic reply burns in my chest. His eyes narrow as he continues to look at me.

"Waiting for my ride."

"Where are you going?" He squats near me, reaching out a hand to my knee, but pulls it back when I scoot farther out of his reach. Not liking my silence, he repeats his question. "Ari, where are you going?" He looks back up at Cal's house and then at me.

"That's the question of the day now, isn't it?" My phone vibrates, and I look at it. A nursery alert. I delete the app without checking the alert. I also delete the app giving me access to the gate. My keys are on the bed, so there shouldn't be *any* excuse to come back here. My heart breaks again, but only because I'll miss the little boy who stole my heart with fishy faces and cups of sand. I've always attached to people too easily, especially the children I've worked with.

My ride pulls up and pops the trunk. I shove my suitcase and two trash bags into the back while Sammy watches as confusion mars his face. He touches my arm lightly to get my attention. "Ari? What's going on? Talk to me." His voice is higher, almost panic sounding. "Why are you leaving?"

"See ya, Sammy. Except, actually, probably not." I flip my hand in something of a wave and get into the car, closing the door. Sammy looks down at his phone, texting someone.

Yep, Sammy, better sound the alarm. Ari's gone, and the tour starts in nine days. And there's no one to watch the asshole's little prince. Better get moving on that.

"Just go," I tell the driver, though I can feel Sammy's confusion as he watches me in the back of the ride share as we pull from the curb. But his confusion doesn't mirror the nauseous rumbles in the pit of my stomach.

Chapter 14

Callum

"Awi?" Gibson looks up to me from the trampoline, his forehead wrinkled. I'm still so livid at her for putting my son's life in danger that even hearing her name from my son makes me want to scream obscenities and hit things, but I have to hold it together for him.

"Ari's bye-bye. Sorry, buddy."

He opens his fist and closes it several times in his version of a wave. "Buhbye Awi!" He kisses his palm and then throws the kiss to her, even though he can't see her.

I'm so fucking pissed at Ari, but I am more pissed at myself. I allowed this to happen. I agreed to let Ari into my home, for the sole purpose of her bonding with my son, caring for him. I should have known something like this would happen. No one can love and care for Gibson like I can.

And what's worse is that she gave me hope that I could make being both a father and a musician work. Yeah, that's not happening. I'm committed to the upcoming mini-tour and the album, but beyond that, I'm done with the Rebels. I can't be doing that shit anymore, not with a young son, and fuck if I'm going through this nanny bullshit again. Ever.

My phone alerts to the gate opening. That would be Ari leaving. I scoop Gibs up with promises of a swim later and head into the house. I'm hungry and still pissed off, which isn't a great combination. I reheat the appetizers that are still in the microwave and get a baggie of Cheerios for Gibs to munch on. We settle in front of the TV to eat and watch Octonauts. But the appetizers from last night have lost their appeal. Gibson settles into my side while he watches, his soft munches the only other sound I hear.

What the fuck am I going to do with him on the mini tour? Sure, the label would probably be able to hire someone to watch him while we are on stage and doing the media events, but the whole point of the nanny was that it would be someone I know taking care of him.

My only choice is Sandy. I love my aunt. She's the only reason Killian and I survived after our mother left us, two eleven-year-old boys, to fend for ourselves.

Our mother left that weekend with her newest boyfriend. He was the asshole that she moved in with us after the last one left. It was her thing. Once one boyfriend got tired of being used by her and left, she found a new one immediately. This last one, Dale, was one of the worst. In the middle of an argument over weed one night, he hit our mom and beat the fuck out of Killian for jumping to her defense. We missed school for a week because of that. Not long after that, they said they were leaving for the weekend. We stayed in the house like we were told.

"She's coming back, right?" Killian asked me as we watched TV on Sunday night.

"Of course. She always comes back." I didn't know this for a fact because she'd never left us alone for a whole weekend before. The moms on TV didn't leave their children unattended. Nor did the ones in the books I read. But I didn't tell Killian that.

His hand clenched mine as we watched TV.

On Monday morning, I made sure Killian and I were at the bus stop ready for school because I didn't want them to send the truant officer out again. They might make good on their threats to call CPS.

By the following Saturday, we'd eaten the last bit of bread and peanut butter in our house. The only thing left in the fridge was milk that smelled funny and one egg. Our situation was bad.

How can I get us more food? And what would happen when the landlord wanted our rent? I didn't even know how much it was, let alone how I could get that kind of cash. I didn't think Killian and I could sneak in and out of the apartment for the rest of our lives. Eventually, we'd get caught. My stomach roiled, thinking about Killian and me being homeless.

"What are you doing, Cal?" Killian asked as I climbed up onto the counter so I can get to the very top shelf of the cupboard. I know mom kept some money squirreled away in the old coffee can up here.

"Just looking for something," I tell him. He continues to watch me as I pull down the old coffee tin. The faint smell of coffee greets me when I pull off the lid. I'm expecting to see some money, but the only thing I find are some expired coupons for laundry detergent.

She took all the emergency money with her. She isn't coming back. I looked down at Killian. We were out of food and had no money.

Gibson and I jump when the front door opens with a bang, my heart beating wildly in my chest as I wrap an arm around him. For the briefest of seconds, I think Ari's come back to exact revenge on me for firing her, and I hug him to me. Gibs stands and wraps his fingers into my hair with one hand and peers around me.

"Why the fuck did Ari just get into a car with what looked like all of her stuff? Where is she going?" Sammy's curly hair is wild, and his high-pitched words match the panicked look in his eyes.

"I fired her." My words are calm and quiet.

"Why the fuck would you do that?" He looks at me like I

just morphed into a horse or something in front of his very eyes. "She was here a month, Cal. Gibson loves her. Hell, I love her. We all do. Why would you fire her? Is this about last night? What about the tour?" The tendons in Sammy's neck stick out in a way I don't usually see unless he's beat the crap out of his drum kit.

I stand, leaving Gibson on the couch to his cereal and Octonauts, and pull Sammy by the elbow into the sitting room.

"Look, I had my reasons, and it's done, but we are seriously fucked right now. Or, I am, anyway. I need to find someone to watch Gibson on tour with us. Entertain him for a bit while I make some calls. I'll be in my office."

I haven't even stepped foot into my office when texts start coming through.

Mav: What the fuck is going on? I'm on my way.

Kill: What did you do? I'm coming.

Kady: Why isn't Ari answering my calls?

I settle behind my desk and call Darren. He answers on the first ring because he knows damn well if I'm calling him, it's an end-of-the-world type of emergency. I explain that I fired my nanny and needed to know what my options were with Gibson for the tour.

"The way I see it, you have three options, Cal. One, you let the label hire someone to look after him while you are busy with things like media and playing. Two, you bring along someone to care for your son, but it sounds like it might be too late for this option." His sigh tells me that I'm not going to like the next option.

"Three, you leave your son behind to be watched by someone, maybe your aunt? The choice is yours, but I need to know what it is by the end of the day. This is getting it down to the wire, man, especially if you need the label to hire someone."

"I have some more calls to make. I'll let you know." I disconnect my call.

Shit. I think I have only one option. Aunt Sandy.

Knock, knock, knock.

I knew I shouldn't have asked the neighbor for something to eat, but it was that or starve, and I couldn't watch Killian die of starvation. And if I died, what would Killian do? He's younger than me. We've never been this hungry.

But now the police are at the door.

Knock, knock, knock.

"We know you are in there, son. It's the police. We're here to help you. Just open the door so we can come in."

"Don't open it, Cal," Killian whispers from behind the couch as the knocking continues. "Maybe it's not really the police. Maybe it's a trick. Or maybe it is the police." His eyes grow big. "Maybe we are in big trouble." His lip starts to tremble.

Our experience with the police hasn't been positive. Usually, they're threatening to arrest my mom for drugs, threatening to take her away and telling her that we'll be thrown into the foster care system. But at least there we'd get food, right?

I open the door.

"Hi." A tall man with dark hair and a bald spot in the middle looks at me, his hand still in the air, ready to knock again. "Can I come in, son?" He's wearing a uniform with a badge and he's alone, so I let him in.

"What's your name, buddy?" He looks around our living room. It's small and kind of dirty, but it's always that way.

"Callum, sir."

"Callum, that's a great name." He smiles at me. The kind of smile that shows all his teeth. The kind that you know he means what he says. "How old are you? Ten?"

"We're eleven."

He tilts his head at me. "We're?"

"My twin." I nod at the couch to let him know Killian's back there. It's always been his favorite hiding place, since he was small.

"Where are your parents?" He looks around our apartment and walks into the kitchen and opens the fridge.

"Our mom left for the weekend with Dale, her boyfriend, but never came back." I didn't want to tell him, but I have to. We have no money for food. I can't feed Killian and me with just one egg and smelly milk.

"What's the last thing you ate and when?" He looks through our empty cupboards.

"We had toast for breakfast yesterday and lunch at school that day too. It was pizza day. Our teacher, Mrs. Nelson, bought our lunch."

"Shit," he mumbles.

"My brother is really hungry, sir, but I didn't want to ask our neighbor for more bread."

The policeman talks in codes into his radio.

"Any units in the vicinity of South Grand, please respond." His radio crackles with responses.

"Can someone drive through and get me two cheeseburgers with fries and two chocolate milkshakes for two eleven-year-olds." He winks at me.

"So, what's your brother's name?"

"Killian." I say it low and glance at the couch. "He's scared."

The policeman nods and sits on the couch. "It's too bad he's not here. He's going to miss when my partner brings those cheeseburgers." He looks over his shoulder, but Killian's not going to budge until he smells the food and maybe not even then.

When the burgers do come, Killian finally comes out from behind the couch. We eat quietly and quickly.

"Thank you," I tell the police officer.

"You're welcome, buddy." He tousles my hair and for a moment, I wish he was our dad. We never had one, but he seems like he'd be a good one.

A short, stern looking woman with brown and silver hair and librarian glasses walks into the apartment. "Are these the boys?"

"Yes, this is Callum and Killian. They're twins." The policeman turns to us. "Boys, this is Mrs. Cooper. She's going to be taking charge of you. Have you found them a placement?"

"Yes. I've found them each a placement. But for tonight, they'll stay at the facility. Then in the morning, they'll get taken to their respective homes until we can find the mother or another relative." She says some more to the police officer, but all I hear is that they are putting my brother and I with different people. That won't work.

"No."

They both turn towards me. "What?"

"I said no. We'll stay here. We'll be good. We've been here for over a week now."

"Don't be silly. You have to have someone looking out for you."

"Don't separate us. Please," I beg them. "He's my brother. You don't understand." Killian's panic is choking me so much I cough. He heard them too.

"We can't do that. Foster families don't want two eleven-year-old boys at the same time."

Our own mom left us to our own devices. And now we have to be split up just so we can live with some stranger who doesn't know us? No.

"We'll run away." I stick my chest out. "He's my only family."

"Callie. I haven't heard from you in over a week. How are you and my Gibson? Killy?"

"We're all good Sandy, all good. How are you?" I close my eyes. I hate asking this of her. Technically, she's our great aunt. But she took Killian and me in back when we were two destitute preteens. I'm convinced if Sandy hadn't come to our rescue, we would have never made it. Three days apart was long enough.

"I'm fine. What do you need, Callie? I always know when you need something." She knows us, the way a mother should.

"It's a lot to ask," I start.

"Spit it out."

"Can you come out on the road with us for three weeks for Gibson? Please." I feel like shit asking her. She's toured with us before, when Gibson was a baby. But he's an active toddler now. She's getting up there in age and isn't as agile as she used to be.

"Of course. I'd do anything for that boy. For you and for Killy too. You know that." There isn't a moment's hesitation in her reply. Just like there wasn't back when she got the call to take us.

"I'm sorry, Sandy. You should be enjoying yourself. Not running after my kid."

"Callie, just tell me when to show up, and I'll be there." Her voice soothes me. "And tell Killy to call his Aunt Sandy. That boy never calls me."

I chuckle. "Yes, ma'am. I'll tell him. Thanks, Sandy. I mean it."

"I know you do. See you all soon." I owe Sandy more than I could ever repay. Yes, Kill and I pay her rent in the retirement community she lives in, but it's not enough. It's not. In the three and a half days we were in separate placements, Killian had already changed. If it had been much longer, I don't think he'd have lasted. And if I lost Kill? I shudder.

At least I can hold out through the mini tour and the rest of the album thanks to Sandy, but I have one more call to make. It's Sunday, so I know the agency is probably closed, but I call anyway.

"You have reached the confidential voicemail of Evelyn Somners. Please leave me a message and I'll get back to you as soon as possible."

"Yes, Ms. Somners. This is Callum Donogue. I have fired Arista. I received photos of her using cocaine in my bathroom. That's not something I mess around with. I entrusted my son to Arista. How can I ever trust her after seeing her with a coke straw up her nose? Not to mention the fact that she obviously told someone where she's been working, since they bring her to and from here every Sunday. I trusted your agency. I will not be repeating this experience."

After I hang up, my stomach burns. Now it's time to face the band, who I have no doubt is all out in my living room wanting answers.

Chapter 15

Arista

hree months later

After restocking the pastry case, I right myself and stretch. The aching knot in my back pulls, shooting a burning pain down my right leg. I can't catch the grimace that crosses my face, but try to disguise it as quickly as I can.

"You okay, Ari?" Letty looks over at me, her lips pulling down at the corners. Letty's my new coworker, and one of my new roommates. "Take your break early. Get off your feet for a few." She's the only one here who lets me take my breaks early. She insists on it when she knows I'm hurting, which is all the time. It's not just my back, which hurts like a mother right now, but my heart too. It's just an empty chasm now. I'm still livid with Callum. Just thinking of him tenses my whole body. The scald of not being believed churns my guts. Callum betrayed me. But it also hurts because I miss Gibson's constant chatter and sloppy open mouth kisses that he gave so freely.

"You sure?" I feel like I'm taking advantage of her sympathies.

"It's dead. Go. Find a book, take a load off, and get lost in someone else's life for a few." She waves past the counter to the adjoining bookstore. I nod my thanks and remove my apron, wadding it up and throwing it in the backroom. I head into the bookstore, but instead of picking a book and flopping down in a chair like I do most breaks, I head out the front door of the small independent bookstore and into the warm day. I walk up a block and a half to a small woodsy park that looks incredibly out of place in downtown Hollywood. I sit on the lawn and stretch my legs out in front of me on the lawn and then bend forward, touching my nose to my knees and hold it.

Stretches and yoga do nothing for the pain anymore because everything is piling up. The pain, not being able to afford my nerve block shots, missing Gibson and wondering how he's doing. Between the standing for hours at the coffee shop, and my night shift waitressing gig at the diner a few blocks away, my back is always killing me.

I do some stretches anyway. They won't relieve my pain, but I've worked hard on my flexibility, and I'll maintain it as long as I can. I lean forward, bringing my forehead to my shins and take a deep, cleansing breath. I'm sick of the pain. Some days, it's hard to get out of my damn bed, but I force myself to because if I don't then I can't make rent and I won't have a bed to worry about getting out of.

My phone chimes with my sister's text alert.

Vi: Dinner Sunday. Please. I miss your face Ris.

Sunday is my only day off from both the coffee shop and the diner. My only totally free day. As much as I miss my sister and would love to hang out with her, the thought of being around Todd makes me nauseous. Right before I moved into my shitty apartment, Todd cornered me in the garage.

"You ready to pay the rent for all the shit you have stored here, Arista? Your sister wouldn't like finding out what a slut you are and what you've been doing behind her back." I couldn't get out of there fast enough. Again.

I shiver at the memory. Even though I'm an adult, Todd still holds power over me, constantly threatening me with telling my sister. If Vi knew, I'd lose the only family I have left.

Me: Picked up extra diner shift. Maybe another time.

Vi: Brunch, then. Come on, Ris- I haven't seen you in weeks.

Me: Sorry- need to do laundry. I'm sure Todd will take you to brunch.

I mute my phone and set it next to me on the grass while I shift into a different position and stretch out, reaching for the toes on my left foot and hold. Then do the same thing on my right. Then back to my left.

"Holy shit, Ari! Is that you?" A shirtless Sammy jogs up to me and squats. "Fuck, it's good to see you."

Startled, I pull up both legs into a ball, hugging my knees to my chest. The motion sends a burning pain that causes my whole leg to pull up. "Shit. Dammit." These cramps are next level lately.

I groan and roll onto my side, my leg still pulling up at an awkward angle towards my butt as the muscles contract so tight it feels like something will snap if I straighten it.

"Are you okay?" His brow is furrowed as he offers a hand as I struggle to get to my feet, the cramp still making it painful to straighten my leg.

I refuse his help. Fuck him. Finally pulling myself to an awkward stand, I put weight on my cramping leg to test it. The muscle tension still pulls at my calf. I don't know what is worse, the pain in my leg or the pain in my chest from seeing Sammy.

"Hey, I just want to talk." He jogs up alongside me as I hobble awkwardly, unable to put my full weight on my leg just yet. I pace a large circle until the muscle finally releases, allowing me to walk more normally. Then I head towards the street.

"I'm on my break and it's over. Gotta go." I hustle towards the sidewalk.

"Ari? You ghosted us! I just want to catch up. I thought we were friends." He stops, his hands on his hips, his unkempt curls plastered against his damp head.

"Ghosted you? What about how your asshole bandmate ruined my whole life, my career? And I ghosted you?!" He has some nerve. Callum's bogus claims that I broke my NDA were bad enough. The accusations of me using drugs in his home and the fake pictures were over the top.

He didn't just fire me, he destroyed my reputation and made damn sure I couldn't even get picked up by another agency. I wouldn't even take the muscle relaxer the neurologist prescribed for my back issues, and I get accused of being a cocaine user. The agency fired me immediately without pay, despite working for him for nearly a month.

"Fuck you, Sammy. And fuck Callum too. Just, fuck each of you. Hard. Without lube."

Sammy drops his head and shakes it like he doesn't under-stand my ire. I'm a little bit lighter from hurling all the venom that's been eating at me towards Sammy. As much I could stay here and just lay into him, work calls. It isn't his fault. Callum is the one who destroyed my career.

"I gotta go. I can't afford to get fired again. No money means no rent." I take off at a slow jog toward the street, praying Sammy isn't hot on my trail. When I get to the light, I press the button, then venture a look behind me. He's still in the middle of the park, staring in my direction, but he doesn't follow. He didn't deserve my ire, and he's right, I did ghost him. I blocked them all as soon as the agency let me go. It wasn't him. It was Callum. The agency wouldn't hear my side of it. They fired me on the spot. Expendable. I've always been expendable.

I jog the rest of the way to the café and let myself in the back door so that I can grab my apron and put it on in the employee restroom. I fix my hair and wash my face and come back out.

Letty frowns at me. Shit.

"Sorry I'm a little late, I got a nasty cramp." Letty's one of the few who know about the injury from the car accident I was in with my parents years ago. I hobble to the back of the pastry case.

She shakes her head at me. "You walk like you're hurting, even worse than normal. Maybe you should go home. Take something and relax."

It's my turn to shake my head. "I can't afford to do that right now, Letty. It'll go away eventually. It usually does." Probably on Sunday night. Just so I can start the whole cycle of pain over again. Without insurance, I can't afford the muscle relaxers the doctor prescribes, the ones I don't usually take but have been lately because I also can't afford the injections that help the most. With the agency, I had decent insurance, but now it's gone.

The rest of my shift goes by slowly and painfully. I start cleaning the counter towards the end of my shift, and when I happen to look up, Vi is standing in front of me, her face etched in concern.

"Ris, you're hurting." What is it with everyone today? If they lived in this body, they'd understand. It's not a matter of hurting or not. It's a matter of how much it hurts today and that's a fucking lot right now.

I shrug. "What do you want, Vi? I mean, from the menu, I'm working." I hiss at her, embarrassed she's shown up here on such a shitty day. But damn, it's also good to see my sister, and it's all I can do not to burst into tears and beg her to take me home. She frowns and orders an iced tea and a brownie from the case.

"The brownies are my favorite," I tell her.

"Then get me two." I ring her up and fetch her brownies, handing them to her on a plate. "I'll be over there." She points to a corner table. "Come sit with me when you get off. We'll talk." I nod while she shoves a twenty into the tip jar. She moves off to the table in the corner and I move onto my next customer.

Fifteen minutes later, I'm lowering myself gingerly into the chair across from Vi at the café, and she slides the plate holding the brownie across the small table at me.

"Have you taken anything for the pain?" She watches me as I crumble pieces of the brownie into my mouth and shake my head. "That's what they're for, so you don't feel so shitty."

"I don't have any left." When I say that, her brow creases. She's worried I've become an addict. "They make me too loopy and throw my balance off, so I shouldn't take them while I'm working." Her mouth turns down and I hate the worry and concern I see painted all over her face. "Look, it's just a bad day." The lie slips out easily.

"How many bad days have you had recently? You're working too much, on your feet too much. You have to take care of your-self," she says quietly.

"I *am* taking care of myself. This is me taking care to make sure I have food to eat and a roof over my head," I snap, then feel a pang of guilt for being so angry at her. It's not Vi's fault I'm having a shitty day. It's not her fault that it hurts to sit, and it hurts to stand.

"I'm sorry. The pain just makes shitty days worse." I push the half-eaten brownie away and grab my purse.

"I miss working with kids." I hate working in a coffeeshop again. I'm so angry at Callum for what he did. I don't under-stand why he felt he had to fire me *and* ruin my reputation to the point of killing any chance I had to work with other fami-lies. I haven't mentioned the ins and outs of why I was let go from my agency with Vi.

"I need to go home and rest before my shift at the diner tonight. I gotta hit the bus stop. You can walk with me if you want."

"I'll drive you. You'll be home in half the time." I nod, grateful even though I know it will take her longer to get home. "Come on, I'm parked around the corner."

"You've lost weight," she observes as we head to her van. She's right, I have, but not on purpose. Between the physical pain, missing Gibson, and the hot seething anger I feel towards Callum, eating isn't high on my list of priorities.

"Did you find my notebook, by any chance?" I miss it, especially now. The notebook is neither here nor there, but it's the leather cover around it that's important to me. Vi gave it to me that first Christmas without our parents. I've refilled the notebook insert many times over the years, filled it with my musings. That cover, with the tree of life etched into it, holds a lot of meaning to me.

She shakes her head. "I looked through some of the stuff in the garage even, didn't see it."

Vi drives me back to my shitty little apartment that I share with two other girls, only one I know well, but at least I feel relatively safe here.

"I don't understand why you insist on living here." She shakes her head as she pulls up. "We may not have the biggest of spaces, but at least the condo is in a good neighborhood, and you know us. You live with virtual strangers, Ris. I worry." Vi turns in her seat to face me. Concern marks her forehead, but it shouldn't. I hate that she feels that even as an adult she needs to mother me.

"Letty's not a stranger, she's a coworker. That reminds me, I think I found someone who'll buy the bug as is. A friend of Letty's brother restores cars and then sells them for a profit. Like car flipping, I guess. She's going to give him my number. I'll let you know." Todd was worse than Callum about my bug. At least Callum kept it in a garage, Todd kept it on the street and kept threatening to have it towed unless I came and moved it. He just wanted me back in his control.

"You love that car." Vi looks at me like I've lost my mind.

"It does me no good without a working transmission, V. It's not practical to keep it. I don't even have a parking space for it here anyway." I don't tell her that the money I make by selling it might be enough to get my nerve block injections.

"I'm okay with it, V. I promise." I pat her leg. "Thanks for the ride." I open the door and slide out of the minivan.

She reaches for my hand. "Ris, you know you can come home, right?" Her forehead is creased with concern. "Anytime, day or night?"

I nod, but it's a lie. I can't live with her, not with Todd there. "I need to be on my own, V. Thanks again for the ride." I shut the door to her minivan and head into the building I now call home, and hope that I can get some rest before my shift tonight.

When our parents died, Vi didn't blink an eye at taking me in. But I was a young teenager, and a grieving one at that. She took on the job of not just being a mom, but being a mom to a surly teenager. She worked hard. Especially after Todd lost his job and never seemed to be able to find another one. She was always there for me. Always. I know that in a blink she would take me in, and having that to fall back on does help, but I need to stand up on my own and to do that I need to be away from Todd, even if it means forsaking my relationship with V.

Chapter 16

Callum

Sammy towels the sweat off his face with his t-shirt, which he then throws behind him. His blonde curls are plastered to his forehead after beating the fuck out of his drum kit for the last twenty minutes. We've been laying drum tracks for this song since he came back from his lunchtime run, but he's been off since he returned. He's moody and snapping at our engineer Dana at every turn, which isn't like Sam. Mav shoots me some side eye after Sam's latest tantrum, then leans forward and presses the mic button on the soundboard.

"Uh, let's take another break, Sammy." He nods at me. My turn. Great.

"Wanna grab a soda or something?" I try to keep it light.

He flops on the couch in the back of the engineering booth. "No thanks." He grabs his phone and starts scrolling. I sit next to him.

"Something bugging you today?" He shrugs and grunts at me. Seems like I hit the nail on the head.

"Wanna go for a walk?" He shakes his head.

"Come on, we'll grab a donut while they work the kinks out

of whatever is going on over there at the soundboard." I nod towards Mav and Dana with his John Lennon glasses, hovering over the soundboard. There's nothing going on except that Sammy's off as hell and grumpier than an internet troll.

"Fine." We leave. There's a donut shop about a block away from the studio, so we head that way.

"How was your run?" I don't know when Sammy started running, but he seems to like it. He did it almost every day on the mini tour. He's been doing it every lunch we spend at the studio.

"Okay." These one-word answers aren't the usual Sammy. We wait for the light to change so that we can head up the next block. As the light turns and we step into the street, he drops a bomb on me. "I saw Ari."

I stop in the middle of the intersection. "You saw Ari? On your run?" It's been three months since I've seen her, and I immediately need to know where she was. And his exact route. She must live or work around here.

"Yeah. Come on, the light's going to turn, dumbass." He coaxes me to the sidewalk across the street.

I tried to get in touch with her through the agency after the tour, but they said she was no longer employed by them and couldn't give me any information. I gave Jax what little I knew about her on Monday.

"How was she? What'd she say? Where did you see her?" I can't help the questions that bubble out of my mouth. This could help me make things right with her.

"She was stretching in a park. Said she was on her break and had to go. Right before she took off, she said we could all go fuck ourselves hard... without lube." Sammy looks hurt and confused. If he only knew the half of it.

"She was limping like she hurt herself. Maybe I should've followed her. I don't know why she was pissed at me. I should've made sure she got back to wherever she works okay." He shakes his head. "I'll never know now."

Ever since Kady got attacked last year after having lunch with Sammy, he's felt guilty about not walking her to her car, blames himself for her attack. "I'm sure she got to wherever she was going, bud." I pat his shoulder and steer him into the donut shop. He orders three different donuts and some sort of frozen coffee shake concoction. I get a black coffee.

He shoves his entire first donut in his mouth. "She was super pissed, Cal. So pissed she spit when she told me we could all go fuck ourselves." He shakes his head as he washes down his donut with some of his drink. "I don't get it. I mean, I could see her being pissed with you. You fired her, but I wasn't any part of that."

Sam's right. He wasn't part of that. That's purely my shit show and fuck if I don't feel guilty. Hopefully Jax'll be able to help me find her so I can fix it.

"She left her phone at the park." He fishes the familiar light purple flowered case holding the phone out of his pocket. "I have no way of getting it back to her. I don't even know where she lives. Do you?"

I shake my head. "I don't. Sorry, man. She was hired through an agency. I don't have any personal information on her. I paid the agency, and they paid her." He frowns and shoves the second donut in his mouth.

"You want this one?" He slides his third donut, a chocolate one, at me. "I don't want it." He sighs and pulls on the straw in his coffee shake. He must be feeling shitty if he doesn't want his donut. He stares at her phone.

I look at the phone laying between us. "We can take the phone to her service provider. They won't tell us where she lives, but they'll make sure she gets her phone. Okay?"

"That's a great idea." He picks up her phone and examines

it. "She has Sprint. Isn't there a Sprint store in that shopping center on the other side of the studio?"

"I think so." I have no idea if there is or not.

"There is! I just checked. Come on, let's go." He bounces on the balls of his feet while he waits for me to get up, almost back to his old self instead of the brooding jerk he's been since lunch.

Ten minutes later, we're walking into a Sprint store.

I hand the phone out to the customer service agent at the counter. "We found this phone in the park. It says she has Sprint. Are you able to get it to her if we leave it here?"

"Sure, we can. But are you for real? Most people would sell it." The agent reaches out for the phone.

"It's not our phone to sell. Do you have a sticky note or something?" Sammy asks the girl behind the counter. "I want to leave a note for the girl who lost it. She's having a bad day." He bats his eyes at her, and she comes back with a stack of sticky notes and hands him a pen.

"Thanks." It takes Sam ten minutes and four spoiled notes to scrawl out a note that he deems perfect before he affixes it to the phone. "Make sure she gets that, okay?" He waits for the girl to nod. "It's important, okay?"

"I'll make sure," she reassures him.

As we walk back to the studio, I can't stay quiet any longer. "I have to know. What did you put in the note to Ari?"

He shrugs. "I just put that I hoped she was doing okay, and that I wasn't sure why she was mad at me, but that I was sorry. And I gave her my phone number just in case she wanted to text or call me." I don't have the heart to remind him that I gave Ari everyone's number in case there was ever an emergency, so she already has it.

We walk into recording studio seven at Monumentus Records.

"You ladies done talking about your feelings and shit so we

can lay these drum tracks?" Mav stands tall next to the sound-board, hands on his hips, with a scowl pointed at us. Sammy scowls right back but nails the next track.

R

GENTLY SLIPPING out of Gibson's toddler bed, I pull his sheet up over his body and leave his nightlight on. As long as I lay with him until he's dropped off to sleep, he'll stay in the bed most of the time. On tour, he'd been sleeping with me in a regular bed, so it was the perfect time to transition him to the toddler bed when we got home. The race car bed from Sammy was a huge hit. He's adjusting to it better than he's adjusted to the lack of Ari in his life. He still asks for her and every time he does, it's like he's stabbing me in the chest again.

I did every fucking thing wrong the morning I fired her. I'd do it all differently if I could go back to that day. I'd have gone over the email more thoroughly. I would have given it to Jax right away to do his investigative shit instead of waiting nearly three months. I would have tried listening to her and my gut. I wouldn't have said what I did to the agency. Hell, I wouldn't have drunk so much the night before.

Even after all that, if I still wanted to fire her, I would've let Gibson at least say goodbye, give him some closure. Instead, he came in from a morning sandbox session with Ari to yelling and then Ari being completely gone. I even took him in her room, and it was devoid of anything Ari. Her keys to the house were on the bed. The only thing she left was her leather-bound notebook, the one she'd scribble in at night. Greta found it tucked under the chair cushion in the corner of her room a few days later. It was so tempting to open it and read what was inside, but I didn't want to know if she'd lashed out about me to her paper confidante. Those are her private thoughts and none of my business, especially now.

Gibson still asks for her about once a day, usually in the morning. It used to be much more. The tour wasn't easy on him or Aunt Sandy. I nearly quit the tour halfway through. Kady finally stepped in with Gibson and sat a show out, giving me peace of mind and Sandy a much-needed break.

I'm leaving the band after the album's done, but the only one who knows so far is Mav. He asked me to wait until we're done recording before making my final decision. I'll finish the album, but my mind is made up. My son needs to grow up with stability and love, and he can't get that if I'm touring the country at the label's beck and call.

I grab a beer and take it out to the patio. Settling into the chair that Ari seemed to prefer, I pull out my phone and open the email Jax sent me this morning. Scanning through it this morning made me feel sick. Tonight, I'll read through it more thoroughly.

Cal- The email you forwarded is from a spoofed account and not easily traced. I can tell you it was sent from a cloned cell phone using your home Wi-Fi. The cellphone cloned was Killian's. I've taken actions on his line to prevent this from happening again, but he needed a new number: 555-545-5426.

Timestamp says the email was sent towards the end of the party. I had my tech guy analyze the attached photos. He says they're all photoshopped. They also traced back to the cloned cellphone.

As for info on Arista Addington: She was terminated from the agency Monday morning following the party. A little digging found she wasn't paid for services rendered due to a clause in her contract about violating the NDA.

Speaking with the director of the agency as a potential employer of Arista, I was told by the director herself that she couldn't in good conscience give a favorable recommendation for Arista.

Financials show that Arista currently works two jobs. One at a café inside of an independent bookstore called Books and A Cup and the other at the Rockabilly Diner on Sunset near Vine. She no longer owns the car with the license plate number you gave me, so that was a dead-end on a possible address. My guess is she's in an under-the-table roommate/sublet situation.

She picked up her phone from the Sprint store yesterday afternoon. The phone is on her sister's family plan. The address comes back to the sister's condo. There's no evidence of Arista living with her sister, however.

Let me know if you want me to keep digging or if this is enough. -Jax

I acted too quickly that morning. I didn't act at all, I reacted. I didn't keep my head. Instead, I saw the pictures of her in the bathroom and fucking lost it right in my kitchen. I was angry I'd made someone who was using responsible for my son. I didn't think about the photos being edited or the anonymous email source.

Why would someone clone Killian's phone? I try to remember who he was with that night. He's always with someone lately, a different someone each time I see him. Was she the one doing drugs in my house, under my roof, with my kid just a floor away? If so, what kind of beef does she have with Arista?

My love and concern for my son clouded my ability to judge the email. I left the director of the agency a scathing voicemail that she returned Monday morning apologizing. She reassured me that Arista had been dealt with in an appropriate but discreet manner.

Now Ari's harboring some mighty big and much deserved hatred towards me, and anyone affiliated with me, judging by how she treated Sammy. I can't text her because she's blocked me and the rest of the band, even Kady and Greta.

Fuck, I don't know what to do. I scrub my hands over my face, trying to decide. I could visit her at one of her jobs, but I don't want her to feel uncomfortable or stalked. And it might be a little too public if she decides to vent. I couldn't even blame her if she did.

Killian's new phone number! She wouldn't know to block it. I immediately text Killian.

Me: New number who dis?

Killian: I know it's you, Cal. Jax ported my contacts over.

Me: I'm offended you didn't give me your new number.

Killian: Jax said he'd update everyone.

Me: Come over tomorrow? I need to use your phone.

Killian: You have your own.

Me: I need yours. You have a new number. Ari won't have it blocked.

Killian: Maybe you should leave her alone. What's done is done.

Me: Just be here.

Killian: See you around 1.

R

WHEN KILL WALKS in the next day, he helps himself to a soda from my fridge, then tosses his phone to me as he joins me on the couch.

"Think about what you're about to do." He looks at me. "She's already pissed at you. This might not go your way. You saw how she treated Sammy, and no one ever gets mad at him. She's fucking pissed. Maybe just let her be."

"Don't think I haven't gone over every possible scenario. This is my only chance." He eyes me.

"I figured." He takes a tug on his soda. "So, what's the plan?"

"When Gibson wakes up, I'll text her a picture of him and ask her if she'll meet us at the park where she ran into Sammy. I figure that must be close to where she lives or works."

Killian blinks, the hesitation visible on his face. "Cal, Gibs is already confused as fuck that she's not around. Isn't that going to confuse him even more?"

I sigh because that's the hundred-thousand-dollar question.

When I don't answer him, he continues. "Leave Gibson out of it for now. If she says no or blows you off, that hurts you. If he sees her and she says no, he'll be devastated all over again. I might not be a dad, but we may as well have written the book on abandonment issues. Don't shoulder Gibson with any more of those than he'll already have because of Becka."

Kill grabs my shoulder and squeezes it tight. "I'm not against you trying to make things right with Ari. I'm against you using your son as bait."

I swallow the hard lump that's formed in my throat. If I don't, I'm going to cry like a fucking pussy, which is something I haven't done since we were kids.

Kill's right, but what floors me is that he's looking out for my son's best interest. That right there may be one of the best things about what's happened with Ari, if anything good can come of this clusterfuck I've made.

The relationship between Kill and me hasn't been the same since the Becka incident. He's been distant and surly and missing from my life beyond the band. Our twin connection we've shared from conception is there, but the emotional one has been missing for over two fucking years. But him standing up for what he believes in his heart is best for my son, it flickers our connection like a neon light coming on. This proves that he's here for Gibson, at least. And that's the most important thing.

"Daddlay? Wakey!" Gibson's tiny voice calls through the app on my cell phone.

"I'll take him to the park that Ari used to take him to. You do what you have to do." Kill stands and makes his way upstairs. I pull up the video of his nursery and watch my brother put his shoes on him. He doesn't even know to change his diaper, so I head up.

Changing him, I hand him back over to Killian. Killian hasn't been around Gibson that much. That was his choice. I'm grateful he's taken an interest in Gibson, but I worry about them going to the park together. He's my brother, my twin, and I know in my soul he wouldn't purposely hurt him, but accidents happen.

"Kiwian," Gibson mutters.

"Let's hit the park while daddy tries to eat a big piece of crow pie." He lifts my son up from the changing table.

"Pawk. Awi?" he whispers.

"Nope, just us buddy." Killian glances at me as if Gibson just proved his point.

I get the stroller out of the closet and set it up, pack it with some snacks and rest my cell phone in the empty cupholder just in case.

"There're snacks and a bottle of water for each of you in his bag." I point to the bag resting in the bottom of the stroller.

"Thanks." I watch as he buckles my son into the stroller. Kill smirks at me as he pushes the stroller out the door. "Take care of things, man." He nods to his phone on the table behind me. "We'll be back."

I watch until they disappear down the walkway, realizing that this is the first fucking time Killian's been alone with my son for any length of time. What if Gibson gets hurt? What if he wanders away because Killian's not watching him? Can I trust my brother? He just proved to me that he's watching out for Gibs too. I have to put my trust in Kill that they'll be okay.

I sigh and flop onto the sofa. I grab Kill's phone and lay back, lifting my socked feet onto the couch.

Me/Kill: Hi. Please don't block me. It's Cal.
Ari: Cal?

Me/Kill: *Technically, it's Kill's new number. I borrowed it. With his permission.*

Ari: *What do you want?*

Me/Kill: *I need to talk to you. Face-to-face.*

Ari: *No.*

Me/Kill: *Please. I'll come to you. Or meet you at the park, the one where you ran into Sammy.*

Nothing. It shows read but no little thought bubble.

Me/Kill: *Ari. I need to talk to you. Please. I'll bring your journal. Greta found it tucked in the chair cushion.*

Me/Kill: *Give me 10-15 minutes of your time. Then you can take your journal and tell me to go fuck myself without lube.*

The little thought bubble appears. Then disappears. Then appears again.

Ari: *When*

Me/Kill: *Whenever and wherever works best for you. I'll make it work.*

Ari: *I have time at 3:30 today. At the park I met Sammy at.*

Holy shit, she agreed! My heart speeds up with the excitement that I'll be seeing Ari today. In just a few hours. I need to see if Kill can stay with Gibs. If not Kill, then maybe Kady.

Me/Kill: *Thank you Ari.*

Ari: *Just bring my journal.*

Chapter 17

Arista

What was I thinking agreeing to meet Cal after my shift at the coffee shop?

I can't believe I left my notebook there. I was in such a hurry to get out that I must have tucked it between the cushions, thinking I was jamming it in the bag on the chair. I thought it was at Vi's somewhere, but apparently not.

I really wanted my journal back, for the cover mostly. It was my Christmas gift from Vi for our first Christmas without our parents. It's a purple leather cover, embossed with a tree, and it means the world to me. I've had to replace the inner note book several times. It's not like I journal every night, but I do it regularly.

At least I got my lumbar injections with my car money. I still hurt, but at least people can't tell just by watching me walk.

Turning the corner and crossing through into the park, I see him. Cal sits alone on top of a picnic table under a tree, not far from where Sammy and I spoke. Shoulders rounded and his long hair shrouding his face, he looks at his boots resting on the bench attached to the table. His hand runs through his long dark brown locks, trying to sweep it out of his eyes. I glance around the park for anyone else he might be associated with, hoping maybe he brought Gibson with him to play in the park. I see no one except Cal. I'm about a quarter of the way to him when he finally catches sight of me. Hopping off the table, he stands with a smile on his face that I can't return.

If it weren't for the sentimental value of my journal's leather cover, I wouldn't be here. I have no desire to be anywhere near Callum. Just seeing the smile on his face makes me want to slug him in the nuts.

The closer I get, the more his smile falls. I'm probably scowling. Letty told me I was scaring the customers away today after I agreed to meet Callum. I thought she was kidding. Maybe she wasn't. I can't help it. I resent that he didn't listen to me or give me the benefit of a doubt. I despise him and the things he's said about me. He's the reason I have to work at a coffee shop and a diner instead of subbing or nannying for someone else.

When I'm within earshot of him, he calls out to me. "Thanks for meeting me, Ari."

I don't reply.

"Let's sit."

I wait for him to sit and slip between the picnic table and bench on the opposite side, as far away from him as I can get. My knee won't stop bouncing, and I can't help but glancing up at him. God help me, if he says the wrong thing, I may throw my first punch ever. I fist my hand under the table just thinking about it.

He slides my journal across the table at me. It's been carefully placed in a plastic bag with a zipper, the kind I used to put cubes of watermelon in for Gibson. "Greta put it right in the bag when she found it, I haven't opened it or anything."

I nod and drag the bag into my lap. "Thank her for me. The cover has sentimental value."

He nods and looks at me. "So, you work near here?" He looks around.

"You're going to waste your ten minutes with small talk?" I snap. He doesn't react to my nastiness, even though it's a side of me he hasn't really seen before. Instead, he twists the skull ring on the middle finger of his right hand a few times before looking up at me.

"I owe you a huge apology, Ar." The casual way he says my name lights my fuse and I can't control myself as I interrupt when he starts to open his mouth to continue.

"No!" I yell so loud, Callum jumps, and people on the other side of the park turn in our direction. "You apologize for yelling at someone or for hitting their car. There is nothing you can possibly say that will make this right. You *ruined* my career, a career I loved. Child neglect, Callum! Drug use!" He winces at each charge he levied against me.

"I never neglected your son. Ever. These are not characteristics anyone wants in the person caring for or teaching their child. I can't even substitute anymore. Evelyn threatened to get the police involved."

My eyes are hot as I strain to hold back the tears, but I'm not giving him the satisfaction of knowing he broke me. I may not understand his sick game, but I'm certainly not going to feed into it either.

"Not only were you an asshole to work for, but you ruined me professionally." I shake my head and rise to my feet. "I didn't deserve that, regardless of what you thought I did. Time's up. Lose my number."

As I walk away, he quietly says, "Gibson misses you."

My heart squeezes at hearing his name because I miss that little boy so much. His soft curls and his toddler hugs and his wet open-mouthed kisses. Thank goodness I am facing away from Callum because there is no way I can stop the tears that fall.

Rage takes over and ripples through me in hot waves. "I miss him. More than you'd imagine a drug user would." Sarcasm coats my words like a winter coat. "You should've thought of that before you fired me. And I should've listened to the little voice in my head that told me not to return, on my first half-day, before I got too invested." I end with that and walk away.

Thankfully, my bus is just pulling up to the stop when I arrive. I didn't want to wait here and chance Callum seeing me. By the time I get to my apartment, I have a pounding rage headache. I flop on to my bed and fall asleep immediately.

The minute I open my eyes, I know I'm late. *Shit.* I throw on my diner uniform, then rush to the bus stop, praying it isn't late today. I enter the diner and grab my timecard just in time.

"By the skin of your teeth, Toots, the skin of your teeth," Teddy, the cook, calls to me with a wink as I'm tying my apron around my waist.

He knows that calling me Toots always makes me smile. He takes our fifties rockabilly diner theme to the extreme, but I love him for it.

"But still on time." I wink at him. It's a Tuesday, one of my slower days on the six to midnight shift, but I look forward to it because I have a couple of regulars who tend to come in around eight. They're usually good tippers and break up the monotony of the shift with friendly banter.

The hostess seats a party of four at one of my tables.

After giving them a few minutes to get situated, I head over to take their drink orders. I get about five feet from the table when I recognize one of the couples as being Mavrick and Kady Slater. The couple with them are people I've never seen before.

I quietly set their waters down in front of them.

"Um, can I take your drink orders or answer any questions about the menu?" When I ask, everyone looks up from their menus and Mav blinks at me, then his lips curl up in a smile as he winks.

"Ari!" Kady squeals, bringing everyone in the diner's attention to us. "Oh my gosh, Mav, it's Ari! Scoot!" she commands Mavrick with a slight push. He slides out of the booth to let his wife out. As he's scooting out carefully, I notice Mav's black baby sling, adorned with tiny gray skulls and the telltale lump indicating there's an infant nestled to his chest.

Kady hugs me tight, rocking me back and forth as if we were long-lost best friends finally reunited.

"It's so good to see you. I didn't think I'd ever get to see you again." She holds me out by the shoulders and gives me a once over. "You look beautiful, as always. Doesn't she, Mav?" He nods, his smile impish as he meets my gaze.

"Uh, thanks? You look pretty too." I reply awkwardly. "So, um, drink orders?" I prompt them.

Kady ignores my request for the drink orders as if we were running into each other in the grocery store and not that they are there to eat and I'm their server. "This is my best friend Hayleigh and her fiancé, Harden."

I smile and nod at her friends. "Uh, hi."

"Nice to finally meet you." Harden holds his hand out to shake mine, which I do.

"You too. Both of you." I smile at them, feeling somewhat awkward in this situation. Since my dismissal from Callum's house, I feel like I have a huge flashing neon sign saying *drug user* or *child abuser* over my head and I can't help but wonder which of them these people see.

"Ari, you haven't seen the baby yet! Oh gosh, Mav, show him to her." She swaps places with Mav. He bends down a little and pulls back the cloth, revealing an adorable baby with his cheek against his father's shirt, lips pursed into a bow. He's so precious, I want so badly to reach out and touch him, but I keep my hands to myself, not sure how that would go over.

"Ari, this is Brio James Slater. Brio, this is our friend, Ari." His voice is low but laced with pride for his son. He called me *a friend*. I don't understand how he could do that after Callum's accusations.

Mavrick's love for his son is evident in how his eyes sparkle and his lips pull back in a wide smile. He runs his finger gently over the exposed cheek of his son and the baby instinctively nestles into his dad's chest and smiles in his sleep, revealing an adorable, deep dimple that matches his father's. Mav pulls the fabric of the sling back up over him so he's completely covered again. "He's seven weeks old tomorrow," Mav shares with a proud puff to his chest.

"He's so sweet and absolutely beautiful." Who doesn't love a baby? And the Slater's baby is the epitome of adorable.

"Congratulations." I squeeze Mav's arm to let him know I appreciate him letting me see the baby. I can't believe they'd even give me the time of day, let alone show me their infant. They don't act like I'm going to sell their secrets to the paparazzi or taint their beautiful baby with my illicit ways.

I step back. "So, what can I get you all to drink?" I plaster on my work smile and do my job.

I deliver their drinks and meals. When I take desserts to their table, I leave the receipt billfold and tell them to take their time. "Flag me down if you want to leave through the back door to the alley." I share quietly. "There're about five paparazzi hanging around out front." I move on to my other tables.

Thirty minutes later, I notice Mav and Kady, along with Hayleigh, standing near the table. I approach. "Back door?"

Mav nods as Kady adjusts Brio into a different sling wrapped around her. He pulls a protective arm around his wife. "Thanks, Ari, Harden's bringing the SUV around."

I lead the trio through the kitchen, down a hall, past the office and storage rooms and to the door that leads to the alley.

"Here you go. Feel free to stay in here until your friend gets into the alley."

I turn to leave when Mav touches my arm lightly. "Ari, wait. The bill." He hands me the black folder with the bill. "I didn't want to leave it on the table." He makes eye contact with me and leans in to whisper in my ear. "Thank you for helping us escape the photogs. Cal's a fucking asshole. We only recently learned what actually happened." His brow furrows and his lips pull down. "Kady's devastated to have lost her friend over his stupidity. If we'd have known the truth sooner, we'd have snapped you up for Brio. Take care of yourself." He squeezes my shoulder, and all I can do is smile weakly at him and nod.

The door to the alley whooshes open. "Come on, Harden's here," Hayleigh says. Mav tucks Kady into his side and shoots me one last glance before walking out into the alley. He must not know what Callum accused me of if he'd trust me with his infant.

I tuck the black folder into my apron and move about the diner, catching up on my tables and orders, then head over to the register to reconcile the tabs that have piled up in my pocket. Three crisp bills slide out of the folder along with his receipt. I discreetly count it out. That can't be right. I count it again. No way. Two hundred and fifty dollars. The tip was paid in cash and is more than twice the bill charged to Mav's credit card. On the receipt, he's scrawled out a note.

THANK you for your excellent service, Arista. We appreciate the extra care getting us out. Kady says please call her. 555-628-5239. – M

FIGHTING to keep my tears at bay, I tuck the receipt away. The extra money is more appreciated than they could ever possibly realize, and just the fact that they extended friendship to me warms my heart. The rest of my shift drags by and I'm so exhausted by the end of it, that I want nothing more than to magically transport myself to my bed.

The temptation to order a ride share instead of waiting for the bus is strong tonight, especially considering my unexpected windfall thanks to the generosity of the Slaters. The bus takes forty minutes to get to my home stop with all the stops between, but ride share would only take about twenty, if that. The sooner I'm home, the sooner I can reacquaint myself with my bed.

It would be an extravagance I rarely afford myself anymore, but I decide I deserve the treat. As I dig my phone out of my purse, a large dark SUV pulls up to the curb and the passenger window rolls down, revealing Mavrick Slater.

"Need a ride, Ari?" He's driving and seems to be alone now. As much as I'd love to, I probably shouldn't.

"I'm good, thanks." I wave my phone at him. "I'm just getting a ride share." He leans over the passenger seat and pops the door open. "Come on, Ari, let me give you a lift." When I stand there hesitantly, he rolls his eyes at me dramatically. "I won't tell anyone where you live, I promise." He makes the motion of crossing his heart with his forefinger and winks at me.

I give in and climb into the passenger seat. I rattle off my address as I buckle my seatbelt, and he pulls into traffic. "How did you know when I got off tonight?" I glance over at him.

"The schedule was written on the whiteboard in the hall, the one with the door to the alley." His lip turns up slightly. Whoops, forgot about that.

"Oh. Well, thank you for the ride home. This is a nice treat." I look down at my hands on my lap.

"I didn't feel comfortable telling you this in the diner, but it wasn't happenstance that we ended up at the diner, Ari. Kady's been missing you, and I was hoping you'd be working tonight." His brown eyes sparkle.

"How did you find out where I work?"

His lips pull up on one side of his mouth and he gives a one-shouldered shrug. "Our head of security is really good about finding out things about people. I mean, technically, it's his job. He used to be special forces in the military. He's got ways we don't question." He winks at me.

"We didn't know why Cal fired you. He originally told us it was because you and he were constantly at odds, and he'd had enough and fired you. We only found out about the email and photos the day you ran into Sammy at the park. Cal had finally forwarded the email, the one with the pictures, to our head of security after we got back from the mini tour. He had someone he trusts investigate the photos. Turns out, they were photoshopped, which I am sure you already knew."

"He didn't believe me. I even offered to take a drug test right then and there at the lab of his choice. I tried to tell him that we were randomly drug tested at the agency, that Evelyn would have my previous test results. Why would he want to listen to me, though, when the pictures told him the story he wanted to hear?" I shake my head. "Even if he didn't want me around, if he truly thought I was using drugs and talking about him, he didn't have to go bad-mouthing me to the agency. The things he said ruined my career." I don't know why I feel comfortable telling Mav all this. Maybe it's because he was nice enough to offer me friendship and a ride home.

"The owner of the agency did more than just fire me without pay. She tells anyone who calls for a reference that I was fired for drug use and child neglect. That agency is the bulk of my references. I've worked for them since I was in college." My eyes burn with tears. "He ruined my career." I can't hold back the sob that rips from my throat. "For his own sick fun."

Mav's eyes are wide with surprise, but I thought he knew all this. Is Mav playing with me too? "No wonder you want nothing to do with any of us." He rubs a hand across his jeans. "You seriously didn't get paid? Does Cal know?" Mav's eyes bug out, looking nearly panicked at the thought of me not getting paid.

"I don't know, and honestly, I don't I care. This is me." I point to my shitty apartment building. I probably should be embarrassed about where I live. I've seen how Callum lives. I am sure Mav's house is just as lavish, maybe even more so. I grab the door, ready to go.

Mav smiles, his eyes back to their warm sparkle. "I can't believe you live here." Great, now he's going to make me feel even shittier for living here.

"You see that building over there?" He points to one just as run-down as mine. A green, two-story apartment building up the street with a palm tree out front. "We lived there as a band. All four of us plus Sammy's sister in this tiny little two-bedroom place on the first floor in the back corner." Mav's face softens. "Man, those were some good times."

I pop open my door and look over at Mav, about to thank him for the ride, when he stops me. "Look, I probably shouldn't tell you this. Hell, I'm the only one who knows, but Cal quit the Blind Rebels. I convinced him to stay on through the recording and release of the new album before he makes his final decision, but I don't expect he'll stay."

Mav probably expects his words to shock me, but I'd expected as much. "I hope you're not putting that on me."

He shakes his head. "No way. That's all his shitshow." He pauses and looks back towards his old apartment building. "I guess I just wanted you to know that he's aware of his mistake. And let you know that we really miss you. Especially, Kady. She doesn't have many female friends, so she holds on to the ones she has. Make sure you call her."

I nod, but I know that I won't. I can't continue my friendship with Kady, knowing how close she is with the band, with Callum and Gibson. It's not healthy for any of us, especially me.

"Thanks for the ride. And the amazing tip. And letting me see Brio. He's gorgeous. Congratulations again." I hop out of the SUV and head inside.

That night, I wake out of a sound sleep to my text alert. I reach over and grab my phone from where it's charging on the nightstand to find it's almost 2:00 am. Who the hell would be texting me at this awful hour?

Killian: I thought you might want to see these.

Killian: 3 attachments

The first attachment one is a photo of Gibson sitting at the top of the slide at the park, elbows up like he's getting ready to propel himself down. The next attachment is a photo of Gibson pouring out a cup of sand in his turtle sandbox at Cal's. The last is a video.

I press play to see Gibson on top of the slide at his neighborhood park, babbling in that sweet way he does.

Killian's voice offscreen says, "Say hello to Ari." And Gibs stops and looks around the park for me.

Killian mutters, "Shit," in the background. "In the camera, Gibs. Ari's in the camera."

Gibson toddles closer to the phone's camera, reaching out for it. "Kiss! Awee! Kiss Kiss!" His lips appear and then, "Luv Awee!" before the video stops along with my heart. I miss my little buddy.

Killian: I thought you might need to see him. He really misses you, too.

Chapter 18

Callum

"Yesss!" Mav hisses his approval as I improvise the solo in the newest song. The music is flowing out of me easily today. Surprising because lately, when I sit down to write, it's crickets.

I hope they're rolling tape, not just for me, I'll remember it, but for the new guy. He'll need it so that he sounds at least somewhat similar.

New guy. The others still don't know, just Mav. This is my last album as a Blind Rebel. The band that Mav and I started as dumb kids in high school. The band that's bonded the four of us together as a family. It was supposed to be for life, but I guess this proves that even the best of families break apart at some point. It's time to say goodbye, for me to forsake one family for another. It'll be me and Gibson against the world.

I wrap up the solo and look up.

"Fuck yeah, Cal. That! Right there!" Mav bounces on his toes in my music room. "That is exactly what I'm talking about. It's some of your sickest shit yet."

Kady slips into the room. "What'd I miss?" She looks at

Mav, who's still bouncing, before she takes her seat behind the keyboard in the corner.

"Fuck, Kade, Cal just wrote probably the sickest riff and solo of his career." She looks over at me and lifts an eyebrow at her husband's excitement. I agree with her silently, because it wasn't quite that sick. Mav's enthusiasm seems over the top. If he doesn't stop this shit, he'll give it all away and his empty platitudes won't sway me to stay anyway.

Killian nudges my foot with his. "He's not wrong. That was intense." He glances at me. I haven't told him, but as always, he knows my time with the band is limited.

"Play it for me." Kady cocks her head to the side as I play through it again, now that she's back from putting Brio down.

"Again." This time I see Sammy hit record, and I play it again as she works to layer her piano pieces on top of it. I'll need to hear it on the playback, but that sounded damn awesome to me.

"This song doesn't even have lyrics yet, and I can already tell it's a fucking hit." Mav flops back on the couch in my music room. "I could read a shopping list to it, and it'd still be the shit."

He bobs his head along as we all listen back through it. I grin because he's right. It sounds even better than it did in my head. When it's right, you just know.

"We earned a fucking break." Mav stands and moves over to Kady, giving her a hug and a kiss on the temple.

I put my guitar on its stand. "I have some burgers to throw on the grill. Gibson's discovered a love of all things meat. Stay. We'll kick it on the patio. I'll set up Gib's old portable bassinette out there for Brio so he can be outside too."

Mav stands back up. "Sounds great. I'll help." He follows me upstairs to the room across from what used to be Ari's. I try not to think about the bed still adorned with the purple comforter she bought. I keep the door closed like she used to, so I don't have to think about it, about her.

"I have some of Gibs's old blankets up here too. And the sheet. I know Greta put it somewhere." I rummage through the shelving units in the closet. "Ah, here they are. You and Kady should take these. They're too small for Gib's new bed."

Mav is looking at me and I've known him long enough to know that look. He's bothered by something and wants to talk about it.

"Kady and I ran into Ari the other day. I just wanted you to know."

"How is she?" It's out of my mouth before I have a chance to stop it. I gulp. She's fucking pissed, and she has every right to be.

"We ended up having dinner where she works." He doesn't answer my question, but continues in his Mav way. "I went back and drove her home. She didn't ask or expect it, matter of fact, she tried to turn down my ride. Anyway, did you know she wasn't paid for working for you? That she's been blackballed from being a nanny? From working with kids at all."

It's all my fault too. I nod and hang my head. "Yeah, Jax told me. As well as where she works. Only thing he couldn't find out was her address."

"I slipped her all the cash I had on me as a tip. This was before I knew she hadn't been paid. If I had known, I would have asked Kady and her friends to cough up all their cash too. I'd have paid them all back just to give her some extra cash."

His disappointment in me is visible with the way his lips are turned down, and in the look in his eyes. "She didn't say anything specific, but, Cal, man, I can just tell she's deeply wounded. Like, to her soul." His emphasis is dramatic in his typical Mav way that he punctuates with intense eye contact. I know he's about to tell me something I won't like hearing.

"You should have seen her face when I pulled back the

wrap so she could see Brio. It was like she couldn't believe I'd even let her see my baby, Cal. Like she wasn't trustworthy or good enough to even look at him. *You* did that to her." He didn't need to drive it home like that. I already feel shitty about the whole situation.

I knew she was angry and hurt. But Mav's words, his descriptions, tell me she's not just pissed, she's broken. Fuck. And I did do that to her.

"Don't look at me like that. You won't be getting her address from me, I promised. Besides, she lives in an apartment complex, and I just dropped her out front. I'm not sure which unit is hers and we don't need you getting arrested for harassing people as you go door-to-door looking for her." He's not wrong, I'd do that. Especially, right now.

"I want to pay her and explain why I did what I did. See if maybe she'd consider being my nanny again, not through a company but directly. When I returned her journal, she was really pissed and wouldn't give me a chance to explain." I sigh. "Not that there's a valid explanation. Maybe this is how it's meant to be."

"Didn't know you gave up so easily." He grabs the portable playpen and starts downstairs.

Mav's words play through my head the rest of the evening, even after everyone left. Everyone except for Kill, that is. For some reason, he's been hanging around my place despite having one of his own near the Palisades. He's taken Gibs to the park a couple of times. But he's still awkward with him, which makes Gibs uncomfortable. Tonight, he's lingering, even though he's usually the first one gone.

"Why do you look like someone ran over your puppy?" Kill kicks my foot before he sits down on the couch next to me. "You wrote an awesome song today, so who pissed on your parade?"

When I don't answer, he continues. "Your son's asleep, by the way. Thanks to Uncle Kill's supremely awesome night-night game." I'm not paying attention. I'm too busy thinking about how I really fucked up with Ari.

He flops down crossways on the couch, laying his head on my lap. "If all you'll do is look at your lap, Cal, I'll lay down here, so at least you'll look at me." I roll my eyes as a childhood ritual comes back around. Fuck, how many conversations did we have like this as kids? Kill's head in my lap, or mine in his, while we talked girls, dreams, ways out, or just listening to music and escaping from the shit that was our life.

Killian sighs and waits for me to make eye contact.

"You're leaving the band." He doesn't ask, he states it as fact. Sadness and disappointment swim in his eyes and damper his voice. We've always known each other on a deep, intrinsic, almost cellular level. It's nothing you can describe to someone who's not a twin. A lot of the time we just know things, about what's going on in the other's heart. And I know in his heart, he's conflicted. He loves me. But he loves this band too.

"I'm not doing the nanny shit again, Kill, and I can't travel with Gibs. Sandy's too old to drag around the country. She deserves a life." He nods in agreement at my assessment of our great aunt, the one who saved us from the system and sure separation. That split would have killed one or both of us, and thank Christ, Aunt Sandy recognized that and took us in.

"You saw how fucked up the tour was. It's not fair to Gibson to drag him around the country like that."

"For what it's worth? I get it. You want him to have the life we didn't. I can't fault you for that, Cal." His lips pucker slightly and pull to one side. It's his tell. He wants to bring something up, but for whatever reason, he doesn't know how to say it. It's not an expression I see often anymore because he's usually the most unabashedly outspoken man I know, such a contrast to him as a kid. He might not be the most outgoing, but when he has something to say, especially to me or the band, Kill usually just says it now, fuck the consequences. He brushes the bangs out of his eyes.

"I kinda did something a few days ago," he says softly, then his eyes focus in on mine. Unsure Killian is not someone I see much of these days, and it reminds me of the boy who used to hide behind the couch.

"What did you do, Bubs?" Another reference to our shared past passes from my lips. I couldn't say brother at first, it came out sounding like bubba. I rest my hand on his chest, so he knows that no matter what, we're always brothers. Whatever he feels he did or wants to say has him faltering. We learned early not to let our vulnerability show, or it'd be used against us. It's making me a little uneasy, but also incredibly honored that he's giving me this gift.

"I texted Ari some photos and a video of Gibs at the park." His eyes beg me not to be angry with him. I may be an asshole, but I know he's trying to help the situation. It's not his fault she's done with my ass.

"She read my text, but she never responded." He's disappointed in his results, his eyes glossy with unshed tears. Fuck, Killian, don't do this to me. He clears his throat roughly. "I thought it might help fix things."

"The Rebels won't be the same without you. We've never not played together." Killian's insecurity catches me off-guard, his palpable fear searing through my chest.

"I might quit too." He closes his eyes and shakes his head ever so slightly, like he can't believe he said it. Or maybe like he can't see himself not being in the band. I know what that feels like. I've been second guessing my decision ever since I told Mav. But there is no way around it. I just can't be what the band needs and what Gibson needs at the same time.

I've had time to come to terms with my decision, to live with it. Kill hasn't. But this is not his decision or his life. We are not the same person. Me quitting doesn't mean he has to give up his music.

"No. You stay," I say with finality, patting his chest. "This is my deal, Kill, not yours. Besides, someone has to keep Mav in line."

A wistful grin passes over Kill's lips with a slight shrug. "He was always more your friend than mine." Quiet passes between us, both stuck in our own heads. His tongue plays with his lip ring as he contemplates what a life outside the Rebels would be like. I think of Ari.

I was so damned worried about falling for her and now I can't think of anything but trying to get her back. For Gibson, though, not for me.

Kill breaks the spell when he abruptly sits up. "I gotta go." He seems even more off now, reminding me that we are not as close as we used to be. We may know each other deeply, but lately all I've been getting from Kill is walls, walls he never used to have. Not with me.

"It's late, just crash here." His head is shaking before I get it all out.

"You're okay, right, Kill?" I look at him. I've been so focused on Gibs, the band, Ari, that I realize I don't even know what's going on with my own twin anymore.

With his back still to me, he nods. "Yeah. I'm okay." I put my hand on his shoulder and he sits there for a second before he gets up. The weight in my stomach tells me he's not okay, but I can't force him to talk to me.

Sometimes I wish I had control over our twin connection, that I could go into his head and figure out what's been up with him lately. But he's always been better at shutting it down than me.

"I'm here if you need me." It doesn't feel like it's enough, my words.

He nods and walks to the front door. "See ya."

R

I SEND flowers and candy to Ari at the café. When I don't hear from her, I send her flowers and candy at the diner. When I still don't hear from her, I show up at the café. I don't know her shift or anything, but I don't want to ask for her either. That's bordering on stalker territory. Of course, so is ordering the biggest coffee they have and a brownie and settling on a chair near the back of the shop and waiting, but it's not stopping me.

Almost an hour later, Ari approaches the bookstore from the side street. She walks straight through the café, into the swinging door that leads to the back. When she returns, she's wearing her café apron and has her hair tied back in a loose ponytail. She leans against the back counter and chats with her coworker for a few minutes before a customer comes up to the counter.

Time to make my move. I get in line behind the current customer. As Ari turns back around to greet me, she freezes as she takes me in. She doesn't give me a greeting, or even a smile. Her coworker's brows pinch together as she notices the tense interaction.

"Can I get another large, medium roast with room? Please. And one of those cake ball things? Actually, better make it two of those. The chocolate ones." She wordlessly rings me up. When she goes to write my name on the cup, I stop her. "Name for the order is *asshole former boss*." She scribbles something on the cup and sets it out for her coworker and turns to take two cake pops out of the pastry case, places them in a bag, and holds it out to me.

"That's $12.00," she says as I stick my credit card in the card reader. It goes through, and I take my card and put it back in my wallet. I grab the envelope from my back pocket and make a show of sticking it in the tip jar before grabbing my coffee as I return to my table.

I sip slowly while pretending to be interested in my book, *East of Eden*. Her coworker takes the envelope out of the tip jar and opens it, then shoves it in Ari's apron pocket. Ari seems to resist it until the coworker leans in to tell her something. Ari's eyes widen slightly at whatever her coworker tells her.

I'm about to get up and throw away my cake pop bag and leave when Ari arrives at my table with another pastry bag. When I look up at her, she sets it down on the table. "For Gibson. I already took the stick out. It's the vanilla one."

I take the baggie. "Thanks." I gulp. Here goes nothing. "Do you have a few minutes? I'd like to talk."

She looks back at the counter. "Actually, I don't." My heart sinks into the acidy pit of my stomach. I sigh and nod slightly while tucking the pastry into my jacket pocket. I knew this wouldn't work.

"The children's program is about to get out, and this café will become a complete zoo in about fifteen minutes." She pauses and then turns to look at me, really look at me. "But if you want to come back after I'm done here, maybe you could drive me home and we can talk on the way?" She moves back and forth on her feet as she waits for my answer.

"I can do that. What time?" I'm overeager and sound desperate, but my heart starts rising back from my stomach into its rightful place in my chest. She's giving me a chance to apologize. Or maybe she wants to tell me to leave her the fuck alone. Could go either way, and that has my chest fluttering. Although it could also be the thirty-six ounces of caffeinated beverage I've consumed in the last two hours working through my cardiovascular system.

"I get off at 4:00." Her nose crinkles again, and I remember thinking about her crinkled nose before. That crinkled nose of hers is still fucking adorable.

"That works for me." I stand. "I'll be back then." She smiles softly and I take it as a good sign. Maybe Kill's texts worked after all. "Thanks for the cake pop. I'm sure he'll love it." She nods and goes back to work.

R

WHEN I RETURN to the bookstore, Ari is already waiting outside. "Sorry. I'm obviously late."

She shakes her head. "Letty let me leave a couple of minutes early."

We walk to my SUV, both quiet as I fight the urge to pick up her hand. I have no right to do something so brazen and caving to it would likely drive her away. It'd work against my ultimate goal, which is to get Ari to come back. For Gibson, not for me, not for the band, or even the tour. Only for him.

"Where do you live?" I watch her as she situates her purse between her feet. She's quiet and tentative, more so than I've ever seen her be before. Even when I was purposely being an asshole to her for the first couple of days, she wasn't this uncertain of herself. I've made her this way. My stomach churns knowing that this is my fault.

"Mav didn't tell you?" She seems surprised when I shake my head. She proceeds to tell me the address. "He said that you used to live down the street," she adds.

"Yeah, that was our place." I can't help but smile, remembering some of the shenanigans that we had in that matchbox apartment. It was the first real taste Kill and I had of what a family could be like. We were four fucked up kids who made music and what they'd all been missing most of their lives, a family, at the same time.

"He had the same expression when he told me." She smiles. "Fond memories."

"Yeah, we had some good times in that little place. Before

we get going, I want to show you a picture of Gibs." I pull out my phone and show her the latest picture of Gibson. He's completely covered in cake pop, even in his hair, his smile wide.

"I think you could say that the cake pop was a hit. I told him it was from you, that's why he's got the big smile." She gently takes my phone and stares at his impish little face, her smile soft and her eyes glistening.

She passes me back my phone. "Thank you." Her words are so quiet they're almost a whisper, and the sadness in them is so thick it matches the heaviness inside of me. Her love for my son is so damn obvious. How could I take something like that away from him? I have to win her back, for him. He needs Ari in his life.

I pull away from the curb and into traffic. "Killian told me he sent you a few photos of Gibs too," I start, not sure where I'm going, or how to break the ice with her.

"He did. They made me smile." She nods her head but doesn't smile now. She doesn't seem to do much of that.

My fault, it's all my fault. "I should've known better than to take that email and those pictures at face value. I was embarrassed about how I behaved at the party. I'm sure you realize I was drunk off my ass the night before. I felt like shit the next morning. It's not an excuse, though, just hindsight. I should've thought it out and listened to you. I shouldn't have fired you on the spot and I definitely shouldn't have left that voicemail with the agency. I wish I could get a great big do-over."

I glance at her from the corner of my eye as we drive. She looks straight ahead out the windshield, no real expression on her face. Not one that I can read anyway. I thought I'd gotten adept at interpreting her before I canned her, but her not looking at me makes it hard.

"In the moment, I was furious with myself for giving someone access to my son when they clearly were doing things detrimental to his health. I see now I didn't give you a chance to defend yourself. I didn't listen to my gut, which was trying to tell me you'd never do anything like that. And let's not even get into the things I said to you the night before when I was drunk. I was so wrong. I'm so sorry, Ari. You didn't deserve any of that." I blow out a breath and remain quiet, wondering if she'll ever speak to me. Was she nice to me at the café just because she wanted me out of there, not wanting a spectacle at her place of business?

"The check in the envelope you put in the tip jar?" Her words are stiff, and she still won't look at me.

"You didn't get paid for working with Gibson. I gave you what I was paying the agency for the month. I know that you probably wouldn't get that much, but I figure you can take the extra and put it towards fixing your car or whatever. Like a bonus for taking good care of Gibson because you were amazing with him."

She's quiet for a while. "I didn't realize the agency made that much off of me."

"They obviously didn't pay you what you're worth." I'm surprised that she isn't in higher demand. There's a good chance she may have been in high demand before I ruined everything for her, though. My stomach drops at the realization.

"Look, Ari, I've been really shitty to you. I can't express how sorry I am for what I've done, and how much I regret firing you. I should have taken a second or two to digest what I was seeing instead of just firing you ten minutes after getting the freaking email." I take a breath.

I decide to just go for it. Get it all out now. "I don't deserve your yes, but I want to hire you back as Gibson's nanny. I'd prefer if you did live-in again, but I would completely under-stand if you'd rather just do days. I'll be fucking grateful to have you with Gibson, whatever schedule works for you."

She doesn't move. She doesn't speak. She doesn't really react at all.

"I'll pay you what the agency was charging me directly, either per week or month, whichever you prefer. No intermediary. Just you and me. We can have my lawyer draw up an employment contract we are both comfortable with, that *you* feel protected by." It's all out there and now I'm hanging on by a thread hoping she agrees.

She's still quiet and the longer she's silent, the further down into my stomach my heart sinks. Staring out the windshield, her face is guarded as fuck, and I can't stand that I can't read it, that I don't know what she's thinking.

"Gibson misses you, Ari. He still asks for you at least once a day. I miss you too." I admit. "We need you."

At the next light, I steal another glance in her direction. We're almost at her place so my time with her is running short. If she says no, this could be the last time I see her, and selfishly that crushes me, but it makes me even more sad for Gibson.

She bites her bottom lip, still not looking in my direction. She's going over her options, the weight of the decision she's making is heavy between us. It's clear that her love for Gibson is the only thing pulling her in.

It's me she's hesitant about. I've put this reluctance into her. I want to slam my head into the steering wheel. Why would she say yes? I've given her no reason to trust me. I sure as fuck wouldn't trust me if our roles were reversed, and it's with that thought I realize this isn't going to go my way.

"Please, Ari." My words are quiet and desperate and remind me of the last time I put myself out there to her in my music room. It's not just because I want the absolute best for my son. I've wanted that since the day he was put in my arms at the hospital. There's a small, selfish part of me that's missed her in my house and in my life, but I'll gladly sacrifice my attraction to her, my desire to know her intimately, for my son, because he needs her more. He deserves her more; he deserves *everything*.

I pull up in front of her building. Her hand goes to the door of the car. "I'll think about it," she says quietly before popping the door and slipping out. "Thank you for the ride."

She pulls the strap of her bag back up on her shoulder and shuts the door. I watch until she disappears into the building. It wasn't a no, but I won't hold my breath that I'll get a yes. It's likely I'll just not hear from her, and that will be my answer. I head to my place in the hills, defeated.

Two nights later, I crawl into bed after a morning of recording and an afternoon of running around after Gibson, then writing more on my own later in the evening. Even after all that, I'm in bed earlier than normal. I grab my book. Still working on *East of Eden*.

I must have dozed off because I find my head snapping up at the sound of a text hitting my phone. I scrub my hands over my face, trying to wake up a little, and set my book off to the side to grab my phone.

Ari: If I say yes, will you be staying with the band?
She's unblocked me.

Fuck, does everyone know I'm planning on leaving?

Me: Depends.

Ari: On?

Me: You.

Me: I won't tour without Gibson.

Me: If you say you'll come back but won't travel, then I'll hire you, but I won't tour.

I watch her thought bubble appear. Stay. Then disappear. Then come back. Then disappear again. Then come back.

Ari: Contact your lawyer to draw up an employment agreement.
Holy Shit.

Me: Is that a yes?

Ari: It is.

Relief and a strange giddiness I've never felt before strum through my body like the most wicked guitar solo ever. *Holy shit. She's coming back.*

It's all I can do not to run into Gibson's room and tell him, but I'm not that crazy. He's asleep and I know better than to wake him up. I'm not going to get his hopes up, just in case something happens, and we can't come to an agreement with the contract. He'll find out when she's back. And I already can't wait to see the relief on his little face that his Awee is back.

Chapter 19

Arista

Moving in is totally different this time. Callum, Killian, and Sammy all help move my boxes from my shitty little apartment back to his place. It took a few days to iron out the details of the contract, going back and forth with his lawyer. I'm confident that I'm more than covered should this not work out, and I think Callum feels he's adequately protected as well. Best part is that the pay is more than I was making through the agency and includes health insurance that is even better than the plan I had when I was with the agency.

Callum's gone to pick up Gibson from Mavrick and Kady's house. I shouldn't be so nervous, but I can't stop moving.

I can't wait to see my munchkin again. It's possible he'll reject me at first. He'll eventually warm back up to me. I did go missing from his life for over three months without warning. I wouldn't be surprised if he gives me the cold shoulder or acts out his confusion in tantrums.

The gate alarm alerts on my phone, Callum reinstalled my apps before he left. I stand in the small sitting room near the door and watch them pull up to the house.

He unbuckles Gibson and carries him toward the door. He's gotten so much bigger. And I can tell he's talking Callum's ear off all the way up the walkway, still my little chatterbox. My heart flutters nervously in my chest the closer they get, and I wring my hands together.

Even though I'm expecting them to come through the door, I still jump slightly when the door opens, and they walk in.

"Look who's here, Gibson." Callum turns him in my direction. When his little eyes see me, they go as round as teacup saucers, and his lips slightly part. His head is still covered with those cherubic blonde curls that I know are soft and smell like lavender.

"Hi, kiddo. Did you miss me?" I ask. I don't approach him even though I want to grab him from his dad and smother him with kisses and breathe in his lavender scent that'll be mixed with a light layer of Callum's spicy smell. I don't want to scare or overwhelm him.

"Awee. Daddy. Awee." He pats Cal's arm, then points at me. "Awee back!" He wiggles excitedly in Callum's strong arms, wanting down. Callum sets him down. Gibs tackles me in a hug around the legs. "Awee! Awee! See wing!" He grabs my hand and drags me through the house to the back door. There is now a small swing near his sandbox.

"Oh, wow, look at that! Did you get your very own swing?" He nods vigorously and babbles something I don't quite understand. "Shammy! Wing peasant."

It takes me a minute to realize he's telling me Sammy gave him the swing as a present. "Sammy gave you the swing?" He nods.

I give in and let him drag me outside and slide him in the swing. I push him gently.

"Moe! Moe wing Awee! Moe wing!" He loves it. He was always afraid of the swing at the park, preferring the sand and the slide the most.

Soon Callum joins us, sitting close on the stone barrier that surrounds the back of the yard from the wilderness of the hills beyond. "Sammy bought him the swing to cheer him up after you left. He was inconsolable for the first couple of days." His dad's stormy blue eyes are wet. "As if I didn't already feel shitty enough. Anyway, Sammy bought him the swing, but he didn't really like it until a few weeks ago."

I nod. "He didn't like the ones at the park when I'd take him either."

The rest of the day, I fit seamlessly back into their lives as if I had never left. Callum explained he did his best to try to keep Gibson's routines the same except for the three-week mini tour they went on. He's hinted that the tour didn't go well with Gibson traveling, but we haven't really talked about it.

Most of the day, Gibson doesn't let me leave his line of sight. He's probably afraid I'm going to disappear again. This only poses a problem when I have to use the restroom or when it's time for him to take his nap.

Callum probably doesn't realize I know that the Blind Rebels have another, longer tour coming in about a month. They leave before the release of the new album. This tour is going to be three months instead of three weeks. I wonder if he's still trying to decide if he wants to stay a Blind Rebel? I'm not getting in the middle of that. It's Callum's decision to make, not mine.

As I slip out of Gibson's room after him finally going to sleep, I run into Callum, who's coming from his bedroom. He's freshly showered and wearing sweatpants and a faded black t-shirt that's snug around his chest and those hard, colorful biceps of his.

"Oh, hey, perfect timing," he says. "Let's go downstairs, we need to talk." Callum's been so different today. He's suddenly way more open with me, and he hasn't let me leave his line of sight much today either.

I lived with him just over three weeks before, and I've never seen him not wear jeans except for when he was in the gym. This version seems more like the real Callum, comfortable in his own skin, in his house.

He sits in the chair he's always favored, and I choose a spot on the couch nearest to his chair. The couch is a soft gray and so comfortable. I've missed this couch.

"He seemed to go down easy for you. I meant to warn you, he's been a bear lately. Getting him to go down." He shakes his head. "I don't know if the tour messed up his sleep schedule, or if it's the new bed, or if he was just missing his Ari." He smiles softly at me.

"I missed him too, so much." He nods but says nothing.

"So, a toddler bed." I break up the silence.

"Yeah, it was time. He'd slept in a normal bed with me most of the mini tour, so I figured I may as well set it up. He's had it since birth. It was," Callum starts, and we finish it together, "a gift from Sammy."

Callum smiles. "Yeah, that's a Sammy thing. I'm surprised he didn't give you a gift for saving his life that day at the table."

I hold up my arm where my angel wing bracelet sits on my wrist and twist it around. "He did."

"Doesn't surprise me. Sammy loves to give people presents. He's like a little kid that way." He examines the bracelet on my wrist. "He made that. Did he tell you that?"

"No! He did?" I examine my bracelet. It's beaded with two metal angel wings on it and a gemstone, amethyst, between them. I've loved it since he gave it to me, a few days before the party where I got fired. Now I love it even more, knowing he made it specifically for me. "It's beautiful."

"He took up metal-working and jewelry-making the year that we broke up as a band to keep himself busy. He made us each one of these necklaces." He pulls his out from under his t-shirt. It's the band logo with a green gemstone in the curled tail of the letter R. "We all have one, but each of our stones is a different color."

"He's so talented." I remember seeing Kady wearing one, but hers is much daintier, with a small pink stone. He must have made that one too.

"That he is." Callum nods and is quiet for a few awkward seconds. Like he wants to tell me something but is unsure how.

"We have a tour coming." He scrubs his hand against his face. "I'm not going to lie, Ari, the three-week tour was hell. Gibson was a pill the whole time. We brought my aunt with us, and I know she loves him, but he was frustrating her. Or maybe she was frustrating him. Maybe he was still distraught over you disappearing from his life, or maybe it was just the rigors of touring, or maybe a combination." He sighs and looks up at me.

"I can only imagine what touring is like for him, stuck in small spaces. Always some place new without knowing exactly where that some place is." He shakes his head. "This tour is going to be longer and more grueling both in terms of travel and media attention. He didn't sleep well, so I didn't sleep well. It was, just bad." His eyes glaze over at the memory.

He sounds like he's trying to talk himself out of touring with the band. If that's what Callum wants, I won't stop him. I can't make that decision for him. This is his life and family. Maybe quitting is supposed to be his course. If he's willing, though, I'd like a chance to try.

"I'm willing to try, if you are, but it needs to be your choice, Callum." If he's not enjoying the touring life anymore, then that's that. But if he feels Gibson is holding him back from something he loves, I can help.

"Are you absolutely sure?" His eyes bore into mine. "I haven't committed to anything yet. The band's waiting for my decision. I hate putting this on you when you've just come back, but we leave in five weeks. If you're not up for it, I'm fine with that, I really am. Just tell me so the guys have time to look for a replacement. Think about it for a couple days, but I need to know soonish."

I grab Callum's hands. "You can't put this on me, Callum. I don't need a couple of days. I'm fine with touring. Just because it didn't work with your aunt doesn't mean it won't work with me. I left his life suddenly, so he was already discombobulated before the mini tour. It'll be different this time." I squeeze his hand. "I think this can work, I really do. But only if you're agreeable to trying. Ultimately, the decision has to be yours."

He nods and squeezes my hand back. "Okay. Let's try. We're a team, right?" He doesn't sound one hundred percent convinced. Once we get into the swing of things, he'll be more at ease.

Gibson welcomed me with open arms and sloppy kisses. Oddly enough, working my way back into Callum's life has been easy too. He seems different now, more relaxed, and comfortable, the way you would expect someone to act in their own home.

A few nights later, I'm curled up in my favorite spot on the couch, balancing my laptop, a notebook and the tour itinerary, a cup of my favorite evening time tea steaming from the coaster on the table. Callum walks in from working at the studio, removes his shoes, grabs a beer from the fridge, and sits in his favorite chair nearby.

He takes me in. "You look like you're studying for a test. What's all this?"

"I'm looking for activities in the different stops on the tour that Gibson might like. Playgrounds, children's museums, zoos, aquariums, kid-friendly restaurants." I set my computer down and grab my cup of tea, even though it's still too hot to drink.

His eyes widen. "Wow. You're going all in."

I shrug. "I might as well have these in my back pocket rather than try to come up with ideas on the fly, when I may be tired. It can't hurt. I want this to be as easy as possible on every-one, even me." I smile.

He nods and settles in with his beer. "The first week of tour is usually interesting. Everyone is getting into the groove of the tour. Then it becomes routine for a few weeks. After that, it's just tiring. We'll all have our moments. We'll bicker, get snippy with each other." He shrugs.

"It's the nature of the beast. On the off days, we all do our own things for the most part. Not because we don't like each other, but because we do. We need the space to be ourselves. Living on a bus can get kind of crazy. There is no privacy. None." His small smile is almost apologetic.

"There'll be five of us on the bus. That's a lot of people living in one small space, even when one of the people is little. We'll have to see how it goes. Mav, Kady, Brio, and Elsie, that's their nanny, will be in a smaller bus. Then it'll be us three, Killian and Sammy in ours. The back lounge on our bus will be Gibson's space. Either you or I will be with him in there. We can switch off or whatever we decide works. The guys and whichever of us isn't in the bedroom will have bunks. The crew have their own bus." I nod along. It's good to know what to expect.

"So, there will be room for Gibson to have some toys on the bus."

He nods. "Oh, yeah. We'll use the back bedroom as his room, and then you and I can switch out or figure out what works best for him. It might work best that you sleep with Gibson, especially on the nights with shows, because we'll roll out so late, it wouldn't be fair to disrupt your sleep to switch out. We'll figure all that out." He shrugs. "But there's no privacy in a bus environment. You'll see and hear things." He closes his eyes, shaking and his head. "I apologize in advance. Sammy and Kill very much live the rock star lifestyle. Hopefully, they'll keep it down." He sighs, and it makes me wonder if he misses those days.

"It'll work out. I'm sure." I have an overwhelming urge to pat his hand or knee, as a show of reassurance, but I'm too far away, and it would just look weird and forward of me.

"It will." I'm not sure if he's reassuring me or himself as he nods. "I'll insist that the label book our rooms as either two-bedroom suites or adjoining rooms if there are no suites available. I hope you are comfortable with that."

"That works fine for me." I'm used to living with Callum and it doesn't bother me as much as it surprises me that he'd want to be that close.

"You'll still get days off. Any day that isn't a travel or show day, unless we have some sort of media thing." He runs his hand through his long hair. He tends to wear it in a low ponytail at the base of his skull. I've seen him wear it down only a few times, and I prefer it that way.

"You'll need them, trust me. It's important for your mental health, just like it is ours. Too much togetherness isn't a good thing." He smiles at me weakly. "Spend time doing you stuff. See a movie, do a spa day, whatever you want. We didn't discuss this, and it's not in your contract, but you'll get your usual pay. The label gives you a nice stipend as well. And anything you need for Gibson, just put it on the credit card."

"This'll all work out. I have a great feeling." I'm excited to get out and see some of the country. I've never been out of California. And I'll have my best little sidekick with me.

The worry-lines that had been non-existent since my arrival have returned this evening. Etched in his face, they make him seem so much older and harder than he is.

Chapter 20

Callum

Somehow, we're the last ones to arrive at the bus staging area, even though I swore we left early.

"You ready to do this?" Mav greets me with a half-hug, half-backslap.

I nod. "As ready as I can be, I guess."

There's a jittery unease in the air. Part of it is the impending tour and the upcoming album release. With both of those things comes an excitement of the unknown. But there is something more that lays on top of the excitement. Something weighing it down. It's settled heavy on my chest.

I feel like I'm being watched. I scan the staging area. The usual crew members mill about; most of these guys are long-timers and have been with our group for years. The security detail mingles amongst them. Darren scurries around, sucking up to everyone. Jeff, our tour manager, stands at the end of one of the semis with a tablet in hand, watching the equipment loading into the trucks, his long blonde hair tied behind his head. He's been with us since we signed with the label. I've never seen him wear anything but jean shorts and a Blind Rebels t-shirt and he's true to form today.

That reminds me; I need to talk to Ari about security. I scan the group until I see Jax standing by Mav's bus, thick arms folded across his chest, mirrored sunglasses on. No doubt he's scanning the crowd. He's been with us forever. His loyalty to our band is something rare in the industry.

"Cal, man, how the hell are you?" I'm tall and Jax towers over me as he man-slaps me on the shoulder.

"Good, man. Good. Who did you decide to assign for Ari and Gibs's detail?" There are a couple of new guys on the band's security team that I don't trust yet and I'm hoping like hell it isn't one of them.

"Aiden will be on Gibson and Ari, backed up occasionally by Luke. The new guys are assigned to the general security stuff until I get a better feel for how they work." He looks down at me and lifts an eyebrow. "That good man?" I nod. He's remembering back when I hated having security around. For me, I don't give a shit if I have a detail or not. I just want Gibson and Ari protected.

Aiden's been with us for a while and is a good guy. "Aiden works. Ari's familiar with him, so that will probably put her at ease. I don't think she's met Luke yet." Luke was brought onto our security detail originally to be Sammy's bodyguard. Much like Sammy, he's a California surfer through and through, his short blonde hair bleached almost white by the sun, which contrasts his deep golden skintone. He's so laid back you wouldn't think he'd make a great bodyguard. That's where you'd be wrong. I've seen Luke in action, and I wouldn't want to be the subject of his aggressive side.

I pat Jax's shoulder, then grimace a little. "I haven't mentioned the detail to her yet. I just wanted to be able to tell her who to expect."

"Maybe I should explain how it works?" he suggests. "She on the bus?"

I nod. "If you don't mind."

183

"Not in the least. Let's go talk to your nanny. Or should I call her your girl?" He lifts that eyebrow again, cocking his head at me.

"She's Gibson's nanny." But I care about her. If I didn't, I wouldn't have gone after her. I remind myself that she's here for Gibson, and not me.

"Sure, man, whatever you say." He laughs gruffly and slaps me on the back again. "Just keep telling yourself that."

When we board the bus, Gibson plays on the floor with his cars while Ari looks for something in the kitchenette.

"Ari." Jax approaches her with his hand out. "I don't think we've been formally introduced. I'm Jax, head of security for this circus." He shakes her hand.

"I was just talking with Cal about your security detail and figured I may as well give you the information myself." Her eyes widen slightly.

"Aiden is assigned to you and Gibson. You remember Aiden? He was at the party." She nods at him, her eyes still wide. "Any time you go anywhere with or without Cal, Aiden will be with you." He looks at her. "If he's not available, his back-up is Luke. This means you need to let them both know that you are leaving. Doesn't matter if you are going for a walk or to get a coffee or on a trip to the zoo, Aiden or Luke go too, every single time. Understand?"

She nods, her eyes wide. "Is this normal?" She looks between Jax and me.

He nods. "The more popular the band gets, the more it becomes necessary. There are children on this tour, precious little souls we must protect. I've got Kady, Elsie, and Brio covered. Aiden has you and Gibson. Luke and Eric will be around too. And I have a new guy, Drew." He reaches out to her. "Hand me your phone."

She pulls it out of her back pocket and slides it into his palm after unlocking it.

"I've added Aiden, Luke, and myself as contacts. Don't go anywhere without one of us. If something happens, anything that makes you uncomfortable or fearful, you tell all of us immediately."

He flashes his phone at her, showing her the text he sent himself and Aiden. "Use it to let Aiden know when and where to meet you for outings. If there's something or someone bothering you, all of us know. Understand?"

She nods and takes her phone back from him. He stands to leave and looks down at her. "We're all friendly, but our job is to keep everyone safe. We take that very seriously. If at times we seem gruff, just remember it's for your protection." She nods again, and he leaves.

"You okay? You look concerned." I squat down and grab a car from Gibson's pile and play with him.

"I wasn't expecting that," she admits. "I mean, I guess it makes sense," she adds wearily and lifts her shoulders in a shrug.

"Don't think this is because I don't trust *you*. It's the freaks out there that I don't trust." I point to the line of fans standing around the perimeter of the parking lot. "I love our fans. They are why we get to do what we love. But there are a few crazies out there too. I don't want either of you in a situation you can't handle. You heard Jax. Mav and Kady have him detailing Elsie and Brio." She slips her phone back into her pocket and gazes out at the line of fans watching us get ready to go.

R

WE ALL GET BACK into the groove of being on the road. After shows, Ari sleeps with Gibs in the back room of the bus, or he sleeps in her room if it's a hotel. It seems to be running smoothly, but the schedule will just get more and more hectic the closer we get to the album release.

The privacy thing... yeah, well, I'm fairly certain Ari walked in on Sammy naked in the bus bathroom once already. It was bound to happen, just a matter of who and when. It'll happen again.

Gibs has been traveling like a trooper. It's Ari that makes the difference. She keeps him on schedule, and he thrives on it. Even on tour, I need to peek in on him every night. Somehow, Ari knows I do this because she keeps the adjoining door or bus bedroom door ajar. I have to put eyes on Gibson before I can even think about going to sleep. It's something I've done since he was born. He's the last thing I see before I go to sleep. How Ari knows this, I have no idea.

We have one more show here tomorrow and then we are onto the next stop, but there is a day in between. Fuck if I even remember what city we'll be stopping over in.

I plan to take Gibson on a hike somewhere. It will do us both good to get some together time in the sunshine. He loves being outside, and that's something I want to encourage.

I knock on the adjoining door before pressing it open. She's showered, dressed, and sitting on the floor of the room, helping Gibson stack the blocks she keeps in her hotel bag for him. He's dressed and comes busting over with his arms up.

"Good morning, buddy." I tickle him, and he throws his head back in a laugh.

"What are your big plans for your off day?" I'm being nosy with Ari, and I don't even care. If she's not busy, maybe she'd like to hike with us.

She shrugs. "I don't really have any. I'll probably just hang around here, maybe read by the pool later."

"Gibson and I will be going for a hike this morning. Would you like to come?" She looks up and appears to be considering my offer.

"Don't feel obligated. I need to get some fresh air and sunlight." I nod to the window in her room. "I want you to do whatever you need today. But if you'd like to join us, you are more than welcome."

She stands and stretches. "I would love that, actually, if you don't mind me horning in on your father-son time?"

"I wouldn't have asked if I minded." I wink at her. "Give me half an hour to get myself together? Have you two eaten breakfast?"

"Yeah, he had his usual fruit and yogurt. I had some eggs."

An hour later, we're strolling into a regional park with a map in my back pocket and Gibson walking freely between us. I picked one of the easier trails so that Gibson can walk until he gets tired, then I'll carry him in the hiking pack.

We take plenty of breaks for him to drink. Ari slathers him with sun block a few times. Ari and I talk about everything under the sun as we walk behind him.

It feels so normal with Ari. I don't know if it's the sunshine warming my skin or being out of the bus and the endless string of hotels and out enjoying the day, but I feel a closeness with Ari I haven't felt with a woman. Not with Becka, though, I tried, for Gibson's sake. How fucking cliché is it that I'm feeling it with Gibson's nanny. I shake my head at myself. I can't even think about entertaining this attraction I feel towards her.

We stumble onto a small creek a few minutes later, and Ari takes off her and Gibson's shoes and stands with him in the stream. He squeals in delight at the water rushing over their feet.

I take a few pictures of the joy on his face. "Squat next to him," I direct Ari and she flashes me a big smile as I snap a few of them together. "That's a great pic." I send it to her phone. "You'll want to keep that one."

A group of hikers pass by and notice us playing in the creek. "Here, let me get a picture of the three of you together," an older man offers. "You three look just like my son and his family." I hand him my phone and join them in the water. "Smile!" he says.

"Mile!" Gibson says back and makes his monkey smile that shows all his little teeth.

The man hands my phone back to me with a friendly pat on the shoulder. "You have a beautiful family, son. Enjoy the rest of your hike." I look at the photos he took. We do look like a family. I send one of those pictures to Ari too.

After Gibson and Ari get their shoes back on, we start our hike back to the car. Gibson's pretty much done with walking and holds his arms up to Ari. "Up. Pease. Up." She bends over to pick him up.

"I'll squat. You slip him into the pack." She maneuvers Gibson into his hiking pack. Once we start hiking again, he sings softly to himself as we continue down the path.

About halfway to the car, I don't even think about it and reach out and interlace my fingers with hers. I only realize what I've done when she doesn't tangle her fingers with mine. When I glance at her, her eyes are wide.

I smile at her reassuringly, and as we walk, she relaxes, and her fingers eventually curl into mine. Her hand is small and holding it feels so right. The warmth, the connection we have, feels simple. It's like walking barefoot through grass. Our connection flows between us and zings in my chest. I start to hear the melody of a song in my head. I hum it softly to myself, trying to get it to stick in my head.

I've imagined love like this but thought it was a myth or something made up for television. Love like this is filled with familiarity and acceptance, with warmth and connection. Like what the hiker who took our picture had with his wife. It's not fucking in the corner of a room full of people, so you can say you bagged a rocker. It's not abandoning your weeks old baby so you can move on to the next bigger, better rock star. It's definitely not letting your eleven-year-old twins fend for their fucking selves because the new guy doesn't want to be bogged down with kids.

I stop our progression. I need to write this down before I lose it.

"Grab my notebook out of the front pocket of the pack?" I ask Ari as I stop.

She hands it to me and watches with her head tilted as I scribble down the notes of the progression and some lyrics, so I'll remember them. They just flow out of me. Inspiration hasn't come to me like this in a while. Once I'm convinced I have it, I slip the pen back into the spiral binding and hand the notebook back to Ari.

"Sorry. A song idea came to me." I shrug. While she's returning my notebook to its pocket in the backpack, it hits me. I'm not just attracted to Ari because she's beautiful, or because she loves my son. It's so much deeper. The person she is vibes with the person I am.

Suddenly, I can't know enough about her, and I pepper her with questions as we walk. I want it all, everything, good and bad. I listen to her talk about how much she admires her sister. It's then that it strikes me that I care what she thinks of me. I always have. She makes me want to be the best me.

It's all about our bond. Every beat of my heart pulses out of my hand and into hers, a heart connection. It's like I'm the guitarist and she's the drummer, keeping me in time and grounded. Fuck if that doesn't nearly knock me over right here in the middle of a hiking trail somewhere in Washington. Or are we still in Oregon?

"Callum?" She looks at me, her forehead and nose crinkled with concern. I didn't even realize I stopped moving when I was struck with my epiphany. "What is it?"

I lean in and kiss her. Her lips go slack and are just as soft as I imagined them to be. She releases my hand and rubs the stubble on my jaw, then works her hand behind my head, her other palm flat on my chest. The warmth of her hand over my heart causes it to beat a little faster, for her. I expect her to push me away, but she doesn't.

I've never kissed like this. Not with meaning in every lick of the seam of her lips and in every gentle tug I make of her bottom lip. There is so much feeling, so much emotion that it causes a deepening of my soul, from just one fucking kiss.

I'm not sure who initiated pulling away, but I feel it deep inside. I look at her closed eyes, waiting for them to open. I have to know she feels this too. When they finally flutter back open, her eyes lock onto mine, dilated. Her tongue dashes out across that sexy bottom lip. She leans back in, taking control, and *kisses me* this time. She fists the center of my t-shirt with both hands. I pull her closer to me, out of instinct, my hand mapping across her back. She moans softly, melting into me just a little bit. We come up for air and she pulls away with a shy blush staining her cheeks.

I re-grasp her fingers in between mine and we head towards the car. Neither of us says anything, both in our own heads, but still locked together hand-in-hand.

Silently, I pray that she doesn't regret the kiss, regret me. I sure as fuck don't regret it.

There's that little worry in the back of my mind, the one that's been tattooed on me since his birth, about how this could affect Gibson. But then there's this with Ari. How real and comfortable it feels holding her hand, and how I just want to kiss her more. Damned if kissing her like this doesn't make me feel vulnerable as fuck. I trust her with my whole self when I stopped expecting others to care for my heart because I learned a long time ago not to trust love.

How the fuck do I deal with this and maintain my son's relationship with his nanny? That's just it, though... Ari is way more than a nanny to me. I've seen the relationship between Mav and Kady with their nanny, Elsie. It's all very employer, employee. They aren't unfriendly with her or feel they are above her, but there is a definite line drawn in that relationship.

It's not like that with Ari and me. We are a family, especially lately.

I snap Gibson into his car seat when we arrive back at the car. He doesn't stir in the slightest. What is it about kids and being outside that makes them sleep like the dead for a few hours?

I start the engine, but I can't put it into drive just yet.

"Ari," I start, turning towards her in the passenger seat.

"No," she says with finality, without even looking at me.

"No?" She shakes her head at my question. I need to tell her how I feel, how I want an us. "I just want to—"

"No!" she interjects forcefully. "I don't want to label it. I don't want to talk about it, just let it be."

"Okay. I just want to make sure you're not mad or disappointed." Shit, this is coming out wrong.

"Disappointed?" There's a slight incredulousness to her voice that is such a turn on. "That was not anything I'd call disappointing." She shakes her head.

"I just don't—"

"Don't second guess it," she interrupts me again. "Let's agree to just let it be for now." She reaches across the console and grabs my hand. "It's all good." Her thumb strokes the back of my hand softly, and it instantly calms the 'buts' and 'what-if's' swirling around in my brain. For now, anyway.

R

ALL I THINK about is her. The way she smells like fresh oranges mixed with vanilla. The way she kissed me right back. The feel of her body pressed against mine. How my body wants so much more of that, so much more of her. I think she wants more too. I want to test this thing growing between us but can't find us the fucking privacy or time to do it.

That's why touring sucks. There is absolutely no privacy. And of course, she doesn't want to talk about it, so I'm not sure how she feels. About me, about maybe being an *us*?

I knew it wouldn't be long before Killian and Sammy decided to entertain ladies in their bunks. It happened last night. How they fit a girl in these bunks with them I have no fucking clue, but I can hear absolutely everything, every giggle, every sigh and whispered moan, every grunt and every single climax.

It never used to bother me, but I'm so wound-up, wanting Ari and needing privacy, that the last thing I need to hear right now are the minute details of their dalliances. I'm thankful when they all finally settle into sleep.

The next morning, I text Mav. It's hard being on a different bus than him.

Me: I need a favor.

Mav: Anything brother. You know I've got you.

Me: I need you guys to take Gibson tomorrow. Please.

When he doesn't answer right away, I think I might be screwed. I need some time with Ari. To explore what this is with her. I know she wants to just let it happen, but I need more than that.

Me: I need some adult time with Ari.

Me: Don't make me beg.

Me: Please man. I'll owe you.

Mav better not be sharing this shit with Kady. I don't need everyone in my fucking business, but I do need some Ari time.

Mav: Cool your jets. Brio had a blowout and then a meltdown.

Mav: You got it. You know we love Gibs.

Mav: And we love you. It's about fucking time. We all feel it between you two.

Mav: Now it's time for you to feel it too.

When we all stop for lunch, Killian sees his new friend to a ride share, then carries Gibson on his shoulders to the diner on the other side of the lot. Gibson giggles and plays with his hair and his necklaces. During lunch, they sit next to each other. I don't know what's spurred on this budding relationship, but I'm fucking loving it.

As we walk back to the bus, Killian again carries a giggly Gibson, and I get choked up a little. I lag behind everyone else as I watch them together. Family is everything, and I want Gibson to know his family is all in for him, especially my twin. Seeing them together like this is everything I could have wished for. Because Killian's been purposely distant since he was born and, honestly, it hurt me that he rejected my son like he did. Witnessing them together, though, erases all that.

Ever astute, Ari notices my sudden case of the feels and touches my arm. "You okay? What's going on?"

I clear the emotion from my throat, and I nod my head towards Kill just as he pulls Gibson's shirt up and raspberries his side. Gibson lets out a hearty laugh that has everyone in the band smiling.

"That." I take a second. "Kill's been so affectionate towards Gibson lately. When he was born, Kill wanted nothing to do with him. He didn't even hold him until he was about four or five months old and even then, it was something I forced on him. He didn't like it and he's never willingly interacted with him. Not like this."

She instinctively rubs her hand up my back, like she understands. I don't know how she can possibly know that this moment is everything I've ever wanted, my twin loving the only other person I've ever really let myself fully love. Until recently, that is.

It's the wee hours of the morning when we finally roll into our destination. I carry Gibs against one shoulder as he sleeps, my duffle slung over the other. A blurry-eyed Ari follows me

193

with her and Gibson's bags. It's a little after 3:00 am when we check into our rooms. We'll be here for the next couple of days and don't play tomorrow. Thank fuck for that.

Mav approaches me near the front desk. He gently removes Gibson from my shoulder and whispers, "We got him. Be fuckin' selfish for once." He takes Gibson's bag from Ari.

"Start your day off with a good night's sleep. Both of you." He nods goodnight towards Ari and pats my shoulder with his free hand as he takes my son with him to the elevator, and Kady carries Gibson's bag.

Ari looks confused as Mav walks off with Gibson. I grab her hand in mine and pull her into the next elevator, but say nothing. The minute the doors slide shut, I lean in and kiss her the way I've wanted since our hike.

Startled, she gasps slightly, and I use it to my advantage, sliding my tongue past her lips to dance with hers. Soon she's fisting my t-shirt, her bag abandoned on the shiny floor of the elevator next to mine.

Her tongue willingly tangles with mine the way I want our bodies to do in my sheets. The elevator doors open to our floor, and I grab our bags in one hand, her hand in the other, and drag her to our door. It takes me three frustrating tries to get the damn keycard to work in the freaking door, but I finally fling it open and toss our bags in the nearby closet without a second thought.

Pulling Ari inside, I cage her against the closed door with my arms. Her knee parts my legs as she grinds herself against my thigh as I harden beneath her. I kiss the fuck out of her, and not gently this time. This has been building in me for days now, and I need her to know what's been brewing in me.

Her hands run under the back of my t-shirt, her nails lightly scoring my skin, urging me on. She inches my shirt up until I have to remove my lips from hers to rip it over my head. In the time it takes me to get my shirt off and fling it away from me,

Ari's removed hers and is now in front of me topless except for her pink lacy bra. Fuck, she's even sexier than I had imagined.

Impatient, she grabs my hand and presses it to her breast until I lightly squeeze. She moans as she leans up on her toes to grab my bottom lip lightly between her teeth. Ari walks backwards, pulling me into the first bedroom. Fuck if take-charge Ari isn't sexy.

Chapter 21

Arista

Callum's usually stormy blue eyes darken as I pull him into the bedroom. Ever since we kissed during the hike, I've needed this visceral connection with him, even though I know better than to even try. It's been impossible to get a minute with Callum since the hike, between Gibson and the band and being all up in each other's business in the bus, the arena, and every-freaking-where. But my body just wants his.

I don't know why Mav took Gibson when we checked in, but I'm going to show Callum that I feel the electricity humming between us too, even if I can't fully give him what he needs.

He dips his finger into the cup of my bra and brushes my nipple with his callused finger. I feel it all the way between my thighs. I back up until my legs hit the bed behind us and I sit. I wrap my arms around his waist and pull him close to me and kiss him right above his navel, his tight, hard abs constricting under my lips. I expect his hands to push me down to his crotch, to demand things, but instead they hold me to him, like he's savoring just being close to me.

"Ari..." My name rolls off his tongue as half plea, half groan, but this is more than just lust. There is need in his voice, sure, but underneath the need is something else, something that sews itself and him to my heart. This could all go so wrong, but right now I care about nothing but Callum.

His thumb under my chin tilts my head up, so he can capture my lips as my fingers work, trying to undo the fly of his pants. Finally able to wiggle my hand down the front of his tight jeans, I lightly rub him. He's incredibly hard. I can only imagine how painful that is in these tight jeans.

His hands grip me under my arms as he pulls me up and lays me back on the bed in one fluid motion. He leans over and kisses me, teases me before pulling back and grabbing the band of my yoga pants. He makes quick work of them, tossing them haphazardly to the side.

Callum walks himself over me, hovering, with one knee between my legs. The only part of him that touches me is the ends of his long hair as it tickles my neck and face. He quickly unfastens my bra, and it goes the way of my pants. "So beautiful."

He leans down and sucks my hard nipple into his mouth, causing my hips to lift off the bed as I gasp at the sensation. Capturing my hip in his hand, he gives me a smoldering grin before he hooks his fingers in either side of my panties before sliding them off.

"Take yours off." I moan and his grin only widens. "Callum, please..."

"Patience, Ari." He bends down and plants a kiss between my breasts and then slowly kisses his way down my body until he's between my legs hovering over me, so close I can feel his breath warming my center. Then, suddenly, he's kissing the inside of my knee and slowly working his way back up my inner thigh.

"Callum... please." My abs clench, wanting him to give me something, anything, to relieve the need for friction. For him.

He stops again, so close I can feel his breath right there and I try to wiggle my way towards him. He chuckles and plants a hand on my lower abdomen to keep me in place. "What do you want, Ari?" His breath blows hot against me.

"You." Before I finish the word, his mouth connects with my clit and I can't help but reach for his head to increase the friction I need, my fingers tangling in the hair on the top of his head. He's too gentle, so I press his head to me, trying to urge him on, squeezing him between my thighs. When he finally slips his finger in me, I almost come, but not quite, not even when he hits a spot inside that nearly takes my breath away.

He abruptly stands and works his snug jeans down. I reach between my legs and touch myself, but it's not the same. It's never the same. And even though I came close with Callum, I know it won't happen. It never happens because Todd broke me beyond repair.

The urgency starts ebbing away as I watch him slide on a condom that I didn't even see him open. He takes himself in one hand and gently pulls my hand away. "I got this, babe."

He rubs himself along me as he repositions over me. Again, his hair tickles the sides of my face. I close my eyes tight and turn my face to his arm, knowing that this will change everything between us.

He'll finally see just how broken I am inside, how I can't connect with him in all the ways I want to, need to. This is the part of me I never want anyone to see, especially him. He'll feel the ruined in me, and the thought of it causes pain in my chest.

He kisses my temple, trying to get me to turn my head. "Ar, baby, look at me." I shake my head. He kisses my cheek.

"Come on, Ar. Look at me." He brings his mouth to my ear "Feel what you're doing to me, Ar." He rubs himself against me again, then rolls my nipple between his fingers.

"I need to see you want me, this, us, as much as I do." I turn my face towards him and open my eyes, praying it's dark enough he can't see the wetness there.

He pulls my lips to his mouth. "God, I want you," he breathes quietly as he kisses me sweetly. The momentum in the room has shifted. I know he feels it too.

"Tell me this is okay. That you want this just as much as I do." He kisses my lips with each word.

"I want you, Callum." My arms curl under his shoulders, and I plant a kiss on his shoulder as he slowly thrusts into me.

"Fuck, Ari." He stops part way in and grips my hips tightly, holding me still. "Just a second, babe." He breathes in my hair and then finally sinks himself fully into me. He stays in me, not moving. He kisses the side of my face and my temple as I hold my forehead to his shoulder, my eyes closed, then he slowly swivels his hips as he starts to pull back out. I push up against him, surprised at my body's own rhythmic clench and release as he sinks into me again and again.

I'm surrounded by Callum. He's everywhere. His scent is strong around us. His fingers dig into my hips and his hair tickles my shoulder. His hard, slick pecs slide against my equally hard nipples while his lips press firmly against mine. He whisper-moans my name in his gravelly rasp. I grip his shoulders hard, trying to keep him right here where I need him. There's an unfamiliar building, a pleasure so intense it's almost painful and I'm not sure what's going to happen because it continues to build instead of fading away to nothing like usual.

"Too much..." I'm not even sure I say it out loud. He readjusts my hips, tugging me even closer to him as he tilts my pelvis up and that's all I need to launch into a freefall over a threshold I didn't know I was teetering on. My vision sparkles as I fall over the ledge as waves of intense pleasure pulse throughout every cell in my body.

"Holy shit, Ari," he pants softly in my ear, still on top of me, still in me.

Breathless, I bury my head in his neck, our sweaty hair mingling, my sandy blonde with his dark brown. He gently rolls us onto our side so we're facing each other and he's not crushing me, but we're still very much connected. His hands come up to my face as he pulls me to him for the gentlest kiss I've ever experienced as his thumb gently strokes circles on my cheek.

My body still zings with the connection we continue sharing, both the physical one I didn't think was possible for me, and the emotional one I never expected. I stayed present with Callum the whole time, feeling everything, wanting to feel everything. Maybe I'm not as broken as I thought.

"That was..." he starts, but can't finish his thought. I want to look at him, but I'm afraid of what I'll see in his eyes, on his face. I can't be disposable to him. Please don't throw me away, I pray silently, not after that.

I press my forehead to his shoulder. There is no way Callum could know what that was to me, but my heart wants to believe that he does now.

My eyes slowly flutter open. He's so close we're almost nose to nose as we lay together still entwined. His usually stormy eyes are a clear, deep ocean blue I haven't seen before. His face is smooth, not mapped with worries or restraint or whatever causes his face to crease so deeply. He looks younger, content.

His lips curl up lazily as our eyes focus in on each other. "There's my girl."

He leans in and kisses the tip of my nose while running a hand up and down my back. *His girl.* That. That is what I needed to hear to finally feel cherished, treasured. I'm not disposable or disgusting. This closeness to him is everything I've needed.

He presses his forehead against mine and pulls me flush

against him. "I can feel you thinking, Ari. Relax. I'm not going anywhere." He holds me close, and I close my eyes and try to accept that he's here and he wants me. *His girl.* "Except to the bathroom. I'll be right back." He slips out of me and out of the bed, breaking the bond I never thought I'd be able to manifest. And now I miss it so much.

I roll onto my back and throw my arm over my eyes to shield them from the bathroom light. Could he tell how much *this* was for me? How he proved to me that I'm not as damaged as I thought, as I've been told, as I've felt for so long.

The bed dips, signaling his return as he pulls the sheet down and gently cleans me. The intimate gesture is caring and catches me off-guard. My breath almost hitches, so I turn my head so he can't see the tears I feel tracking down my cheek. He leaves and comes back, this time stretching out in the bed beside me, pulling me to him, my back to his front and nuzzling his chin into the crook of my neck. "Ari," he whispers so quietly I almost don't hear him, despite our close proximity. I'm dropping off, my body completely relaxed as he holds me to him, the security I didn't know I was longing for now cocooning me. "I think I love you."

Chapter 22

Callum

I can tell the exact moment Ari stops fighting sleep and drops off because her body finally relaxes fully, so I feel her weight in my arms. She's since turned so she faces me instead of away from me, head against my shoulder as I lay on my back, my arm clutching her tight to my side, her leg thrown over mine.

I should be exhausted. I *am* exhausted, but fuck if I can sleep now. Not after what we just shared. That was so much more than fucking, even more than making love. I was surprised when Ari took charge when we first got to the room. But in the bedroom, the dynamic totally changed again. She was steeling herself, preparing herself for disappointment. That doesn't make any fucking sense to me, because she is amazing.

When she finally let herself trust me, it was fully rewarded with the most intense connection I've ever experienced. I didn't know such a deep connection existed. She had to feel it too; there was no way she couldn't.

Then she opened her eyes, and I could tell she felt it. She was rocked by it just as much as I was. The intensity scared her,

I think, but it doesn't scare me. It healed me. And it seared her into my heart. Ari's not a nanny; she's my world, where Gibson is my purpose.

Waking up to Ari, still in my arms, her lips parted slightly as she breathes softly, is like a dream. I've always thought she was gorgeous, but in sleep, she exudes a peace that's eluded me since our mom left and I was in charge of keeping Killian and me alive.

I didn't want her to work for me in the beginning because of her beauty. She knocked me off balance during her interview. I didn't think I'd be able to stay away from her. I was right about that, but, fuck, this girl is in me now. She's part of me. I've never felt like this before. I tried, I forced a relationship with Becka because of Gibson. You can't fake or force what Ari and I have.

My hand tingles from a decrease in circulation caused by our position, so I clench and unclench my fist slowly a few times. This slight movement jars Ari awake despite my best efforts not to disturb her.

"Gibson." She starts to sit up automatically, not remembering he's with Mav and Kady today.

"Shhh, he's with Mav, remember?" I lean in and kiss her forehead, and she blinks at me a few times. "Nope, not a dream."

I kiss that beautiful mouth of hers.

Her cheeks pink slightly when my movement causes my morning wood to rub against her leg. "Sorry, not sorry."

I kiss her again, softly at first. She surprises me by rolling up to straddle me, settling just above where I really want her, so I'm firmly nestled against her ass.

If waking with Ari in my arms is Heaven, and it totally is, then her gorgeous pert breasts right there waiting to be kissed while she straddles me mean I've died and gone to Heaven. Her knees squeeze me on both sides as she leans down to kiss me, but I divert and capture her nipple in my mouth instead, my hand automatically kneading the other one. She releases a throaty moan, then grinds against my lower abdomen. It nearly does me in.

"Condom?" she gasps.

Reaching over to the nightstand, I grab one, thankful I grabbed the extras from my bag last night. She takes it from me and repositions herself so I'm in front of her. She carefully rolls it down my shaft and gives a squeeze that has me rushing to think of guitar tabs, so I don't let loose like a fucking teenager before anything really happens. She squeezes again.

"Ari!" I grab her hips to help her position herself over me.

She slowly takes me in. Once seated, she leans down to kiss me, and as our tongues mingle, then she slowly starts moving. She sits back up, her hands on her breasts as she starts to move faster.

"Callum." She draws out the *m* in my name into a hum as I replace her hands with mine, needing to touch more of her. When I gently squeeze her tits, her fingers dig into my shoulders as she gives herself the balance and leverage she needs to really start moving. I slip my hands down to her hips to support her bucking against me.

"Oh God, Ari." I can feel her slowly starting to tighten around me. I'm not going to last much longer. I reach a hand over and brush my thumb against her clit lightly at first and then with a steady pressure. Her legs tense around me, fingers digging into my shoulders.

One more light graze of her clit and she's clenched around me so fucking tight. Her body shifts, and she bites down on my shoulder hard as she finally tips over the edge. With her eyes squeezed shut, she goes boneless in my arms as I thrust up into her one more time as she milks my release from me. "Fuck! Ari, yes."

We collapse together into a sweaty mess, sliding against each other on the sheets. "Now that's a fucking wake up call."

The notes of her giggle work their way into my heart. Then her stomach lets out a growl, her eyes growing wide.

"Me too. Let's order breakfast." I kiss her nose as her cheeks heat.

We feast on waffles and bacon after the sexiest shower ever. When we finally dress, I turn to her. "What would you do right now, if you could do anything?"

She thinks about it, biting her lip while she ties the laces on her white and black checked Vans. "I don't know." She sits up and looks at me. "What would you do?"

"I don't even know what state we're in honestly," I reply. "But whatever, wherever, I want to do it with you." I'm being so fucking honest right now my chest tightens. Why is this so scary? I hope she can see it. I hope to hell she can feel it.

A grin grows over her face. "I think we might be in Idaho. But it could be Wyoming. I'm not sure either." She giggles again.

I pull her to me on the couch. "I know it's probably too soon to say this, Ari. But I fucking love you." Her eyes go round and her lips part at my admission. "I think part of me has since that day you walked into my sitting room for your interview. Fuck if I didn't fight it, though." I run my hand through my hair. "I'm tired of fighting my feelings." I admit. "I can't do it anymore. I want an us, Ar."

Admitting that feels like I'm on stage in front of thousands of people, balls to the wind, with not even a guitar to hide behind. But no, I'm fully dressed, sitting here on this couch next to Ari in Ida-fucking-ho, confessing things I didn't think I'd ever say.

She seems to understand my discomfort with sharing my feelings because she reaches over and squeezes my hand.

"I want us too." She squeezes my hand again. "Why don't we go get Gibson and take him on another hike?" Her hand squeezes mine again.

"You don't want to have the day to us? Mav and Kady have him all day." I'm surprised by her suggestion.

She shakes her head. "I want *us* to go hiking again."

℞

THE NEXT SEVERAL days are a haze of media, shows, piling into the bus, sleeping and doing the same thing over again the next day. Ari and I steal a few moments here and there, but I don't have the time I want for either Gibson or her. The days are blurring together, and it's even harder for me to keep track of where the fuck we are or what day it is. But I do know we have two days off in two more days. I keep telling myself that. Because those two days off will mean time with my son and my girl.

Between radio interviews, my phone vibrates in my pocket. It's probably Ari texting me my daily pictures of Gibson. I love her updates throughout the day. On busy days like today, it takes away a little of my guilt and stress and adds in some joy. I always look forward to these texts. Doesn't matter if they are exploring somewhere new or are just hanging at the hotel pool.

It vibrates a few more times while we're on air. As soon as we're off air, we hit a conference room with a handful of fans that are prize winners for promotions from the station. As we've finished with them, we're rushing down the hall with our road manager and into a waiting car, then I pull out my phone to find a bunch of texts from Ari.

I scan through them, my heart dropping further towards my stomach the more I read.

Ari: Staying in today, Gibs doesn't feel well. Hardly ate breakfast.
Ari: Gibs is def not feeling good. He's clingy.
Ari: He's gotten sick a few times and has a fever.
Ari: There's a pediatric urgent care nearby. Aiden is driving us.

Ari: Back. Doctor says it's a virus and he has to ride it out. I'm keeping him in my bedroom – we don't want you to get sick.

"Fuck. Swing by the hotel first," I demand as I slide into our waiting car.

"No time. We're already late for soundcheck," Jeff pipes up from the driver's seat, looking at me through the rearview mirror.

"My kid is sick. You *will* take me to the fucking hotel, Jeff. Now," I growl to our longtime tour manager. He knows I never miss soundchecks. This is my kid, for fuck's sake.

"Geo can stand in during soundcheck." Mav leans forward between the seats and glares at Jeff. "Cal needs to check on his son. Drop him at the hotel first, dammit. It's his kid."

He rests his hand on my leg, understanding I'm about to jump into the front seat and drive this fucker to the hotel myself if I have to.

As soon as the SUV pulls up, I'm out the door and jogging into the hotel. I hit the elevator call button, but it seems stuck on the fifth floor. What the fuck?! I hit it again and again.

Finally, the damn elevator arrives. Getting in, I press 6 and wait. This has to be the slowest fucking elevator. It stops on the second floor.

"It's going up. Get the fuck on or let me shut the door." A middle-aged lady recoils from getting onto the elevator as I repeatedly jam the door close button. Fucking people. It's an elevator, not rocket science.

I fling open the door to the suite, startling both Aiden and Ari, who are sitting in the common area.

"Where's Gibs?" I'm practically yelling, but I can hardly hear over my heart beating in my ears. My son is sick, and I was chatting at a fucking radio station.

Ari puts her hand on my chest, patting it softly. "Shhh. He just fell asleep." She takes me to the open door of her bedroom. Gibson's sleeping smack in the middle of Ari's bed in just a diaper and t-shirt that's riding up slightly. "Sleep is what he needs. The doctor said to keep him comfortable, quiet, and well-hydrated. We stayed here while Luke went to the pharmacy and got baby acetaminophen and lots of Pedialyte."

Her hand rubs my back with light circles as I watch him sleep from the doorway. I can finally breathe.

"The acetaminophen is already working. His fever is starting to go down." I nod and move away from the door and drop onto the couch. Thank fuck, he had Ari to take care of him.

"He was so miserable, poor little munchkin. I hope it was okay that I took him to the urgent care for kids. I used the credit card for his copay."

I should've been here to take him to the doctor and to comfort him. But at least someone who cares was. He wasn't alone. He's not Kill and I.

"Callum, shouldn't you be at soundcheck?" Ari looks up at me from her phone.

I shake my head. "Couldn't after I saw the texts. My guitar tech is standing in." I glance through the bedroom door at my son. "He's never been sick before." The slow circles she caresses on my leg calm my racing heart.

"He's going to be fine. I wanted you to be informed. I didn't mean to frighten you."

"No. You did everything you should've done." I swallow hard. "I'm so glad you were here. Not just to take him to the doctor, but to comfort him too."

I stare at him sleeping on the bed in her room, lying on his back like a starfish, legs and arms spread wide, taking up as much room as he can.

"It's not something Kill or I got much of as kids. I just panicked a little, I think." Ari nods as if she understands, but what I'm telling her is new information to her.

He wakes up an hour later. Ari gets him to drink some of his "new juice," which he does gladly and wants more. His fever is nearly gone, and that's without another dose of acetaminophen. He's quietly stacking those damn blocks she carries with her.

"He's way peppier. Before the doctor, he just wanted to be held and whined," she tells me, laying her hand on my leg. "You can head to the arena. He's good. I'll text you if that changes."

It kills me to leave him when I know he's feeling crappy. I flop down with him and help him stack his blocks for a few minutes. Ari knows what she's doing. She loves my son and cares about him and his well-being, but it doesn't make it any easier to leave him when I know he's not feeling well.

He'll likely be sleeping while I'm onstage anyway. I try to convince myself that he'll be okay, but I'm doing a shitty job of it. I have tonight's show and tomorrow's show and then two days in a row off. I should do something nice for Ari for taking good care of Gibs. She looks tired. I pull out my phone and text Jax to get my plan in motion.

Chapter 23

Arista

A violent, acidic roil in my stomach wakes me. How is it possible to feel both hot and cold at the same time? It's still dark, and no light seeps under the curtain in the hotel as I kick off the heavy, scratchy comforter. I roll to my side, my body achy for no reason. Another rush of acid has me scrambling for the bathroom, barely making the toilet before hurling so much I feel like I'm drowning in everything coming up. I drop to my knees on the cool linoleum as another wave hits me. By the time the third wave hits, I'm ready to die right here in this hotel bathroom.

Wherever I am, this is it. I'm dying. Where could all this possibly be coming from? There is no way I've eaten this much. I lurch forward, unable to stop it as my whole body jerks as it works to purge more of the evilness out.

Gibson's crying. Shit. I woke up Gibson. But he quiets down quickly, so maybe I'm imagining it.

"Ari? Oh shit, baby." Cal sounds so far away, but he must be close because he carefully gathers my hair behind my head and rubs my back in a firm but gentle motion as the purge turns into dry heaves and finally ceases for the time being. He releases my hair and then squats down next to me as I rest against the toilet. A cool cloth wipes my face and then he holds out a glass with a little bit of water.

"Rinse." His sleepy rasp is laced with concern as I bring the glass to my lips.

I take a small mouthful of the water and swish it before releasing it into the toilet with everything else. The motion sets my stomach roiling again, and I heave a few more times, even though my stomach is completely empty.

His cool, rough hand touches my forehead. "Shit, Ar, you're burning up. Let's get you back in bed."

When I shake my head, the room spins a little. "I'll sleep here. It's easier." I lean against the tub, relishing its coolness through my thin tank top. He leaves me in the bathroom to my gross misery.

Maybe he knows I'm going to die here. Or maybe I'm already dead, but my brain just doesn't know it yet. I hope Callum tells my sister.

"Arm around my neck." He has one hand under my knees, the other gathering me to his chest. "Come on, babe."

"You'll get sick," I try to tell him as he flings my arm over the back of his neck. Then I'm floating through the bathroom against Callum's warm, hard chest. He sets me on the bed and pulls the sheet up to my chest, but not the scratchy spread. My eyes get heavy, and I drift off into a quiet nothingness.

R

*T*ODD WAKES *me up in the middle of the night again. It's so dark and he's so close. I can feel his thick, sweet breath as he hovers over me, his hand fisted in my hair.*

"We're going to try something different this time. Open up."
I clamp my mouth shut and turn my head away from him.
"No. Leave me alone. I don't feel good."

"You'll feel better. Take it." I hear the shuffling of his pants going down.

"No!" I try to be as forceful as I can, even though I know it's a mistake. Whenever I fight back, he just gets rougher. "Vi will be back soon."

"She's working the overnight shift, which she changed to so she could be here for you during the day. It's your fault she's not here, so now you'll make up for it."

His hands grab my shoulders and pull me up out of bed. "You'll do as I say."

"Vi!"

"She can't save you, you little bitch. I swear if you say anything to her, one word and I'll tell her how you seduced me. You think she'll want to be around the person who killed her parents and stole her husband? You'd be out in a heartbeat." His hand is closing in on my throat, and the darkness turns into a black oblivion.

R

"Ari, open your eyes for me, baby. Come on, babe, wake up."

"Vi?"

"No, it's not Vi, it's Cal. I need you to wake up, the doctor's here. He's going to check you out, okay?"

"Todd?" I can hear the fright in my own voice. I can't let Vi find out what he's done.

"No, not Todd." Callum sounds frustrated. "A doctor. He's going to check you out, babe. Maybe give you some fluids."

I want to answer, but I'm so tired and everything aches, and I just want to be left alone.

"You were right to call for me. She's dehydrated, which could be the cause of her hallucinations. I'm going to give her some IV fluids. Hopefully that and some sleep will pep her up, but I can't suggest traveling for her. Not like this." The doctor's voice is far away, like he's down the hall.

"Arista? I'm Doctor Taylor. Your friend tells me you're not drinking anything. Hon, we have to rehydrate you. It'll just be a little stick." I close my eyes and go back to sleep, just for a little while.

R

"Just a little sip, babe." Callum props me up and brings a straw to my cottony mouth. The overly sweet smell of the orange drink causes my stomach to bubble with acid and my body tries to heave again. My abs ache with the motion, tired of heaving.

I turn my head away from the glass and close my eyes. My head feels like it's stuck inside an off-balance washer.

"Dammit, Ar, you'll get dehydrated again. You need to drink." I hear the concern in his voice, but I can't make myself drink it. I know the minute it hits my mouth, I'll throw up. I don't have the energy to vomit again. I just need to rest for another minute. I close my eyes.

"Ar, come on. Wake up." He jiggles me just hard enough to keep me from drifting back off. "Just a few sips."

"No," I croak. My bottom lip burns as another tiny crack shoots down my lip as I move my dry mouth to speak.

"Try this, it's different." Another straw pokes at my burning lips. There's no smell this time, but I think my head will explode if I throw up again. "It's just water, Ar. You need liquids, or you'll end up in the ER. Please, one sip?"

His voice cracks, and even though my vision's blurry, I can see the deep crevices lining his forehead. He's worried about me.

I pull a tiny sip of water through the straw just to make him feel better. The cool water coats my mouth and throat. The slipperiness feels so good that I don't even care about throwing up again. I swallow and take more in until he pulls the straw away.

"That's enough for now. Don't want you nauseous again." He rests his hand on my head. "You're still hot." He presses his lips together in a thin line.

I hurt all over and my mouth feels like I licked the desert, cactuses and all. He sits on the edge of the bed, his eyes scanning over me, occasionally pushing my hair out of my face.

I drift off, but he keeps waking me up to put the straw between my lips. I feel like death and don't really know how much time passes between sips or sleeps. A few times he makes me swallow something. Sometimes he lays his palm on my head and I think I hear him talking. I can't tell if he's close and mumbling or if he's far away and talking to someone else. Maybe it's a television.

When I wake up again, I'm so hot that a sweaty dampness makes the sheets stick to me. My tank top sticks to me too, and I feel gross and sore. I don't even know where I am, but it seems like the same hotel. It also feels like more time has gone by than one night. We shouldn't still be here. We should be on the road somewhere.

I push the sheet off. The big chair from the sitting area is in the corner of the bedroom now and Callum's sprawled in it sideways. His head lolls to the side, and he's sleeping with one leg over the chair's arm, the other stretched down to the floor. It looks wholly uncomfortable, but he's sleeping soundly, complete with little snores.

My cup with the straw is on the nightstand, but it's empty. I wander into the sitting area, wondering where Gibson is if Callum's sleeping in my suite. I hope there's a bottle of water out here. I don't want to drink sink water, but I will if I have to.

As I shuffle to the couch, Killian moves out of the other bedroom, the one Callum should be sleeping in, rolling Callum's suitcase towards the door.

Not expecting me, he jumps about a foot when he catches sight of me from the corner of his eye.

"Fuck, Ari. You scared the living shit out of me," he says in a hoarse whisper, grabbing at the collar of his black t-shirt and taking a deep breath.

"You look like you feel better. Cal still sleeping?"

I nod towards my bedroom. "He's in there. I feel like I got run over by a truck, though, so I don't know about feeling better."

I finally sit down on the edge of the couch, suddenly self-conscious of the fact that I'm only wearing a tank and boy shorts in front of Killian. But he doesn't seem the least bit phased by my attire.

"I bet. Fuck, you were sick. Do you remember the doctor coming in?" Killian stands, fiddling with the handle to Callum's suitcase.

"I went to the doctor?" I don't remember leaving the bed after Callum carried me from the bathroom.

Killian shakes his head. "The doctor came here. House calls are a perk of being on a record label. He ended up giving you an IV bag of fluid because you wouldn't drink anything." He points to the band-aid on the top of my hand.

"That was yesterday, about noonish, I think. The doc told him if you didn't drink anything by 9:00 last night, Cal should take you straight to the ER. He finally got you to drink some water after that. He tried some of Gibson's leftover Pedialyte, but you refused it." He looks over at me.

"He woke you up and forced you to drink a little every thirty minutes or so." He motions to the wet bar in the corner littered with empty water bottles and an ice bucket with small, half melted cubes of ice that I want to shove into my mouth to ease the dryness and the roughness of my voice.

"Where's Gibson?" My heart starts to beat faster, realizing that I haven't seen or heard my favorite little germ monster since I've been awake.

"Kady's playing with him while I get Cal's stuff together.

He's fine, it's all good." He points at Cal's suitcase at his feet. "We sent the busses ahead last night and stayed an extra night here. We have to fly out in an hour and a half for the show tonight." How long was I sleeping?

"I was trying to let you guys sleep as long as possible. I just got done throwing Cal's stuff together and was about to wake him. Maybe you should shower first since you're up so he can sleep a few minutes longer. Kady packed your stuff, and it's already downstairs, but I think she left you fresh clothes in the bathroom." He shoots a small grin at me, then opens the door and wheels Cal's suitcase out with him.

The warm water feels so good cascading over me that I just stand under it and let the sweat of sickness run down the drain and try to make sense of time. If there's a show tonight, it means it must be Wednesday. We were scheduled to roll out of town around 3:00 pm yesterday. It's almost noon now. I can't believe they changed travel plans for me. I dry and dress in the clothes that Kady laid out for me. She even left my toiletry bag so I can brush my teeth and hair. I feel almost human again.

When I reenter the bedroom, Callum's still lounging in the chair, but he's awake and looking at his phone. When he sees me, tension leaves his body as he looks me up and down a few times.

"You look so much better." He shifts, so he's sitting upright in the chair instead of across it. "But how do you feel?"

His eyes assess me again from head to toe and back again.

"Better since I showered. My head still hurts. I'm kind of tired and hungry but afraid to eat." To prove my point, my stomach gives a little rumble. I'm hoping it's just complaining because it's empty and not because I'm going to start vomiting again.

He nods at me. "Kill says we only have about forty minutes before we have to leave for the airport. I'm going to grab a shower. There are some crackers by the wet bar. You might

216

want to try nibbling on one but go kind of easy at first." He heads off to the bathroom.

"Awee! Awee so sick. Poor Awee." Gibson calls to me as I get on the small private plane the label chartered for the band. He's buckled in next to Killian, but starts squirming and pulling at his belt when he sees me in the aisle.

I pass them on my way to find a seat. "I'm doing better, buddy." I reach over and tousle his hair. Pretty sure the little booger is why I was so sick. I must have caught whatever he had.

I take a window seat in the middle of the small jet. Callum told me on the way to the airport that the doctor gave them all some sort of antiviral shot, but Brio was too young for one, so Mav and Kady are keeping their distance with Brio just to be safe. I wave at them at the very back of the plane.

"You look so much better," Kady calls from the rear of the plane.

"Thanks for packing my stuff for me." She waves me off like it wasn't a big deal, but it was to me. I'll do something nice for her to thank her.

Callum comes down the aisle behind me with his duffle bag. He hands me a container of Goldfish crackers and a bottle of Sprite before flopping into the seat across from mine. "You need to keep up your hydration." He nods at the bottle he just handed me.

"Thanks." I crack the soda to let the bubbles fizzle out.

Once settled, Callum leans his head back on his headrest, his eyes half shut. I have no doubt he'll be out like a light before the landing gears go up. Gibson gets a similar look when he's fighting sleep.

I can't believe he took care of me for two days while I was sick, or that the whole band held everything up as long as they could for me. Part of me feels bad for causing a problem, but part of me is amazed that they cared enough to change plans so drastically.

Callum lets out a soft snore as the plane lifts off, as I expected. I think it's only a two-and-a-half-hour flight. As soon as I can, I take my seatbelt off and curl up with my crackers and soda and watch the clouds float by my little portal window.

Sammy drops into the seat next to me. "Hey, you doing okay?" His voice is quiet to not disturb Callum.

"I feel a lot better." I offer him a cracker, but he shakes his head.

"You look it. I seriously expected to wake up this morning and find out that Cal had taken you to the ER. You were so out of it yesterday. You wouldn't drink anything, and you were mumbling incoherently. Then the doctor came and gave you fluids." He shakes his head. "I was so sure you were heading for the ER. I'm so glad you're better." He squeezes my arm. "We're lucky no one else got it. Seemed like a nasty bug."

"I hope Cal doesn't get it. I guess the doctor gave you all antivirals, but it doesn't mean he won't get it, since he was so close to me before he got his shot." I look over at him sleeping sounding, mouth slightly open. "He obviously didn't get much rest."

Sammy shakes his head. "He was up taking care of you. Kill and I brought him breakfast to make sure he was eating yesterday. Mav made sure he got dinner and tried to convince him to nap, which didn't happen. He's wiped." Sammy looks over at me. "I've never seen Callum worry about someone like that who wasn't Gibson." He shrugs.

"Even before Gibson?" I can't believe I let that come out.

Sammy snorts. "Definitely not before Gibson. You realize that Gibson's mom used to be Mav's fiancée, right? As in, she was still Mav's fiancée when Gibson was conceived."

"I probably should've known that, but I didn't." While I knew who Callum and The Blind Rebels were before I ever stepped foot in his house, I didn't pay attention to the gossip rags. I vaguely remember something about the sex tape, but nothing more than there was one.

"It's the whole reason the band broke up for a year." Sammy looks wistfully at Cal. "There was some major bad blood between Cal and Mav. But that's water under the bridge now, or mostly anyway." Sammy smiles at me.

I nod, wondering how any band can get past the constant gossip. It's got to be very tiring to be constantly part of the rumor mill like that.

"But what I'm trying to tell you is that Cal over there"—he motions towards his sleeping friend—"grumpy ol' bastard that he can be sometimes. He likes you, as in *likes you, likes you.*" Sammy waggles his eyebrows at me and leans in, bumping shoulders with me. "And something tells me that you might *like him, like him* right back."

When I don't respond, he dives a little deeper. "Life's too fucking short to ignore shit like that. Trust me." He squeezes my arm again before returning to his seat across from Killian and Gibson.

We're dropped off at the busses parked outside the arena. Callum looks less tired after his nap on the plane. He's talking to Mav, Kady, and Elsie while Gibson busies himself, sliding his fingers through his dad's loose hair and babbling to himself quietly. I want to hold Gibson, but Callum passes him off to Elsie with a kiss on his head before returning to me.

"Don't worry about Gibson today. I want you resting and hydrating. Kick it on the bus, take a nap. Drink lots of water or even better, some of Sammy's sports drinks, okay?" I nod.

Callum runs his hand through his long hair, bringing it behind his head and tying it in a low ponytail with the wrap on his wrist.

When he finally looks back at me, it's more than just concern. There's something that looks a lot like fear on his face.

219

"You went kind of goofy on us when you were dehydrated, Ar. Hallucinating and shit. It was... scary."

I have no memory of this, but the fear creasing Callum's face has me wondering what the hell I said or did that upset him so.

"I'll bring you some food later, after soundcheck. Rest, okay? If you start feeling bad again, text me. If I don't answer immediately, text Jax."

"I think I'll be fine." He turns to walk towards the guys. "Callum, thank you for taking care of me."

He nods and opens his mouth like he's going to say something, but Killian interrupts. "She'll be fine, Cal. Come on. We gotta do some interviews before soundcheck." Callum flashes a soft, half-smile at me, but his eyes tell me he wants to say so much more before he turns to join the rest of the band.

Without Gibson, I'm bored on the bus. I line my empty water bottles on the counter so Callum will know I've been following his instructions when he comes back with food.

Stretching out on the floor of the common area, I do some of my easier yoga poses, which feel good after being in bed for two days. When done, I curl up with a book to catch up on my reading, but I must have fallen asleep because I jerk awake at the feel of someone's hand on my head.

"Hey, just checking in on you." Cal gives me a tired smile. The bags have returned under his eyes. "How ya feeling?"

"I'm okay." I shrug. "A little bored. I miss Gibson and his antics."

He lets out a half-chuckle as he sits with me on the couch. "Antics is right. I see you've been keeping hydrated. Good." He looks over at the small kitchenette table across from us where there now sits a paper plate covered in foil. "I brought some of the blander stuff they were feeding the band and crew today. If there's something different you want, text Aiden. He'll get it for you."

He's absentmindedly rubbing my leg that he's pulled into his lap, while staring out the one-way window that looks out on the back of the arena. I like it. Callum has changed how I feel about myself and how I feel about him. I more than *like him, like him*, as Sammy said. He has a lot of love to give.

He says he loves me, but I worry about Gibson. And I know Callum does too. But I'd love to try for an us.

I look over at him as he continues to stare out the window at the comings and goings in the parking lot. He looks as if he could almost fall asleep.

"Who's Todd?" His sudden question startles me so much that I don't respond right away. Why is he bringing up my asshole brother-in-law? He looks over at me, brow furrowed with concern. He's stopped rubbing my leg. "You mentioned him a few times when you were sick. You thought I was him."

No. Just no. Callum is definitely not Todd. What the hell was I thinking? He can't know. No one does. Not even Vi. "My brother-in-law." I say it slowly, my stomach churning with acid but for a different sickening reason this time.

Callum's brows crease even deeper and his jaw clenches so tight the muscle tics. "And Vi's your sister, right?" I nod. He's silent for a long time. He pats my leg. "You asked for her too."

"Viola raised me after our parents died. She's fourteen years older. My parents had a hard time getting pregnant after Vi. They lost a couple of pregnancies in between," I mention. "Vi's my big sister and something of a mom now too." I shrug as he looks over at me. This is probably the most personal I've gotten with Callum about myself.

"Makes sense, you'd ask for her. Probably wanted the comfort of something familiar when you were sick." He pats my leg again but doesn't make eye contact. Dammit. I want to know what I said, but I can't ask. What if I had inadvertently mistaken him for Todd *that way*?

"I gotta get back to the arena. Rest up. We're rolling out

right after the show." He gets up, his back arching as he stretches, arms above his head.

"Callum? You take the bedroom tonight with Gibs," I say, nodding to the room at the rear of the bus. "I'll sleep in the empty bunk." He opens his mouth like he's going to disagree. "I think Gibson should be on the bus with us, so his routine isn't disrupted. You stayed up for two days taking care of me and need the rest. Sleep in the big bed with Gibs, get the rest you need. That way, tomorrow I can help with him."

Chapter 24

Callum

We're on an adventure today at a local park geared towards kids Gibson's age. Ari found this place when she did her research before the tour, and I'm excited to spend the whole day with her and Gibson. I have a surprise for her that I think she'll really enjoy.

I grab her hand and intertwine our fingers as we watch Gibson climbing around on one of the interactive apparatuses. She shoots a shy smile at me and holds back firmly. We spend a few hours together following Gibson around while he climbs and slides and plays in the sand. While he's playing with another kid, I pull her in front of me and kiss her like I've been wanting to. She wraps one arm around my waist and wraps the other around the back of my neck, keeping my lips close to hers. When I run my tongue along her lips, she opens her mouth and our tongues dance together. We finally break apart to catch our breath, and I put eyes on Gibs, who's still happily playing in the sand.

"Wow," Ari breathes out.

I tip my forehead down to press it against hers. "Hmm, wow

indeed." I kiss her nose before nipping at her lips a few more times before we're interrupted by Gibson.

"Uh-oh. Potty." He takes Ari's hand. She's been helping us work on potty training, but he's a stubborn cuss like me. The upheaval of being in a different place all the time probably doesn't help. The potty training frustrates the hell out of me. But Ari tells me that him noticing his accidents is part of the process. He just has an uncanny ability to need the potty at the most inopportune times. Like when I'm in the middle of trying to kiss his nanny senseless.

"Okay, buddy, let's go to the bathroom." She takes him with a new pull-up and sets off for the bathroom.

I lean against a nearby tree, checking my phone while I wait. A group of five women approach me, one of them in front of the rest. "Aren't you Callum Donogue from the Blind Rebels?" She's obviously the bravest of the friend group.

I push off the tree. "I am. I'll sign stuff for you or take selfies or whatever, but when my nanny and son come back, we'll have to move along. Deal?" They seem agreeable and I take some pictures and sign some things. As soon as I see Ari and Gibson coming out of the bathroom, I pull back slightly from the group. "I hope to see you ladies at the show tomorrow."

"Can we meet your son? Is that him?" A lady pulls out her phone and aims it at Gibson and Ari.

I put my hand in front of her phone. "That's my son. Don't take pictures. Please." She's not happy with me. "I mean it." I glare at her before walking away.

I swing Gibs up in my arms as we walk in the opposite direction of the fans. "You ready for our picnic lunch with Ari?"

Gibs nods and once I'm convinced they aren't following us, we find a spot on the other side of the park on the grassy area near a big tree. Gibs and I set up the blanket and lay out the food I packed. We eat to Gibson's continuous chatter until he finally settles against me and drifts off.

I lay him down at the end of the blanket wrapped in my jacket so I can kiss Ari some more. And kiss her, I do. She surprises the hell out of me by shifting and rolling on top of me.

"I like kissing you." Her voice has taken on a new husky quality that has my balls pulling tight. She tosses her head to the side so her hair cascades over one shoulder, then leans down over me and kisses me softly at first, but I can't help myself, I deepen it. She groans and grinds her hips against mine. She leans down and aggressively kisses me. I want this girl like I've never wanted another. I'm so hard against my pants that I feel every slight shift she makes.

I take my tongue and run it up her jaw to her ear and then nibble my way down her neck. She gasps my name quietly and pulls my head up to hers for another soul-merging kiss. After a few minutes, it's not clear who's kissing who anymore.

Gibson stirs, and we shock apart. I check my watch. "Shit. We have somewhere we need to be." She nods and we start to put our picnic away.

"This."—I motion between us—"is so not over." Her lips pick up in a mischievous smile that tugs on my insides.

R

WHEN WE GET to the airport, Ari turns to me, her eyes narrow.

"What are we doing here?"

"Gibson and I have a surprise for you."

"Suppize!" Right on cue, Gibson calls from the back of our rental.

"Good job, buddy. We are here to pick up your sister and brother-in-law."

Her eyes go round and start to sparkle as she squirms in her seat.

"Really? Vi's here?" She can't get out of the SUV fast

enough. I can't help but smile, because this is the exact reaction I was hoping for. It's also not lost on me that she asked about Vi and not Todd. I want to meet him and feel him out, because my gut is telling me there is something off about this Todd guy.

We rendezvous with Ari's sister Viola and her brother-in-law Todd. Vi looks a lot like Ari, only older. They both have the same sand colored hair and similar hazel eyes. Ari's slightly taller and thinner, while Vi has longer hair.

The way Ari holds on to her sister as they embrace at the airport makes me happy that she has someone like that in her life since her parents died.

My parents aren't dead, well, last I checked, anyway. Having Killian around helped cushion the blow that neither of our parents cared for us enough to be there with a simple hug or to chase our nightmares away.

Killian probably has no idea that having him kept me alive and mostly sane. Our bond may be somewhat strained right now, but there is nothing I wouldn't do for my twin. And I know he'd help me in a heartbeat. He might question me, like he did when I borrowed his phone to contact Ari, but he always has my best interest and that of my son in his heart.

Ari absolutely glows in her sister's presence. She mentioned how worried her sister was after telling her about getting sick last week. Her sister is a nurse in a multispecialty practice back in LA. Vi questions her about being sick like a worried sister and nurse. I already love her and am glad I had Jax arrange this.

I can't wait to tell them about the surprise I have for them, but I'll wait until dinner. When we get to the hotel, Ari retrieves Gibson and I get her sister and her husband checked in. I take Gibs from Ari and he rears back. "No! Awee! Pease. Awee. Okay. Fank you."

Ari smiles softly at him and kisses him on the head.

"Sorry, buddy, you're stuck with me right now. Ari's going to visit with her family. You and I are going for a swim." He calms at the mention of a swim because I have a fish for a son.

"We'll meet in the lobby at six for dinner. Be prepared. I might have a surprise or two up my sleeve." I wink at her when I really want to lean in and kiss her. I don't think Vi and Todd know about our relationship. I would be surprised if they did because of the NDA. The guys have gotten used to us kissing randomly here and there, but I don't want to spring us being a couple on her family if she's not ready.

She squeezes my arm and Todd's eyes narrow at the action. "See you then, Callum."

Chapter 25

Arista

There is a sparkle in Vi's eyes as she puts on some makeup before dinner. One I haven't seen in ages. It makes me happy to see it, so happy she is here with me.

"How glamorous is it, traveling around the country with a rock band?" Vi adds a second color to the lids of her eyes. She stares at me through the reflection in the bathroom mirror before moving on to the other eye.

"Glamorous?" I can't help the snort that comes out. "I wouldn't exactly call it glamorous."

She turns around. "Traveling all over for free, staying in nice hotels? Seems pretty posh to me, Ris."

"That's only because it's what you are seeing right now. We only stay in hotels on the days there are more than one show in a city or sometimes for an off day. The rest of the time we're on a bus with four adults, one toddler who still hasn't mastered potty training, and whatever groupies Sammy and Killian have picked up the previous night. There is absolutely no privacy, so everyone knows all your business. The guys probably even know when I'm on my period; it's that kind of no privacy. It's a lot of late nights. Some days Callum doesn't even see Gibson when he's awake."

"But free concerts, Ris." She kind of rolls her eyes at me like this isn't tiring or even really work.

"Tomorrow night will be the first time I've seen them live." Her face tells me she doesn't believe me. "I'm here to take care of Gibson, keep him happy. To do that, I have him on a schedule that doesn't include concerts. I see the occasional soundcheck so we can all eat together. But even then, I'm watching a toddler, so I'm usually making sure he hasn't ripped off his earmuffs or isn't wandering off and getting into things."

We move back out to their room. Todd is eating a bag of eight-dollar potato chips and drinking a little bottle of some sort of alcohol from the minibar while watching golf on the television.

Vi pulls out different shirts for my inspection. "I brought this one for you. You should wear it, Ris, it'll make your eyes look so pretty." She holds up a purple, off the shoulder top, garnished with sparkles. It's a beautiful top and it's new because it still has the tags on it.

"It's gorgeous. Are you sure you don't want to wear it?" She shakes her head and throws the purple shirt at me before bending over and rifling through her bag and pulling out a red top this time.

"And you should wear this one tomorrow, so you'll totally look rock 'n' roll." She giggles. Her lighthearted laugh makes my heart happy. I love light and free Vi. She's not stressed, like after mom and dad died, when she suddenly had a teenager to raise, and I know I was a handful. She didn't have to choose to raise me, but she did. She uprooted her whole life for me. First by transferring to nights at the ER and then changing over to a local specialty clinic instead of the hospital. All because of me.

My hug catches her off-guard. "Woah, Ris." She pats my back gently. "It's just a couple of shirts. No big deal."

229

I shake my head, unable to get the words out. I never thanked her for taking me on. She didn't have to do that after our parents died. She was newly wedded and off living her adult life when suddenly, she was tasked with raising a surly, hurting teenager. "Thank you. Not just for the shirts, but for being there after Mom and Dad. I know I wasn't an easy kid."

I hug her and she hugs me back tighter. "We were both grieving. You know I'd do anything for you." I nod. "What brought that on? You're not normally so emotional."

I shrug. "I dunno. Guess I just miss you." She hugs me again.

"Where's my thank you?" Todd stands and holds his arms open for a hug too. Not wanting to cause a stir, I move to his arms, praying it's just a brief hug. My stomach threatens to dispel my lunch as his fingers press into the flesh of my back. I try to pull away after just a few seconds, but his hold lingers a little too long.

"Don't ever forget all I've done for you too," he whispers in that voice, the one that makes me feel thirteen and scared. I nod to appease him. If I don't, who knows what he'd do.

"I'm heading to my room to change. This shirt will look great with my black jeans." I pull away hard and head directly for the door. "I'll be back in a few." I rush down to the suite at the end of the hall, needing to get away from Todd so I can breathe.

Callum and Gibson aren't in the suite. They're probably still down at the pool. I wiggle into my favorite black jeans, the ones with the jeweled back pockets. I pull on my black boots, glad I packed them. I tug on the purple top that Vi brought and style my hair. I'm almost done, when I hear Callum enter the common room with Gibson who's babbling about blocks and sand and SeeSee, which I finally figured out is what he calls Elsie.

"Daddy and Ari have a special dinner tonight, buddy, so

you get to have dinner with Elsie and Brio," Callum tells him. "Let's pick a few toys to take with you."

"BeeOh." I can't help my giggle. He tries so hard to say Brio, but it still comes out sounding like B.O. and that makes me laugh like a twelve-year-old boy.

"Oh, hey, I didn't know you were here." Callum sticks his head into the bedroom at my giggle.

"I just wanted to change. Vi brought me this shirt. Pretty, right?" I look down at it.

"You look stunning." His voice is husky, and his eyes are my favorite deep ocean blue. I feel my cheeks flush under his perusal.

"Come here." As I enter his hug, he tips up my chin and kisses me softly at first, but then with a pressing urgency.

"Awee pitty. Awee kiss kiss!" Gibson tugs on my leg, not wanting to be left out.

Callum chuckles before pulling away. "Already trying to horn in on my girl, huh, bud?" Callum picks up his son. I love that boy and his father. And seeing the two of them together is irresistible.

He called me *his girl* again. It warms my heart, makes me feel safe and just like that, any residual grossness I felt from Todd dissipates. *My girl.* I love how it sounds coming out of him.

He tips Gibson's face to mine so he can kiss my cheek. "Pitty Awee." Gibson pats my cheek. He's about to go in for a fishy face, but Callum pulls him away.

"Let's get those toys to take to Elsie's." He leans back and kisses my cheek again. "I'll see you downstairs, beautiful."

R

WE MEET in the lobby and walk together to the valet. I want so much to hold his hand. To feel his warm palm against mine and the steadiness and connection we have just in that small gesture. I don't want Vi to know I'm sleeping with my boss, though.

When the valet pulls up in the rental SUV, Callum's hand at the small of my back has me relishing in the comfort I was desiring minutes ago.

"Would you like to sit with your sister in the back seat or the front seat with me?" Callum asks me. Todd's gaze burns into the side of Callum's head.

"With Vi, please." He opens the back door and I get in and scoot across the seat so Vi has room. Todd stands at the front passenger door like a dumbass. Did he think Callum would open his door, or is he just fuming because I'm sitting with my sister?

At the restaurant, Callum and I sit across from Vi and Todd at a table tucked into the back corner. There are crisp white table clothes and a soft flickering candle in the middle of our table. After drink orders are taken, Callum clears his throat. "I was going to wait until after dinner, but I can't wait anymore."

My leg tenses up. Is he going to out us? That'd be a bad idea in front of Todd. He will find a way to exploit it and take advantage of the situation. He'll either try to use Callum for his money or somehow turn Callum against me. If Todd knows I'm serious about Callum and he is serious about me, he'll try to end it. It's not like he hasn't scared away guys before. Especially when I was younger. Vi always said he was just being protective of me. If she only knew how far off she was.

"I have a surprise for you and your sister." Callum hands me an envelope. Puzzled, I open the envelope with our names penned on the front in his block print. The card inside is from a local spa with our names and an appointment time for tomorrow.

"Woah, Callum! This is amazing. Look, Vi, a spa day tomorrow!" I hold out the card for her to see while looking over at

Callum, who's grinning at us. "I've never been to a spa before. Thanks!" I reach over and hug Callum without thinking about it. Thankfully, he keeps it short and friendly.

"You're welcome. I wanted to do it for you after Gibson was sick as a thank you for taking such good care of him. Having you there to comfort him when I couldn't be meant the world to me." He looks over at me, concern creasing his brow.

"I arranged a spa visit for earlier, but you got sick, then the schedule was crazy busy. So I thought I'd treat you both tomorrow instead. I want you two to have a good time together. I know Ari misses her weekly lunches with you, Viola." He smiles at Vi. I look across the table at my sister who's glowing, she's so excited. But Todd's face is sour.

"Don't worry, man," Callum says to Todd. "I have some fun stuff planned for us too. It'll be awesome."

"Sure, cool." Todd tries to sound grateful, but by the look in his eyes, he's anything but. I'm intimately familiar with this look. I gulp and fiddle with my silverware. At least I'm not going to be alone around him any time soon. This is something he'd try to make me pay for, even though I knew nothing about it.

Dinner with my sister is fun, despite Todd glowering at me whenever he can. Callum tells funny stories about the tour and Gibson. Vi tells stories of our childhood and cringeworthy stories about me being a terror of a teenager. If she only knew the kind of teenager I really was.

I love seeing her have fun, and the food is so good.

Throughout the night, Callum's hand drifts to rest on my thigh. The thrill of that makes me happy. And nervous.

Vi probably wouldn't care about my relationship with Callum, especially now that she knows him. The longer I'm with Callum, the more I realize that I love him. He spelled out his love for me almost immediately. But I have trouble saying the words back. Not because I don't. I do, so much. But I can't make myself say them, not yet.

We ride up to the floor when we get back to the hotel. I stick my hands in my back pockets because I can't stop from wanting to interlace my fingers with Callum's. We've been doing it more and more when we're together. It comes so naturally now that it's hard to stop.

I hug Vi goodnight and make plans to meet her for tomorrow's appointment. Todd leans in and kisses me on the cheek, whispering quietly, "Slut. I know you're fucking him." His words rob me of my breath.

He pulls back and grins widely at Callum. "See you tomorrow, man." He tucks Vi under his arm and they walk down the hall one way, while I quietly follow Callum the other way towards our suite.

Chapter 26

Callum

"No! Daddddaaaah!" Gibson arches his back against Elsie's grip as Kady cuddles a sleeping Brio in a baby wrap. I take my helmet off and head towards them, not able to take his fussing anymore.

"I'll sit this race out. I'll take on the winner."

"Pussy." Todd mutters under his breath as he rolls his eyes and heads to the go-cart assigned to him. We've only been here an hour, and he's already shown himself to be not so good with kids.

I walk Gibson around the track as he weaves his fingers into my hair and lays his head on my shoulder. I know he's tired because it's well past nap time. If I can get him to fall asleep, that'd be great both for Elsie and for me.

The next race is Todd, Mav, Jeff, and I. We zip around the track, Mav pulling out to an early lead, the fucker. I'm just about to catch him when Todd fucking punts my ass right into the wall.

If you're going to race me dirty, I'll race you dirty right back, dude. I catch back up to him and return the favor. We get black flagged for aggressive driving and are forced to pull our carts off the track.

"What's your problem, Donogue?" Todd hollers over at me as he jerks his helmet off.

"You dumped me first." My lips pull back into a smirk. I can't resist poking the bear. "Seemed like a fair play to me." I shrug.

"Whatever." He slams himself onto a bench near his cart.

I sit on the other end. Instinctively, my eyes find Gibson in the glassed room across the way. He's still asleep near Elsie.

Todd notices this and shakes his head. "Having a kid must suck."

"Nah. He's the best thing I've ever made." I say it simply because it's the truth. I don't miss life without him because he *is* my life. Him and Ari.

"So, Ari lived with you guys after her parents died?" I'm trying to be nonchalant, trying my best to give off a shooting-the-shit kind of vibe. I don't need him figuring out that I'm on a fact-finding mission.

He nods and looks over at me. "Started a couple of months after we got married. I think she was thirteen or something." He rolls his eyes.

I have to be careful how I tread here, to seem curious but not grill this asshole the way I really want to. "That had to be hard. A grieving teenager can't be easy to take on, especially in a new marriage."

"Pffffttt. You aren't kidding. It certainly wasn't my idea. Vi insisted. Personally, I'd have sent her to CPS or wherever the hell orphans go." He blows out a sigh and I'm having to hold myself back already. He wanted to turn away his wife's mourning teenage sister? How could he do that when family is fucking everything? My jaw tightens to the point of pain.

"Fuck, she was a handful back then. Had to learn her

lessons the *hard* way, that one." My stomach turns at the sick smile that crosses his face while reminiscing.

"But I handled it. God knows her sister couldn't. I love my wife, I do, but that woman was always coddling that thick-headed little sister of hers. At least my wife was able to get that mothering thing out of her veins on Arista. I'd hate to be saddled down like you are."

He looks off to the side and then back at me and lowers his voice. "You need to pay attention to what I'm about to tell you. I know you're involved with Arista in an intimate way." He shows me a digital rag on his phone with a photo of us kissing at the park yesterday.

"Everyone knows you're screwing the nanny except my wife. Don't let Arista make a fool out of you. That little bitch is feisty, and she'll bite."

The things this asshole just said about Ari have me wanting to draw back and pop him hard in his smug fucking face. If he talks about her like that to someone he's just met, if he talks about a fourteen-year-old child like that, I shake my head. I can't fathom anyone talking about a teenager like that, especially the one charged with her care.

I get right in his face, so close our noses nearly touch. "You have some nerve talking about Ari like you know her," I seethe at him.

"Oh, trust me, I *know* her." A twisted grin lifts up his cheeks and I fucking snap.

I pull back, ready to take my shot. "You stay the fuck away from her. You hear me?" My voice is steel despite the hot rage flowing through my veins.

Someone from behind catches my punch before I release my fury on this asshole.

"Cal? Everything okay?" Kill steps between us, facing me but keeping a strong hold on my right arm. "What's going on?" He asks the second part low, so only I hear him.

237

The corners of Todd's mouth twitch up in a slight smile. "Think about it this way. Is the little bitch worth your career or your son?" The evil grin starts to creep across his face again until Killian releases my arm and flips to face him. Kill's face must be as murderous as my thoughts, because the evil grin on Todd's face turns into a grimace of fear.

"What the fuck did you say?" Killian stands chest-to-chest with Todd, Kill having about three inches on him. Now it's my turn to be the pacifier.

"I must need my ears checked because I swore you just threatened my nephew and called his nanny, your own sister-in-law, a bitch." Kill's fists are already balled as he purposely bumps chests again with Todd.

My hand is on Kill's shoulder, holding him back from Todd. Kill isn't a fighter, and it's rare for him to go off on someone, but when he does, he doesn't stop until he's pulled off. With how I'm feeling about Todd right now, I may "accidentally" let my twin go.

Todd throws his hands up as Sammy and Mav approach. "It's all a misunderstanding, man."

Misunderstanding, my ass. Was he seriously threatening me with my son because I love his sister-in-law?

Todd must realize he's outnumbered because he immediately backs down. Maybe he understands the band is a family and that we'll side with each other right or wrong, without even knowing the why or how.

"Who's taking on the winner of the first heat?" Sammy tries to defuse the testosterone-fueled tensions running high between the three of us.

For the rest of the time at the go-kart track, Mav and Sammy are vigilant in making sure I am not alone with Todd and vice versa. Somehow, we get through the day without throwing down, despite my intense need to punch Todd's fucking face.

The best part of the day is the selfie that Ari texts me of her and her sister with some brown goop all over their faces. Despite the goop, their smiles are big and easy. I zoom in on Ari's face. She's so beautiful, even with that stuff smeared all over her. I'm glad I could give this bonding time to them. They seemed to need it, especially my Ari.

Todd comes to the arena with us for soundcheck and heads to the green room and goes right for Mav's whiskey, opens the bottle, and helps himself. Mav gives me a look and I know I'm going to owe him a bottle of Breckenridge or some shit. It's not like he's drinking the bottle, but he likes to take them home with him to enhance his home bar. He also helped himself to Sammy's beef jerky, but I don't think Sammy cared.

Right now, he's "watching" soundcheck from the empty venue seating and I use watching very loosely because he seems more content to mess around on his phone while we run through some songs to make sure everything sounds right.

We're about halfway through soundcheck when I notice he's chatting with Bryanna, the lead singer of our opening act FemmeDepot. Even from here on the stage, I see the intimate way he's touching her.

My body language must be a neon sign flashing *pissed off* because Killian checks my line of sight. Seeing what I see, he saunters over to me, still strumming his bass, and says, "Not your circus, not your monkey."

He nods at me, then saunters back over to his tech to switch out basses. I continue to watch Todd put the moves on Bryanna, knowing what will happen if he pushes too far. She's in a committed relationship and is a take-no-shit kind of chick. Just as I thought, she pushes him away and gets up and walks away, shaking her head. I'm too far away to hear what she says when she turns back, finger pointing at him, no doubt giving him a piece of her mind.

I can't help my chuckle, knowing Todd just got served up a

plate of mashed karma potatoes. As much as I hate it, Kill's right, this isn't my circus. I swap out guitars and focus on making it through soundcheck without throttling Ari's asshole brother-in-law. This is not the place or the time.

R

WE'RE minutes from going on and I can't fucking sit still. I really want Ari to love the show. Since it's her first, I want it to be perfect. I'm almost as nervous as the time we found out record company scouts were in the audience.

But I also have this sinking feeling in my gut, telling me something bad is going down while I'm onstage. The sudden appearance of the paparazzi at the hotel only adds to it. It almost makes me not want to take the stage for the first time in forever.

I seek out Aiden and pull him aside. "Stick extra close to Ari and Vi tonight." He nods, his face stone serious. "Whenever possible, stand between Ari and Todd. I know it sounds like a weird request, but humor me. And don't let Ari go anywhere alone, not even to the bathroom."

"I got your girl." Even Aiden knows she's my girl. He turns on his heel to catch up with her. Knowing he's going to be extra vigilant tonight gives me a little peace of mind.

Onstage, I pour my everything into the strings of my guitar and my backing vocals, knowing that Ari's eyes are on me. Ari's dancing in the front row with Vi and both have big smiles on their faces. True to his word, Aiden stands between Vi and Todd, making him the odd man out while the sisters dance together.

Chapter 27

Callum

After Vi and Todd fly home the next morning, we have a long drive and then four consecutive shows. By the time I'm walking off stage after night three, I'm wishing we didn't have VIP experiences for each concert on this tour. Mav's voice is starting to suffer from the back-to-back shows. The average fan probably couldn't hear it, but I sure can.

I pat Mav on the shoulder as we head into the green room to sign autographs and take selfies with the fans.

"Mav's voice is a little rough tonight," I announce loudly to the room as we enter and before we get started. "Don't be offended if he doesn't talk much. He's trying to save it for tomorrow's show in Pittsburgh. You have questions, Sammy, and I have your answers." I grin. "Besides, he's just the fucking lead singer. Clearly Sammy and I are the life of the band."

"Hell yeah we are!" Sammy jumps up and down as he says it, pumping himself and the crowd up. The room laughs, including Mav. We split off for different areas and people line up to walk through to each table.

By the time I hit the bus that night, every bone in my body

aches with exhaustion. I push the door to the back room on the bus open to take my nightly peek at Gibson.

Ari's sound asleep in something of a fetal position on the bed facing Gibs, who's not far from her sleeping on his back with one arm reaching above his head and the other at his side. The green sheets are pulled mid-way up Ari but aren't covering Gibson at all, so I quietly sneak in to cover him over.

I can't bear the thought of climbing into the bunk and sleeping alone tonight. I want to wake up with Ari and Gibs.

I softly shut the door to the bedroom at the back of the bus. Shucking off my shirt and pants, I slide in between the sheets and snuggle up behind Ari's warm body. I breathe in her orange vanilla scent and wrap an arm around her waist as I tug her into me. She lets out a sigh and mumbles something I can't make out as she relaxes against me. She might wake up mad in the morning, but this will be the best night's sleep I've had on this tour bus yet.

"Daddee. Daddeeee. Awee." Gibson's singsong greeting lets me know he's awake. Ari's still in my arms, and the moment she awakens, she starts to stretch and then freezes and grabs my arm that's still firmly holding her against me. I tug her to me even tighter. "Morning, beautiful," I whisper in her ear.

"Callum!" She rolls to face me. "You're in here." I nod and take her in. Her cheek has a red pressure mark from the hand she had tucked under it, and her hair's messy in that just woke up kind of way, but she's so beautiful it almost hurts to look at her and not touch her.

"You realize the band knows about us, right?" I rub her back reassuringly.

She turns pink and nods and lays a gentle kiss in the middle of my chest.

"Us." She looks up at me as she says it. "There is an us."

I gather her up and hug her hard to me. "Yeah, there's definitely an us. I love you, Ari. And I don't care who the fuck knows." Her eyes are moist, like she might cry, and she shakes her head ever so slightly.

"But why?" Her voice is so quiet that I almost don't hear it. "Why me?"

"Why the hell not you?" I kiss her, but I can see there is something that makes the question very real to her. She seriously doesn't understand why I love her. That stops now.

"There's been something about you since your interview. I was against hiring you because I felt it then and it scared the shit out of me. It's partially why I was so gruff and hard on you in the beginning. I could see that you were good for Gibs, but I worried about what would happen if I somehow messed things up between us." Shit, this is not coming out right.

"I need you almost as much as he does." I sigh while she looks at me. "I love you, Ari, because of who you are. You're beautiful. You're smart and driven. You've worked hard to get where you are now. You have my son's heart. And you have mine." I run my nose from the shell of her ear down her jaw, peppering it with little kisses along the way, stopping only when I get to her lips. I swipe my tongue across them, and she parts them for me so I can deepen our kiss.

Tired of being in bed, Gibson launches himself over Ari and crawls in between us. "Moanin. Kiss kiss." He puckers his lips up, trying to get in on the kissing action. After Ari peppers him with kisses and I do the same, he sits up. "Okay. Bekfist time. Pease. Fank you."

His language skills are off the charts for someone his age and they keep getting better. I'm convinced that Ari has a lot to do with that. She's constantly chatting with him and asking him questions. I chuckle and dig some sweatpants out of my suitcase and pull them on.

I pick up Gibson as Ari straightens the blankets on the bed. "'Mon Ari Bekfist!" Gibs calls out at her.

"Yeah, come on, Ari, it's time for breakfast." I stroll with Gibs out to the empty common area.

Ari stretches out on the floor and runs through some of her yoga poses while Gibs eats, preferring to get them out of the way before the area fills up with Sammy, Kill, and whoever his newest friend is. Ari's so flexible. I fucking love watching her stretch. It's a turn on.

"I think that we should continue to share the bedroom. You know, if that's cool with you." I smile as I watch her contort into whatever upward cat child pose she is doing now.

She transitions between poses and then looks up at me with a grin growing across her face. "Very okay." After tonight's show, we have a marathon road trip. We'll be on the bus for eighteen hours or so, including a rest stop for the driver. Sharing the back bedroom in the bus will make the trip easier. Plus, I hate those damn bunks. They feel like coffins.

At the second radio station appearance of the day, Ari texts me a picture of her and Gibson making what I assume is roaring lion faces with the lion exhibit right behind them. I love the texts she sends me of their adventures, and I know I'm grinning when the DJ asks me, on air, what's got me smiling.

"A picture of my son at the zoo." I hold up the phone so he can see. I think he was trying to scold me for checking my phone, but ever since Gibs got sick, I try to check it every time. This time it ends up leading to a discussion about parenting on tour, with Mav and I both giving similar takes. It works out well because the callers are talking about parenting too. It ends up being the best interview of the day.

Ari rushes into the green room, clutching Gibson, to say hello and grab some food. As soon as she sets him down, Gibson runs up to Sammy with a new stuffed toy, a lion.

"Hey, you." I pull Ari down onto my lap. "Did you have fun at the zoo?"

She nods and relaxes against my body. I fucking love that I

bring that calm to her just by holding her. "Gibson loved the lions this time."

"I loved the pic you sent. Thank you for that, for all the ones you send when I can't be there." I look in her eyes, wanting her to know that I really do love them, but what I see reflected back stops me.

"What's wrong?" She looks pale, and her eyes dart around the room like she's looking for something.

"There were people everywhere. Fans or paparazzi? I don't know. They kept crowding around us. Saying lewd things. I had to hold Gibson with one arm and drag his stroller with the other. I mean, Aiden was there, thank goodness, and the zoo helped, but it's like they knew exactly where we were. How did they know?"

"Shit. I mentioned it at the radio station. The DJ called me out for checking my phone, so I said it was a picture of my son at the zoo." Fuck, I should know better than that, putting Gibson and Ari into the thick of things like that.

"I don't know, maybe. But it seemed like a lot of people. And they all seemed to know who we were. I mean, do your fans even know what Gibson or I look like, really? They were firing questions at me about if I was sleeping my way around the band. Some of the things they shouted were plain lewd, considering I had a child in my arms." Her voice rattles as she speaks, and it causes my chest to tighten. I look for Aiden, who's huddled with Jax just outside the door.

I squeeze her to me tight. "I'm glad Aiden was with you. Fuck. I'm sorry. I'll be more careful." She nods and leans her head against my shoulder.

A few minutes later, she moves to get up from my lap. "Let me get Gibs some dinner so you two can eat together."

She works her way around the food spread, getting Gibson his favorite foods, and I make a plate for myself. We sit on the floor by the couch and eat together, the three of us having our own little floor picnic in the midst of this chaotic green room where people come and go all around us.

After the show, I slip into the bedroom at the rear of the bus and crawl under the green comforter with Ari and Gibson. The bus stops in the early morning for the mandatory rest stop. We sleep until Gibson gets up, then the three of us walk to a nearby park to play with Aiden in tow. Twenty minutes later, the park starts crowding with people. People without kids. Aiden notices it too and steps closer to us.

There's no way this park would be this busy at 10:45 on a random Tuesday morning. Very few of these people have kids with them. They're fans. We are in a Podunk town somewhere near the Tennessee/Virginia border. It's not a scheduled tour stop but an in-between layover, so it's not like this stop is posted anywhere. It's our break in the middle of our long-ass road trip to Miami.

Ari's brow creases when she notices them, and she picks up Gibson. "Okay, park time is over."

"No, Aweee. Stay. Pease. Stay." He arches his back and whines. "Pawk pease stay!"

Aiden and I flank Ari, my hand resting firmly on her lower back as we walk with a quick clip to the corner and head back for the parking lot of a mall a few blocks away from where the busses are parked. I don't want to get back on the bus this early, since we have almost five more hours to kill before we head back out on the road. But the mob of people are not only following but gaining on us.

Aiden can handle the pursuing crowd, but I'm relieved to see Luke from the security team jogging towards us from the direction of the busses. He joins our group and walks with us, him behind us as we continue to the bus staging area at a steady quick clip. When Gibson realizes he's not going back to the park, he grabs a handful of Ari's hair and gives it a hard yank.

"Mean Awee. Mean," he screeches.

He yanks it a second time. I immediately take him from her and hold his hand down to his side. "No. You do not pull hair, Gibson. No." I say it firmly without yelling. But he's not used to being reprimanded by me, and his eyes widen and his lip trembles.

He looks down. "No hairs," he repeats quietly to me.

"That hurts. You don't hurt people." He shakes his head. "Tell Ari you're sorry." I'm mortified at his hair pulling. He's never done that shit before. To anybody. That he'd do it to Ari because he's mad is not excusable.

"Sowee Awee. Sowee. Ouch." Mirroring Ari, he rubs his hand on his head, then sticks out his bottom lip. "Sowee." He says it quietly, reaching out a hand to pet her hair.

"Apology accepted." She pats his hand as we walk into the parking lot and head straight to the bus. I take Gibson right to the bedroom and sit with him on the bed until he falls asleep. No story, no Ari cuddles, no Octonauts. Nothing. When he's out, I leave the door ajar and return to Ari, who's reading on her Kindle as she sits curled up on the couch. I sit next to her and rub her leg.

"I'm so sorry he pulled your hair. I don't know what got into him." I'm still mortified that he'd treat Ari like that. She gives him her whole heart, and he yanks her hair.

"He's frustrated and not even three. He doesn't mean it. You reacted in exactly the right way. Swiftly and with authority, but didn't go overboard." She gives me a soft smile, but I still feel like crap.

"It had to hurt. Hell, my head hurts just thinking about it." She smiles and reaches over and pets my head. I can't help but lean into her touch.

"It hurt like hell. Especially that second pull." She winces at the memory. I lean over and kiss her temple. "You can kiss my booboos anytime." She winks at me.

Chapter 28

Arista

Everywhere I go with Gibson lately, it's a matter of minutes before we are surrounded by a crowd. It's not happening to the band members, which makes no sense. The band gets followed around by the usual media and fans. But Gibson and I are constantly inundated with grabby fans and sleazy paparazzi every single time we go out. They say vile things, not caring there's an impressionable child who often gets mad and scared when his activities are interrupted. It's gotten so bad that we've started taking a second security person when we go out. Usually, it's Luke. Sometimes it's Jax, who's been trying to figure out why we've suddenly become so interesting.

Jax personally scouted out the park by the hotel earlier this morning and sent me the location. Gibson really needed to play like a kid, and I needed the sunshine. Luckily, it was sunny and warm without being too hot. I think we are in North Carolina today. Aiden, Luke, and I got to the park with Gibson. Settling into the sand with Gibson and his favorite cups, we play together. We weren't there fifteen minutes before people started showing up. I tried ignoring them as we played, but still kept an eye on the growing numbers. Then the taunting started.

"Are you sleeping with the bodyguards now too, slut?"

"What's wrong with the kid? Doesn't he talk?"

"Who haven't you slept with in the band, you whore?"

As I gathered up Gibson's toys, a box of condoms is hurled at us, coming damn close to hitting Gibson in the head as he played. I couldn't take it anymore, so I snapped him up and ran to Aiden, who escorted us to the car while Luke quickly collected the rest of the toys and joined us.

It's too much to go out anymore. Even if it was just me, I couldn't do it. But a toddler shouldn't be subjected to the constant lewd comments. So today, Gibson and I are hanging out at the venue with the band. This venue is a huge arena, and Sammy and Killian spent hours setting up a makeshift playground for Gibson. It might not be as fun as the park and it's not outside in the fresh air, but it's fantastic in its own right.

This large unused, empty concrete storage space has some of Gibson's scoot toys set up, a few empty road cases open for him to crawl in, and an epic blanket fort for reading, snuggling and hanging out, tucked into a corner. I'm not even sure where the blankets or pillows came from, and I don't even care. I'm taking advantage of the fort today as much as Gibson is.

Gibson's not interested in the book I brought in with me. He's content to sit on the floor with his dark green truck and another car he brought. I'm happy to just sit in the fort buffered from the nastiness of the real world.

"Voom voom," he hums quietly with his toys. Over his soft playing, I hear someone enter our indoor playground. Their boots scratch across the concrete floor. I momentarily freeze, hoping that whoever has found us is friendly and not someone who's going to tell us to take the fort down.

"Ari? Gibs?" Mav's voice calls out quietly.

"Mads." Gibson returns his call.

"In the blanket fort." I start to crawl out towards the outside.

When I pull the blanket back, Mav is squatting at eye level at the entrance. "This is an epic fort. Did you build it?" Mav's eyes sparkle as he takes in the roomy yet cozy interior of the fort.

I shake my head. "Sammy and Killian did."

"Damn, they're good." I nod in agreement. "Cal's finishing up with a photographer. Then we're all going to lunch. We have a back room at a nearby diner reserved."

"Come on, Gibs." I reach my hand back to him. "Let's go potty and get ready to go to lunch."

"Potty." He nods. I grab his hand and rush him to the bathroom in Callum's dressing room since he's agreeable to sitting on the potty. Usually, it's a fight. He's an active ball of energy and getting him to take time away from playing to use the restroom isn't something he likes to do. I squat next to him as I hold him on the potty since he doesn't have his little seat handy. I'm expecting another exercise in futility. But I hear the telltale sounds of him actually using the potty.

"Good job! You did it!" It's the first time he's recognized that he had to go and used the toilet.

"Did it!" he parrots as I dig through my bag for his prize. I show him the sheet of stickers I pull from my bag.

"You get to pick a special sticker! Which one do you want?" He looks them over and points to a puppy sticker. I carefully peel it off the sheet and stick it to his shirt. "That is your special good job sticker for using the potty! Daddy will be so proud of you!" He smiles at me.

We emerge from the bathroom, and I stop dead in my tracks because Callum is standing there shirtless. His inked skin highlights the rippling back muscles underneath as he pulls on a shirt before turning to us.

"Hey, buddy. You ready for lunch?" He looks over at Gibs, who is studying the sticker I put on his shirt.

"Wook. Speshul. Good job!" He pulls out his shirt a little so Callum can check out his puppy sticker, too.

Callum squats down and takes it in with him. "That is a special sticker, buddy."

"Gibson got it for going potty on the potty," I explain, so he knows it's a good day.

Callum smiles and hugs Gibson to him roughly and nuzzles his neck. "You went potty in the potty? Great job, buddy! I'm so proud. This is definitely something to celebrate! You're getting to be such a big boy." Callum looks up at me, his eyes sparkling with pride for his son.

At the diner, Jax informs us of a growing crowd outside as he closes the shades on the windows in the private dining room. How they found us before our meals are even on the table is a mystery. How does word move so fast? I wonder if it's the band's true fans out there or the ones that have taken to following just me and Gibson.

The diner is thrilled their dining room is chocked full of people, most hoping to get a glimpse of our group. Luckily, this room is completely separate from the main dining room, with Luke and Drew standing guard at the door. I seriously doubt anyone will be disturbing our lunch.

Sadly, though, it takes all four bodyguards to get us to the waiting SUVs. The crowd is ridiculous, and the vehicle starts to rock as I am attempting to buckle Gibson into his seat. I glance up and every window has multiple faces pressed against it. We are completely surrounded. The safety of the SUV feels more like a box that's getting smaller and smaller.

Chapter 29

Callum

I t's been a shitty week. I sing a few bars to give the sound guy an idea where my mic levels are as I play during soundcheck, but my eyes don't leave Ari and Gibson. They're playing on the concrete floor of the arena with the blocks, building some sort of elaborate structure that Gibson is parking his cars in. Gibson is wearing his earmuffs.

Ari hasn't taken Gibson out anywhere in over a week. For the last several weeks, it seemed that no matter where she tried to take him, a group of so-called fans would show up and harass them, each time worse than the last, with the fans getting aggressive and rude with Ari. Jax is trying to figure out how the fuck they seem to know where they are going, but so far, no luck.

Meanwhile, my son and Ari don't go anywhere that isn't the bus, arena, or hotel. It's not that security won't go with them, or that I forbid them from leaving. It's all Ari. She doesn't want to expose Gibson to the vile comments. She hasn't told me about them, mind you. I only know because Aiden told me what they shout at them. Just hearing what they are subjected to makes me really question why I'm doing this. Do I love playing live music? Absolutely, but not at the detriment of my son and girl.

I'm not looking forward to telling Ari the label extended our tour. I found out during our impromptu meeting in Mav's bus before soundcheck. Seven additional weeks of shows that will cross back over the middle and southern states that we missed the first time around. That's a long time and she might refuse.

When done, I hand my guitar off to Geo, my guitar tech, and hop off the front of the stage. Ari pops up from the floor as soon as I arrive. "Can you take over for a few? I have to use the restroom."

"Of course." Aiden follows her as I settle in with Gibs.

As I watch her retreat, I can't help but notice she walks stiffly, like she hurts. These damn concrete floors can't be helping her back issues. Another thing to add to the list of things I need to discuss with her. But during the rare moments we are alone, I tend to fill them more with touching, kissing, and making love. Fuck talking. I can't get enough of Ari.

"Voom Voom." Gibson makes his car go in and out of the structure he and Ari built. He knocks into the wall of the block structure, and it shifts.

"Uh-oh. Cwash!" He pushes the car into the wall on purpose and laughs as the wall breaks apart. Soon Sammy and Killian are sitting with us, and we each have a car in hand and are playing with Gibs. Kady grabs her camera and takes some photos.

Not only is Kady a member of the Rebels, but she's also our band photographer. When she was first dating Mav, she used to show up taking pictures, and it would give me the creeps. But now her photos are the most prized items on the wall of my home.

Ari comes back and Kady shows her the pictures she took

on the camera's display. "You boys look so cute playing cars." She chuckles and turns back to Kady.

"That one should be posted on the band's social media as a behind-the-scenes of the tour picture." Kady agrees.

"Speaking of the tour," I say while standing up. I cross over to Ari and put an arm around her waist, and pull her to me. "It's been extended by seven weeks." Ari grimaces. Shit, I knew she'd be disappointed.

"I know you've been miserable lately. Maybe after New York, things will calm down fan wise." I kiss her temple, and she closes her eyes as if she's cherishing it. "We'll be there for four days, and I'm taking you on a date. Just you and me. Okay?" She nods.

After the normal pre-concert schmooze fest with the label's VIPs, I head to my dressing room, hoping to find Ari and Gibs, but they aren't there. I check the little play area that Sammy set up for him in his dressing room and they aren't in there either. I slip quietly onto the bus and Ari is curled up with her e-reader in her lap and a cup of tea in her mug. She isn't reading. She's staring off into space.

"Hey," I greet her as I slip onto the other end of the couch. "Gibs is napping?" She nods and gives me a tight smile. "Good, I wanted to talk to you about the tour extension."

She takes a deep breath and sets her cup on the counter behind her. I mentioned it in front of the guys because I took the chickenshit way out. I should have brought it to her in private.

"I'm sorry I told you in front of everyone. I just didn't want to forget to tell you. We have so little private time."

She nods. "I understand. It's just..." Her voice trails off. I know she's thinking about how hard it's been on her and Gibson lately.

"I know. Jax is working on figuring out what is going on with people harassing you everywhere you go. I just need you to hold on, and as soon as he figures it out, I'm sure everything will go back to the way it was before." I'm pulling this totally out of my ass, but I can't risk her quitting on me. Who the hell knows if Jax can fix this? If he could, I think he'd have done it by now. I don't want to lose her. And if she quits, I can't tour anyway.

"When we're in New York, I'll need to find a doctor there who can give me my nerve block injections. I'll call my doctor and see if he has any recommendations for someone there." She looks out the window, avoiding my gaze. Nerve block injections?

"What are you talking about?" My head is spinning because I don't remember anything about injections.

She turns towards me and tucks her legs under her. "I was in a car accident when I was thirteen and injured my back. Nerve blocks help with my pain management. They usually last about five months or so. But last time my back was really irritated from being on my feet at the diner and the café. So, this time it's only lasted about four months." She looks up at me.

"You're in pain?" My gut clenches tight when she nods. She's in fucking pain and hasn't said a word. Dammit. "How long have you been hurting?"

"It's been at the level where I know I need a shot for the last five days or so." She says it like it's no big deal, like she hasn't been in fucking pain for nearly a week and hasn't said a damn thing to me. My chest tightens as I wonder just how much pain she's been in.

"My injury doesn't affect my ability to take care of Gibson. Running around after him is good for me. It keeps me limber." She's worried I'm going to fire her. I know she can take care of Gibson, but who is taking care of Ari? It should be me, and I'm failing.

I shake my head, disappointed in myself, but she misunderstands the gesture.

255

"I'll just need to take an hour or two off in New York for my injection. I'll try to make it for an off day."

There's a knock on the bus door and Mav sticks his head in. "Cal, we gotta get to the appearance."

I forgot we have another appearance at a radio station to sign autographs and do a Q&A for fans.

"Text me the name of your doctor." She reaches for her phone. "We'll talk later." She nods as my phone vibrates with her message. I want to tell her I love her, but not in front of Mav.

I don't get back to the bus to talk to Ari, because after the appearance, there is another station that wasn't on the schedule. By the time we get back to the arena, we're in the green room getting ready for dinner.

"Darren, I need something." Our label rep stops in his tracks in the back corridor of the arena. It's not like I ask much, so I've already piqued his curiosity.

"Ari needs a doctor to administer her a nerve block for her back. I just texted you the contact for her doctor in L.A. She said she can hang on until New York, but I want this for her as soon as possible, Darren. No buts. Just make it fucking happen."

I rarely pull the rock star card. This is one time I am glad to do it. Darren scurries off with a nod to do whatever the fuck it is that he does, and I join the band in the green room. I flop on the couch next to Mav.

"That seemed like an intense convo with Darren. Everything alright?" He looks over at me, forehead wrinkled. He knows I usually avoid Darren. I'd tell him, but I don't want someone to overhear, so I shrug. "Talk to me, man."

Mav's eyes are on me as I scan the room. He knows me well enough to know I won't air issues in front of others. I'm upset she didn't tell me sooner. Knowing she's been in pain and hasn't mentioned anything has been playing over and over in my head. He pats my knee and gets up. He says something to Kady, then stands by the door and motions for me to follow.

We walk, him leading, me following. I'm not sure if he knows where he's going or if he's just wandering around until he finds a place that's private.

"Talk to me, man. You've been a headcase all day." I hop up to sit on the counter in this empty room that looks like it's used as some sort of concession area or kitchen. Just like Mav to get right down to business.

"I'm worried about Ari." Mav's my brother and I know I can dump this on him. I need to dump it on someone and get it out of my head.

"What about her?" he asks as he leans against the same counter next to me.

"You know how the fans have been with her." He nods as I talk. "Jax is working on it, but, man, Aiden's told me some of the shit they say to and about her. It has to bother her. She's not a robot. She has feelings. She hasn't taken Gibson anywhere in over a week. I'm worried about them not getting out. What that's doing to them."

"Okay," he says slowly. "This isn't new; it's been going on for weeks. What's different about today?"

"Ari confided in me that because the tour's been extended, she needs to find a doctor in New York or somewhere to give her some nerve block injections for her back. She's mentioned back pain before, but never anything about getting nerve blocks." I pull the rubber band out of my hair and re-do it.

"Mav, man, she's been in pain for almost a week and hasn't said a fucking word. That's what's bothering the fuck out of me."

Mav gives my shoulder a squeeze. "Because you love her." I nod. "Have you told her that?"

"I have, a few times, actually. But she's, I don't know, guarded. I'm pretty sure she loves me too." I sigh. "It bugs the fuck out of me that she's been in pain and hasn't said anything. The whole thing makes me angry with myself. I should have noticed." I sigh.

He squeezes my shoulder again. "You're taking this too personally, man. She's probably not used to having someone to tell, someone who cares."

I relax a little. I can always count on Mav talking me off the ledge. He's probably right.

"Callum! Where the fuck are you?" Sammy's urgent holler is loud and desperate. We hear it at the same time and head for the door.

"Thank fuck!" Sammy's eyes are wide with panic and he's grabbing my shirt. "Come on, it's Gibs. He sliced open his chin." All I hear is Gibs and I'm at a dead run. *Gibson.* As I turn down the long concrete hall that leads to the green room, my son's cries echo down the hallway towards me. This isn't his "I fell and scraped my knee" cry. This is much worse. I run faster than I ever have. The frantic cries of my son are muffled by my heart pounding in my ears.

He's sitting on Ari's lap when I get to the green room. But all I see is blood. She's holding a towel under his chin, but it's covered in red. My son's blood. Suddenly, I feel like I'm going to be sick. "What the fuck happened?"

Kady stands in front of me, hand to my chest. "It looks worse than it is. The medic said facial wounds bleed a lot." She pats my chest a few times, trying to get me to look at her and not that bloody towel.

"He's okay, Callum, but the medic said he probably needs a few stitches in his chin. Jax is bringing a car to the back door. Calm yourself, or you'll upset Gibson more." She's been a mom for two minutes and she's reminding me to stay calm?

When he sees me, he hiccups a few times, then starts crying again. "Daddee!" He's been crying so hard his face is red and shiny from his tears. I scoop him out of Ari's arms and take over holding his towel to his chin.

He rests his head on my shoulder. "Owie."

"I know, buddy. We're going to go have a doctor look at it, okay?" I rub his back and he sniffles and cries a little more. I'm about to turn to Ari when Jax comes in.

"Car's waiting." We follow Jax, and I slip into the backseat. Fuck the car seat. I'm holding him. Ari sits in front with Aiden, and Jax slips in beside me. "The ER's not that far. About ten minutes."

The ride is a blur. I concentrate on the feel of his little warm body against mine and slowing my racing heart. *He's okay.* I kiss his head and he sniffles again. Ari hasn't said a peep since I got into the green room. I'm about to ask her what happened, when Jax announces our arrival at the ER.

Jax and Ari hit the check-in desk, while I follow, carrying Gibson and his chin towel and beloved green blanket. He starts whimpering and by the time we get to the desk, he starts fully crying again. We're immediately escorted to a curtained off area and a nurse starts trying to get vitals on Gibson, who wants nothing to do with her while I sit on the bed with him on my lap.

"Nooo!" He squirms and tries to climb up onto my head.

"She just wants to listen to your heart, buddy. Remember how Dr. Peterson listens to it?" I try to reassure him. The nurse lets him play with her stethoscope and he listens to my heart while she takes his temperature and gets him to lift his chin to show her his wound.

It's the first time I've seen the actual gash. It runs from one side of his chin to the other, and I see layers of skin and shit. Is that bone? I blink hard.

The room slants, and the outer edges of my vision darken. "Fuck. Take him."

The nurse says something about being squeamish. The

next thing I know, Ari's holding Gibson on her lap across the room while something squeezes the fuck out of my arm. Am I lying on the bed I was just sitting on?

"Welcome back, Daddy." The nurse who was trying to get Gibson's vitals pats my shoulder. "I'm taking your blood pressure. You fainted on us." She smiles sympathetically. "I know your first reaction is to sit up, but just lay back for a few minutes. If you sit up too quickly, you might faint again. I'm going to get you some juice. Don't sit up." She sends me a firm look and heads out of the curtained room.

I lay back and close my eyes. Could this day get any worse? Ari's in pain, my son has a fucking gash, and I'm such a fucking wuss that I fainted. I shake my head at myself.

The nurse returns with a juice box for me and one for Gibson, so he didn't feel left out. She insists on helping me sit up slowly, and I don't say anything, but I am glad she did because my head still feels a little off kilter. I suck on my apple juice box as instructed.

As she's leaving, a doctor comes in. "Hi, I'm Dr. Rossini. So, it looks like Gibson here split his chin open and needs some stitches. I'm the on-call board certified plastic surgeon."

She moves over to where Ari holds Gibson on her lap and squats down to his level. "Hi Gibson. I'm Dr. Rossini."

"Seenee." She smiles at his attempt to say her name.

"Close enough, kiddo. Can I see your owie?" He nods and lifts his chin, already proud to show it off. He got that gene from Killian. I immediately look away. "Can you tell me what happened?"

"He tripped over a toy and fell onto the concrete floor. I applied pressure right away. It bled a lot. The medic that looked at it said he needed stitches." Ari's quick to answer since I have no clue.

"Did he lose consciousness?" the doctor asks.

"No. It stunned him for a half a second and he started

crying, then screaming when he saw the blood." I peek over at the doctor, and she is nodding along as Ari is talking.

"Are you comfortable holding him while I stitch his chin? I can have a nurse do it, but it might be easier on him if you or dad hold him." Ari looks over at me for the first time since this whole thing happened, clearly asking for my permission.

"You hold him. I might faint again." This gets a chuckle from the doctor, and I wonder if the nurse told her I fainted once already. Of course, holding a juice box might be a clear indicator.

"The shot to numb his chin will probably cause him the most discomfort. Maybe distract him with something?" Ari starts singing one of the songs from the Octonauts and he mumbles along with her, still content to play with the stethoscope the nurse gave him. He tries to listen to Ari's heart. Then the doctors.

The doctor takes a needle and sticks him under his chin near the wound and his lip quivers, but he doesn't cry full out. "That's the worst part, buddy. I promise. We'll just give that a few minutes to take effect."

Fifteen minutes later, Gibs is the owner of seven teeny stitches in his chin, covered with a bandage to keep it clean. He also gets two Snoopy stickers from the nurse for being brave, which he immediately sticks to his shirt like Ari does with his potty reward stickers. I didn't get a sticker because I fainted.

The nurse gives us care instructions and he'll have to have the stitches removed in a couple of weeks. I pick him up from Ari's lap. She shouldn't be carrying him if her back's bothering her. He weaves his fingers into my hair and lays his head on my shoulder, sighing as I sign his paperwork.

I rub his back as we walk out, not really watching where we are going. That was a mistake, because we're instantly inundated with people as soon as we exit the ER. Somehow, Gibson, Jax, and I are separated from Ari. I can only see the top of her head over the crowd as they inundate us, and I hear the nasty words being hurled at her. "Whore." "Child abuser." "Cunt." "Loser." "Homewrecker." I can see her being pushed around. Someone knocks into me, and I almost lose my grip on Gibson. He whimpers and grasps my neck with a death grip. Fuck.

"Leave me the fuck alone," Ari screeches. I've never heard her cuss or scream before. I need to get to her. I jerk open the door to the SUV and deposit Gibson on his feet into the back, him wailing as I shut him in to protect him while I turn to go get Ari.

"Get in the fucking car, Callum. Now," Jax growls at me as he pushes me back toward the SUV and past me to get to Ari. He pushes a few people out of the way before I duck back into the car. Gibson jumps into my lap.

"What the fuh..dge," I mutter. Gibson looks around frantically, probably for either Ari or his blanket, which she has. The front passenger door opens and Jax shoves Ari in. She holds Gibson's blanket up around her head so the animals that have us surrounded can't see her. Her head's bent forward into the blanket, and I swear I hear her sniffle as Jax gets in beside me.

"Get us the fuck out of here, Aiden," Jax commands from the backseat.

When we pull up at the arena, I have just enough time to carry Gibson into the bus for Ari before I have to be on stage. He flops back onto the bed like a noodle and grabs RuffRuff for a snuggle after I set him down.

I pull Ari into my arms and hug her tight against me. She returns my hug, resting her head right over my heart as she tightens her grip around my waist. I kiss the top of her head. "You okay?"

She nods her head against me. Then she whispers, "I'm sorry."

"For what?" She won't meet my gaze, instead, she keeps her head buried into my chest.

"Gibson got hurt." Her voice is soft and small.

"Did you hurt him?" I know she didn't, but I'm trying to prove a point.

She lets out a small gasp. "No! He was playing—"

I kiss her to stop her. To reassure her. To show her I trust her and love her. I pour it all into the kiss. When I finally pull back, she still looks upset.

"Then there's nothing to be sorry for," I tell her.

"But—"

"He's a kid, Ar. They have accidents. They get hurt. Killian got stitches on his upper arm after jumping off a doghouse and impaling it on this big, gnarly stick when he hit the ground. He was eight. Broke that same arm when he was ten falling off his skateboard trying to jump a fire hydrant. Broke his other arm when he was fifteen jumping off a roof on a dare. Hopefully, Gibson won't be quite that dare devilish or accident prone." I chuckle as I hold her to me tight. "It's not your fault. As much as I'd like to, we can't wrap him in bubble wrap."

She's about to say something, but someone pounds on the bus door. "Come on, Cal! We go on in like, shit, three minutes, man." It's Kill.

"Speak of the devil. I gotta go." I kiss her forehead. She nods and squeezes me one more time, and I squeeze her back before I head out to Killian.

"Gibs good?" He looks back at the bus as we head back towards the arena.

I nod. "Fine. Seven stitches in his chin." My gut gives a slight churn as I envision the gash, the layers of his skin and meat and bone. Shit. I close my eyes, feeling a little woozy again. Like I drank too much when I haven't had a drop all day.

"You okay?" He grabs my shoulder and squeezes it hard, bringing me out of my thoughts. I nod and his gaze on me softens. "You fainted at the hospital." It's a statement, not a question.

"Did Ari tell you?" I glare at him. But I know she didn't. He just knew. No one had to tell him.

"You fainted when I got that stick stuck in my arm." He pauses to look me in the eye. He squeezes my shoulder again.

"You know I feel you too." He's always been more intuitive. I have that twin connection with him too, but Killian feels it more than I do. Or he pays more attention to it maybe. "Don't worry, I won't say anything."

"Mav will find out somehow and never let me live that shit down." He's a fucker like that.

Killian chuckles. "You're probably right, but he won't hear it from me." He slaps my back as we head up the stairs to the stage where the guys are waiting in the dark.

Mav looks at me hard. "Gibs okay? You good?"

I nod. "Let's rock."

Chapter 30

Callum

Two days later, somewhere in Connecticut, Killian and I are entertaining Gibson in a grassy area adjacent to the doctor's office where Ari's getting her nerve block. Jax has us under his watchful eye, with Aiden stationed outside the doctor's office. Oddly enough, there haven't been any paparazzi or fan sightings today and she's been in there for about forty minutes now. I didn't know that getting the nerve block shot required light sedation. The nurse said she'll stay awake, but she'll be very relaxed while they give her the shots.

I've asked Killian to help me with Gibs while I make sure Ari rests and takes care of herself. Surprisingly, he was more than willing.

Aiden texts Jax that Ari is done, so I walk over to the office. She's sitting in the waiting area looking all kinds of out of sorts. "Hey, pretty girl, you ready to go relax at the hotel?" She smiles, but it's not her usual smile. This one is sloppy, like she's drunk.

A nurse comes up. "She's still pretty loopy. I went over these instructions with her, but I'll go over them with you too, just in case." She looks up at me and I nod eagerly, wanting to know exactly what Ari can and can't do.

"She can eat now if she's hungry. Make sure she drinks plenty of water all day. No alcohol today. No driving for twelve hours. No strenuous activity for twenty-four hours. If the injection area hurts, she can ice it for fifteen minutes at a time and take acetaminophen as needed. She can shower tonight if she wants. Take the bandage off before the shower. No need to cover it back over after unless it's bleeding, which it shouldn't. Call us immediately if she develops signs of an infection like fever or any redness or oozing from the injection site." She hands me a paper with all this information on it. Thank God, because she spewed it so fast, I could barely catch it.

"She's had these before, so she probably knows all this, but I appreciate this because I'm a newbie." I wave the paper, and she smiles before leaving.

I help Ari stand and she sways, her smile still sloppy. "You hungry?"

She nods. "I want eggs. Breakfast eggs."

"When my girl wants eggs, she gets eggs. I'm sure Aiden can find us an all-day-breakfast place. Gibson's probably getting hungry too."

We head back to the hotel after eating. Gibs and Ari both seem ready for a nap. I could probably use one too. Such a badass rock star thing to do; take a nap on your day off. Kill takes Gibson into my bedroom of the suite with my iPad, while I settle Ari on the couch with a bottle of water.

"Smuggle with me." She smiles softly at me, not realizing she messed up the word because she's still kind of off from the sedation.

"Gladly." I kick my boots off and slide in next to her. She leans against me, resting her head on my shoulder as we watch some stupid show about people looking for their dream house after winning the lottery or some shit. I'm not paying attention to what's on the TV. It's all about the girl whose warm body is snuggled up against me. I can't believe how much I love her, how well she fits with me and Gibs. She's the first person I want to see when I wake up, when I walk off stage.

It seems too soon to feel this strongly for someone. After Becka left, I swore off women completely. I was so wrapped up in learning to be a fucking dad and balancing giving Gibson what he needed with being a rock star that I didn't have the emotional or physical energy to do anything else. I didn't want to let anyone else in. But Ari's everything we needed and nothing I fucking expected, because who the fuck would have thought I'd fall for my nanny?

Ari's dropped off, head still against my chest, and I'm not far behind her, when someone bangs on the hotel door. Kill shoots out of the bedroom muttering something about a sleeping toddler and I can't help but chuckle at his sudden paternal leanings.

Jax strolls in, taking in the fact that I'm curled up with Ari on the couch. I motion for him to keep it down so Ari can sleep. He squats down next to me.

"Where's your girl's phone?" he whispers.

I nod at the bedroom. "In there, I think. Why?"

"Did she take it with her today?" Jax asks.

"I don't think so." He nods and strolls into Ari's room. He returns minutes later with her phone.

"Unlock code?"

"213112."

"I'm taking this with me." He pockets her phone. "I'll be back after I confirm my suspicions." I'm much too comfortable here with Ari to question him. He leaves. I doze on the couch, snuggled up with Ari for more than an hour, awaking only when I hear Gibson and Killian stirring in the next room. It's my dad superpower. My ears are always tuned into Gibson, even when every other part of me is asleep.

Kill comes padding out of the bedroom with his feet bare, his black hair sticking up at odd angles. He ended up getting sucked into the nap vortex with Gibson. It's easy to do, but not something I'd expect from Killian. He's always stayed as far away from Gibs as possible. Now Mr. Rock star is fresh from a nap with his nephew, complete with a wicked case of bedhead. It warms my heart that my brother is finally taking to my son.

"He's hungry. Do you have those fish crackers he likes?" Kill's voice is a loud whisper.

I nod towards the big bag Ari carries with her almost everywhere that has everything Gibson could ever need in it, usually in triplicate. He nods and rifles through it until he finds a box of the crackers and grabs a bottle of water from the minibar.

"Is it cool if I take him down to the pool after his snack?" he asks. My gut initially clenches at the idea of my son at the pool with someone who isn't me. When he was born, I had nightmares of him falling into my pool. They were so intense that I had a pool net installed so that the pool can be covered in a way that prevents him from drowning. But this is Kill. He'll watch him. It'll be fun for both of them, and good for Kill to get some nephew time. I'm trying everything I can to foster their relationship.

I nod. "Should be a swim diaper in that bag too." Kill goes back to the bag and pulls it out. "Put sunblock on him, please. Make sure you take Aiden or Luke with you. Oh, and you might want to brush your hair before you go downstairs. You have some serious bed head man."

He flips me off as he returns to Gibson. I drift back off with Ari, not even hearing them leave.

I wake up again when Ari begins to stir. She starts by stretching her arms and moves away to stretch her back, wincing a bit.

"Injection site?" I ask, and she nods and reaches behind her to rub the spot. "You want an ice pack? Maybe some acetaminophen?"

She shakes her head. "It only hurts when I stretch. I'm okay. Where's Gibson?"

"Kill took him to the pool about an hour ago. I imagine they'll be back any minute." She nods and I get a text. It's a pic from Kill of Sammy and Gibson in the pool.

Kill: Mav took Gibson with him up to his suite because he wanted to see Brio. Is that cool?

Me: Yeah, I'll get him in a bit.

Me: Thanks for being such a big help with Gibs today.

Kill: I love him.

Me: He loves you too.

Kill: You good tonight? Sammy and I were gonna hit a club.

Me: Golden. Thanks again. Have fun. Remember, no glove, no love.

Kill ends our exchange with the middle finger emoji. I show the texts to Ari, who laughs when she gets to Kill flipping me the electronic bird. I shoot Mav a text, telling him I'll be by in about an hour for Gibson, and he replies immediately with a thumbs up.

"How are you feeling?" I kiss Ari's temple and breath in her orangey scent.

"Pretty good. Sorry I was crappy company."

"I slept almost as much as you did." She shrugs at my comment. "Sleep is healing. I'm just glad I didn't go in with you. I'd have probably fainted again if I had to watch them insert a big needle into your back."

She giggles hard. "I never expected you'd be squeamish, Callum. Here you were, holding your scared, injured son while being the calm, collected parent I've come to expect. Until you saw his chin. I've never seen someone turn so pasty so fast. You mumbled something about taking him, then your eyes rolled back, and you slumped over. Thank goodness the nurse was there to grab Gibson. I guess it was because he's your son?"

"It wasn't the first time." She looks at me quizzically.

"Remember when I told you Killian impaled his arm on that stick? I fainted then too. And when Gibs was born." It's ridiculous that I'm a grown man, but I pass out when things get a little gory. It always knocks me down a peg or two. I let my hair fall in front of my face and shake my head at myself.

"Well, your secret's safe with me." She rubs her foot against my leg. "It's just something I'd never expect."

"Killian knows I passed out at the hospital," I tell her and peek at her to gauge her reaction. I've never shared this part of me with a woman. Not outright.

"You told him?" she asks softly.

I shake my head. She cocks her head slightly as she looks at me to explain. "Because we're twins." I fidget in my seat and clear my throat. "We just know things about each other sometimes."

I don't usually tell people. Sammy and Mav accept it because we've been around each other long enough that they've seen it in action. We don't share it because most people don't understand and ask us to do stupid shit like read each other's minds.

Ari's eyes widen and she sits more upright on the couch. "I remember reading about that in one of my child development classes. About some twin siblings being able to experience each other's emotions. Is that what it's like? Like you feel sad when Killian is sad, kind of thing?"

"Not quite. It's more like we just know some things. Almost like it's happening to an extension of yourself that's not really you." I shrug. "I've never been very good at explaining it. If you're truly interested, talk to Kill. He seems to be more in tune to it or pays more attention to it or whatever."

She continues to rub my leg with her foot. "Interesting. I might talk to him if that doesn't make you uncomfortable."

"Nah, I wouldn't have suggested it if I was uncomfortable with it. It's not something we brag about or share. It's just something between the two of us." Others have asked, but I just usually deny this connection because honestly, it's between me and Kill, and not their business. But I want Ari to know everything about me, because I want to know everything about her. She nods and rubs my arm.

"We should get Gibson soon. Feel okay enough to go out to dinner? The three of us?" She probably doesn't realize how much her face lights up when I mention Gibson. It's one of the reasons I love her.

"I'd love to. Give me a few minutes to change?" I nod and she heads off into her bedroom of the suite. I head to the other bathroom and pull my hair back into a low ponytail and grab a hat. We'll go casual. It's less conspicuous this way. Just as I send Jax and Aiden a group text about us going to dinner, there's a knock on the door and Jax walks in.

"We aren't quite ready yet." He looks at me, puzzled. "Did you get my text about Ari, Gibs, and I going to dinner?"

He shakes his head, and it's then I notice he's holding Ari's cellphone. I'd completely forgotten he had it.

"I found out some shit, man." He grimaces at his own words as I feel my stomach drop. This can't be good. "We need to talk."

"Okay. I'll get Ari." He nods and settles into the sitting area as I get Ari.

"Jax took your phone earlier. I forgot to mention it. I was half asleep when he came. He had some ideas about how the fans keep finding you and Gibson. He's back and wants to talk to us." She nods and follows me out to the sitting area. She sits next to me and grabs my hand, and we both look over at Jax.

"It dawned on me when we were at Ari's appointment today that no fans showed up. This got me wondering what was different about this day compared to others, and it dawned on me that maybe you didn't have your cell phone with you today."

271

Ari nods. "I didn't need it. Callum was there, and so were you and Aiden."

"I started investigating before we even left the appointment. I found a private Facebook group that I was able to join. Someone with an anonymous profile posts your location all the time. That led me to wonder how the anonymous person knew where the fuck you were." We both look at him and he looks away. He doesn't like what he's about to tell us.

"When we met at the busses on the first day of the tour, I installed a tracker app on your phone. It's something I've put on everyone's phone, so if you go missing, I can find you quickly." This is fucking news to me. He is our security, but it's none of his goddamn business where we are. He must know I'm pissed because he shoots me a look that tells me he knows this isn't over.

"There's a second functionality of that software. It can help me track other app activity on the phone it's installed on just in case we need to prove something to law enforcement. I've never used that part of the app before. Using it today, I found something very interesting. Right before each of the posts in the group with your location, the family locator app was activated on your phone, Ari."

She stiffens against me.

"I wasn't doing anything. I swear." Her body's super tense against mine. I rub her back and try to listen to what Jax is saying.

Jax shakes his head. "I know. Someone was using the app to find your location."

That fucker Todd. He better be glad he's on the other side of the fucking United States right now, because all I want is to cause him physical pain.

Ari gasps and then jumps off the couch. "I... that... I mean... is that even legal?" She paces back and forth behind the chair that Jax is sitting in.

Jax shrugs. "It's a gray area and is something addressed in the family plan agreement that you likely signed when you got your phone. You know, in the small print that nobody reads."

There is agony in her eyes when she looks at me. "This is my fault. We were accosted at the fucking hospital, and it was my fault. Gibson could have gotten hurt in all that pushing and shoving. He's heard terrible words because of me."

I've never seen her so pissed off. Her face is red and her fists are balled up at her side. She looks like a murderous firecracker. She snaps her phone up off the table and spikes it into the floor. When that doesn't do much to it, she walks over to the open balcony door and sails it off the balcony as hard and as far as she can.

"I should have known. Always strings. Always!" She wheels around and kicks the chair closest to her with one foot and then the other over and over while tears roll down her face.

Petrified she's going to injure herself, I wrap my arms around her to stop her aggression. "Don't hurt yourself because of him. It's over." She shakes her head, but eventually relaxes in my arms.

"You don't understand," she mutters as she flops onto the couch when I release her.

"I was going to suggest cancelling your service and getting your own plan." Jax stands. "But that works too." Motioning to the balcony where Ari sent her phone flying. "I have a feeling that things should get a lot better now. As long as you don't activate another phone on the same family plan, they shouldn't be able to track where you are going."

I walk Jax to the door. "Get her a new phone with a case and everything. Service in her name but bill the plan to my black card." I say it quietly, so Ari doesn't hear me. He nods and leaves.

"Ready to get Gibs and head out to dinner?" I ask her, where she's still slouched on the couch like a sulking teenager.

She looks up at me. "You're not angry with me? I put your son in danger."

"Not on purpose. You had no idea you were being tracked." I sigh, trying to figure out how to word this. "You love Gibson. You'd never hurt him; it's not in your DNA."

"Let's go. I'm sure he's getting hungry, and Mav's probably ready to have one less kiddo to deal with." The spunky light in her eyes is gone. I take her hand as we walk down the hall to the Slater's suite and find Gibson sitting on the floor with Mav, happily pounding away on the keyboard Mav brings with him everywhere while Kady changes Brio on the nearby bed.

"Cal, you seriously need to get this kid some piano lessons. He's very into it." Mav smiles up at us, proud as Gibson continues to pound away.

"He's not even three yet, man. I'm not signing him up for piano lessons." I scoop Gibson up. "Ready for dinner, buddy?" He nods and reaches out to Ari to be held. "Ari has an owie and can't hold you right now. Let's go eat."

Chapter 31

Arista

After not being allowed to carry or hold Gibson at all today, I'm grumpy and jonesing for some time with my little guy. At least Callum lets me cuddle with Gibson and sing with him until he falls asleep. I love his lavender and Callum-scent that permeates my nose as we lay here. He's been asleep for about ten minutes now but snuggling with him makes me feel better. Because Todd has things stirred up in my head. I'm pissed. Hurt. And then even more pissed.

"I think he's out." Callum's low voice is raspier than normal at the door. He hitches his head toward the sitting area. "I'm not tired yet. Are you?"

I shake my head as I carefully remove myself from the bed Gibson's sleeping in. "The nap left me well rested." I have visions of Callum and me naked in my bedroom as I walk behind him, but he returns to the sitting area that he's rearranged so we can snuggle. There's a gift bag sitting in the middle of the table. I know it's a phone. I shake my head.

"Is that what I think it is?" I nod at the bag.

"Take a peek and see." His eyes have a mischievous glint that I see in Gibson's sometimes.

I pull the paper out of the bag and indeed there is a brand-new phone, complete with a case that's similar to my old one. "Callum, you didn't have to do this. I can't accept this—it's too much."

"I wanted to. Jax has it all set up. Your phone number is even the same, and your contacts have been ported over. The service is on a different carrier and under your name now. I'm paying the bill, since you're my nanny, but it's not part of my plan. Jax probably installed his tracking app, though." His thoughtfulness has tears forming in my eyes.

The plan is in my name, to reassure me. I shake my head, unable to express what that small gesture means to me. "Callum..." I don't know what to say. He knew enough to get me my own plan. He's paying for it, but oddly enough, I'm okay with that. I set it back in the bag.

"You need a phone, especially on tour, but you should have a phone anyway. So you can call your sister and stuff." He's trying to talk me into it. But he doesn't have to. I stand on my toes and plant a kiss on his still moving lips.

"Thank you." I kiss him again and pull him to me. He deepens the kiss and pulls me to him with that gravelly turned-on groan of his, but then pulls away.

"No strenuous activity. Doctor's orders," he states, looking pained. "Let's sit and order a movie and snuggle." I want him so badly, but I know I won't get my way. He's not going to give in. He settles on the chaise part of the couch and pats his lap. Somehow, he's even got popcorn in a bowl that I didn't see before.

I snuggle up between his legs and lean against him as he stretches us out on the couch. He sets the popcorn next to us and flicks through the available movies and lets me choose. I don't really care what we watch. I just like being close to Callum.

"I don't think we can get any closer without taking our clothes off," he moans.

"I offered, but you turned me down." I look up at him behind me with a smile.

"The nurse stressed it when I picked you up." His eyes are that deep blue ocean color I love but are edged with a deep passion.

"Since when are you a rule follower?" I tease and rub my back against his front again, feeling him stiffen against me.

"You're saucy tonight." He leans down and kisses me, and then deepens the kiss until I'm clenching my thighs together and cursing his resolve to be a rule follower.

"Tell me about your back. How bad is it?" His voice has shifted from his impassioned gravel to a concerned tone. It was inevitable that he'd ask.

"I'll probably need surgery eventually, but right now, this works for me. Surgery isn't a guaranteed fix anyway." I turn so I'm sitting across his lap, so I can see his face. "The pain is really not that bad most of the time. Until the shot runs out. There have been a few times where I have a flare up or I couldn't get a shot and the pain was excruciating. It was so bad I could hardly walk. But it hasn't been that bad in a long time. It was getting that way, after the agency dismissed me because I couldn't afford my injections until I sold my car."

"You sold Penny to pay for your injections." He repeats my statement. I'm surprised he even remembers her name since he hated my car so much. He nods his head like he's piecing something together in his mind. I miss my Beetle. I loved that car—she represented my freedom and losing her was like losing part of me. I just hope whoever ends up with her loves her and appreciates her as much as I did.

"Yeah. I couldn't afford to fix it, plus I was in an under the table roommate situation and didn't really have a place to park it."

It's quiet between us, and I have this urge to tell him all about the accident. As in the gritty details that I never share. The things I never talk about. Ever. Not even with Vi. She's asked a few times, but it's always been too much to go there. Too painful. But Callum gives me security and strength I didn't know I had. I want to tell him. I need to tell him.

"It's because of the car accident." I clear my throat. "I was in the car with my parents when the accident happened, the one that killed them." My voice sounds tiny, even to me. I take a deep breath and feel the hitch already. Callum bands an arm around me and hugs me to him tight. I'm not sure if it's because he felt the hitch in my breath or because he somehow senses I'm about to tell him something I don't talk about.

"I snuck out that night. I was grounded because I got a D in math. I really wanted to go to this party. I tried to bargain with my parents to let me go, but they were all about grades, plus I was only 13 and they didn't think the party was something I should go to anyway. I slipped out of my window and walked to my friend's house anyway. She was a year older than me. I was in way over my head at this party. I had never even had alcohol before. We both ended up drunk. I called my parents. They weren't happy, but even though I was drunk or maybe because I was, I sensed that my mom was relieved that I called them instead of trying to get home another way."

I swallow hard, thinking back to arguing over the seatbelt, to when my dad decided to pull away.

"We were four blocks from our house when a car ran a red light and slammed into the driver's side of our car. I wasn't wearing my seatbelt. I was so embarrassed that they took me from the slumber party in front of all my friends, even though I was the one that called them. I got into an argument with my parents and refused to wear it."

"I remember the tumbling. The grinding every time the car contacted the cement. Then everything was eerily quiet and still. It took me a minute to realize I was lying on the ceiling of the car." I take a deep breath to force myself to remember I'm here with Callum and not there in that cramped wreckage. He squeezes my shoulders and I find the strength to continue, even though I don't want to go back there.

"I crawled out my window in the back and then into the front from the passenger side because the driver's side was too damaged to squeeze through. My parents were hanging in their seatbelts at an angle because the car was tipped with the nose up on a utility box. I released my mom's seatbelt and dragged her out through her window opening. I went back in for my dad, but it was hard for me to get his seatbelt to release. He was heavier and I couldn't get my hand in the right spot between him and the center console to be able to push the release button hard enough to get unengaged. But I finally got it. He was heavier than my mom and harder to fit through the window."

"My mom was still breathing. I knew because I could, um..." I screw my eyes shut and can't help the sob that escapes, remembering the wet gurgles that came with each released breath and the gasps each time she took another one in. It was a horrible, gruesome sound. I didn't know it at the time, but I was hearing her last attempts at life. "I could hear it, um, bubble out each time she exhaled. But my dad wasn't breathing, and I couldn't find a pulse, so I started CPR on him. I had just learned it two weeks before when I took the babysitter's certification course from our city. It seemed like I was doing it forever, and it's hard. Even harder than those dummies they use in class. Someone came along and called 911 for me. It was too late. They were both..." I gasp again and Callum hugs me tighter to him, his chin on my shoulder as he rocks me slightly. "Gone by the time the ambulance got there."

He's quiet, and the emptiness, the same aloneness I felt on the road that night, engulfs me. The bustle of the scene. Police,

EMTs, other people who happened upon the accident walking around, talking amongst themselves. I was so alone and so empty, watching as they did their jobs like it was a movie. But it wasn't a movie. My whole life was gone. They didn't have to tell me. I already knew.

The EMT in the back of the ambulance had icy blue-gray eyes and short spiky blonde hair, and she was wearing Batman earrings. Why do I remember her fucking Batman earrings, but I can't remember the sound of my own mom's voice?

"You're so lucky you survived, hon." Lucky? It wasn't lucky to lose my parents because I was selfish and went somewhere I wasn't supposed to. It wasn't lucky at all. I shake my head slightly. Nope, not lucky.

"They think I hurt my back when the car was rolling since I didn't have a seatbelt on. I've had problems since then."

I swallow hard as memories I've worked years to quell try to come flooding back.

"Fuck, Ari," Callum blows out next to my ear in a whisper. "I'm so sorry that happened to you." He pulls me tight against him as he continues to rock us, reminding me I am here with him and not back there on the road.

His warmth envelopes me, reassures me, the leathery, spicy smell that is uniquely Callum replacing the smell of rubber and oil and carnage. I focus on his comfort and love, on being here with him. Not on the last gurgling sounds of my mom's life. Or of the feel of pressing down repeatedly on my dad's chest with all my weight, willing his heart to start beating again. Not on the heartbreak of that night, or the breaking of the rest of me that came later.

I shift on Callum's lap so that I face him and lean in to kiss him. I need to connect with him somehow and if this is the only way he'll let me today, then I will take his comfort however he'll give it to me. His warm lips softly find mine, tentatively at first, but the kiss grows stronger and more affirming than ever.

Our tongues tangle in a dance that reassures me that I am here, and he loves me. No, that he cherishes me. When we break for air, he presses his forehead to mine as we gasp for breath.

"I've never talked about it before. Not even with Vi," I whisper between us.

"Why not?" He can't hide the surprise in his voice at my confession.

I pull away. "If she knew that I snuck out? She'd blame me, and I needed her. I didn't want the social worker to put me in a group home. Vi was all I had left. They were her parents too, so how could she not blame me? We wouldn't have been in the accident if I had stayed home like I was supposed to." Keeping the horrors of that night to myself was my own secret punishment.

His jaw muscle tics as he clenches his teeth but says nothing. Maybe I shouldn't have said anything. Maybe my selfishness back then has made him reconsider us. *Us.*

He rests his chin on my shoulder. He's tender and loving. Not mad or disgusted like I thought he'd be. It's here in this tiny moment, in this small show of support and comfort, that I feel the urge to tell Callum more. Tell him the rest. Let him see all the broken, smashed pieces of me, so maybe he can help glue me back together.

But I just can't make my mouth say the things I've locked away, the ones I can't tell anyone. So, for now, I allow myself to take all the comfort he gives me as he holds me to him. I listen to his heartbeat steady in his chest, a calming, soothing rhythm that lulls me to sleep.

R

I sit upright, gasping for breath. "Woah, Ari?" a sleepy, rasp of a whisper asks while a hand squeezes my thigh. "You okay?" I can't catch my breath. I can't figure out where I am. It's so dark in here. It takes a few seconds for my eyes to adjust to the dark. Familiar things come into sight. A suitcase, not mine, in the corner of the room. The time in red from the bedside table tells me it's 3:37 am. Callum sits up next to me and wraps a tentative arm around me as I finally catch my breath.

"Bad dream?" His sleepy words are hushed. On the bed next to ours is the lump made by his sleeping son. He rubs small circles in the middle of my back, near the site where I got my injection yesterday.

I nod and scoot away from him. I can't handle the comfort and touching right now. I stumble from the bed into the attached bathroom, closing the door behind me. I turn the light on. Closing my eyes, I splash cold water on my face. As I lean down, I'm struck again with the vision of Todd undoing his belt. I shake my head. *Not here. He's not here.* I gasp and stumble against the shower, knocking into the glass.

There's a soft rap, and the door opens a crack. "Ar? You okay, babe?" Callum's face is a combination of concern and confusion as he slips into the bathroom with me. I pat dry my face, giving myself a few seconds. As I set down the towel, he pulls me to him. His scent comforts me, as does the feel of his arms around me.

I need to tell Callum. I can't deal with this secret anymore. I can't take the dreams when they come, or the shame that burns through me. I should have just told him last night. He has the right to know before this goes any farther between us. When I tell him, when he finds out what I've done, this will change our relationship.

I take one more deep breath of Callum, just in case it's my last one, then look up at him. "I need to talk."

He squeezes me tight and nods. Leading me out to the sitting room, he relaxes back on the chaise we were in just hours ago and holds his arms open for me to take my place nestled between his legs like earlier.

Wrapping his arms around me, he helps me settle between his legs and kisses my temple softly, leaving his lips there. "What's on your mind? Is it about the dream?" he whispers into my temple.

I take a deep breath and it rattles within me as I release it. "Remember when we were talking earlier, and I told you about the accident and that I'd never told Vi?" He nods against me. "There's something else I haven't told anyone. I have to tell you because it's not right that you don't know. It's, um, it's even harder to talk about."

My stomach clenches tight, and I'm suddenly both light-headed and nauseous. Callum kneads firmly at the tight knots between my neck and shoulders, leaving little kisses in the wake of his massages.

"You don't have to," he says quietly in my ear. "We can talk about it later, if that's easier."

Maybe this is a bad idea. Maybe talking about it won't make it easier. Maybe saying the words will only change things between Callum and me for the worst. What if Todd finds out I told and hurts Vi?

"I, um." I look down at my lap, and Callum's hands move down. He envelops me in a hug from behind, pulling me against him hard and tight.

He's trying to support me, to comfort me, but I don't deserve it. How the hell do you give something a voice when you've buried it so deep, you'd hoped it could never be found? When you've been so ashamed you can't look your own sister in the eye?

"Um." My eyes burn with tears as I look out the dark window, imagining the world going on out there, none the wiser of the guilt I'm about to purge myself of.

"I've messed around with Todd." My head hangs from my shoulders as I release the words on a quick out breath. It's out there now and I can't take it back.

An advantage, or maybe it's a disadvantage, of this position is that I can't see Callum's face. Is there disappointment? Disgust? Is he repelled that I've had relations with my brother-in-law?

His body tenses around me, yet he doesn't disengage from our intimate position. He takes a few measured breaths, while my own are shallow as I wait for him to say something. Anything. *Please don't be done with me.* I blink hard with the realization that my secret is now out as hot tears make their way down my face.

"What do you mean by 'messed around', Ar?" His words are quiet and slightly wavering. But they're also unexpectedly comforting despite my confession implying that I'm a whore who betrayed the only family she has left.

"Does it matter? He's married to my sister. I'm the other woman in my own sister's marriage. I betrayed the one person left on earth who loves me. What kind of person does that? What kind of monster am I?" I try to pull out of Callum's grip with my sob, but his arm is like the bar on an amusement park ride, so I'm forced to cry in his arms.

Instead of letting me go or cursing me, he pulls me tighter into him and rests his chin on my shoulder like he did last night. This morning. Whenever that was.

"When did it start? When did it stop? Has it stopped?"

The only sound is my ragged breaths as I try to keep from completely breaking down. "You don't want to know. Trust me," I whisper. *No one loves a whore like you, Arista. That's exactly what you are. You're the other woman in your own sister's life.*

I cover my face in my hands and sob while Callum continues to hold me to him.

"I love you, Ar," he murmurs quietly, then presses a long kiss to my temple, keeping his lips there. "You can tell me anything."

"Two weeks after I moved in with them." His jaw tenses

next to my ear at my words. I should stop, but he needs to hear it all and I need to get it all out. I can't stop it from spilling out.

"It stopped when I moved into the dorms for college. He tried a few times when I'd come home during breaks, so I stopped going home for them. That's when he started threatening me, threatening to hurt Vi if I told anyone. When I went back to my sister's to sell Penny, I got there early to clean her up. I didn't think he'd be there. He cornered me and asked me if I was there to pay him rent, *that way*, then proceeded to remind me how it was all my fault. That I made him do these things to me and that Vi would be disgusted with me. And that if I told anyone, she'd never want to see me again."

Chapter 32

Callum

I'm so fucking angry I don't know what to do with the white-hot rage that hums through me. I need to move around to dispel it, but Ari needs me to hold her, so I keep my arms tight around her. I want to pick up my guitar and chuck it through the television. I want to turn shit over and break shit. I need the destruction under my fingertips, to get the satisfaction from breaking something. Because there is so much rage in me, I need to fucking do something with it.

What I want to do most is find that fucker Todd and break his fucking face with my bare fist. Then beat him some more for taking advantage of a grieving kid and twisting his role in her life. Then maybe deal out a few kicks to his ribs while he's down just for the hell of it.

My jaw is clenched so fucking tight that my molars might actually crack. But I have to stow this shit away, get it under control for Ari. I take a deep breath to try to loosen myself. There are more important things right now. Namely, Ari. I don't want her thinking the tension winding me up has anything to do with her and what she's just confessed.

Why she equates what that fucker did *to her* as *a betrayal on her* part and not as the fucking abuse it really was is beyond me. Todd told me as much at the go-kart track! I didn't pick up on it. I wish I'd beaten his ass when I had the chance. I should have known then. Fuck, part of me *did* know then. But it didn't soften the blow to my heart, hearing it directly from her.

Ar's body hitches against me with huge sobs as she releases some of what's been bottled up inside her. I move her so she's cradled on my lap instead of between my legs. I press my lips to her temple and just hold her gathered up against my chest. As much as I need to fix this for her, I can't. Instead, I hold her tight and hope I give her a semblance of peace and comfort, of security. I whisper occasionally that I love her. But mostly I just hold her.

Her sobs eventually subside into occasional hitches.

"Ar—" I have an overwhelming need to tell her things, but I don't know how much she can handle right now. She's just expunged a huge anchor weighing down her soul. She tips her head up to me, her eyes red and puffy with tears, but she's still my beautiful girl. I kiss her forehead.

"I love you. What you just shared, that has no effect on my love for you. It's something that happened *to you*, but *it isn't who or what you are*. You prove that every day with every breath you take." I lock eyes with hers, wanting her to see how much this is true to me. Her eyes widen slightly and her lips part.

"But—" she starts, but I interrupt her.

"Nothing you can tell me will change my mind. I love *you*." Her eyes well with tears again. "The only thing it changes is that I wish I had kicked Todd's ass at the go-kart track when I had the chance. The things he said about you, the way he said them, I should have known what was going on. I should have put him in the hospital then."

"But I need you to listen because this is the important part. It might be hard to believe, but what happened to you?" I blow

287

out a breath. "Fuck, Ar, that is *not* your fault. That's not 'messing around with Todd.' That was straight-up abuse, baby."

There's an argument on the tip of her tongue. I can see it as she opens her mouth slightly, but I continue before she has time to give it voice.

"I don't need the specifics to know that you were a kid and what he did was wrong, so fucking wrong. The fact that you were an injured, grieving teenager, makes it even more despicable. You didn't betray anyone. You didn't cause someone to cheat, just like you didn't cause the accident by sneaking out."

She just stares at me, eyes wide, like she's trying to process my words. I rub my hand up and down her arms soothingly. Why this came out now, who the fuck knows. But I am glad it did, if only so I can help her shoulder the burden of these heavy secrets that have been weighing her down, so she doesn't feel so damn alone. No one would even guess the shit she's endured. You can't tell by looking at her, by talking to her, that she's had this secret so long.

"One more thing." I lay a soft kiss on her forehead. "You need to talk to your sister."

"No." Her response is quick and defensive.

"I'm not saying it has to be today or even tomorrow. She loves you, Ar, and she needs to know all of it. The accident. The stuff with Todd. Especially the stuff with Todd." Her head continues to shake. "I'll help. I'll go with you and hold your hand while you do it, but you need to talk to her."

"No, no, no, I can't." She mutters it quietly and puts her hands over her ears like a child. It's too much for her, so I don't push, not yet. But Vi needs to know what kind of person she married.

I pull her to me tight and remove her hands from her ears. "We'll talk about that part another day, another time. Okay?"

She nods hesitantly, then relaxes against me. She's completely spent from the emotions she finally let out.

"Let's go back to bed." I pick her up and carry her to the empty bed, setting her down gently. I turn around and cover Gibson over on his bed, but then I slide in with Ari, her back to my front. She drops off quickly, exhausted from unburdening herself from secrets she's held onto for way too long.

When I'm sure she's out, I grab my phone from the nightstand and send a group text to the guys. I also loop in Darren and Jeff.

Me: Shit came up. Need tomorrow off. I'll be there for the show but count me out for the media shit and whatever else is going on. Turning my phone OFF.

I'll catch hell for it tomorrow, especially from Darren. Jeff knows I wouldn't blow stuff off for no reason. Before I can power down a flurry of texts start coming in from Kill.

Kill: Gibs Ok?

Kill: Ari Ok?

Kill: You?

Me: Gibs is fine. Ari will be okay. Me? I'll be right as rain after I beat the fuck out of Todd.

Chapter 33

Arista

I t's been nearly a week since I confessed everything to Callum in the middle of the night in Connecticut. On the one hand, I feel lighter having someone that knows my secrets. On the other, I'm waiting for Callum to use my confessions against me. He hasn't given me any indication that he would, and I'm starting to realize that the expectation is a response that Todd conditioned into me.

I expected Callum to treat me different. But he doesn't. He still looks at me the same, touches me the same. He even kisses me the same. If he's repulsed or disgusted by me or worried for Gibson, he hasn't indicated it. So, I try hard not to let that expectation ruin what I already have.

I've never been to New York, and it's exactly like I expected, but also more. It's tall, the sidewalks are crazy busy, and there is just an energetic buzz that seems to run through it, like the whole city runs on massive amounts of caffeine. Oh, and there is always this underlying funky odor outside.

Tomorrow the guys have a show, then an off day, then we go upstate and do another show. We'll pile back onto the buses and head up to Vermont and then Maine. Then it's off to start the extension of the tour by swinging back through some of the southern states until we are back in California for four shows, the last one ending back home in LA.

Callum's thumb strokes the top of my hand in his lap as we sit on a bench watching Gibson dig in the sand with his little dump truck at one of the many playgrounds here in Central Park. It's a simple but comforting gesture on his part. It's not a conscious action, though. He does it while he stares across the park. I wonder what's got him so deep in thought, and my stomach clenches at the thought it might be me he's thinking so deeply about.

I'm about to ask when Gibson jumps up and runs to us. "Potty, Awee! Potty!"

"I got it." Callum swoops him up with his diaperbag and heads to the nearby restroom while I sit on the bench and wait. I bet it's another sticker day. He's having more and more sticker days. I start digging through my purse just in case he earned another sticker. Out of nowhere, a woman approaches and sits next to me on the bench.

"Hi," she says, but doesn't look at me. She faces the park.

"Hi." I pay her no mind and continue to dig through my purse.

"Your son is adorable." I look up at her. She has chin length brown hair and, even dressed as conservatively as she is in her brown sweater and tight jeans, I can tell she has legs for days. The kind I would kill to have. She doesn't seem to be a nanny or even a parent, as she doesn't have the large bag filled with anything and everything a child in a park would need like I do.

"Oh, thank you. I'm not his mom, I'm his nanny, but I agree. He *is* adorable." I smile at her. "Do you have children?"

"Oh yes, over there." She motions to a group of children playing on the climbing dome. "Oliver is six." I glance at the group of children, but none of them appear to be that old. I look back at her and she's staring at me with this weird expression that I can't place. It's almost vacant, with a hint of jealousy.

I smile at her despite the fact she gives me the willies and I hope that Callum comes back soon. "I'm sorry, what did you say your name was?" I ask.

"I didn't. I gotta go." She walks off quickly in the opposite direction of the group of children where her child is supposedly playing.

From the corner of my eye, I see Callum on his way back from the restroom, Gibs on his hip. "Sticka! Sticka pease." Gibson does a little dance waiting for me to produce the sticker sheets I carry in his bag of tricks. He especially likes to find Sammy or Killian on a sticker day because they usually give him a piece of candy if he has a sticker on him.

"It's a two-sticker day," Callum tells me as he rejoins me on the bench.

"Two stickers, Gibson?" I ask him and he nods. "Way to go, buddy! High five!" I hold my hand out and he slaps it.

"Tomorrow is going to be crazy busy for me. We are booked with all kinds of media appearances all over the city before the show." Callum sighs. "I'm glad we have today to just kick it together."

"Don't worry about us. I am going to bring Gibson back here and take him to the petting zoo and maybe do that carousel again. And I read that there is a puppet show going on too. I bet he'll like that. Although maybe not, when I was little puppets always scared me." I glance at Callum, and he's amused at my confession about puppets. "This place is so big. There will be plenty for us to do."

Callum grins at me. "I love seeing the city through your eyes, Ari." He pulls me to him. "I'm really looking forward to our date tonight." He kisses the side of my head. "Speaking of, we should get going. We'll grab lunch and then you need to go shopping. We'll come with you."

"I need to go shopping?" I narrow my eyes at Callum. "Why?"

"You need a fancy dress for tonight." His eyes sparkle mischievously. "And probably shoes to go with the dress." He shrugs. "Don't worry, Gibs and I will make sure it's appropriate." He chuckles at my expression.

"Why wouldn't I get something appropriate?" Is he serious?

"Because that sounded a lot less creepy than I really want to see you in your skivvies in the dressing room." His eyes sparkle as they scan my body while he mentally undresses me.

"Skivvies? Who says skivvies anymore?" I giggle at his wording.

He shrugs, and his eyes return to mine. "I am a lot older than you are."

I can't help the snort that flies out of my mouth at the absurd comment. "You are not. Six years is not that much, Callum." He blows out a slow breath and looks over at me and shrugs. "You act much older than you are."

"Someone has to be the responsible one in the band."

R

RUNNING my hand down the smooth copper colored fabric, I look at myself in the mirror in the second bedroom of our suite in New York. Most nights, we end up together in bed now. Sometimes, all three of us, especially on the nights of Callum's shows. He'll slip into bed, and we'll just wake up together to Gibson. It's comfortable, even if I have to take Gibson out of the room so Callum can actually get some sleep because he's joined us just a few hours before his son wakes up for the day. But for tonight, Gibson is with Kady and Mav, and I'm getting ready in my own bedroom of our suite because Callum wanted to be able to have a door to knock on.

I have no idea where we are going. Just that I needed a

dress. Shopping with Callum and Gibson was fun. I modeled a few dresses, but I knew that this was the one the minute I saw it. I love the coppery color and the cool feel of the fabric. He insisted on paying for the dress and shoes. But I drew the line at the perfect little purse that I had to have to complete the ensemble. I even put on a little makeup for tonight. Kady came over earlier and helped me put these luscious loose curls in my blonde hair. How she did it, I have no idea. My hair has a slight wave naturally, but nothing like this. She knows hair.

The quiet knock on my bedroom door sets my stomach fluttering with butterflies, even though I know it's Callum. This feels different somehow. I take a nervous breath and open the door.

Callum stands in front of me holding a small bouquet of white daisies. His long, dark brown hair is down, a surprise since he almost always pulls it back when we go out. I love it down, though. It makes me want to run my fingers through it. Gone are his usual jeans or leather pants and shirt. Instead, he wears a dark gray fitted suit jacket with a metallic leathery look to it. I have to hold back from reaching out to caress the fabric between my fingers. The tie matches the dark filigree pattern on his silver waistcoat. His fitted suit pants are tight in all the right places. He looks amazing, yet still very rock-n-roll. He's rebellion personified.

He holds out the daisies to me, looking so much like a little boy that my heart squeezes. I take them. "Thank you, they're beautiful." I add some water to a glass from the wet bar and put the daisies in the glass.

"You look stunning, Ari." He holds his hand out. I take it, and he spins me slowly to take in the full effect of me all dressed up. He lets out a low whistle. "So fucking sexy." His tongue wets his bottom lip, and his eyes darken as his pupils dilate.

"You clean up well yourself, Callum." He offers me his arm

and we head down to the lobby. We turn heads as we walk through because he looks hot, so hot. I can't help the smile on my face knowing that he's mine. We slide into a waiting car.

He continues to hold my hand, his thumb gently rubbing the back of it as he nuzzles my neck, his slight stubble scraping my neck and only adding to my desire for him. "You always smell so good," he whispers with a groan in my ear before gently kissing directly behind it.

I cross my legs and clench them, part of me wishing we were heading back to the hotel and not out for our date.

We finally arrive at our destination, and our driver opens our door. Callum exits first, holding his hand out to me. We are near the water's edge, and he walks me to a cute restaurant front for The River Café.

We're taken right to a corner table along the bank of windows that face the river. The lights are twinkling along the darkened river and my heart skips a beat that he brought me here. The view, the ambiance, are both amazing. This has to be the best table in the restaurant, and even if it isn't, it's still the best because Callum's with me. He holds my chair out when we reach our table.

"Callum, the view! It's amazing." I gaze out the windows after I sit.

"Stunning." I glance up at the gravel in his voice and he's looking at me and not out the window. My cheeks heat slightly, but it feels good to be the object of his attention.

I need to touch him. Reaching across the table, I take his hand and he smiles softly, looking at our hands clasped on the table. We order our food. He holds my hand the whole time. We talk quietly about the shows coming up, about Gibson, about the song he's been writing with Mav. But mostly, I concentrate on the feel of his hand interlaced with mine and this closeness I feel with him. There's an intensity when he looks at me, I feel it all the way to my heart. He finds excuses to touch me through the whole meal. It's all brushes of his hand here or his leg there. He's everywhere and everything. And I wonder briefly what he has planned for after dinner, because I want him for dessert.

At some point, the bill comes, and Callum pays it. I didn't even notice until he's handing the billfold to our waiter and thanking him.

"Ready, beautiful? Our car is waiting." He holds his hand out to me and we walk back out to the car, holding hands.

When we're both inside the limo, Callum pulls me against him, exactly where I want to be. I don't pay attention to where we are going, I don't really care, although part of me hopes we are heading back to the hotel. He lays a line of light, sweet kisses down my jaw, down my neck to my shoulder.

His voice is a low gravel next to my ear. "You're so amazing." His hand caresses my upper thigh in light circles before he pulls me onto his lap.

I want to run my fingers over his defined chest and back and feel his warmth. But his suit coat, waistcoat, and shirt thwart me. Instead, I weave my fingers into the hair at the back of his neck and pull his face closer to mine. His lips smile against mine briefly before returning my kiss, lips warm against mine. His tongue swipes gently over my lips and I part them, and our tongues dance together. He releases a low rumble into my mouth that makes me want to strip him down right here in the back of the limo. I press against him, getting as close as possible as our kisses deepen and intensify. Nothing exists except for Callum.

A knock and a clearing of the throat from the driver as the partition glass comes down separates us, and the driver speaks. "Mr. Donogue? We are about to arrive, sir."

Callum pulls away slightly. "Thank you, Gary."

His deep blue eyes sparkle as he looks at me. "We're here." He grins at me. "Ready?"

Having no idea where here is or what we are about to do, I nod and bite my bottom lip.

He chuckles. "Don't worry. More of that later." He winks. "Much more."

The door to the limo swings open. Callum helps me out of the limo and onto the sidewalk. I look up at the Empire State Building. I've only seen it before in pictures and movies.

He chuckles at whatever my awed expression looks like. "Come on." He pulls me closer to him and we walk in holding hands and go directly to the elevator. He pulls out a card and hands it to the attendant.

"We've been expecting you, Mr. Donogue." We ride the elevator up to the 86th floor. It doesn't take as long as you would think to get to the 86th floor, that's for sure. We walk onto the observation deck and the attendant directs us to a second elevator.

Callum flashes his magic card again, and we are taken up to the 102nd floor observation deck. It's glassed in and the view is both stunning and incredibly scary. I immediately freeze. We are really high up. I fight the urge to sit down, as if being closer to the floor will make it seem that much less high and I'll be less frightened. My heart races. I squeeze his hand, afraid to move.

He stops when he realizes I'm frozen in my spot in the middle of the room.

"I didn't know you were afraid of heights, Ar," he says quietly and comes back to where I am.

"Me neither," I gasp, slightly dizzy as I try to rationalize that I'm not going to fall, despite what my head keeps trying to tell me.

He chuckles softly and hugs me to him from behind as we look out the windows from where we stand in the middle of the room. There are just a few people up here, and no one seems to be paying any attention to us. Whether it's because that is just how New Yorkers are or because no one recognizes Callum here, I'm not sure. It's late, so maybe no one expects a rock star dressed to the nines at the Empire State Building.

"Do you want to go?" His voice is quiet in my ear as he rests his chin on my shoulder.

I shake my head. "No! Just give me a minute. I think I'll be okay." I breathe out slowly, trying to calm myself. With his arms wrapped around me, I start to relax a little.

"You have all my minutes, Ari." His voice is so quiet I almost don't hear him. My heart races. *All his minutes*. We stand together like this, taking in the night from the middle of the room.

After acclimating to being so far above ground, I take a half step away from him. "I'm okay now. I want to go see. But slowly."

He holds my hand and lets me be in control of how close we get to the windows. I edge closer slowly, taking a few minutes to stop and get accustomed to being where we are before I take a step farther, but try not to draw attention to us either. We do this until we are right up at the window. The view is stunning with all the lights flickering. Being up here is still kind of scary, but I'm almost glad it's dark because it makes the height a little less in your face.

"So pretty," I murmur.

"Yeah, you are." His voice is warm on my ear. I knew he was close, but not that close. When I turn my head to look up at him, he kisses me. This one isn't the fiery, needy kisses like we shared in the limo. This one is soft and slow and has meaning and feeling. It's not lusty need. It's even more than love. It's filled with deep connection, longing, and trust.

He pulls away first and stares at me with that twinkle in his blue eye. "Come on." He puts a hand on my back, and we walk over to a non-descript door, the kind you don't notice until you're walking through it. He shows the attendant standing at the door his card and the man opens the door. "Watch your step Mr. Donogue. Ma'am." The man tips his head at me as I follow Callum.

It's a dimly lit work room, with cabling running over plain concrete walls. There's a steep black attic staircase on one side.

"Go slow, it's steep." I climb the staircase slowly, with Callum right behind me, and step up onto an open-air balcony. I freeze up again. There isn't anything here but a short cement wall. What if we fall off?

Callum joins me just outside the doorway and like he did below on the glassed-in observation deck, he hugs me to him, my back to his front. "Breathe Ari," he reminds me softly, and I release the breath I've been holding. It's slightly chilly up here, but it feels refreshing.

"Give me another minute. I'll be okay." Even though I can't see his face as it's next to mine, I can almost feel his smile.

"I told you, all my minutes are yours, Ari. Every. Single. One." He kisses my temple and just like downstairs, I start to relax into being this high up out here with just a small retaining wall between us and certain death. Especially with his arms around me.

"I'm okay now." He loosens his arms from around me, and I step closer to the edge. "You didn't bring me up here to throw me over the edge, did you?" I look over at him. I'm kidding, but he obviously doesn't realize that, judging by the horror on his face.

"No! I thought—" he starts, panicked.

"I'm kidding, Callum." I rest my hand on his chest. "I know you'd never do that." He visibly relaxes.

"I didn't think that you might be afraid of heights," he says, hands shoved into the pockets of his gray pants.

"It's never been an issue before. But then again, I don't know that I've ever been this high up before. Well, except for the plane, but that's different." I shrug.

He closes the distance between us and pulls me to him again. I can't get enough contact with him.

"Not everyone can come up here, I take it?" I look up at him.

He shakes his head slightly. "It's heavily restricted. But I know some people who know some people." He shrugs. "I just wanted a romantic, real date. Just us." He looks out over the city's sparkling lights. "I'm trying to show you how important you are. How much I love *you*, Ar." His blue eyes are watching me with an intensity that causes me to go all warm and gooey on the inside. He does this to me a lot lately, reduces me to a warm and gooey girl.

Somehow, the stressed-out single dad from earlier in the year has challenged everything about love that I thought I knew. He's stripped me, crumbled my walls and now stands beside me. Letting him in, being that vulnerable with him, is scary. It's as if I'm exposed and naked for the world to see. He knows the things about me that I've never spoken out loud to anyone but him. Not even to my sister, especially not my sister. He *knows* and loves me *as I am* anyway. I rub my hand on the side of his face, the start of his stubble lightly scratching my palm.

"It's working. I know you love me." I squeeze him hard around the middle and he smiles. "Thank you for bringing me up here. It's beautiful and peaceful and a little scary. I'm so glad we're up here together."

He leans down and touches the tip of my nose with his. "Me too."

We watch beneath us as lights flicker on and off, adding to the sparkling quality of the city. He removes his suit jacket and pulls it around my shoulders. It smells like leather and spice, like Callum, like I'm home. Enjoying being surrounded by him, I slip my arms into his suit jacket. He chuckles because it swims on my frame.

"As much as I love looking at you out here, I'm dying to be

with you, in you, Ari." Callum's gravelly voice cracks. He lays a hand on the small of my back and guides me to the door with the stairs. "I'll go first." He quickly descends the steep metal stairs and stands at the bottom to assist me. As soon as he can, he wraps his hands around my waist and lifts me off the step and onto the floor like I weigh nothing. At the bottom, he leans in and kisses me. "So sexy, especially in my jacket."

In the limo, I lean into him. His arm pulls me into him, and I revel in how I fit perfectly like a missing puzzle piece. Our hands are clasped on his lap, his rough and callused, mine soft and smooth. I lay my head on his shoulder.

"You're not getting too sleepy, are you?" His voice is quiet. "I'm not quite done with you yet."

I shake my head. "Just thinking."

"Good things, I hope." He kisses my temple.

"The best things." I snuggle into him and sigh as he wraps me to him tightly.

When we arrive back at the hotel, there are some fans waiting outside when we step out of the limo. I am surprised they are still here, considering how late it is, but I guess some fans will do anything to get a glimpse of the guys. Callum pulls me into his side and smiles brightly for the fans. "Not tonight, ladies." We stroll through the lobby holding hands, me still wearing his jacket.

Chapter 34

Callum

She's so fucking adorable wearing my suit jacket. In the elevator to our suite, she leans against the back wall, grinning up at me from my too-big-for-her jacket. I have a feeling she might not give it back, and that's okay with me, even if it is my favorite fucking suit. She swims in it, which just adds to the adorableness, and she grins while holding her chin up high, as if wearing my suit jacket is akin to wearing a ring, like it's something she's proud of. *Shit. A ring.* I really need to think about getting her one of those soon. Because that's coming. I need her to know I'm fucking serious about her, that she's mine and I want the world to know it.

"I love that you're so comfortable in my clothes." She smiles when I say it, her eyes sparkling like green-brown gems.

"It smells good." She shrugs as if it's no big deal.

"Oh yeah?" I look at her. Smells good? What a little weirdo.

Her cheeks tinge pink. "It smells like you." She nestles into the way-too-big jacket as she says it, as if she's reveling in the scent.

It's so damn sexy I can't help the growl that escapes me, which causes a light giggle to bubble out of her just as the doors open to our floor. I grab her hand and walk her quickly to our suite. No passing go. No peeking in on Gibson.

I swipe the keycard and pull her into the room and immediately trap her against the door. My lips graze her jawline, leaving nips and kisses along the way. She arches her back and presses against me. One hand on my chest, she stops me, only to take my hand with her other and pull me into the bedroom of our suite. At the bed, her hands immediately start undoing my suit pants while I slip my jacket off her shoulders. I then take off my waistcoat and dress shirt.

Her fingers are urgently fumbling with the fly of my suit pants. "Where's the fire, sweetheart?"

"Between my legs." She's breathy and flustered as she continues to work on my fly, and I can't help my chuckle at her desperate answer.

"I got you." I put my hands over hers and move them up to my chest while I rid myself of my pants and underwear.

"Lift your arms for me," I growl, and she does. I pull her dress over her head and toss it gently onto the chair. She's so stunning standing in front of me in just her bra and panties. She bites her lip and her skin flushes pink as I drink her in. I've seen her before, but she's something to behold each and every time.

"You're so damn beautiful." Her chin lifts slightly with my words as she throws her shoulders back. I grip her hips as I pull her into me. She snakes her arms around me. One hand comes to rest on the back of my head and the other bands across my back as she lifts to kiss me again. I walk her to the bed behind her. She sits and scoots up the bed and I crawl up until I'm hovering over her. I lean in and kiss her again. I can't get enough of her kisses. They start off soft and sensual, but then turn urgent and fiery. She's got both hands around my neck and is leaning up to meet me as I hold myself up with one hand and work her bra off with the other. Kissing my way down her neck and chest, I plant a kiss between her breasts, and she releases my neck and returns to the bed.

When I lean down and suck in a nipple, her hips rise up off the bed.

"Callum, please." The way she moans my name makes me want her even more. I work a finger into the band of her underwear and work them down her leg and she flips them off with a flick of her foot.

I reach over to the condoms I put on the nightstand, hoping this is where we'd end up tonight. She grips my arm. "I'm on the pill. I trust you."

"I'm clean. I swear. I—"

"I trust you." Her hazel eyes lock with mine and there is no doubt in her kaleidoscope eyes. She trusts me, with all of her, and if that's not a revelation, I don't know what is. She trusts me with all of her. All of her. Even the fragile pieces she lets no one else see.

I kiss her again, and she pulls me to her. Sliding in feels even more intense with her than before. It's always heavenly with her. But this is it. There is nothing but us, nothing but our bodies sliding against each other and her sexy as fuck little moans egging me on.

"Callum." She draws out the last syllable in my name like she does when she's close like this, as she clenches around me.

I pull her up to me as she cries out, and soon I'm following her with my own release.

I roll to my side, so I don't crush her with my weight because I am spent. As we catch our breaths, she curls into me.

"Thank you." Her voice is breathy.

"Thank you?" I lift an eyebrow. "I don't think anyone's ever thanked me for sex before."

"Not for sex. Although... yeah, that was good. For today, tonight. For it all." She presses her soft lips against my jaw. "I love you. And I love you showing me you love me."

And just like that, she takes my breath away, and I'm grateful for the darkness in the room because my eyes tear up. I was confident of my standing in Ari's life before and didn't think I needed to hear her say the words she's been hesitant to say, until she actually said them. It's like both sides of my heart start beating in unison, one side for her and the other for Gibson.

Chapter 35

Arista

Gibson loves the carousel in Central Park. We ride it three times throughout the course of the day. I text Callum pictures of him sitting on a different horse each time. We might ride it one more time before we leave. I've always thought puppets were creepy and apparently Gibson doesn't care for them either, so we ditched the puppets for extra time in the petting zoo.

He loves playing in the sand and has settled into a digging session with another child about his age. I love watching him because he doesn't really play with the other child, more like he plays alongside him. He hasn't had a lot of interaction with children his age, so this is great for him.

"Hello again." The woman with brown hair sits next to me on the bench. She was here last time we were in the park when Callum took Gibs to the bathroom.

"Oh, hi." I scan the park for her child, and again see no one that would match someone his age. Most of the kids here are too little. I scan her face, trying to find something remarkable about her. There is something that isn't right about her, but damned if I can figure out what.

"Your son likes playing in the sand," she remarks, watching him play with the sand molds we brought with us. The other child takes a mold and uses it after watching Gibson make a few frogs in the sand.

"He's not my son, I'm his nanny. But yes, he loves playing in the sand. I have to keep an eye on him, so he doesn't dump sand on the other child's head. He does that sometimes." I face Gibson but keep an eye on her. Aiden is standing near a tree with his eyes on Gibson and me, so I have no doubt if she tried something funny, she wouldn't get away with it. A glance up at him tells me Aiden must have noticed her since he's moved closer to my bench.

"He'll be turning three soon." She says it as a statement, as if she knows him. Yet her voice is void of any intonation, any emotion at all. Like she's a robot. I have an urge to snatch up Gibson and run in the opposite direction of this creepy lady.

"How did you—"

"It was nice to see you again. I better go." She's moving down the walkway before I even have time to finish my sentence. How did she know that he'll be three in a few months? I mean, he's of average size, so I guess she might have figured it out. But just the way she said it with that flat voice gave me chills.

"Everything okay, Ms. Addington?" Aiden is right behind me. Never blocking either of our views of Gibson.

"Yes. We should get back to the hotel. Callum will be back soon, and he wanted to have some time with Gibs before the show tonight." I gather his toys. He doesn't put up too much of a fuss because I tell him we'll get a balloon before we go back to the hotel.

At the balloon vendor, he picks a bright green one. He favors green things. His green truck is his favorite. His green blanket is his favorite. The green blocks are always the first ones he uses. It must be his favorite color.

When Callum walks into the suite, Gibson runs into the bedroom and comes running out with his balloon trailing behind him.

"Look at that balloon and two stickers on your shirt, too? You had a really good day!" Callum wraps him into a hug. I watch the stress of his day roll off him in that simple contact with his son. The lines on his face lessen and the smile on his face broadens.

"Good." Gibson nods, and fiddles with the stickers on his shirt.

"A dog and a penguin today I see" Callum points at each sticker as he says the animal names. "I'm so proud of you, buddy. You had fun at the park with Ari?"

"Fun. Awi. Fun. Roun and roun," he explains.

A smile stretches on Callum's face as he looks up at me and shoots me a wink. "You went around and around on the carousel again? Wow. Ari must love you to let you do that."

Gibson turns around with outstretched arms and rushes to me. "Loves Awee. Loves." I pick him up and he throws his arms around my head and gives me an open mouth kiss on the tip of my nose.

"I love you too, kiddo." *So much.* I kiss the end of his nose in return.

"What do we feel like for dinner? Between room service and delivery, we can get just about anything." Callum sits on the floor, so Gibson sits between his legs.

"Shickin," Gibson says as he fingers Cal's BR logo necklace Sammy made.

"Why am I not surprised?" He laughs. We order room service, making sure that Gibs gets his daily dose of chicken. Afterwards, Callum gets ready to head to the show for the night after reading Gibson a story.

"At least we don't have to be on the bus tomorrow until 1:00pm. We can sleep in a little since the show tonight will run long. We have a VIP afterparty at a club somewhere, so I probably won't be back until late. Later than normal, late. I'll be quiet."

"We'll be in the two-bed room, so don't be a stranger." I wiggle my eyes at him, then give him a big hug.

He kisses that spot where my ear meets my head and whispers, "You can count on me snuggling up with you tonight no matter how late."

He leaves and I get Gibson ready for bed. We read one of his books and then sing about twinkling stars quietly, twice through until he finally drops off halfway through the second round. I snuggle with him until he's good and asleep and build his little pillow fort, so he doesn't roll out.

I snuggle into the other bed with my e-reader and read until I awake with a start when I drop it on my face. I deposit my e-reader on the nightstand and am quick to fall back asleep. I don't even know what time Callum came in. I have a vague memory of his weight on the bed and him pulling me to him, of his scruff scraping against the crook of my neck.

I find myself still wrapped in his arms this morning, surrounded in that spicy smell that is pure Callum. I want to turn and face him, snuggle into his chest, and breathe him in. Kiss him until he's awake.

But he's sleeping soundly. His steady, deep breaths make me want to curl into him and drift back off to sleep with him. He's very relaxed except for the arm slung over me, keeping me against him. As gently as possible, I lift his arm from me and scoot out from under him and off to the bathroom.

When I return, I can't help but stare at him while he sleeps. Part of his soft, dark brown hair is spread out on his pillow since he's rolled onto his back, the other part is draped across his face, hiding one of his closed eyes. The sheet's only covering part of his legs as he sleeps in a pair of boxers. But it's his arms I can't stop admiring.

I love his arms and their strength. They're covered in a colorful mix of tattoos that sleeve up each arm and spill onto his shoulders and part of his chest. One arm is slung across his abdomen and the other is bent at the elbow, his arm where my body was before I got up. It's like he's searching for me, even in his sleep.

In the other bed is his son, also sleeping on his back, but in a starfish form, arms and legs stretched nearly as wide as they'll go. Head turned to the side, his curly blonde locks are wild in his sleep. I want to pick up Gibson and take him to his uncle's room and have my way with his father. But instead, I crawl back in with Callum for a few more minutes.

"Hmmm, there you are." He rolls back onto his side and pulls me to him and kisses my forehead. "I missed you. Now go to sleep. I'm tired."

As much as I loved sleeping in with Callum, it wasn't a great idea because we had to rush around to get to the bus call.

As we are waiting our turn to get in the car that will take us to the busses back at the arena, Gibson twists in Killian's arms and reaches past his shoulder.

"Bawoon! Bawoon!" He reaches and cries out right as Killian gets into the SUV with him. I snap him into his car seat before getting my own seatbelt situated. When I look up, the lady from the park is standing amidst the other fans. I can almost hear her monotone voice as she stares at the darkened windows. She holds a small bouquet of helium balloons in different shades of green and watches the SUV as it starts to pull away. The windows are tinted dark, so I don't think she can see us, but I am completely unnerved as chills run down my arm and my stomach turns to a block of ice.

"Christ, Ari, are you sick? You're super pale." Callum turns in his seat and reaches over it to feel my forehead, his eyes narrowed as he assesses my face.

I shake my head. "No. The lady with the balloons. She was

at Central Park. Both times. She talked to me, but she gave me weird vibes. She was just watching us pull away! The lady with a bouquet of green balloons."

Callum's eyebrows pull closer together as he frowns, trying to understand what I'm saying. I know I'm not making much sense. "The person who sells balloons at the park was just here watching us?"

I shake my head. "No. She was from the park. She tried to talk to me about Gibson, but she seemed sketchy. I didn't really say much to her. But she seemed to know Gibson would be three soon. And then she showed up at the hotel with green balloons, like the one I got him. She's weird."

"Did Aiden see her?"

"Yeah, he came over and asked if I was okay, but she was already leaving. Why is she here at the hotel? And with green balloons?" My voice is rising in pitch, but I can't help it. "Am I being followed again?" I can't keep myself from trembling. She's skeeved me out with her bouquet of balloons. There is something not right about her. About this whole situation.

"Text Jax right now. Everything you remember about her. Both of you." Callum points to Aiden and me. When his dark blue eyes lock on me, they calm the quaking I didn't even realize I was doing. "It's probably just some fan, but we should take it seriously."

I'm still thinking about it when we board the buses still parked at the arena for our trip back down south. We finally start heading down the highway. Today's a long travel day and I'm comforted by the fact that we are putting a lot of distance between us and creepy balloon lady.

Chapter 36

Arista

The buses pulled into The Staples Center a few hours ago. We're home, but not yet. First there's the LA show. The last on the docket for this tour. I'm both excited and nervous somehow. I asked Callum if we should just go home and wait for him, but he wants us here. There's a feeling in my stomach that something's up. Callum's been busy with media since before we even got here, doing phone interviews with local radio stations, and it didn't stop when the buses pulled in.

Gibs and I go on a treasure hunt in the bowels of the arena. Luckily, Elsie watched him for twenty minutes while I hid some of his small animal toys throughout the halls and dressing rooms. So, he runs out in front of me.

"Hmm. Where it at?" He keeps muttering to himself as he looks for his toys.

"I dunno. Where's it at? Did you look under that chair?" He runs to the chair and looks under it.

He shakes his head. "Not dere." He stands up and throws his hands up in the air.

"Well, I'm pretty sure there is a pig toy in here somewhere."

This tub of small plastic farm animals was ridiculously cheap, but he loves them almost as much as he loves his green truck.

"Oink, oink." He scrunches up his nose as he makes a pig noise. It warms my heart how stinking adorable and happy this boy is. He continues his search, throwing in random oinks. "Ahh Awi. I finded!" He rushes over to the corner and picks up his pig.

"One more room. This time, it's the cow. Do you remember what the cow says?" I ask as I lead him down to Sammy's dressing room, where his plastic cow sits on a table amid various snacks laid out for the always hungry Sammy.

"Moooo," he demonstrates as we go into Sammy's dressing room. "Where cow?" He throws up his hands.

"I'm not sure, buddy. Let's find out." He walks around, stopping to look under the table and in the small bathroom. "Moooo," he calls out as if he's hoping to call his plastic cow toy home. "Moooo."

Sammy walks in while we are searching. "Shammy, moo!"

Sammy looks at him, shrugs, and moos right back at him, which makes Gibson laugh.

"We are looking for his plastic cow that's hidden in here." Sammy knows this game, as we've played it on long haul trips in the bus.

"Let's see if we can find it, then." He helps Gibson look all over his dressing room for it. They even check Sammy's duffle bag.

"Not hewe!" Gibs exclaims and throws his arms up again. It seems to be his favorite gesture today.

"Oh, I am pretty sure it's in here somewhere."

Sammy picks him up. "Let's have a snack and think about where your cow could hide." He walks Gibson over to the snack table and bends him over the table as he pretends to peruse the selection of snacks.

"Der is!!!" Gibson bounces in Sammy's arms as he reaches

for the cow that I've artfully hidden next to Sammy's beloved beef jerky.

"I guess cow was hungry. He was with the snacks." Sammy laughs.

"Thank Sammy for helping," I say.

"Fanks helping Shammy!" He reaches out to give him a hug, which Sammy gratefully takes.

"You're welcome, bud. You're my favorite Gibson." He hugs him tight.

"Squishing Gibshon." He squirms and laughs with Sammy. "Fabborit Shammy." He gives Sammy another hug, tight around his head.

"Squishing Sammy," Sammy tells him, and he giggles some more. Sammy meets my eyes over Gibson's continued squeeze. "This kid. He makes every day better."

"That he definitely does. Let's go find Daddy, buddy." I relieve Sammy of Gibson's death grip around his head.

"Oh, um, Cal and Kill are doing some sort of interview. Just the two of them." Sammy looks down.

"They are?" I don't remember seeing anything in Callum's schedule today.

Sammy nods. "Yeah. It's last minute for some magazine doing an article on rock brothers or something." Weird. Callum usually texts me if something like that pops up. Maybe he didn't have time.

"Well, we'll get out of your hair. It'll be dinnertime soon, and I want to pack up his stuff on the bus." I wink at Sammy as I gather my chicken-loving charge to head back to the bus to clean up and pack up some of our stuff, since we'll be heading home after tonight.

"Uh, you sure you guys don't want to hang with me and eat some snacks?" Sammy's eyes are wide.

"Aww, thanks, Sammy, but I really want to get Gib's stuff packed up, so we'll be ready to head home after the show." I leave with my munchkin and his bag of found toys from our little hide-and-seek game.

"Umph." Gibson and I smack right into Killian as we enter the hall. "Sorry, Kill."

He grabs my arms to make sure that I don't tumble with my precious cargo. "Oh, hey."

"How did the brothers interview go?" I ask and look past him, hoping to catch a glimpse of Callum.

"Brother interview?" He looks at me quizzically. He checks his phone and continues to walk with us and guides us to his dressing room.

"Oh, you mean the twin one with Cal. It was okay." He shrugs. "They always ask us about that twin thing. You know, do I know what Cal's thinking? Can we do it in front of them? Like we can do it on command like a trained seal. It makes him uncomfortable, and I don't particularly love feeling like a circus freak."

This is my opportunity to bring up the twin connection. I've been wanting to find time with Killian to chat like Cal suggested, but never had a chance.

"Cal told me about that." I nod. "I remember reading a couple of studies when I was in school about twins. It fascinated me. Do you know what he's thinking? And no, I don't think you're a freak. I'm truly interested." He leads us to his dressing room, and I put Gibson down and he grabs the cow and horse and starts playing with them on the floor.

"He told me you might ask about it. The best way I can explain it, is that it's like there's a second part of me that's out there experiencing things that I'm not necessarily experiencing. But that part is Cal, so it's not really me." He peeks over at me through his hair. He's not used to sharing this part of himself either.

"Callum told me, for instance, that you knew he passed out when we were getting Gibson's chin stitched at the hospital."

"Yeah. Sometimes I just know things. Like, I knew that he'd decided to leave the band before you came back. Sometimes it's a physical feeling, like when Callum passes out, I feel woozy and upset." He shrugs. "The more intense the emotion or feeling, the stronger it is."

"I mean, you can't feel everything... right?" I'm instantly mortified as I flash on some pretty intense and emotional feelings exchanged between Callum and me. Can he tell when we are intimate? My face instantly heats.

"Not that, Ari!" Killian turns as red as I feel. He shakes his head. "Usually, we feel the things that are distressing for the other. Although, sometimes, I just get how he feels about situations or people. Like his feelings about you, those are all very good feelings, very strong feelings. I assume it's because he thinks about you a lot. Whatever he's preoccupied with, maybe? But no, I don't feel it when you and him, are, uh, you know, intimate." He looks down at his feet and turns even redder, like an embarrassed teenager.

It's not something I'd ever expect from this dark, brooding man. He's always with a woman, a different one each night, typical rock star. Killian is a conundrum of sorts. He's known as being the quiet one, the dark one by the fans. And maybe with fans he is a little standoffish. But he's been nothing but warm and welcoming to me, if not a tad shy, maybe.

"I mean, sometimes it is physical. When I had food poisoning a few weeks ago, I had the headache from hell. He had a headache too. He mentioned it to me a couple of times. That hopefully once I ate, 'our' headache would go away. But usually, it's more the emotional things we feel." He pauses like he's thinking.

"For instance, Gibson's birth. From the moment his son was born, Cal's thinking, his whole state of being, shifted dramatically, and I felt that deep in me." He taps his torso, lightly grabbing his shirt.

"It altered him on a deep internal level, and that's probably normal for most people with the birth of a child. But I felt it on that deep internal level too. Feeling him with all this new angst and turmoil on top of my own conflicting emotions was a shit ton to deal with." He sighs a deep, resigned breath and looks up with me. At our eye contact, I can almost feel his weariness.

"It can be so exhausting, Ari, almost painful, to deal with his emotions on top of my own. Sometimes they get confused and I can't tell which are his and which are my own. To the point that it's really hard for me sometimes. It was like that when Gibson was born and I had to step back, distance myself from both of them. And that, of course, hurt Cal. It's set us off-balance somewhat. And now I feel bad about that disconnect."

He sighs. "I'm not as good as Cal is about turning this connection shit off. He says he doesn't feel it as deeply as me, but I think he's just better at turning it off than I am. Tuning it out expends a great deal of energy in me, sometimes to the point that it hurts." Killian's words haunt me.

The twin connection has always fascinated me since I read about it in my child development class. It takes an obvious toll on Kill's state of mind and well-being, but he just accepts it for what it is.

"Gibson was seventeen days old when Becka left. That morning, I woke up feeling nauseous, scared and alone. My gut told me something was up with Gibson. Cal wasn't reading or replying to my texts, so I decided to head over to his place. On the way there, I started feeling this intense anger that burned in my gut. It was so bad I had to pull over." He glances over at his nephew playing on the floor. We sit facing each other on the small couch in his dressing room, so I lean over and pat his knee.

"I hadn't felt that kind of anger from Cal since we were young teenagers, right before our Aunt Sandy took us in. I don't know how to explain the feeling. It's a deep, burning anger mixed with fear and self-loathing. When we were teens, I understood it because we experienced a lot of the same things. We were in the same place, physically and emotionally, so our feelings jived because our situations jived. But as an adult? It's a fucking scary space to be in. I wasn't living it, so I didn't have that level of context for the feelings I was experiencing." His voice breaks and he wipes at his eyes with the back of his hands. His love for his brother emanates off him when usually he's so aloof and cool.

"Cal and I, we've never ever really talked about any of this connection shit. It just is. And we accept it as such."

He takes another shuddered breath. "Please don't tell him."

"Tell him what, Kill?" I squeeze his knee.

"How messed up it makes me that Gibs has most of Cal's thoughts and now you take up a good portion too. That I feel replaced or less important? I'm not sure. It's stupid and I shouldn't feel this way, that much I know. Gibson *should* be at the forefront of Cal's thoughts. But it's more than that. It's more like he has something that I don't. That I can't." His face scrunches as he pulls in a shaky breath, and tears leak out the corners of his eyes. I grab Killian by the shoulders and pull him into a hug. He's rigid at first, but eventually relaxes into it.

Killian always seems like the most standoffish member of the band. Now I know why. He feels too much, too deeply, and it takes its toll on him. He needs the walls he puts up to maintain that space and his composure. For whatever reason, he doesn't feel like he can talk about how alone he feels or how he doesn't want to be alone.

"I know I've said this to you before, Kill, but you can talk to me any time, about anything. And I promise it goes no further than us unless you want it to."

He nods and mutters, "Thanks Ari." He takes another shuddered breath, then pulls back and swipes at his eyes with the back of his hands. He stands and quickly moves into the small bathroom just off his dressing room.

Gibson continues to play with his cow and pig happily on the floor, softly mooing and oinking as he does. My phone vibrates in my pocket.

Cal: Meet me on the bus ASAP. Bring Gibs.

"Kill, you okay?" I can't leave him alone until I've made sure. Thankfully, he opens the door. His eyes are a little red, but his lips turn up in a small smile and he gives me a nod.

"Yeah. I'm good."

"Just wanted to make sure. We'll get out of your hair." I hold my phone up and shake it slightly. "Cal wants to see Gibs before the show."

I gather up my little charge and hold him. "Tell your uncle goodbye."

Gibson reaches out for Killian, and he takes his nephew. "Bye bye, Unka Kiwi." He goes in for an open mouth kiss on his cheek. I can't help the giggle that bubbles out at Killian's new moniker. Uncle Kiwi. That's a name that'll go over well.

"Come on, you little rapscallion, let Uncle Kiwi get back to getting ready." Gibson willingly comes back to my arms after Killian kisses his temple. Gibson gives Killian his trademark wave where he closes and opens his fist.

"Bye, kiddo." Killian says as we hit the door. "Oh, Ari?"

I turn back to look at Killian.

"Thank you, for the talk and stuff." His smile is diffident and small.

I nod at him. "Any time, Kill. I mean it."

I hurry down the corridor of dressing rooms and hit the back door to where the busses are staged outside the arena. I head toward our bus.

"Ari! Ari!" Elsie appears out of the Slater's bus and rushes up to me.

"Hey. What's up?" Not really in the mood for a chat, I'm more focused on getting Gibson to the bus.

"I'm here for Gibson." She holds out her hands and he goes to right her without a fuss, despite my trying to hold on to him.

"But Cal wanted to see him." I hold out my hands, but he's latched on to Elsie, already entangling his fingers into her hair.

She nods. "Trust me, he wants me to take him. We're having chicken nuggets and carrots. Cal has it all planned out."

"Shicken!" Gibson cries out gleefully and bounces in Elsie's arms. I could probably feed him broccoli if I called it green chicken.

When I look back towards the bus, Callum's standing in the door. His arms are propped up on each side of the door frame, his long hair is loose and hangs below his shoulders. His t-shirt is pulled up slightly, giving me a peek of those well-toned abs that I love so much, black jeans hugging his hips perfectly. His feet, oddly enough, are bare. He gives me a smirk when I stop to take in the sight of him just a few feet in front of the doorway.

"See something you like, Ar?"

No, I see *someone* I love. I look him over one more time as he stands there, and he lets go of the door frame and turns sideways while he jerks his head.

"Get in here already. We don't have much time, and I've got a lot…" His voice trails off.

I step up the stairs into the living area of the bus. The blackout blinds are pulled, so the interior is darkened, but it's also lit up with strings of delicate white fairy lights tacked to the roof of the bus.

"I thought we could have dinner under the stars, even though it's still light outside. Just the two of us." He gestures towards the ceiling that has small white Christmas lights running the span of it. One of Gibson's blankets is stretched out over the floor. There is a bottle of champagne chilling in an ice bucket that Killian stole from one of our hotels next to a bag emblazoned with Giolli's Deli.

"Wow! Look at that, stars during the day." He put so much work into this, for me. He shows me how much he loves me in small ways and big ways. I love them all, just like I love him.

He walks over to the indoor picnic he's set up and drops down on the blanket and pats it. "Join me?"

I kick off my shoes and join Callum on the blanket.

"This is nice. Unexpected. When did you have time to do this?" He shrugs as he pulls out some champagne from behind the large basket.

"We didn't have an interview this afternoon. Kill helped me rig this all up." I can't help my flinch when he pops the cork on the champagne and starts pouring out two glasses.

"Sammy lied to me?" That little booger.

"He did. Surprising, huh?" Callum nods and hands me a flute of champagne. "I didn't think he could pull it off. I was sure he'd ruin it, but he didn't."

"I'm completely surprised between him and Killian. Both were quite convincing when talking about the interview." The champagne bubbles pop on the surface of the flute, giving off a sweet fruity smell.

Callum looks at me and then takes my flute away. He sets it on the table behind him next to his.

"I'm getting ahead of myself." He shakes his head and turns to face me. He fidgets with the edge of Gibson's blanket with one hand, his other lays on his lap.

"Ari," he sighs my name with reverence. "I love you. I didn't want to at first. You know I fought it. But that was never going to work because, well, I love you. Shit, now I'm repeating myself." He runs his tattooed hand through his hair.

"You love Gibson. And me. But you loved Gibson first. You cared about him despite me. You don't even realize how important that is to me." He chuckles softly. "Because I gave you quite a few reasons to hate me." He shifts on the blanket and re-crosses his legs.

"Man, why is this so hard?" He runs his hand through his hair again while letting out a long exhale. "I can write songs that hit number one, but trying to express that you mean the world to me, I screw it up." He mutters to himself and shakes his head again, then reaches to take my hands in his.

"What I am trying to tell you, Ari, is that you've wiggled your way under my skin and into my heart. I love you so much, Arista. So much." He squeezes my hands in his. "Will you marry me?"

Did he just? Marry him? He did say marry me, right? Callum? Holy canoli, he just asked me to marry him!

Callum's hand shifts back to the edge of the blanket and uncovers a small black box and opens it, showcasing a beautiful glittery ring with shaky hands. I've seen these hands do a lot of things, hold and comfort his son, weep emotion through his guitar, tune me up and push me over the edge. But I've never seen them tremble like they are right now.

Tears burn my eyes, but these are the best kind of tears. Callum loves me, all of me. He's the only person who knows all of me and loves me anyway. And he wants to keep me. My breath catches in my throat. *He wants to keep me.*

"You're worrying me, Ar." He chuckles and his Adam's apple moves in his throat. The pink-stoned ring shines up from his still quaking hands. I've seen this man scared for his son, bone-tired, and concerned for me. I've watched as he worries about his brother and seen him high on post-show adrenaline. But I've never seen him nervous, and he's waiting for my answer. *Shit. I need to answer him.*

"Yes! Yes! So much yes!" I lunge across the blanket at him, wrapping my arms around his neck. Thankfully, he's quick enough to catch me, but my momentum topples us back onto the floor and he laughs a deep hearty, carefree laugh that I don't think I've ever heard from him before. And just like that, I fall a little farther in love with this man, when I already thought I loved him completely.

"Thank fuck." He grasps my head and pulls me to his lips. The minute our lips touch, all the twinkling lights fade away and there is nothing but Callum.

I pull back from his kiss, needing a breath. "You really thought I'd say no?"

He pulls one shoulder up in a half-shrug. "I worried you'd think it was too soon."

I put my head on his chest as we lie there on the floor. Listening to the thudding of his heart through his t-shirt, I feel like I'm finally home.

Chapter 37

Callum

Fuck, the crowd tonight is on twelve. There is nothing like playing L.A. These are our people, the ones that have been with us from the beginning. The crowd is making so much fucking noise I can barely hear Mav as he talks to them. But all five of us are eating it up as they move in unison to every one of our songs. The entire arena is on their feet, jumping, swaying, clapping, fists pumping, as they move to our music. Between this and the fact that we get to sleep in our own beds tonight, it's a great night.

I glance over at the side of the stage. Ari stands next to Aiden, her smile huge as she claps along with the song. Her ring sparkles on her hand from here. This means Jax is with Gibson. And it means the next song we do is one I wrote, despite the fact that Mav will be singing it. I can't give it the kind of justice it needs, that Ari deserves. It's her song. I nod at her and wink, so she knows I see her. If she only knew what was about to happen next.

We wrap up 'Crushed Dreams,' one of our hardest and most popular songs, and Mav returns to center stage and snaps his microphone into the stand. I walk up closer to Mav after switching out my guitars. This teal Fender I hold is one of my favorites and is named Sevyn, after Sammy's sister.

"How ya doing out there tonight, L.A.? Still hangin' in there with us?" The crowd roars their response to Mav, and he grins out at them and nods his approval. "Good to hear you all. And we do. We hear every single one of you. We fucking love it. We love you."

He pauses for the crowd to die down a little. "We love playing here in L.A. because this is our home. Home is where your family is. So tonight, we are all family, am I right?" Another raucous response from the crowd.

"As part of our family, I have some serious news to report to you all." The crowd quiets, hanging on Mav's every word. "As of a few hours ago"—he turns over and looks at me—"our brother Callum is officially off the market!" He smiles and throws a hand in my direction.

I lift my arms up in a V as the spotlight shifts to me for a second. The crowd roars, but I see a few sad faces out there as well.

"Ladies, Sammy and Killian are still taking applications if you want to put in your resumes." The crowd goes crazy again as Sammy rolls a quick drum roll and Kill just shakes his head and blushes a little.

"Because love has made our Cal all mushy tonight, he's asked that we change things up a little bit. What do you say?" He nods at their appreciation.

"This is a new song Cal wrote all on his own. We've never played it live, so forgive us if it's a little rough around the edges. This one's called 'Together.'"

I lean into his microphone and turn my head to the side so I can look at Ari. "This one's for you, Ar." I point to her and then we start our newest song.

This one's a rocker for sure, Killian's strong bass chords are deep and set a good foundation with Sammy. But the words, all mine, are more melodious. Mav kills the emotion of the song, just like I knew he would.

He wraps it up with a quick, "Welcome to the Blind Rebels family, Ari." Then we launch right into our last song, "Burn It." I play it from muscle memory because my eyes keep glancing towards the side of the stage where Kady is hugging Ari. I'm ready to hold my girl and take her home.

We let the crowd call us back out for a second time since it's L.A. and the last show for a while. Then we bow, Sam gently tosses out a couple of his sticks into the crowd and Kill and I each toss several picks out into the crowd.

Filing off stage, I gingerly hand my guitar over to Geo, and as soon as he has her in his hands, I'm tackled from the side by Ari. I wrap my arms around her. "Thank you for the song. I love you!" She peppers me with kisses, and I pull her against me. Her telling me she loves me never gets old.

Her legs wrap around my waist, and I carry her into my dressing room. She continues to kiss my jaw, then nibbles my neck along the way. I want nothing more than to lay her down on the couch in here and have my way with her. But home is calling too and having her in my bed where she belongs is top of my list tonight.

With her legs still wrapped around me as we continue to kiss, I pull back. "Let me shower quick, then we can go home. Let's do this in our own bed, while Gibs sleeps down the hall in his own bed." She nods and reluctantly pulls away.

The after party is probably already ramping up down in the green room. A slight guilt pulls at my gut, telling me I should go down there and enjoy the fruits of a long ass tour. Celebrate with my brothers and Kady.

Kady: Don't you dare come to this after party. You take that girl home.

After the quickest shower ever, I throw on some jeans and make my way back into the dressing room for a fresh shirt. I catch Ari looking at her ring, moving her hand slightly side to side as she watches the light bouncing off it from different directions. Her face has a soft smile. Glancing up at me, her eyes then travel down to my chest and work their way even lower to my abs, then flash up back to my eyes with a spark of lust dilating her pupils as her tongue wets her lips.

"Hey, now, not until we've put Gibson in his bed. Then you can look *and* touch." I wink and pull on my favorite green shirt.

Gibson snores lightly from his car seat as we sail down the highway. Glancing over at Ari, she's still grinning. I haven't seen her smile this much ever, so I think she really likes the ring. She keeps glancing down at it, like she's making sure she's not dreaming.

"I know we just got engaged, but I've already been in contact with a family lawyer. He comes highly recommended by our entertainment attorney."

Ari's eyes widen and then shift so she's sitting taller in her seat. "I'll sign any prenup or whatever you need. You need to protect yourself and Gibs. I understand." Her words are honest and don't hold even a hint of disappointment.

I didn't expect that kind of reaction, but the fact that she's not hurt at the thought of signing a prenup tells me that she is in this for the long haul.

"That's not why. He's drawing up paperwork so that once we're married, you can officially adopt Gibson. If you want to. You don't have to. These kinds of things take time, so I wanted to make sure everything was ready. He's also working to change things like my will and life insurance and some other stuff, but we can talk about that shit later."

Her mouth is ajar, her eyes are wide, and she's almost frozen that way. I lean in and kiss her gently before returning my eyes back to the road. "You okay, Ar?"

She blinks a few times and pulls back. "You really want me to adopt Gibson?"

I nod slowly. "Only if you want to."

"Of course, I want to. I love him."

"I know."

R

"I WISH YOU WOULDN'T." I stand near the door as Ari snaps Gibson into his stroller.

"Pawk, daddy. Pawk." Gibson points to the door when Ari stands back up.

The media attention after our engagement was announced at the concert had been steady for the first week but finally died down a few days ago when some starlet entered treatment for her eating disorder. I've met her a few times. I wish her nothing but the best. But I feel slightly guilty that her trials are giving us the reprieve we've been wanting from the paparazzi.

Since the press has backed down and shifted their attention, Ari is determined to take Gibs to the park today.

"He doesn't understand why we've been keeping him at home. Plus, his little friend, Ryder, is going to be there, Cal. He needs to socialize with kids his age. Aiden's coming with us, and Ryder's mom will be there. It's not a big deal."

"No beeg deal, daddy. No beeg deal. See Wider. Pease. Fank you. Okay?" Gibson cocks his head at me.

I bend down and kiss my son. "Okay. You have fun with Ryder and be a good listener for Ari and Aiden, okay?" He nods his head and fiddles with his plastic camel. He's been picking a different animal out of his safari bin every day this week. Today must be camel day. Ironically, it's even Wednesday.

Gibson nods his head.

"Be careful."

"You know I will be."

"I know. I love you."

"I love you too." She leans up on her toes and plants a

chaste kiss on my cheek. We've jumped right into full displays of affection in front of Gibson. He doesn't seem to notice or care. My entire world heads down the walkway with Aiden, who gives me a curt nod as he walks behind them. But I can't help the anxious ball of nerves that sits icy in my stomach as I watch them go.

"Hey, bring me a coke when you come back." Sammy sticks his head out of the music room where we're all sequestered, working on some new music. I nod and grab something for everyone to take back.

R

WE'VE FINISHED THE SONG, but my phone remains dark. No pictures of Gibson and Ryder in the sand. No pictures of my brave boy finally conquering his fear of the big slide. Nothing. It's been a good two hours, possibly more since they've left and not even a gate notification of them returning. My phone's dark and it's bugging the fuck out of me.

Killian's hand latches around my forearm, squeezing so fucking tight that I look up, about to tell him off for getting upset that I'm futzing with my phone instead of paying attention, but his expression stops me cold.

He's whiter than when he broke his arm jumping off the roof as a teen, his face creased with worry lines on his forehead and his mouth is pulled into a tight grimace I've never seen on my twin before. It's an odd expression for Killian, and he's unnaturally still. His eyes aren't really focusing on me, but when they finally do, I feel nothing but terror radiating from him.

"Gibs," he gasps it out in a short breath.

Then my phone starts ringing. Aiden.

"What?" I bark into the phone as I watch Killian watch me, his eyes wide with panic. Looking around, my music room is filled with somber faces. They already know what my brain is slow to figure out. Killian felt something distressing about Gibson. But how?

"They're gone, Mr. Donogue. Fuck. I'm sorry. We're looking for them now. But they're gone. Jax is tracking Arista's phone." Aiden's breath comes in quick clips like he's running. He better be running because when I find him, I'm going to fucking kill him.

"What the fuck do you mean, they're gone?" My roar reverberates off the soundproofed walls and if I didn't already have everyone else's attention, I do now. "How the fuck do you lose the only two fucking people you're supposed to be keeping safe? You're fired. Immediately."

By the time I hang up, everyone is standing. Kady puts a soft hand on my shoulder. "Let's head to the park. Jax is already there. The police are on the way."

She nods towards Mav who talks quietly into his phone, when I didn't see him pull it up to his ear to begin with.

"I'll drive you and Kill." Sammy's hand is outstretched, palm up, waiting for my keys. Once he has them, he's up and bounding towards the driveway before I'm completely standing.

Gone? My son and my fiancée are gone? Maybe they decided to walk to Ryder's house? Although Aiden would know it if they had.

A wave of cold overtakes me. Where did they go? Why? And how did Killian even know?

We're at our community park in minutes. Police cars and fire trucks are arriving and jumping into action as we pull up. I'm out before Sammy even has the SUV in park. Jax stands over a sitting Aiden in the middle of the park on a bench by the sand. When he sees me jogging in their direction, Jax pushes Aiden's shoulder to indicate he should stay on the bench before striding towards us in a commanding way.

"What the fuck?" I lead the charge forward, about to take Aiden apart with my fists. Jax blocks me and grabs me by the shoulders.

"Calm the fuck down, Callum. Jumping Aiden won't help." He holds me in place.

"Where's my son, Jax? It's his fucking job to know. I pay him to protect them."

I point at Aiden over Jax's should and direct my shouts at him. "Where the fuck are they, Aiden? What the hell happened?"

My breath heaves and my muscles are threatening to give out because I'm so ramped up. Jax strengthens his grip on my shoulders and shakes me slightly, drawing my attention away from Aiden and back to him.

"If anything happens to Gibson, I'll tear him the fuck apart." I lock eyes with Jax and then holler over to the bench at Aiden again. "Piece by fucking piece, you hear me?" The wall of a bodyguard I pay to protect my world cringes in on himself, looking defeated and out of sorts on the park bench. He won't even look at me. Fuck him.

"Callum, pay attention." Jax shakes me until I bring my eyes back to his. "They were ambushed. Aiden was incapacitated with a taser and then cold-cocked. He never saw it coming. When he woke up, he was alone in the park." Jax steadies his glare at me.

"Whomever set this up must have been lying in wait for them. I'm convinced of it." Jax looks at me. "This is not Aiden's fault."

I'm about to tear into Jax and Aiden again when Mav approaches us with a police officer.

"Cal, they need to know what they were wearing. Do you remember?" Shit. What were they wearing? I close my eyes tight. The doorway. I told Ari I didn't want her to go. Fuck. I knew something bad was going to happen.

"Gibs has a green dinosaur shirt on, denim shorts, and his converse. The black ones. Like mine." I wiggle my foot. "He might have his floppy straw hat on, since Ari usually makes him wear it at the park."

"Good." Mav squeezes my shoulder. "What's he weigh now, about thirty pounds?"

"Twenty-seven. He asked me to weigh him during bath time the night before last. He likes to watch the numbers on the scale change."

"What about Arista? What was she wearing?" The officer looks up from his notepad.

"Fuck. I don't remember." I squeeze my eyes shut again.

"Think, Cal. Ari. You said goodbye to her. What was she wearing?"

"Black yoga pants, maybe? A faded red shirt?" I don't remember, but that's probably not what she was wearing. That's what she had on this morning. Those were her comfy clothes. She wouldn't go out of the house dressed like that, especially not if she was meeting Ryder's mom there. Fuck, why can't I remember.

"No. She was wearing jeans and a light green shirt with buttons," Sammy pipes up. "I'm positive. I saw her right before she left. Remember, I popped my head out of the music room and asked for a coke?" Sammy looks at me. "I remembered the buttons because she doesn't usually wear button-up shirts." Sammy wrings his hands. "It was a little big, I think it might have actually been one of your dress shirts," he says to me.

Jax's and my phone signal a text at the exact same time. I pull my phone out and look at it.

Ari: Don't call the police. I have Gibson.

Ari: Need to clear my head. I'm not sure this is the life for us.

Ari: I'll be in touch.

"Fuck. She just turned her phone off." Jax pulls at his hair with his free hand. "My app says it was sent from about five miles from here. She's probably on foot."

"So, your fiancé took your son?" This police officer is an idiot.

"My fiancé wouldn't do that. She wouldn't."

"If he's with his mother, it's not kidnapping, sir." The officer looks down his nose at me.

I'm really starting to get pissed off. Do none of these officers communicate with each other?

"Ari is not his biological mother. His bio-mom relinquished her right when he was seventeen days old, and I haven't seen her since she left us. Ari is my fiancé, and she loves my son like he's her own. We are working on the fucking paperwork so she can adopt him. She wouldn't do anything to hurt to Gibson. She wouldn't just take him away from me."

"This text seems to say she did." The officer hands me back my phone.

"Is this guy for real?" I ask no one in particular.

Jax senses my exacerbation and escorts the cop away from me, bending his ear, likely about his theory about Aiden being ambushed. I don't know if he really thinks that or if he was just trying to keep me from beating the fuck out of Aiden.

"We'll find them," Mav says from behind me and clasps my shoulder. "We'll find them, man," he repeats.

Totally out of gas, I drop to my knees right in the middle of the park. I don't even have the strength to search for my son. My life, my heart, gone just like that. And Ari's in on it? Those texts, they sound so unlike Ari, but so does going missing with my son. Is she using me after all?

No, I have to stop thinking like this. We were fucking fine. We just got engaged. Everything is wrong with this situation. I don't understand why she would do this. I love her. She loves us. She wouldn't take him. She wouldn't.

"Does this belong to your son?" Another officer approaches

with a jacket he holds out with his gloved hands. Gibson's green rainslicker that Ari keeps tucked into the stroller.

"It's his rain slicker. It's usually in the bottom storage of the stroller, just in case. Ari always plans for just in case." The officer nods and wrestles the jacket into a bag marked "evidence." It wasn't until the officer turned that I noticed the blood all over the jacket.

"Is that blood? Blood on my son's jacket? What the fuck? Where was it?" I can hear the screechy quality of my own voice, but I can't control it. I can't pull in a deep enough breath, so I breathe faster. This isn't fucking happening. Gibs is gone and now he may be bleeding.

My chest constricts even tighter. I need to look for them my fucking self. But I can't even get up because I can't catch my fucking breath, and now my chest is tight as fuck. The world starts to spin.

Someone grabs my shoulder hard, fingers digging hard into my flesh. "Breathe, Cal. Slower. Like me. In— two three four. Hold— two three four. Out— two three four. Come on Cal, breathe with me."

I emulate Kady's breathing pattern and concentrate on her fingers as each one grips my shoulder to the point of near pain. My breath starts to come back to me.

"I've got to find him. Them." Something's happened to them. *The blood.* Fuck. Why would they be taken? Who would do that to Gibs? And why the fuck would they hurt him? Please God, make that blood not Gibson's. But if it's not his, then it's Ari's.

"We have to consider that Arista Addington might be the one who took your son, sir. I know it's disconcerting, but considering the text, just realize we have to keep every possible angle in mind. Did you two have a fight recently? Has she been doing things that are out of character for her?" He eyes me hard.

"No! No, you don't understand. Ari loves my son. She'd never put him in jeopardy." The look he gives me turns my stomach. It's the look of a man who's seen caretakers do just that and much worse to the people, the children, they were supposed to love.

I can't believe this about Ari. I won't. That's not her. Even though the texts say different.

"She wouldn't do this." I'm starting to feel like a broken fucking record.

"I don't think there's much we can do but wait." Mav gives my back a hard pat. My eyes search out those here that I know. Sammy's pacing the park, searching even though the park is mostly open, and you can see most of it from right here. Kady's talking with Aiden, who still sits on the bench talking with an EMT. Aiden shakes his head, and the EMT doesn't look pleased with him. Jax did say he got clocked, and for a moment, I feel bad for him. He should have been watching. How did someone like Aiden get snuck up on?

Kill sits on a bench on the other side of the slide. He's pale and all out of sorts, exactly like I feel on the inside, but he shows it on the outside. I don't know how I could have ever discounted his love for my son, because I see and feel it now. And that makes me feel like a shitty brother.

Jax, head of fucking security... how did he get here so quickly? Aiden must have called him first to give him time to get here before calling me. That's fucking time I could have been looking for my son. Jax is striding towards me yet again, a different officer in tow.

"Cal. Officer Jacobs wants to ask you a few questions." I nod at the officer.

"What do you know about the people meeting your fiancée here in the park?" He's got a notepad at the ready, like a stereo-typical television cop. How is this my life? I'm done talking. I want to start looking. I'll go door-to-fucking-door until I find them if I have to.

"Um... Ryder is his name. He's a few months older than Gibson. His mom's Selina Huckabee and they live a few blocks over that way." I point. "On Breeze Circle. I think that's the name of the cul-de-sac. First house on the left." He nods. "Selina works in real estate, her coworker sold me my house five years ago. I'm not sure what her husband does. His name is, um, Randolph, I think? He's a suit somewhere."

He nods again. "We believe the play date was a ruse to lure your fiancée and son to the park. We don't think the Huckabees were involved in the crime. Seems Mrs. Huckabee's phone was cloned, and the text was sent from that cloned phone to arrange for the play date."

This is all sounding too familiar. "Wait. Killian's phone was cloned months ago. Jax knows all the details. Could the incidents be related?"

"It's possible." The detective looks to Jax.

"I'll get you the info I have. We have a whole file on the incident." Jax starts texting someone immediately.

"Also, Ari, her brother-in-law Todd would track where she was. He leaked her location multiple times to several fan pages so the fans would end up wherever she went with my son." Officer Jacobs jots it down in his notepad and nods his head.

"All things to look into. Thank you, Mr. Donogue." He turns and heads off somewhere.

Jax returns. "They want us all to go back to your place. They are sending a few units there. They want you there in case Ari or someone attempts to call, like, for ransom." Ransom? Ari didn't care about money. She offered to sign a fucking prenup. "It's a good idea. Look." He nods to one end of the park where onlookers have started to gather at the crime scene tape along with the press. This is a fucking mess. The last thing we need is more paparazzi getting involved in our fucking life.

Sam slings an arm around my shoulder. "Come on. Let's get you home."

R

SOMEONE SUGGESTS GETTING LUNCH, but I'm not hungry. I don't even bother to unwrap the submarine sandwich Greta sets in front of me. I play with the edge of the butcher paper around it.

What's Gibson having for lunch? Is he hungry? Is he scared? Is he fucking bleeding? Are the police right and Ari's done this to him?

Thinking about him being hurt makes my chest grow tight again. I'd know. I'd feel it if he was hurt. I just can't figure out Ari. My gut tells me she wouldn't do this. She loves Gibson and me both, and she'd never hurt either of us on purpose. The texts point to her and the few police that I've heard make it sound like she's the prime suspect. That makes my stomach churn because they know what they are doing, right? They are the police.

Kill doesn't attempt to eat either. Everyone else only picks at the food, even Sammy. Greta's here, cleaning up, urging us to stay hydrated, and keeping the officers who mill my house caffeinated and fed.

Every time my cell phone rings, I jump. I answer every unknown number, when before I'd send them to voicemail. So far, every call has been media related. Word is out that my son's been kidnapped. I hope they aren't saying shit that will spook whoever has him and jeopardize my son's wellbeing. How did they even get my number?

Every hour that passes seems to last a year. Every hour he's gone is another hour marked against his much too short life. Every hour he's gone is another fissure breaking my heart. If anything happens to my son, I won't survive.

Chapter 38

Arista

"Awi. Kiss, kiss." Gibson's voice is far away and blends into the constant thumping and vibrating my brain, but my cheek is moist with his open mouth kisses. It takes me a hot minute to realize the constant thumping isn't from the outside but is the inside of my head pounding slow and steady, just like the pain.

Taking a deep breath, I force my eyes open. An unfamiliar bedroom. Then I remember in brief flashes, like pictures. The park. Gibson on the slide. Aiden dead on the grass. A green balloon. Hot burning buzzing through my body. Can't move. The woman from New York carrying Gibson. The park sliding by me sideways.

Gibson's beautiful curly hair frames his face as he brings it up to mine. "Waked up!" He smiles and pats my shoulder, causing a white-hot pain to shoot through me, then kisses me again. "Aww better, Awi."

Groaning, I sit up from where I am on the carpeted floor. I'm in pain, and each slight movement is agony. This is definitely a bedroom, seems like one for a preteen girl. It's still innocent, with its light lavender walls graced with butterflies.

But no toys are visible, so not a child. I can't raise my left arm, it lays limp at my side, my elbow and shoulder screaming at me with every slight adjustment I make. There is no comfortable position, but if I stay still it dulls to a near-constant throbbing.

His little lips turn down in a frown. "Owie, Awi!" He gently touches the side of my head and his fingers come back bloody. On top of everything else, apparently, I'm also bleeding.

"I'm okay, baby." I reassure him, even though I am not okay. I can't take a deep breath because a sharp pain shoots through me when I try. My head feels disconnected from the rest of my body and everything just hurts.

Gibson climbs into my lap. "Home, Awi. Home. Okay. Pease. Daddy?"

"I want to go home and see Daddy too, buddy." I hug him with my right arm, and he lays against me.

"Home. Daddy." He whimpers. "Pease."

The door to the room opens and the woman with dead eyes from New York comes in with a bottle of water and squats down in front of us.

"Are you thirsty?" She tries to hand Gibson a bottle of water, but he buries his head in my chest, refusing to even look at her, let alone take her offering.

Her eyebrows pull in at his rebuff. "He's got to be thirsty by now." I say nothing because I'm not sure if she's talking to me or herself.

"Home. Daddy." He whimpers into my chest again.

"He's scared," I tell her. "Let us go. We won't tell anyone, I promise. Just let us go home."

"He's mine now." She grabs him around the waist and tries to take him from me, but he tightens his grip around my neck. I tighten my grip on him as best I can with one working arm.

"Noooo! Awi." His grip around my neck tightens to the point where it's getting hard to breathe. He's so young, yet he seems to understand our dire situation.

339

"Leave them alone and get out here. We've got an issue." She stiffens and drops her arms from Gibson. The voice causes my stomach to clench tight. *Todd.* A wave of nausea runs through me. Todd's part of this too.

"I don't have a say when it comes to what happens to you." She looks at me but doesn't really, her eyes still hollow. "But he's mine now." She nods towards Gibson, who's still clutching me with a death grip, then gets up and leaves, closing the door behind her.

I sniff the water in the bottle she left. It smells of nothing foul or unusual. I take a small taste. It's just water.

"Have some water, buddy." I hold up the bottle to him. He takes a few sips and then pulls away from it.

"Look bawoon." He points to the ceiling, and there floats another green balloon, just out of my reach as I sit. She distracted him with it at the park. And it's my fault he went to her. In New York, I bought him that damn balloon and now he associates parks and balloons.

She must have been sent by Todd to keep eyes on me, whoever she is. How long has she been watching us? My stomach turns again. This is all my fault. I've put us in this position. Callum will never forgive me. I'll never forgive me. My only hope is that I can save Gibson before Todd, or the woman, hurt him.

Using my right hand, I push myself up. I grab the balloon and pull it down to Gibson. Every movement I make hurts my left arm.

"Bawoon!" He stands and runs in a tight circle with his balloon, our dire circumstances forgotten for the moment.

I search the room for a way out or a weapon I can use. This room isn't lived in, it's staged. Every drawer is empty. The books on the shelf are papier mâché and not even real books. Everything is fake, so possible buyers can envision what the room would look like. There's nothing I can throw through the window to open it and the window doesn't open, no matter how much I try. I pull on the window release one more time, trying to get it to slide open.

There's a dark, deep chuckle from behind me.

"You think I would be stupid enough to put you in a room with a window that would open, Arista?"

Todd blocks the door out of the room. At his appearance, Gibson runs straight to me and tries to crawl up my leg in a panic.

"It's me you want, Todd. Let Gibson go home to his dad." I wrap my right arm around Gibson protectively to steady him on me, but he keeps grabbing at my left arm and every time he does, pain shoots across my chest and down my back at the same time.

"He's just a little boy, Todd. He's not part of this. I'll do whatever you want. Just please let him go."

"I'm not concerned with the boy. He's all hers. She can do whatever she wants with him. That was our deal," he sneers, his hands balling up.

"It's you that I'm concerned with, Arista." He advances, and I instinctively clutch Gibson tighter to me. "You've been talking, and I told you what would happen if you talked about us."

I nod vigorously, trying to placate him. "You always have. You can do whatever you want to punish me. Just please give Gibson back to his dad, and not that awful woman. Please. I'll do anything, Todd. Anything."

He grabs me by the hair, and I instinctively let Gibson go, so he slides down my body and isn't part of this. Fisting my hair in his hand, Todd pulls me so close to him I can feel his hot breath on my face. My left arm screams at me for the movement.

"You're fucking right, you'll do anything, Arista. You have no fucking choice, no control here. Do you hear me?" The snarl on his lips let just enough teeth show to know he means business.

I close my eyes and nod, just wanting the pain to go away, to wake up and find this is all some twisted dream. But I can't fade away right now, Gibson needs me to protect him.

He releases me.

"No. Bad man! No be bad!" Gibson, in all his almost three-year-old might, tries pushing Todd's leg and when that doesn't work, he bites him hard.

"You little shit." Todd lunges to grab him.

I throw myself onto Gibson before Todd can get to him and wrap myself around his little body. Todd can kill me, but while I'm still breathing, I will not let him hurt Gibs.

"Let him go, Ari. Let him go." Todd tugs on my shoulder, the hurt one, sending blinding pain down my arm. When I refuse to unwrap myself from around him, Todd decides to try to go through me. He kicks me in my ribs hard, hoping I'll let Gibson go, but I only squeeze him tighter to me with my good arm.

"What are you doing to him?" The screech was loud, and I chanced a look up to see the woman grabbing Todd's arm. "He's mine. Do not hurt him." Todd turns to deal with the woman, and I just keep myself pulled around Gibson until they leave.

There has got to be something I can do to get Gibson out of here. I'm at the point where I don't really care what happens to me. I'd rather take anything they have for me than let them hurt Gibson in any way. There is nothing in this room I can use as a weapon, even the stupid closet is totally empty, not even a bar to hang clothes on.

Gibson naps on me as I sit propped against the bed, his soft snores comforting me. It's starting to get dark here now. I really have to pee, so I imagine Gibson does too, if he hasn't already.

I move him onto a pillow I've dragged off the bed with my good arm and get up, my ribs and left arm hurting so much it nearly takes the breath from me with each step. I open the door and peek out. Our room is midway down a hall, and to my right looks like more bedrooms, probably the master being on the end. The other end of the hall opens into what I assume is a living room or kitchen. I wonder what they've done with his stroller.

The woman passes by the hall and sees me peering out. Maybe I can gain her favor. She comes to me.

"What are you doing out?" She peers into the room behind me.

"Um." I look around to see if Todd is near and lower my voice to a whisper. "I have to pee, like, really bad. But I was also wondering where his stroller is? He probably needs a new pull-up. We're still working on potty training. He was doing so good, but this whole thing might have messed that up."

"The bathroom is there." She points to a door just a few feet away. "I'll wait here. You pee and come right back here. When you're back, I'll go get you what he needs."

When I'm in the bathroom, I pee, but I also check for anything I could use to defend myself. My heart sinks when I find there is nothing in here either. All the drawers are empty. There isn't even a shower rod in the room. I wash my hands with no soap because there is none and return to find the woman standing there watching Gibson sleep on the pillow.

"Thanks. The stroller has a diaper bag in the bottom. He has pullups in there. If you can't bring me the stroller, can you just bring me a pullup and some wipes, just in case." She nods and comes back with just what I asked for.

"Shit. We've got company. Dammit. Did you tell someone where we were?" He comes fleeing into the hallway. "There is an unmarked van across the street. They are watching us." He raises his hand to his partner like he's going to hit her.

"Or it could be a soccer mom that just got home. Who are 'they' Todd? The police? The FBI? Callum? He doesn't have a van. But you realize that's his son, and he's a celebrity, right? It could be paparazzi." He says nothing.

"What about Vi? Does she know what you've done?" I press

on. I shouldn't poke him, but I'm tired and hurting and want Gibson safe.

He turns around slowly to look at me, his eyes slowly narrowing. Before I can react, his hand strikes me across the cheek as hard as he can.

My cheek stings so much I can't help the tears that fill my eyes almost instantly.

"All Vi will know, all anyone will know, is that this is all on you." He stops and cocks his head like he hears something. Maybe the van is some sort of police vehicle. Maybe they'll save us both. He leaves and then comes back.

"You're right, Arista. It is just a soccer mom." His words drip with sarcasm. "That's why marked cars are arriving now. How did you signal to the cops?" He pushes me into the door face first and starts frisking me. His hands are all over me, causing me to gag when he touches me down there.

"Don't touch me." I try my hardest to wriggle out of his grip.

He slams me into the wall near the door even harder. "You are not in control here, Arista."

Gibson whimpers, his eyes wide, watching Todd accost me.

Todd's eyes focus in on Gibson, and I have a quarter of a second head start getting to him. I tuck Gibson onto the pillow and lay on top of him, careful to leave him enough room to breathe, before Todd gets to us.

"Is that kid really worth your life, Arista?" He kicks me like he did before. And all I can think is that he is. Gibson's health is worth my life.

Each kick is harder than the last. Each one takes my breath away for longer until a blast of pain in my head turns everything bright hot white while squiggles swim in my vision.

I hold Gibson, trying to figure out what to do next as the sparkles slowly dissipate like fireworks.

I don't know how long we stay huddled up with the pillow. Gibson's quietly chattering about owies and kisses. My vision is dark on the edges. The only thing keeping the dark from taking me is Gibson talking to me.

Bang. Bang.

Sluggishly, I realize it's gunshots. I huddle around Gibson tightly, hoping to be able to stay awake long enough to protect him.

Chapter 39

Callum

I t's getting dark, and all I can think of is that Gibson is out there and not here. I squeeze his RuffRuff that's somehow made it into my lap. Every squeeze of the soft toy releases a little reminder of Gibson, the mix of his baby smell and his lavender bath soap. He's probably hungry, tired, and scared.

And Ari, if she did this? I shake my head. I can't even go there, so I concentrate on Gibson and him coming home to me. He's got to come home to me. Whoever has him can have everything I have. I'd give them the keys to my house, if only I could just walk away free and clear with Gibs.

Fuck. I'd gladly let them kill me if whoever has him could guarantee my baby's safety. He could be with my brother and be fine, and that would be enough for me. I'd trade my life for his, because fuck, my baby hasn't lived long enough.

"No!" Killian yells at me from across the room. Everyone in the room jumps, and a few of the cops reach their hand on their weapons while they turn to the commotion in the otherwise quiet house.

He stands up, grabbing a pillow and chucks it at my head.

"Don't fucking think like that, asshole." He stalks off upstairs, Sammy on his heels.

The television in the great room flickers, but it's on mute. Everyone's still here. Sammy's upstairs with Killian. Kady sits on Mav's lap in a chair, her head on his shoulder, their hands intertwined. They should go home. They have a baby of their own to worry about. They should be with him.

We all know that the longer we go without hearing from someone, the worse the outcome will be. Each minute that passes without knowing where my son is, is another strike against him. Each minute that passes steals a beat from my own heart.

An officer sits on a stool at the breakfast bar. She quietly chats with another officer who leans on the bar next to her. She has no idea that's Ari's spot, where she has her morning tea before Gibson wakes up.

The officers are talking about my Ari. Making assumptions that aren't true. She wouldn't take Gibson. She was happiest with us. She isn't into this for money or notoriety, like they suppose she is.

Each breath I take is a rattled mess. My head feels like a watermelon with about twenty rubber bands around it, and at any moment, it may blow.

Sam and Kill return from upstairs. Killian flops into a chair and gives me a hard, terrible glare. Sammy stands behind him, a comforting hand on his shoulder. But when Kill doesn't respond, Sammy ruffles his hair trying to piss Kill off, get him to react to something. Still nothing. Sam pulls him into a hug and murmurs something I can't hear.

The phones of all the officers in the house ring simultaneously. They are talking at once and watching us closely as we wait. I clutch RuffRuff tighter. Something's happening and not knowing what grinds in my empty stomach.

The female officer approaches me from the kitchen, her lips

347

in a tense line. "There's been some developments. We believe your son and fiancée are barricaded inside a house not far from here. So far, we've been unable to establish communication."

I stand. They're close. I need to get them.

"We want you at the scene to make a plea over the loud-speaker. We're hoping that will get them to communicate, if not surrender." I stuff RuffRuff in my jacket pocket as I stand. Gibson will want something familiar. I won't be coming back without my son. Everyone else moves with us towards the door. The cop stops and turns.

"We can't have any other people on the scene. The rest of you will have to stay."

"He's my twin. I'm coming." It's the first thing Killian's said since his outburst a few hours ago. It feels like sandpaper when he talks and like we might both hurl at the same time. "If something goes sideways, he'll need someone there." His last words are whispers and Sammy grips his shoulder tight again.

"Fine. Just you. I'm sorry, the rest of you will have to wait here."

In the back of the police car, Kill squeezes his fingers around my balled-up hand. He says nothing. He doesn't have to because what's going on in me goes on in him.

We drive up a barricaded street. Press and onlookers crowd a cordoned off perimeter. There's a fucking helicopter circling overhead, its rotors beating in time with the throb in my head. Kill rubs his hand on his forehead and glares at the police chopper while he walks with me as we're escorted under the tape and up the middle of the street. We're only about six miles down the hill from mine. There's a bouquet of green and white balloons tied to the mailbox and a banner that says "Welcome Home" hanging in the window. The sight of the balloons makes my stomach churn.

We're escorted to a command center set up in the back of a

vehicle that looks like a cross between an armored truck and a tank.

"Best we can tell, there are three adults and one child in the house," the officer in charge tells us.

He hands me a radio. "Just let them know you're here, that you want your son and to pick up the phone when it rings. Say nothing else." I nod.

He nods at the radio, encouraging me. I press the button. "This is Callum." My words echo from the speakers on the top of the armored vehicle. "You have my son. I just want my boy. Please answer the phone. We want to talk." The officer nods and motions for the radio back. But I can't give it back without letting Gibson know I love him. "Gibs baby. It's daddy. I love you, son. Daddy loves you so much."

The officer snatches the radio from my hands, cursing at me. Someone in the back of the vehicle calls the house. The phone rings and rings on speaker, but no one picks up. *Please pick up. Anyone. Answer the damn phone.*

Waiting here is worse than waiting at home because it's all I can do not to charge that fucking house. Three to one? No, three to two because Kill would be right next to me, and I wouldn't even have to ask. Our odds are fairly even. They may have guns, but they have my kid and that makes me fucking invincible.

There are no signs of life in the mostly darkened house, except the slight fluttering of a curtain.

The officer in charge has me repeat my request, and I do.

Officers dressed in tactical gear begin to assemble at the front of the vehicle we're in. It's fully dark now but their movement is highlighted in the lights outside the vehicle. It all looks like one of those police dramas on television. Except not, because my whole world is in that house. *Daddy's here, baby. Hold on for daddy.*

As I watch the officers mill about outside the truck, I catch a glimpse of a rifle, and that's when it hits me. They are getting ready to breach the house.

"Fuck no! No guns. He's just a baby. I haven't had enough time with him. I'll go in, not them. Not with their guns." I point at the growing assembly of officers in front of the command vehicle. I stand, but the other officer blocks the door.

"Don't make me handcuff you to that chair, son," an older cop says.

Killian stands behind me and wraps his arms around my shoulders, restraining me from behind. "Let them do their job, Cal. They know what they're doing."

Kill's quiet words take the fight out of me. He turns his restraint into a hug. "They know he's in there. Let them get him back, okay?"

I nod, and he squeezes me. They make us stay in the armored command vehicle or whatever it is. They're probably worried I'll rush in behind them after Gibs. They'd be right. I'm going in for my son; I've already decided it. Shifting in my chair, I plan my escape from this vehicle.

"Don't even think about it, son." The lines around the cop's eyes are deep. How could he possibly even know my plan? The only person besides me who might know is Killian.

"Let me go over with you how this is going to go down. First, we're going to knock. If that doesn't work after about fifteen minutes, we'll fire a flash round into the house. You'll hear that, maybe even see it. Don't be alarmed. It's meant to disorient the captors. It won't be fired into the room with your son. Infrared tells us he's in a room at the back of the house. One of the adults is in the same room with him. The other two are in the front. Once the flash round has been fired through the window, the SWAT team will breach the door. Officer Sanchez here," he points to one of the officers at the rear of the assembled group. "His assignment is to get to your son. That's his only job. Get Gibson and bring him out."

350

I rub the officer on the screen of the monitor we're watching, my way of giving Officer Sanchez extra mojo to get my son the fuck out of there in one piece. Kill stands behind where I sit in front of the screen and squeezes my shoulders again.

"Who's getting Ari out?" I want to give him the same mojo.

The officer in charge responds. "We aren't sure if Arista Addington is an accomplice or a second victim."

"Bullshit is she an accomplice!" Not my Ari. No way is she part of this. She loves Gibson.

"We don't know that. She'll be detained and taken into the department and interviewed."

I'm too tired, too focused on Gibs. But Ari needs me too.

Officers mill about in their SWAT gear, but what the fuck for, I don't have the slightest idea. Are they gathering the troops? Has the situation inside the house changed? Not knowing is killing me. I just want to hold my family and not let them go. It seems to take another hour before they start to advance toward the house.

Time speeds up and stands still at the same time. I hear the blast of the flash rounds. One, two, three. They're in the house. Then the officers are shouting "Police. On the Ground. Get the fuck on the ground." All I hear is muffled, angry shouts. I can't see anything. I watch the busted down door through the little porthole window like it's a movie. Flashlights move around the room erratically. An officer passes by the doorway with a rifle drawn on someone in the front room.

Kill's fingers dig into my shoulders as we wait, watching. I draw in a breath, having to remind myself to breathe.

Dammit, Sanchez, where are you? Where's my son?

More yelling. More movement. Officers yelling a muffled "Clear!" every few minutes.

Then I see a flash of Gibson's blonde curls just inside the door. He's clutched tightly to the chest of Officer Sanchez, who has his arms wrapped protectively around my son, one hand holding and covering his head to the officer's vest. He jogs down the three stairs and starts across the lawn over to a waiting ambulance.

I tear out of the command center vehicle, working my way through other officers on the scene towards the ambulance.

"Dadddeeee!" he screams, hiccups a few times and then starts again. "Dadddeee! Daddayy!" The piercing sound pushes me to run faster towards him. The officer sets him down on a waiting gurney and immediately turns to me, catching me as I reach out to snatch up my son.

"He's okay! He's okay!" Officer Sanchez says loudly in my face. He blocks me from reaching Gibson.

"You need to calm down. You're going to scare him more than he already is, okay? Take a breath, man. Just take a breath."

He breathes in deep, encouraging me to do the same. I try to copy the officer, but I don't look at him. I can't take my eyes off my son. He looks fine. I mean, his whole face is red and wet with tears as he hiccups with his cries every few minutes. But he's okay.

Officer Sanchez steps aside once he's convinced I won't come unglued and steal my son off the gurney and run all the way home with him. I so want to, though. I want to get him the fuck out of here, take him home, and never let him out of my fucking sight again. Ever. But not without Ari.

The EMT attending him grasps Gibson, and it's a good thing because when my son catches sight of me, he practically leaps off the gurney at me. I pick him up and hold him to me tight.

"Daddy's here, buddy. Daddy's got you." I rock him back and forth and bury my nose in his curly hair. He still smells like my baby, and he feels so fucking good in my arms. So good.

His cries eventually lessen to the occasional hitch, his hands intertwined in my hair as I sway, trying to comfort him and myself, my desperate grip too strong, but I just can't loosen it. I don't think I can ever let him go again.

I turn to watch the door, hoping to see Ari.

"Sir, we need to take him to the hospital. You can come with us. Just come on up into the ambulance with him."

"I thought he was okay?" I look him over, trying to figure out where he's hurt.

"He's fine. It's standard procedure, just to make sure." The EMT holds his hand out to help me steady myself as I step up into the ambulance with my son. He makes me sit on the gurney and then belts us both onto it. The back door of the ambulance is still opened wide, as I watch as officers move back and forth on the scene. Then there's action at the front door as officers lead Becka out of the house, hands cuffed behind her. That fucking bitch. And right behind her, out comes that fucker Todd, also in cuffs.

They better be glad I'm strapped to this gurney, because I'm about to pass my son off to my brother and kick some serious ass.

Kill appears in the doorway of the ambulance, blocking my view. He waits until I make eye contact with him. He's doing it on purpose. Pulling me out of my head and out of the ways I want to hurt that fucker, Todd, and Becka.

When I finally give Killian my attention, he speaks. "I'll meet you there. We all will." I nod and squeeze Gibson to me just a little tighter as he whispers, "Uncle Kiwi."

"Wait, Kill!" He stops and turns. "Find out about Ari." He nods as they close the doors. The ambulance drives slowly down the crowded street.

"Awi owie." Gibson starts crying again. "Awie owie."

"Ari hurt you?" Bile threatens to come up, as my worst fear comes to life. If Ari hurt him, then it's my fault and I'll never forgive her.

He shakes his head hard. "No. Awi owie. Awi owie. Kiss kiss Awi, aww betta." He shakes his head and starts crying.

"Ari kissed your owie?" He shakes his head, flaying back against me and arching his back. He's frustrated. I'm not understanding him, and I'm frustrated too.

"Ari's got an owie?"

He starts crying again.

"They'll take her to the doctor and make sure she gets all better."

I suddenly remember RuffRuff and dig him out of my overstretched pocket. "Here, look who wanted to see you."

"UffUff!" He hugs his stuffed dog to him and lays his cheek against him. "UffUff."

R

"Shicken, daddy? Pease? Fank you!" He's been asking for chicken for the last half hour. He's hungry, but we are stuck waiting on the results of his X-rays. Those X-rays had me donning a lead outfit so I could sit with him because I couldn't let him out of my sight, but also because he didn't want me out of his either. And I still don't know a fuckin' thing about Ari. Gibson seemed to think she's hurt and because I haven't found out anything about her, I'm worried. If she's hurt, then likely, she's not an accomplice.

Kady gets up from a chair in the corner of our small room. The hospital gave us a small private room instead of leaving us in a curtained bed in the open emergency room, and I'm thankful for the privacy.

"Mav will come stay with you. I'll go to the drive through across the street and get him some nuggets. He'll be right in, okay?" She leans in and gives Gibs a kiss.

"Kaykay." He whines when she leaves, but peps back up when Mav strolls in a few minutes later. He looks ever like the rock star, his hair perfectly messy, but his forehead is uncharac-teristically wrinkled, and he looks like he could sleep for a year. I know I fucking could. I'm starting to come down off the worry and adrenaline, and exhaustion is starting to seep into me all the way to my bones.

"He okay?" He looks at Gibson hugging his RuffRuff while watching Octonauts on my phone in the hospital bed.

"Seems to be."

"Kady says he's asking for c-h-i-c-k-e-n? That's got to be a good sign, right?" He reaches over and squeezes my shoulder.

"Yeah. You haven't heard anything about Ari, have you?" I'm desperate for information on her. Killian's been searching, but I haven't seen him yet.

His lips pull into a frown as he shakes his head. "Sorry, man."

"When Kady gets back, you guys should split. Go home to Brio. Hug him tight for me." My breath hitches and I almost lose it, right here in my son's hospital room, in front of my baby and my best friend.

"We're good, man." He squeezes my shoulder again, harder this time. "We want to make sure you *all* get home. Brio's with Elsie. I just checked in with them before Kady came out."

The door swings open, and Killian jerks his head into the hallway, wanting to speak with me. I look at Mav, who nods and moves into my seat on Gibs's bed, tipping his head to watch the cartoon with him.

"Ari's here in the hospital somewhere. Officer Sanchez, the guy who brought out Gibson, says they're pretty sure she wasn't part of it now. He said he had to pry Gibson out of her grip. She was huddled around him, like maybe she heard the flash bangs and thought people were shooting and was trying to protect him. He hinted at the fact that she was in rough shape, but no one will tell me a damn thing since I'm not family."

He gives me a quick once over and then glances through the door into the room. "Gibs is good, right?"

I nod. "Yeah. He's been asking for chicken for the last half hour. Kady went to get him some. We're just waiting on a doctor to go over his X-rays. We need to contact Ari's sister. She can find out her condition for us, and tell them we're engaged."

"On it." Kill leaves towards the lobby, poking at his phone.

Gibson starts crying in the room behind me. I rush back in.

"He just noticed you were gone," Mav said. "I told him you'd be right back." He's holding my son, bouncing him and trying to console him.

"I'm right here, buddy. Right here." I take him from Mav and sit with him on his hard hospital bed.

A few minutes later, the doctor strides back in. "Nothing's broken. Here are his discharge papers. I put a rush on them because I'm sure you are ready to get him home." He hands them to me. "I stapled some pamphlets and business cards to the back. I suggest a therapist that specializes in childhood trauma. For both of you, maybe even your whole family." He pauses as Kady slips in the door with the chicken and scoots along the edge of the room.

"Because he's so young, he doesn't have the ability to talk about what's bothering him. He might not even understand himself. Be prepared for unusual or unwarranted aggression, frustration, hostility. He might start lashing out by biting or kicking or regressing with things like potty training and foods he'll eat. He might start asking for bottles or pacifiers or other things that soothe him. It's his way of showing he's upset." He looks over at Gibson, who's still on my lap.

"Think of him as overtired but dialed up to level ten all the time. There might be night terrors and other sleeping issues. He'll probably be clingy. A therapist can help you all work through it and any issues that you have as well."

"It's important you be patient with him, but with yourselves too. This was a trauma to all of you, you should treat it as such. Let us know if you have any questions, Mr. Donogue. Make sure you check out at the desk." The doctor ducks out of the room.

At the checkout desk a few minutes later, I'm trying to balance Gibson, who's holding onto me like a baby spider monkey and filling out some stupid form I can't concentrate on. I'm worried about Ari and can smell Gibson's chicken, which is making me hungrier and grumpier than hell.

"Here, let me." Killian takes the pen and starts filling out the forms. The admin lady looks over disapprovingly when Killian starts filling out the forms, but he breezes through them without even needing to ask me for anything but my hurried signature here and there.

I turn my head to nuzzle Gibson's sweet, soft neck when Vi catches my eye. She's in a glassed-off room talking to a doctor in the ER. She's pallid and pulled in on herself. Her lips pulled down in a grim frown, as she nods at whatever the doctor is telling her.

"I'll be right back." I kick Killian's foot, so he knows I'm talking to him. I adjust my grip on my son and go find out what the fuck is going on with *my* Ari.

Chapter 40

Arista

I'm just under the surface of the water. Waves of light filter through, giving me just enough light to know I'm here, but it feels good to be down here. I'm floating along in the in-between, not close enough to the surface to break through but not dragging along the coarse bottom either. I should come up for the air and light at the surface, but the closer I get to breaking the plane of the water into the world, the more I hurt everywhere, and the brightness makes my head throb. Down here, the beating in my head slows to a peaceful nothing.

Rista? Ris, come on, wake up. I need you, Rista. Wake up. Please. For me.

I'm sorry. I didn't know. Rista, please wake up.

Viola needs me. Her voice sounds small and so far away. I need to get to Vi. What's he done to her? I try swimming closer to the surface as hard as I can so I can get to Vi. I must protect my sister from Todd.

But the more I try to break through, the deeper I go until I'm scraping along the uneven bottom again.

R

THE VOICES URGING me up are different today. Three different ones all jumbled together, but I'm down too deep. The light from the surface is so far away I can barely see anything.

Ari, I miss you. We need you so fucking much. Gibson needs you.

She just squeezed my hand, Cal, I swear it.

Can you squeeze my hand, Ar? Just a little squeeze, baby.

Fight to come back, baby.

I try to fight up to the surface, but it's so far away and I'm too tired.

Rista. Wake up for me. Please.

I let them go, floating back into my peaceful darkness.

R

MY TONGUE IS THICK, like it's wrapped in gauze and dry like the sand in Gibson's green turtle sandbox.

Gibson. Something about Gibson. Gibson?

"Gibson!" I gasp, breaking out into the brightest light. It blinds me as I try to sit up and my eyes slam shut to protect me.

I have to find Gibson. I can't see and my head throbs like it might detonate at any moment, but I force my eyes to open just a little bit, so I can find him.

"Gibson?" My screams tear at the dryness in my throat.

"He's okay, Ar. Gibson is okay. You are too, baby. You're safe too." Strong arms encompass me. *Safe. I'm safe.* My breath is hard to catch.

"He's sleeping at home. Kill and Sammy are with him. He's safe. Lie back. Come on, baby." *Callum is here.* He guides me to lie back in the bed.

I blink and squint; the lights overhead hurt. A nurse hovers over me.

"Do you know your name?"

"Arista." My tongue sticks to the roof of my dry mouth, making it hard to enunciate the s sound. I smack my lips, trying to conjure up moisture, but can't find any.

"Can you open your eyes for me?"

"Too bright. Hurts so much." I try to keep them open but have to squint to keep out the light that makes my head hurt more.

"Let's get you a sip of water." A white and yellow bendy straw appears in front of me and memories of Callum trying to get me to drink the sickly-sweet orange liquid when I was sick. I lift my head to take a sip and my bed magically starts moving to sit me up.

"There, that's better. Right?" The nurse reminds me of my sister. She encourages me to take a few sips of water.

"Vi?"

"Your sister went home for the night, but she'll be back. Your fiancé's here. Do you remember his name?"

"Callum." My mouth sticks at his name. *He's here.* I look for him, careful not to turn my head too fast, but the room spins anyway.

I finally find him sitting on a chair pulled up close to the other side of my bed. His eyes are wide and his lips agape, but the rest of his face tells a different story. There are purplish bruises under his dark blue eyes and a few days' worth of scruff on his chin and jaw. His t-shirt is rumpled, and his hair is pulled back in a loose ponytail, strands pulled out of it here and there instead of smooth like it usually is. He's on the very edge of the plastic chair, elbows on his thighs, blue eyes staring at me, unblinking.

"How do you feel, hon?" The nurse watches me as she offers me another sip. The cool water lubricates my mouth.

"Easy, not too much," she says softly. "How do you feel?" she repeats.

"Hurt, ugh." Everywhere, I want to add, but I can't seem to make my mouth do the work to say the word.

"The doctor should be here any minute now. He'll need to give you a look over and then he'll prescribe something for the pain." She smiles down at me.

"Kay." I sag back into the bed, my body feeling like it weighs five hundred pounds. My eyelids pull down, attached to anchors. "Hurt." I close my eyes for a few minutes.

R

"Arista? Can you open your eyes for me?" It's easier to open them this time, and the room is darker, only a soft light over the sink across from my bed is on this time.

"I'm sure you don't remember me. My name is Dr. Marks. I was here when they brought you in. Do you remember what happened?"

"Took Gibson to the park."

"Good. Do you remember what happened after that?"

What happened after that? Todd has Gibson. My heart beats fast. I chase them and then I'm on the ground in the park. Pain. Darkness. Gibson kissing me. A strange room I can't get out of. Nothing's making any sense, the machine is beeping fast, and it's hard to breath.

"Todd. Has. Gibson."

The doctor nods again.

"Do you remember anything more?" My head's spinning with images that don't make sense. Aiden dead in the park. Darkness. Pain. Gibson kisses. More pain. Shooting. The beeping gets faster.

"Stop with the questions. I'm not a doctor, but all that beeping can't be good." Callum's voice is deeper, rougher than normal. I turn my head slowly to look at him and he's standing, his hands balled up in fists that rest on my bed. He looks like he's about to throttle the doctor.

"It means her heart rate is elevating. She's probably a bit worked up, anxious. Totally normal, considering the circumstances. I'll send the nurse in with something for the pain. Rest is the best medicine for you right now. Rest and time. I'll check back in on you later."

I nod as he leaves. My eyes are already heavy again, but the friendly nurse is back with a needle that she sticks into the IV.

"This will help the pain. It'll also make you a little sleepy."

"Is that wise considering her head injury?" His words are harsh and gruff.

"The doctor knows what to prescribe. She needs rest. Don't keep badgering her." The nurse gives him a look, and he chuckles without any humor.

"You and the doctors are the only ones who've even talked to her." He smirks at the nurse, but he's not happy.

The nurse walks out, and I glance at Callum again. He's standing there, his eyes squeezed shut, fists still balled.

I want to tell him something, but I can't remember what because everything starts to get fuzzy and dark.

R

CALLUM'S PACING back and forth, from the window of my room to the door and back again. It's dark outside still or again, I'm not sure which. The room is quiet except for the beeps and the shuffling of Callum's tennis shoes on the linoleum floor.

Despite his tight, rigid posture as he moves, everything about him screams exhaustion, from his still rumpled clothing to his disheveled ponytail.

"Callum?"

He stops and turns, swaying slightly on his feet.

"Sit before you fall asleep standing up and hurt yourself."

His tense face softens as he gingerly sits down on the edge of my bed, like he's afraid to jostle me. He picks up my hand and brings it to his thigh, lightly rubbing the back with his thumb.

"You're the one in the hospital, yet you're worried about me." He shakes his head like he can't believe it. He continues to rub the back of my hand, watching me, assessing me.

"Do you know what my injuries are?"

He cringes as if thinking about it gives him pain in his belly. "Moderate concussion. Your face looks like you took a boot to the side of the head. You have a gash along your hairline, stitched closed now." He fists his hands and clenches his teeth before carrying on. "Three broken ribs that thankfully didn't puncture your lung or you might not have made it with as long as it took to get you two out of there." His face pales at his own words as his eyes become shiny.

"Dislocated shoulder and elbow on your left side. They think he must have dragged you across the park by them." He nods to my arm on the other side. "They're watching your spleen. Originally, doctors told us they'd probably have to remove it, but the bleeding seems to have stopped, so maybe not." He closes his eyes for a minute and then looks at me. "Lots of fucking bruising and swelling. Lots."

He takes in a ragged breath and then visibly steels himself before bringing his eyes back to mine. The emotion in them makes my own eyes well with tears before he says anything. "Thank you. For protecting him. He didn't have so much as a scratch, Ar."

I try to smile up at him. I want to tell him that, of course, I'd protect Gibson. I love him, love both of them. But I'm so tired I can't seem to open my mouth to make the words I need to say. My eyes keep closing without my permission. Everything is slowly dulling, even my awareness. Callum leans over me and brushes the hair from my eyes. "Sleep, beautiful. You heard the doctor, it's the best thing."

His voice sounds so far away as I close my eyes, but I squeeze his hand hard. He squeezes mine back. "Don't worry, you won't be alone. I promise."

R

THE NEXT TIME I wake up, Kady is futzing with a beautiful bouquet of flowers on the small windowsill.

"Pretty."

She twirls around at my words, a bright smile on her face.

"Good morning. I wanted to get these here so you could see them. I'm a little early, but the nurse let me in anyway."

I look around the room for Callum, but he's not here.

Kady looks at me sadly. "Cal went home to rest and be with Gibson. He'll be back later this evening, though."

"How is he?"

"Cal? Exhausted. Worried. Anxious." Looking closely at her, it seems that she is the same. She sits.

"I meant Gibson."

She sighs and looks back at me. "Clingy. Whiney. Exhaustively asking for you." Her smile is sad. "The ER doc said he was fine physically, if that's what you mean. Gibson's dealing with the kidnapping the only way he can. Cal's working on getting them in to a therapist, but the waiting list for an appointment with the one he wants is long."

"Breakfast has arrived!" The cheery nurse moves my little bed table towards me with the plate. "Enjoy."

I lift the cloche from the plate to find blueberry pancakes and some scrambled eggs. Also, an accompanying box of juice and a cup of coffee that's making me nauseous just smelling it. I push the coffee aside. I'll have to remember to tell them I don't like coffee.

I didn't realize I was hungry until I saw the pancakes. I take a bite, and immediately want to spit them out, but Kady's watching me.

"Oh no, that good, huh? I guess hospital food is terrible everywhere."

Kady watches me struggle through the rest of my breakfast while we chat about everything but Todd, Becka and the reason I'm here in the first place. But I start to get tired after a fresh round of pain meds and eventually slip off, even though Kady's still in the room with me.

Sammy is sitting next to me when I wake up the next time.

"Hey, look at you, all awake and stuff," he whispers with a smile, and scoots his chair a little closer.

"Why are you whispering?"

He nods at the other side of my bed, where Vi is curled up in a ball, sleeping on the other side of my room.

"We couldn't get her to go home after she found out you woke up and were talking, but she's beat."

"So's Callum." I remember he nearly fell asleep on his feet.

"Yeah, Kill just texted me a pic of Cal and Gibson napping together. Thank fuck he finally fell asleep." I'm unclear if he means Cal or Gibson. Sammy hands me his phone. Gibson's asleep on his race car bed in just a diaper and t-shirt. Next to him, Callum is jammed onto the bed, curled around his son, encasing him in a protective bubble.

"What's even more ironic? Flip to the previous picture. It's from last night, while Cal was here with you." The next picture is the same, but different. Gibson's wearing his dino pajamas in this one and the person curled around him is Killian, not Cal. But he's curled around him in the same protective bubble.

Sammy shrugs at me when I look up at him. "Kill and I were on Gibson detail last night. Kill went up to check on Gibs and never came back downstairs. I went up, and that's what I saw. Cal has no idea. I didn't show the picture to anyone but you. Kill just needed to be close to Gibson, I think. He was pretty shaken up. We all were. But Killian took it as hard as Cal." Sammy's usually laidback smiling face takes on a bleakness I never suspected he was capable of.

"Cal's place is very crowded as of late. Killian and I have been crashing there. When Vi leaves the hospital for the night, she comes to the house and sleeps in your old room. Mav, Kady, Kill and I take turns sitting with Vi or Cal and you. You can only have two of us at a time." Sammy flashes me a sad smile.

"It's killing Cal, though. He wants to stay home because Gibson needs him. Gibs is clingy as hell, just like the doctor said he'd be. But Cal wants to be here with you too. He worries about you when he's there. He worries about Gibs when he's here." He shrugs.

"He's running himself to the ground. I'm worried he'll end up in the room next door at the rate he's going. Cal's being Cal, though, taking care of everyone but himself." Sammy frowns as he lets out a little sigh.

Callum needs to take care of Gibson and himself. I'll be okay. He needs to have at least one full night's sleep. I don't want to be the reason he ends up dropping from exhaustion.

"Kady wanted me to tell you not to eat dinner if it gets here before she does. She's bringing you something after she saw the crap they tried to feed you for breakfast. Was it really that bad?"

I nod.

Vi stretches out of the ball she was curled up in. "Hey, Vi. Glad you got some sleep, even if it was in that chair." Sammy grimaces. "That's not even a comfortable chair; it couldn't be a very comfy bed."

The nurse and an aide come in, and Vi and Sammy go for a walk while they take their readings and help me freshen up. I can't wait until I can take a real bath.

Vi comes back alone and sits on my bed, the same way Callum did last night.

"Ris," she breathes out, and something in her voice makes me look up at her. Her eyes are full of tears. "Oh, Ris, I had no idea that Todd was doing those things to you." She looks away and shakes her head. She grabs my hand and holds it tight. A little too tight.

"I wish you'd have told me." She looks down. "It makes me sick, knowing what he did to you. I'm a nurse. I should have known." A loud sob escapes her as she squeezes my hand tight. "Forgive me for not realizing what was going on." She pulls in a shuddered breath and shakes her head. Her face turns red as her body tightens. and blinks away the tears in her eyes.

I squeeze her hand. "Vi, you did so much for me. I wanted you to be happy."

"You think that I'd ever be happy with someone who molested my little sister? Seriously?" The red in her face deepens. I pull back. There's that word. *Molested.* But was I molested? Todd made me feel like it was my fault. That I was the instigator, the whore.

"I can't believe Cal told you." I shake my head. "Talk about kicking you when you're down."

"Cal knows? You told Cal about this, but not me? I'm your sister, Rista. I was supposed to be protecting you." The anger in Vi turns to something I can't identify.

"Cal didn't tell me. That fucking scum bag I married did at the jail that night. He's damn lucky there was a plexiglass partition because if there hadn't been, I'd have jumped him right there." Her face flashes with anger, something I've never seen on my sister, not like this.

"I still don't understand why he did this. Or who the lady with him was. The one from New York."

She puts a hand on my arm. "Ris. That was Becka. Gibson's mom."

She was stalking us! No wonder she knew so much about

Gibson. "But how does she know Todd? What did she want with me?"

"We don't know everything. But from what the police have told us, they met online in the group Todd used to release your location. They had different ultimate goals but figured out they could work together to get what they both wanted." She squeezes my hand and I get the sinking sense that she doesn't want to tell me their goals.

"What did they want?" My words are soft because as much as I don't want to know, I need to know.

"Becka wanted Gibson. Todd wanted you."

"But why?"

"They think on some level Becka regrets signing away her rights to Cal."

"And Todd?" Vi winces, and I'm not sure if it was the shrillness of my question or the answer that causes it.

"He wanted to separate you from Callum. The police seem to think he was worried you'd tell him what Todd had done to you. That Callum would convince you to come to me or the police. If he could frame you for Gibson's kidnapping, he thought Callum wouldn't want anything to do with you." She stops and looks at me.

"One of the things he told me at the jail was as soon as he figured out his original plan wasn't going to work, he was going to kill you, Ris. Because of what he did to you. If he killed you, he figured we wouldn't find out about, about the things he did to you." She lets out a sob and bends in to hug me. "He figured he'd be safer in prison as a murderer than as a child molester. A child molester, Ris. He told me all this at the police station. He was being recorded. It's all on tape."

"I can't believe I was living with—" Her voice breaks, and she catches herself. "Why didn't you say something, Ris?"

"He told me that what I had done was the ultimate betrayal against you." I can't meet her eyes, even though I know she

368

doesn't see it that way. "That you would side with him, that you wouldn't believe me. That he'd tell you what else I'd done." My last words are whispered.

Vi pulls me in for a gentle hug. "You're the only person I would've believed. You're the only family I have left. I love you, Ris."

She shouldn't love me. I was the one to blame with Todd. I killed our parents. It's my fault they're dead. If I hadn't snuck out, they wouldn't have had to come get me.

"Vi, you should hate me. I killed mom and dad." The words just come out, followed by streams of hot tears flowing down my face. I can't bear to look at her. I can't even stand the contact with her, so I pull back. She'll hate me now.

"What, Rista? No, hon. You didn't. You didn't run that red light and hit them. You were in the car with them." She gives me that look I get when I mess things up. My memory's still a little scrambled thanks to the boot in the head. Most of the stuff is still there, just the order is messed up. It's been getting better slowly. The neurologist thinks I'll get most of it back.

"It's my fault they were out of the house to begin with. I was grounded and snuck out. I got drunk at a party. They wouldn't have been in the accident if I hadn't snuck out."

"No. That was not your fault."

"But—"

"No buts. It wasn't your fault, Ris. You didn't do anything that almost every teenager has done at least once in their life. What happened to mom and dad was terrible. I'm sure what you dealt with at the scene was more traumatizing than I can ever imagine and I'm a nurse, so I can imagine some gruesome things. None of that was your fault, Ris. *Not. At. All.* You need to let that go right now."

"Easier said than done." I still won't look at her.

"I always knew, Ris. About why they were out. You had alcohol in your system at the hospital. Mom and dad didn't.

Hell, mom still had her slippers on. I never once blamed you. You need to stop blaming yourself for someone else's careless mistake. Of course, they came to get you. If you called me, I would have come to get you too. Should I blame myself because you didn't call me for a ride?"

I shake my head back and forth. Like hell should Vi blame herself for that.

"I'd never blame you for that. Ever. If you know anything, know that. You are not to blame for their death, Ris. God." Her sigh is so heavy, I feel it. "You've carried this with you all this time? I was a shitty parent to you. I tried so hard to make sure you had everything you needed. And I overlooked that my scumbag husband was doing those things to you." She shakes her head and looks over my bed and out the window.

"I thank God every day that you made it, that you didn't die too. Because honestly? Statistically, you shouldn't have made it. Mom and Dad were both wearing seat belts. You weren't." She hugs me to her so hard it hurts to breathe.

R

CALLUM BRUSHES my hair off my face. "I'm glad you talked to your sister. Do you feel a little better?"

I nod. "I do. But now I've got to talk to you." This won't be fun. He'll put up a fight. But this is important. For all of us.

He tips his head to the side and examines my face. "What do we need to talk about?"

Just as I'm about to tell him, Sammy strolls in with a big bag in one hand and a pillow under the other arm.

"I'm here with everything we need for our party. You"— Sammy turns towards Callum—"hit the road, Jack. You're not invited to movie night in room 314." He hooks his head at the door.

"I don't know what the fuck you're smoking, Sam." Callum

rises to his feet, his face folded up in anger. He's so quick to anger lately, even I've noticed it. I think of what Kady told me about Gibson and his agitation and wonder if something similar is happening with Callum. Exhaustion and the stress of the kidnapping, it's starting to catch up with him and he's taking it out on everyone around him.

"This is what I needed to talk to you about. Sam, give us another minute, please."

Sam sets his bag and pillow down in the empty chair and strolls back out.

"What's going on, Ari?" Callum picks my hand up and rubs it. When he's here, he's always holding my hand, caressing my leg, touching me somehow. He needs the reassurance I'm okay as much as I need to know he's here with me.

"I need you to do me a favor. I need you to go home tonight and really sleep." I flip my hand over and squeeze his.

"I sleep fine here."

"Bullshit, Callum. I don't sleep fine here with the nurses coming in all the time and all the noise and I'm in a bed. You're scrunched into a hard plastic chair. I'm fine. I need you to be fine too." I pause. He's showered, yes. He looks more like the put together rock star I know. But his face tells a different story. He's got permafrown lines lately, deep creases in his forehead and baggy, exhausted eyes.

"Callum, you can't keep going the way you are. Go home. Sleep in your own bed, get restorative rest. I know you're worried about me, so Sammy's agreed to stay with me tonight. If I don't get sprung tomorrow, Killian will spend tomorrow night. You can visit me for a while, like you did today."

"But I want to be here. Ari, I miss you." His frown pulls at my stomach and makes me sad. "I love you, Ar. Don't make me go."

"I love you too, Callum. The doctor said today that I'll be released tomorrow or the day after. Physically, I'm a mess and most likely I'll need you to help me on top of taking care of Gibson. You need to get some real rest. Please. Do this for me."

"You really want to spend the night with Sammy?" He looks at me dubiously, the corners of his mouth still pulled down.

"I really want you to sleep at home in your own bed. Get some real sleep."

He stands up, leaning over me, and gently kisses my lips. He presses his forehead against mine. "I don't like this. But I'll do it, for you. If you're sure." He locks eyes with me as I nod, then he kisses me one more time before standing up.

Sammy peeks back in. "All good here?'

"Yeah." Callum walks towards the door and looks back at Sam with a hard glare. "You'll call me if something happens?"

"Of course. But nothing's going to happen, Cal." Sammy locks eyes with Callum, his face the most serious I've ever seen. Callum seems to approve of what he sees and pulls his eyes back up towards mine.

"I'll text you good night when I go to bed. I love you."

"Love you. Bye."

Sammy pulls both chairs together to create something of a bed and drags it near my bed. He pulls out a laptop and pulls up Netflix.

"Whatchya wanna watch?" He smiles over at me before bending over to dig through his bag.

"You thought of everything, haven't you?"

"I did." He sets a bag of popcorn on the bed close enough to the edge so he can reach it too. "I figure you for a Junior Mints girl. But if you're not, I also have Reese's Pieces or Raisinettes."

I smile so big my face gives a throb on my left side where it's bruised to hell. "You guessed right. I love Junior Mints." I take the box when he offers them. He settles in with the chocolate-covered raisins.

Chapter 41

Callum

hree months later

As soon as Ari got home, she started planning our wedding. I suggested hiring one of those planners who do it all, but she insisted she wanted to plan it all herself. So, she threw herself into it and planned a full wedding in three months, in between her physical therapy sessions, Gibson's play therapy, our couples therapy, our individual therapies for Ari, myself, Gibson, and Vi. We are all chocked full of therapy right now. The only one who refused therapy is Kill. I even offered to pay.

All this therapy and all I know is I'm fucking pissed, or as my therapist says, "Displaying signs of hostility and anger." Hell yes, I'm angry. It's disrupting my sleep and has me snapping at people around me, some of whom are suffering from their own shit because of what happened.

Even before the kidnapping, it would have been a huge hell no to Becka being part of Gibson's life in any way. I don't know what was going on in her warped brain that made her think stealing the son she signed away her rights to would get her back into my good graces. I've thrown some very expensive lawyers at her, because I know damn well she's going to try to get off claiming I took advantage of her "fragile postpartum mental state" or some shit.

And don't even get me started about that fucker, Todd. Just the sound of his name makes my blood boil. For what he's done to Ari and Gibs mostly. But also, for what he's putting his soon-to-be ex-wife through as well. Viola's living with us. The aftermath of what he's done is playing out in her life too. Not to mention that the fucker kidnapped my son in an attempt to keep Ari from disclosing her abuse.

Fuck. I need a vacation. Luckily, tomorrow afternoon, I'm leaving for Aruba with Ari, Gibson, and Vi on our honeymoon. I couldn't leave Gibson here. Not only did his therapist think it was a bad idea, but I *can't* leave him, or Ari, for that matter, for more than a couple of hours without breaking into a cold sweat and rushing home no matter where I am or what I'm doing.

So, Ari suggested her sister come with us. Viola would get a much-needed escape for a couple of weeks, and she'd be there to watch Gibs when Ari and I need some adult time.

I unknot and then reknot my tie for the third time in Gibson's bathroom. Vi's and Ari's giggles float down the hall from our bedroom. It's something I never thought I'd hear again. My Ari's light, infectious giggle. I smile as I smooth my hands over my hair. It's pulled back in a simple, low ponytail. I'll take it out for our ceremony and the reception because Ari likes it loose. And today I want her to have everything she wants and needs to be happy. Because her wedding should be. I turn back and go into Gibs' room, which I'm using as my dressing room, so Ari and her sister can use the master, to find that Gibson has taken off his shoes. Again.

"No, Gibs. You have to keep your shoes on. You can take them off after the ceremony, I promise." I wiggle his feet back into his black converse.

"No shoes!" He takes one off and throws it at me.

"Please, buddy. I want Momma's day to be the best. She really wants you to wear shoes. Please."

"No Shoes! Sim!" He tries to untuck his shirt from his little suit.

"Sorry, buddy, no swimming. Not today."

"Yes, sim! Sim!" he yells, his face red, his hands balled up. He arches his back and goes completely stiff. He starts holding his breath, which scares the fuck out of me every time he does it.

His tantrums are one of the things we're working on with his therapist. The ER doctor knew what he was talking about. At least his night terrors seem to be getting better, thanks to Killian. Uncle Kiwi took it on himself to help with Gibs' night terrors, spending most nights curled up protectively around my son while I spent mine curled up around Ari. I don't know whose nightmares gut me more.

The first night Ari was back home with us, I made an exception and let Gibson sleep in bed between us. That was a huge mistake. Ari woke up screaming, which woke up Gibson, who joined her, which woke up both Vi and Killian. We learned the hard way that having Gibs in his own room was better for everyone. Killian slept with him to combat the night monsters, as Gibs called them. Night terrors still happen for both of them. Hell, I even have the occasional nightmare about that day, but with a lessening frequency. I think when we get back from our honeymoon, Killian will return to sleeping at his own place.

I pull Gibs into my lap, gently holding his balled-up hands in mine. We rock gently, like the therapist suggested. It might not be helping me much, but at least it gives Ari and I ways to help Gibson work with issues.

"I know you're angry, buddy. But Daddy and Momma Ari love you. So much." I continue to rock him and hum. Thankfully, this seems to help, and his warm body starts relaxing against mine. I kiss the top of his head, leaving my lips on the crown of his head as we continue to rock back and forth.

"Hey, you guys ready?" Mav sticks his head in the door, his tie around his neck untied. Concern flashes through his eyes as his grin turns down to a frown. He knows what our position means, that Gibson's had another meltdown, and I'm trying to soothe the tension out of him.

"Mostly." I stand up, still holding Gibson to me.

Mav grabs Gib's little shoes. "Let's go. We should have left like twenty minutes ago." He stands in the hall and waits for us while another round of giggles filters down the hall from our bedroom.

"You didn't peek, did you?" His eyes narrow. "Because that shit's bad luck and that's something you don't really need any more of."

"I didn't peek, but I'm not going to be late to my wedding if my bride is still getting ready."

He follows me down the stairs. Gibson puts his head on my shoulder. It's almost his naptime. "He really needs a nap, or he'll have a complete meltdown during the ceremony. I can't deal with that. Not today, not on our wedding day."

"We have it covered at the church. That's why we need to get there." Mav leads me out the door to his waiting SUV.

I snap Gibson into his car seat but before I slide in. "Mav, let me tie your damn tie before it flies off and you lose it." He stands still and lets me get to work on his knot.

"How did you learn to tie a tie, Callum?" He tips his head at me. "Couldn't have been your dad."

"Mr. Hunter," I say simply.

"Our biology teacher?" He tilts his head to the side.

"Yeah. He came to court with Sandy and us that time Killian got in trouble for shoplifting. He taught us each to tie a tie. He was a cool dude, actually, for a teacher." I shrug and get in.

At the church, our aunt Sandy has a corner of the

groomsman room set up for Gibson, including a little pup tent and some pillows. He crawls into the tent with his favorite green blanket and falls asleep quickly.

We sit at a table, each nursing a tumbler of bourbon. We're all dressed, and all ties have been tied. We've been shooting the shit while we wait for things to start happening.

"The best part of the wedding," Mav says confidentially, setting down his empty tumbler. "Is the moment you lock eyes with her as she's coming down the aisle towards you. Swear to God." He looks over at me. "Be prepared, man, because you'll catch all the feels, right here." He taps his chest.

There's a knock on the closed door. "Fifteen minutes," Kady yells from the other side of the door.

Mav stands and buttons his jacket. "That's my cue. See you fuckers at the altar." He cuffs my shoulder.

"Where the hell are you going?" He's supposed to be with me at the altar as one of the groomsmen.

"You'll see. I'll be there. But I got something I need to do first." He leaves the room.

"Where the fuck's he going?" Sammy and Kill shrug simultaneously.

This is not in the plan. Arista has a very specific, detailed plan for every part of this wedding, and Mav leaving fifteen minutes before he's supposed to be at the alter with me is not in those plans. I don't want anything to go wrong today, because then I might have a wife and a child both having meltdowns.

Sandy wrestles my son from the tent. I join them over in the corner. "Hey buddy. You're going to look so handsome for momma in your little suit." I button his little jacket and slip his Converse back on his feet.

He touches his foot and I cringe, worried he's going to yank them off. But then he leans over and touches mine. "Same. Wike Daddy."

"That's right buddy. And like Uncle Killian and Uncle Mav. But not Uncle Sammy. Because he had to be a rebel."

Gibs gets up and touches Kill's shoe. "Unka Kiwi same." He then touches Sammy's shoe. "Wed. Bad Shammy. Wong Shoe." He shakes his head.

Killian's head tips back as he laughs hard. "Wrong shoe. Bad Sammy." Kill coughs he laughs so much.

"That's classic, little dude. Knuckles." Kill holds his hand out to Gibs, who makes a fist and touches his knuckles to Killian's. The two of them have forged a bond this last year that I've dreamed of them having and I honestly think that is due to Ari.

"Nuckas." He nods his head in his serious Gibson manner.

R

I PULL on the collar of my shirt slightly, trying to cool down. I'm pretty sure the wedding march should've started by now. It feels like I've been standing here at the alter for an hour, with my real and chosen brothers. Except Mav, who's still missing in action. At least Gibson isn't screaming.

"Quit fidgeting," Kill whispers in my ear. "Relax. The music will start, and they'll come down the aisle."

"But Mav said he'd be here."

"Mav isn't the one getting married. If he misses it, he misses it. That's on him."

"But—"

The music starts playing. Everyone in the pews stand and turn towards the door. The bridesmaids start their way down the aisle. First Kady, who holds Gibson's hand. He waves to our guests, getting laughs and smiles out of everyone. They take their place at the altar, Kady holding Gibson up so he can see when Ari comes down the aisle. Then comes Vi. She takes her place next to Kady and kisses Gibson.

And then comes my Ari.

"Here she comes," Kill says quietly.

I haven't even locked eyes with her and mine are already wet. Her dress hugs her hips and flares out into a shimmery full skirt. Her hair's been braided back with small white flowers. I catch her eyes and her smile grows, making her eyes sparkle. My heart stops for a second, then speeds up. Fuck, she's beautiful. And she's being escorted to me by Mav. The fucker. He grins a huge grin and mouths, "Told you. All the feels."

"Awi so pwitty. So pwitty Awi Momma."

I'm still trying to get him to call her mom. She's fine with him calling her Ari. So far, the closest I've gotten is the occasional Ari Momma.

Mav puts her hand in mine. "Congratulations, brother." He pats my back and takes his place between Sam and Kill.

The minister starts talking, but all I'm paying attention to is Ari. The glistening of her eyes as she looks at our clasped hands, the light pink gloss on her lips that she licks at tentatively. The slight shake of her hands when she slides the dark tungsten band down my finger.

I'm just waiting for the permission to kiss her because it's all I want to do.

After we exchange our vows, it's finally time.

"I present to you, Mr. and Mrs. Callum and Arista Donogue. You may kiss your bride." I put my hands on each side of her head and pull her towards me. Our lips touch and lightning shoots straight through me.

"Kiss Kiss! Awi Momma. Kiss kiss!" Our friends and family chuckle. Leave it to our son to steal the show at our wedding. She giggles and leans over and kisses him on the cheek.

I pull her to me and kiss her again. Touching foreheads, I whisper, "I love you, Mrs. Donogue."

"I love you too." She kisses me.

"Kiss kiss, daddy." I pick up my son just after kissing him

and I discover his feet are bare. "No shoes." He grins his biggest smile.

Epilogue: Callum

Six weeks later

"What is it?" Ar looks at me. We're walking out the front door, holding hands while I carry Gibson with my other arm.

Seconds after her question, she spots her beloved and now fully restored Volkswagen Beetle parked in the middle of the driveway, with all our friends standing around it. Penny's now all one color, a deep purply red and she shines like a damn mirror.

"It's my car." Her hands cover her mouth as her tears start running down her face immediately. "My car."

"Oh no. Momma cwyin'. Poor momma. Kiss kiss. Aww betta!" Gibson puckers his lips and starts wiggling to be put down. He's always concerned for Ari, wanting to kiss her sadness away.

"It's my belated wedding present to you. It wasn't quite done before we left on our honeymoon."

Ari looks over at me and then rushes to the car and sits in it. It's been fully restored, right down to the black leatherette seats. It took Jax no time at all to track the car down. The guy she sold it to was going to restore and sell it anyway. So, I paid him for it in advance. He does amazing work.

"She runs like a dream." Sammy comes up and puts the keys in her hand. "I drove it all the way up the hill, even. No problems."

Sitting in it, she honks the horn and smiles, waving like she's in a parade. That makes Gibs want to toot the horn, so I let him down. He runs to the car and Sammy places him in Ar's lap.

The shoulder and elbow double dislocation Ari suffered when she was dragged through the park caused some damage. Certain activities, like lifting Gibson using her left side, are still a little tough for her. But she's getting stronger every day. We've even included her PT into our daily visits to our home gym. Because this is now *our* home. Ari's on the deed and everything.

We're all getting a little better. Although it's still fucking hard for me to let either one of them out of my sight for more than a few hours. Kill finally moved back to his place after we left for our honeymoon. I don't think a day goes by that he, Sam, Mav, and Kady all drop by. Vi still lives with us while we settle, getting her out of the condo and divorced from Todd, who is in jail, along with Becka, hopefully for a long ass time. Because if I see either of them? I might kill them.

Our friends stay for a casual backyard barbecue and Gibson eats up all the attention that Sammy and Killian shower him with.

That evening, after everyone's either gone back to their homes or are in bed, Ari picks up Gibson's building blocks. I bend over her, shadowing her. "Shouldn't he be doing that?" I whisper and plant a kiss behind her ear. I slip my hand up the front of her shirt and squeeze her breast gently.

"Callum! What if Vi comes downstairs?" Ari gasps huskily, her back arching slightly, pushing it into my hand further.

"She went to bed an hour ago. She won't."

"Then let me finish picking this up and then we'll take it to our bedroom."

I help her get the dimpled blocks back in their tub. As soon as the lid snaps, I whisk her into my arms and carry her up to bed.

"I can walk, you know."

"I know." I kiss her.

We undress and slip under the covers of our king-sized bed. We roll on to our sides, looking at each other. Ari's got bags under her eyes and she yawns, despite the fact that it's early.

"Are you okay?" I brush her hair out of her eyes as an excuse to touch her head.

"Just tired."

I pull her to me." You've been tired a lot lately. You feeling okay otherwise?" She doesn't feel hot.

"Actually, I've been meaning to tell you I'm late." Her words come out faster than normal and when she's done, she sucks in a breath and holds it.

"Wait, what? Really? Do you think?" Another baby? My chest clutches. Hell yeah. This is even better than making her cry over her Volkswagen.

I pull her in tighter. "Breathe, beautiful. That baby needs oxygen just as much as you do."

She lets her breath out.

"I didn't mean to. We didn't talk about it. I think I forgot my pill a few days with all the wedding stuff."

"Shh. This is okay. More than okay." I pull her to me and kiss her neck lightly. "Have you taken a test or anything?"

She shakes her head. "I didn't want to do it without you."

"I'll get us one tomorrow morning, okay?" She nods, and I pull her hips flush with mine to hold her to me. She's asleep in minutes, her long even breaths calming the excitement flooding me.

If it were up to me, I'd go to the store right now to get a test. I'll get up early and hit the drugstore.

Pregnant. A second baby. This time will be different. Everything will be different because this time I'll have the woman I love beside me.

R

Shivering, I can't get warm. I'm cold and wet. What the fuck? The water is everywhere. I gasp like I'm fucking drowning and my arms burn with exhaustion. I'm too tired to keep paddling.

"Callum? Callum, what's wrong?"

I heave, trying to open my eyes. Finally, my air comes, and I sit straight up. I'm still cold. I cough like I have water in my lungs.

Ari slaps my back.

"Are you okay? Callum? Are you sick?" Ari's hands touch my forehead. Fuck! I slept late. I was supposed to do something this morning. Get a pregnancy test. That's right. *We're pregnant.*

My breath comes in hard gasps, like I've been running.

Something's wrong.

I'm not really wet, but I still feel drenched and *so fucking cold.* Fuck. *Killian.* But not. *He's okay.* Fuck.

"What is it?" Ari sits up and watches me jump out of bed and start throwing on clothes.

"You need to stay here with Gibs. I've got to go check on something."

Ari's eyes widen. "Is it? Is it Killian? Is he okay?" Her voice is small and laced with panic. Her eyes grow wide as she figures out what's going on. *The connection.*

I shake my head. "Kill's okay. He needs dry clothes, but something *is* wrong." I'm not making any sense to her. It's not making any sense to me either. I've just got to get to Kill with some dry clothes before he ends up with pneumonia.

I drop my pants I was picking up.

Sammy. The beach. A broken surfboard. Blonde hair plastered to his head. His parted lips are blue. Eyes are open but blank. No! Oh, fuck no! Not—

"It's Sammy." I gasp "Fuck. It's Sammy. Kill needs me." I jerk my pants up and grab a shirt, a dry pair of pants, and some socks for Kill.

My phone starts ringing with Kill's ringtone.

I don't wait for him to speak when I pick up the phone. "Where are you? I'm on my way."

The Playlist

I've made playlists for each of the books. The playlist for Blending Chords can be found on my Spotify.

This is a small sampling of the music on the Spotify playlist for 'Blending Chords' (BC):

1. Don't Treat Me Bad- Firehouse
2. Looks That Kill- Motley Crue
3. No Ring Around Rosie- Kix
4. Enemy- Jet Black Romance
5. Bad Company- Five Finger Death Punch
6. Here I Go Again- Whitesnake
7. While My Guitar Gently Weeps- Jeff Healey Band
8. Kristy, Are You Doing Okay?- The Offspring
9. Tonight- Jet Black Romance
10. The Ballad of Jayne- L.A. Guns

The full Spotify playlist for BC is 58 songs and is one minute shy of being four hours long. I listened to it while writing but also while editing and sometimes while procrastinating.

You can find me on Spotify: Amy Kaybach

Reviving the Rhythm

Want to know which of the Blind Rebels boys is up next? That'd would be Rebels drummer extraordinaire Sammy Denton.

Sammy

After high school, three things mattered to me: my sister Sevenya, my drum kit, and my surfboard. With Sevenya in the passenger seat, we hightailed it to Los Angeles so I could chase my rock and roll dreams. But I left a part of my heart back in the valley.

Just as the Blind Rebels were gaining popularity, I suffered a crushing loss. One I didn't think I'd ever recover from. I tried running to the ocean for solace only for an accident to turn it against me.

Melody

When it comes to relationships, I've learned it's best to keep my distance. Heartache takes many forms, so I avoided it by perfecting the art of not getting too close. Instead, I focus on my career as a fire paramedic to help others the only way I can.

When I saw the surfer go down in the water, my instincts and training kicked in. Never did I expect that the life I'd be saving off-duty would be that of my high school sweetheart. He broke my heart then. I keep his beating now. Haunted by pains of our pasts, we're left wondering if a second chance is even possible after all these years.

Reviving the Rhythm- coming **September 2022**

Acknowledgments

These people are my village. The ones who make these books possible. They read early copies. They boost me when I'm down or when one of my characters isn't talking to me. These are the people who make these books a reality for me.

Misty: My bestest friend. Thank you for plugging my book wherever you go and for being so excited about my Blind Rebel boys. Hearing your ideas and thoughts about my characters is so fun. I especially love that I have to stop myself from spoiling future books for you because I know you'd kill me for doing it.

Jamie: Thank you for always being a sounding board for my writing ideas. And for planting the little seed that maybe I should consider publishing them!

Tricia: For your undying and enthusiastic support and reads in the rough form.

Shayna Astor and Sherry Bessette: Thank you both for all your suggestions and help- both specifically with the book and with other "author" questions I have. These books would not be the same without either of you.

Emily Wittig: For these amazing covers that all look so great and for being so kind and patient with my questions. I can't wait to have all the books together on my shelf so I can see your art all in one place!

Caelan Fine: Thank you for helping me with the graphics that fit the vibe of my story. I'll gladly book Tatum's package for books three and four. And now I can't stop looking for excuses to say Tatum's package.

Hayleigh of Editing Fox: Of my four Rebel Boys, Callum's story is where I made the most painful cuts in editing, but your help and suggestions made it a little easier. Thank you for helping me make this story flow. And for recommending The Affair.

Mackenzie of Nice Girl, Naughty Edits: One day I will master commas. Maybe.

Charli of Charli's Book Box: Thank you for getting my store up and running for me but also for being the first to interview me and for supporting the books so much!

Pat Vassar: Thanks for the vocabulary suggestions. Can you find all *three* instances of your favorite word? Let me know when you do, and I'll send you a present. Keep up being the Jeopardy grand quiz master, but you really must stop giving Misty a throbbing headache at work.

Marie: I love your enthusiasm about my books and your willingness to help spread the word about them makes me smile. That makes you the bestest sister-in-law ever and yes it's in print for the world to see.

My ARC readers & Bookstagrammers who help me get the word out: Thank you for reading and for loving the Rebels like

I do! I appreciate you sharing all my teasers and other posts! I love reading your reviews. Your support means the world to me because this is how word gets out about my books!

My parents: You read my first book with such enthusiasm. I hope you like this one too.

About amy kaybach

Amy Kaybach has been writing since she learned to hold a pencil at three. When she's not daydreaming about sexy rock stars and how to put them into print, she's working in IT or planning her next great adventure with her best friend since junior high. She lives on the central coast of California with her two obnoxious, but well-loved beagles.

As a motorsports fan she loves her cars loud and fast and as a music fan she loves her music hard and loud.

She loves to connect with her readers

 facebook.com/RockinAuthorAmyKaybach
twitter.com/amykaybach
instagram.com/authoramykaybach

Made in the USA
Coppell, TX
03 May 2023

16347779R10236